Re-Reading *Harry Potter*

Second Edition

Suman Gupta

Professor of Literature and Cultural History
The Open University

First published 2009 by
PALGRAVE MACMILLAN

Palgrave Macmillan in the UK is an imprint of Macmillan Publishers Limited,
registered in England, company number 785998, of Houndmills, Basingstoke,
Hampshire RG21 6XS.

Palgrave Macmillan in the US is a division of St Martin's Press LLC,
175 Fifth Avenue, New York, NY 10010.

Palgrave Macmillan is the global academic imprint of the above companies
and has companies and representatives throughout the world.

Palgrave® and Macmillan® are registered trademarks in the United States,
the United Kingdom, Europe and other countries.

ISBN-13: 978–0–230–21957–1 hardback
ISBN-10: 0–230–21957–8 hardback
ISBN-13: 978–0–230–21958–8 paperback
ISBN-10: 0–230–21958–6 paperback

This book is printed on paper suitable for recycling and made from fully
managed and sustained forest sources. Logging, pulping and manufacturing
processes are expected to conform to the environmental regulations of the
country of origin.

A catalogue record for this book is available from the British Library.

A catalog record for this book is available from the Library of Congress.

10   9   8   7   6   5   4   3   2   1
18   17   16   15   14   13   12   11   10   09

Printed and bound in Great Britain by
CPI Antony Rowe, Chippenham and Eastbourne

Re-Reading *Ha*...

'NIVERSITY OF

Also by Suman Gupta

LITERATURE AND GLOBALIZATION

SOCIAL CONSTRUCTIONIST IDENTITY POLITICS AND LITERARY STUDIES

THE THEORY AND REALITY OF DEMOCRACY: A Case Study in Iraq

THE REPLICATION OF VIOLENCE: Thoughts on International Terrorism after 11 September 2001

CORPORATE CAPITALISM AND POLITICAL PHILOSOPHY

MARXISM, HISTORY, AND INTELLECTUALS: Toward a Reconceptualized Transformative Society

V. S. NAIPAUL (Writers and Their Work Series)

TWO TEXTS AND I: Disciplines of Knowledge and the Literary Subject

Contents

Acknowledgements

I am grateful to colleagues of the Open University Literature Department for allowing me the space and time to write this book. The School of Arts at Roehampton University has provided me with access to the facilities of that institution. I have used these extensively and am grateful to colleagues at the School. Thanks are due to numerous friends – even those who were noncommittal or dismissive – with whom I have discussed parts of this study. Readers and editors for Palgrave Macmillan have made significant contributions in finalizing the book. As always, and despite her doubts about these formal gestures, I particularly acknowledge Xiao Cheng's contribution to the process of writing this. I have thrashed out most of the ideas here with her before committing them to paper. My son, Ayan-Yue Gupta, played a substantial part in my thinking about the area of this study.

Part I
The Text-to-World Approach

1
Book Covers

I begin, as most readers must, with book covers. Book covers are drawn into the interstices of reading, as inattentively observed or casually overlooked as a pub such as the Leaky Cauldron might be in London. The images and words on book covers convey a fleeting first impression of what may be in the book, arouse expectations; book covers draw certain readers in, select them as they select the book; book covers tacitly mould readers' expectations and influence reading by the fulfilment or failure of those initial expectations. Every time a book is opened yet again the reader's gaze passes thoughtlessly over the covers and something of their first influence is rekindled. Yet the part of book covers in making a (quite possibly lasting) formative impression on the reader may be forgotten under the weight of their all too tangible and constant material usefulness as the recognizable surfaces, protective coverings, of particular editions. The materiality and material usefulness of book covers often obscure their role in the process of reading. Yet book covers are implicated in the process of reading even before the reader engages with the text that is 'contained' between them. On book covers the covert machinations of the industry that mediates the passage of books between authors and readers are obviously and yet disarmingly casually presented to view. The point is hardly worth labouring: so I begin, as most readers inevitably do (but perhaps more attentively than is usual), with book covers.

I have two Bloomsbury copies of each of the following[1] before me as I write this: J.K. Rowling's *Harry Potter and the Philosopher's Stone* (*Stone* hereafter), *Harry Potter and the Chamber of Secrets* (*Chamber* hereafter), *Harry Potter and the Prisoner of Azkaban* (*Prisoner* hereafter) and *Harry Potter and the Goblet of Fire* (*Goblet* hereafter). One of the two copies of each is directed at children and the other at adults. I know this because the covers of children's copies of *Stone, Chamber, Prisoner* and *Goblet* have quite different images from the adults' copies of the same titles. This is especially intriguing because that is the only significant difference between the children's copies and the adults' copies. In every other respect the differences are minor: there is a slight price difference (the adults' copies cost a jot more), the print of the adults' copies is marginally smaller, the reviews quoted on the back covers are not the same (but similar). The texts within – from bibliographical details and dedications to conclusions – are identical in the children's copies and their adults' counterparts. The images on the covers mainly identify the children's copies as being for children and the adults' copies of exactly the same texts as being for adults. Images, in brief, distinguish the ostensible readerships of these particular editions.

The texts are the same but the images tell different stories, and therefore may lie at the interstices of reading and mould the process of reading, in unobtrusively different ways. The children's copies have sharply defined and cheerfully coloured paintings, cartoon-strip in effect, crowded, action-packed images presented with self-conscious artifice. Images spill over from the front cover onto the back, colours clash with each other vividly in the letters of the title and their backdrops. The flashy images appear to move towards the reader in unexpectedly engaging ways: the Hogwarts Express of the children's *Stone* seems to rush headlong towards the reader and a somewhat exaggeratedly myopic Harry; Mr. Weasley's flying car charges straight through the clouds at the reader on the children's *Chamber*; the Hippogriff of the children's *Prisoner* flies just over the reader's nose (sharply focused before a gigantic moon like the ET bicycle of Spielberg's film); the Hungarian Horntail dragon looms threateningly over Harry and the reader on the children's *Goblet*. Harry is easily recognized by the lightning scar on his forehead. The action places Harry and the reader in close proximity: the reader is not a voyeur who participates in the desirable action from a titillating distance, but someone who is visually and immediately so close to Harry that they could well merge. This reader can vicariously become Harry. This is presumably the child reader, innocently captured by the flash of colours, the whirl of action and naively drawn into empathizing with the hero who is in the midst of it all. Some of the same motifs appear on the adults' book covers, but the images are dark and subdued. These are black-and-white photographs or photo-collages, confined within a geometrically defined space on the front cover. There is a quaint steam train puffing along on the cover of the adult *Stone*; a 1950s-looking car emptily wading through clouds on the adult *Chamber*; a lonely and somewhat awkwardly assembled half-eagle half-horse suspended over some cotton-wool clouds on the adult *Prisoner*; and a photograph of what is distinctly a Chinese dragon (stuff of myths) on the adult *Goblet*. The motifs are the same as on the children's book covers, but dislocated from the action of the story for there is no Harry and friends in their midst: no Harry looking astonished, or Harry being matey with Ron, or Harry with an alarmed Hermione clutching on to him, or Harry dodging dragons. The motifs are dislocated from their instrumental roles within the novels and stand out stark and lonely on the adult covers, held at a distance by their quaintness, made remote by the nostalgic tint of black-and-white photographs. Revealed thus in all their strangeness they appear to acquire mysteriously symbolic meanings, connotations that are reminiscent of something that cannot be remembered. The reader is held at a distance, invited to retreat into a past, black-and-white world, left alone with some faintly intrigued feeling and some mildly questioning sensations. This is presumably the adult reader, a wistful, self-possessed, thoughtful person with a black-and-white past.

The child reader and adult reader so characterized are the 'implied readers' of these book covers; these book covers predispose the reader to the books and thereby also predispose the books for the reader.

Old theoretical quarrels lurk behind the phrase 'implied reader'. It was reasonably clear to Wolfgang Iser (responsible for that phrase) that a dialectical relationship exists between the reader and the text of a literary work (and to some extent any text).[2] A reader brings certain necessarily unique associations, attitudes, beliefs, experiences to her reading; the literary work presents a juxtaposition of words, phrases, sentences, descriptions, narratives, etc. The two interact and readings are produced which are necessarily different for different readers. And yet readings (insofar as they relate to particular literary works and some common ground in human experience and expression) also open the possibility of discussion and exchange about what is accepted as being the same text. It is the latter that primarily interested Iser – a literary work is always that particular literary work (despite different possible readings) because the given text guides the process of reading to some extent. In other words, the text of a literary work has an 'implied reader':

> He embodies all those predispositions necessary for a literary work to exercise its effect – predispositions laid down, not by empirical outside reality, but by the text itself. Consequently, the implied reader as a concept has his roots firmly planted in the structure of the text; he is a construct and in no way to be identified with any real reader.[3]

This concept of the 'implied reader', which is naturally attractive and useful, gave rise to a series of disagreements. Stanley Fish argued that to derive the reader so single-mindedly from the text of a literary work is to miss the point. The process of reading is more comprehensively directed by certain assumptions about how to read and understand texts that exist among specific critics (or the 'interpretive strategies' that are agreed upon by an 'interpretive community'), so much so that it is questionable whether a particular text can be said to have any discrete and determinative existence at all.[4] A waspish exchange followed between Iser and Fish.[5] Others felt that both Iser's and Fish's were rather fanciful and abstract ways of trying to come to grips with the process of reading: the thing to do is to study carefully how actual readers read – to actualize the reader.[6] And yet others maintained that this whole business of focusing on reading alone at the expense of everything else was misguided and overstated.[7]

With the Bloomsbury covers of the *Harry Potter* books in mind it is immediately evident that though I have found it convenient to use Iser's phrase to clarify their effect – and have made that an excuse for a brief excursion into some pedantic-sounding arguments from the 1970s and 1980s – nothing else about Iser's thoughts are relevant here. And nor, for that matter, are those of his immediate opponents. Readers, in this instance, have not been implied by the text (as written words) but by the covers. There is no point in turning to anyone else who pondered Iser at that time to come to grips with this curious phenomenon. All of those mentioned above shared at least this with Iser: they were concerned with the status of the text in relation to the reader and vice versa, and not with covers of particular editions. Their understanding of the text of a literary work never included the book covers. Book covers were too trivial for their attention.

But book covers do matter for the *Harry Potter* series. What is clear here is that different 'implied readers' have been distinctly and discernibly suggested without any reference to what is conventionally regarded as the text of a literary work. This is certainly not unique to the *Harry Potter* series (think of all the different book covers for the same text that we constantly encounter as readers). But the confidence and simplistic clarity with which this is done on the *Harry Potter* books is striking. The effect of this brash confidence in the impact of book covers, in the shells of books, is one of diminishing the substance of the text – those written pages – to some extent. It makes me aware, quite against my usual habits, of the degree to which the *Harry Potter* series, and what Jack Zipes has called the *Harry Potter* 'phenomenon',[8] are about something that appears not to be confined to the text or its 'implied readers' or, for that matter, actual readers or even the 'interpretive strategies' of 'interpretive communities'. It seems to have more to do with images and the production of images and the place of images in producing, advertising and marketing books. Is that indeed the case?

For the moment I simply leave that question suspended there.

But have I revisited those somewhat rusty reader-response theories only to say they are not relevant to me? Did I need to take so circuitous a route to make my rather obvious point? Well – not entirely. I am actually primarily interested in the question of *reading texts*, and what that means for the specific matter of reading the *Harry Potter* series (the printed pages thereof). My discussion of book covers here is mainly to lead into the written words and their reception. I have ideas to ponder about reading texts, especially apropos the *Harry Potter* books, for which this brief prelude on reader-response is bound to be useful – eventually.

Much would get clarified when I get down, gradually and unhurriedly, to explaining what exactly this essay is about. I wish to say no more for the moment than that this essay is about *the political and social implications of the* Harry Potter *books, or the political and social effects that constitute the* Harry Potter *phenomenon.* I say no more for the moment (what did that mean?) and instead allow myself to be distracted by what the book covers have conveyed to me: the distinction between adult readers and child readers. I should try to clarify what this distinction between adult and child readers consists in outside/inside the book covers.

2
Children and Adults

Perhaps the *Harry Potter* phenomenon, the enormous success of the books, is not a matter of book covers and things outside readers and texts; perhaps the phenomenon is one to do squarely with texts and readers. Perhaps the books are so successful because they have received extraordinary approbation from the readers they were primarily and ostensibly directed at – children. Everything is clear and above board then: the success of the *Harry Potter* books proves that they are genuine articles, books that are really for children, that children actually enjoy. The scale of success might indicate that these are more *genuinely* books for children than other books that are produced as such. Perhaps the whole *Harry Potter* phenomenon devolves from a perfect match between text and intended readership, and this has to do with the books being for children and being read with pleasure by children. There is nothing more complicated about the phenomenon, everything else follows logically from that. This is the view that is unsurprisingly championed in a feature in the *Advertising Age*:

> The popularity of *Harry Potter* emerged with the schoolyard chatter, not with marketing hype. Today, two-third of kids ages 8 to 18 have read at least one in author J.K. Rowling's series of *Potter* books – properties that initially arrived with comparatively little of the fanfare we've come to associate with new book titles.
>
> A generation that has been marketed to its entire life birthed its own buzz, took ownership of the *Potter* brand and declared it genuine. Until now, virtually everything marketed to kids has been saturated by hype, and they're hyped out. *Harry* grew organically, and it is the purity of these origins that has created real equity for the brand.[1]

Perhaps I was misguided in dwelling upon images on book covers.
If this is true, then the *Harry Potter* books are worth examining for one special reason: they should give, more than any other recent book, adults some indication of that magical thing – the kind of textual qualities that grab children. What is that factor X that gets *Harry Potter* books an extraordinary endorsement from children? But before following that line of argument any further, we need to draw back a bit. That *Harry Potter* books exist with adult covers is not purely a matter of wishful thinking. Adults (above 18, even above 35) have taken to *Harry Potter* books with extraordinary enthusiasm too. This is familiar territory now. When the *New York Times* Book Review created a separate children's fiction best seller list in August 2000 and relegated the *Harry Potter* books to the top of it (these had held the top three slots of the adult fiction best seller list for more than a year before that) Barbara Marcus, President of the Scholastic Children's Book Group, noted bitterly that 30 per cent of the first three in the series had been bought by and for readers who were 35 or older.[2] On the same occasion, Craig Virden, president of the Random House Children's Books, reportedly said: '3.8 million copies: that's an adult number! And even though I think anything that draws attention to children's books is great for business, I have to say that this is really unfair to Scholastic.'[3] The figure quoted by Barbara Marcus originated from the NPD Group, which conducts market research for 12,000 households in the US. The NPD Group has in fact been producing an interesting range of statistics since on the readership of the *Harry Potter* books, and on interest in the films, and consumption of *Harry Potter* memorabilia (published in NPD's *Harry Potter Prophet*), all of which indicate a high degree of interest in these at all sorts of levels among adults. Irrespective of actual readership, adult interest in, contribution to and engagement with the *Harry Potter* phenomenon has certainly been substantial, judging from a cursory glance at figures such as those gleaned from surveys and shown in the tables overleaf.[4]

Another survey carried out in May 2001 (announced by NPD on 26 June 2001) showed that of the 1,373 respondents, 57 per cent of children and 47 per cent of adults were planning to buy Harry Potter products; and of the adults 32 per cent admitted that they were buying some of these for themselves. And, finally, a survey carried out in May 2002 in the UK showed that despite the *Harry Potter* books, seven to fourteen year olds were buying fewer books than before; and for the *Harry Potter* books themselves the ratio of adults reading them compared to children is increasing (whereas in 1999 71 per cent of these

Table 1   The *Harry Potter* popularity meter survey, in which 1,511 respondents aligned themselves to one of the positions in the left column

	Children (6–17) per cent	Adults per cent
Harry Potter is the best	17	3
I really like Harry Potter	21	8
I like Harry Potter	23	16
I don't care for Harry Potter	28	66
I don't like Harry Potter	5	1
I really don't like Harry Potter	2	3
I can't stand Harry Potter	4	3

Source: NPD, 28 March 2001.
(If taking a position – i.e. not not caring – indicates some effort to read or think about *Harry Potter* books, then this shows that at least 34 per cent of the adult respondents had done this.)

Table 2   Kids and adults who are aware of and plan to see the film *Harry Potter and the Sorcerer's Stone*, from 1,403 respondents in July 2001

	Kids (6–17) per cent	Kids that read Harry Potter per cent	Adults per cent	Adults that read Harry Potter per cent
Aware of movie	65	75	50	86
Plan to see movie	47	66	21	75
Not sure	29	25	25	13

Source: NPD, 26 September 2001.
(Survey results on this for September 2001, announced on 8 November 2001, showed that awareness of the movie had increased for kids in general to 75 per cent, and kids who read *Harry Potter* to 88 per cent, and for adults in general to 65 per cent, and adults who read *Harry Potter* to 93 per cent.)

were bought for 7 to 14 year olds, by 2001 this had fallen to 36 per cent with 15 to 35 year olds accounting for most of the remaining).[5]

Even insofar as children are primarily the readers of certain books, it is generally accepted that adults have a substantial mediating role in that interest (the above figures certainly indicate that adult mediation has been an important element in making *Harry Potter* books popular among children). Adults buy books for children, encourage children to read those books, sometimes read those books to children; children buy books written ultimately largely by adults, published and marketed by adults, following often the example and enthusiasm of adults. It is very difficult indeed to gauge to what extent the *Harry Potter* books engage children in any unique fashion, untouched by adult interests and motives. The collections of children's responses to the *Harry Potter* books that are available[6] express little apart from enthusiasm and the ubiquity of these sorts of adult mediation. The enormous sales figures of these books in a range of different cultural contexts cannot be said to reflect as clearly the endorsement of children as the fact that adults are buying them in large quantities ostensibly for children (mostly adults buy books): these sales figures indicate that *adults have given extraordinary sanction to these books as appropriate reading matter ostensibly for children.* If there's a factor X involved, it is surely not one that relates to *extraordinary endorsement from children,* but one that explains the *extraordinary sanction from adults for children;* the clarification of that factor X lies within the adult readings of *Harry Potter* books, not the children's reading.

But the issue here is more complex. The market research indicates (doesn't prove, for ultimately those figures depend on the quirks of sample surveys and questionnaires) that adults are reading and endorsing these *Harry Potter* books not just *for* or *on behalf* of children, but for themselves. A large number of ecstatic reviews have attested to the pleasure that adults have derived from reading these books:[7] though this is often justified by such sentimental and ultimately meaningless notions as making up for a lost childhood or rediscovering the child in oneself. Those reviewers who are not able to derive such pleasure themselves recognize instinctively that they have to argue with adults, not children, for adults are the main consumers and endorsers here. Some are simply bewildered by the phenomenon of this extraordinary adult endorsement and wonder why it has occurred, others direct their arguments against *Harry Potter* to adults and for adults. It has even been suggested that the extent of adult interest in *Harry Potter* books shows a gradual regression in reading habits among adults (adults are becoming less 'grown-up' in their reading habits).[8]

It is, it seems to me, impossible to tease out, verify and analyse what exactly children are *reading* in the *Harry Potter* books. It is possible to affirm that significant numbers of children have unravelled the words and sentences and chapters in a basic mechanistic manner: as a mode of storing up information (enough to answer Potter trivia quizzes or play Potter board and card and computer games), as a part of learning to read and acquiring some grasp of language (something adults are grateful for amidst fears about literacy which have simmered constantly since the 1960s)[9] or to chime in with or disagree with adult or peer suggestion (to answer those perennial questions, 'Did you enjoy it?' 'Was it fun?' 'Why did you like it?'). These indicate that the pleasure and benefit that children have derived from engaging with the *Harry Potter* books are to a determinable extent *outside* the text, so to say – it is the pleasure of competing in games intelligently, or the benefit of learning to read fluently, or the joy of impressing an adult or a peer. Undeniably, children do get pleasure from their reading (I, and many adults, will attest to having experienced such pleasure, but that's an adult memory of something that is not recoverable as such and only analysable in retrospect) – my point is that that aspect of children's reading is irretrievable in any *unmediated* sense. Any retrieval is a critical act of adult reconstruction. The fact is that adults have perfectly naturally and in accordance with custom spoken for children insofar as the *Harry Potter* books go, inferred their pleasure for them and discerned the moral (or immoral) lessons for them – and in the process it is not unreasonable to assume that adults have spoken for themselves. Large numbers of adults have done so without the subterfuge of speaking on behalf of children.

For critical purposes it is prudent to assume that there is no factor X that we can hope to reveal that would tell us anything about children from the *Harry Potter* phenomenon. Let me be clear about this. I am not asserting that large numbers of children are *not* getting pleasure in reading *Harry Potter* books, or are not enchanted by and 'hooked onto' them. It seems very likely, judging from asseverations from children and adults alike, that they are. What I am saying is that that pleasure or enchantment is not analysable in terms of the relationship between text and reader; insofar as verifiable evidence allows for analysis of what children read at all it either takes us out of the sphere of the text and reader as a closed relationship (to the world of proliferation in media, learning and competitive activities and entertainments and the industry that capitalizes on these, or response to stimuli provided by educational institutions and interests), or rebounds into adults speaking on behalf of children and thereby actually saying something about themselves or something about the world that adults (more determinatively than children) self-consciously inhabit.

Let me call my stance here what it is: *it is a prudent critical decision not to examine the* Harry Potter *phenomenon as something that peculiarly devolves or emanates from and with effect on children. I think that can only be asserted and not examined beyond the assertion. As far as this study is concerned the* Harry Potter *books, and the phenomenon, are addressed because it is likely to tell us (adults mostly, especially the readers of this essay itself) something about us and the social and political world we inhabit.* If *children* as a category, as a collection of subjects, enter this world in any analysable sense it is most likely to be on adult terms as a category or collection of subjectivities with social and political effect.

3
The Seriousness of Social and Political Effects

When I asserted that in talking about 'children' as readers of the *Harry Potter* books (actually any book) we – primarily adults – are presenting 'children' as 'a category or collection of subjectivities with social and political effect', I am aware that I have stepped into the, in this context frowned-upon, register of the *serious*. I have done this already by stating earlier (with what was, I hope, a tantalizing lack of explanation) that the main interest of this essay is the 'political and social effects that constitute the *Harry Potter* phenomenon'. Such statements could all too easily become fodder for negative perceptions of academic jargonizing, the pretentiously intellectual, the nit-pickingly pedantic... – all terms replete with a sense of the mismatch between object and analysis. This perception could take two forms. It could be observed that the *Harry Potter* books are aesthetically too slight, too much the sphere of light reading, too attuned to an uncritical child world, too removed from the here and the now in their content to deserve such hefty critical apparatus as political and social analysis. Or it could be asserted that there is something perverse about trying to expose the delight of (especially children, but also children-within-adults) reading *Harry Potter* books to these worldly and responsible matters: there is something pristine and innocent about these books and the enthusiasm they generate which should be admired and valued, not exposed to weighty scrutiny. A mismatch is gestured towards in such arguments: the mismatch of meeting the light-hearted with killjoy seriousness, the unthinking with analytical rigour, the obviously trivial with the expectation of depth, the mass-market product with elite literary taste.

If I took such arguments seriously I would have nothing to write here. Both the assertion that the *Harry Potter* books do not deserve analytical attention and the desire to maintain the innocent joy of reading them are indicative of something that itself needs serious consideration: both are indicative of a determination not to realize the possibilities of reading beyond a point, not to read *thinkingly*. (I briefly elucidate the connotations of reading *thinkingly* in the next chapter.) These do not confirm that the *Harry Potter* books cannot or should not be placed in the happening material world; these do confirm that there is a widespread determination to keep these books away from all that. The embarrassed grin and excuses with which a serious academic who happens not to be a specialist in children's literature or fantasy writing admits to reading these books (almost like admitting to reading pornographic magazines), and the supercilious surprise and condescension with which his serious colleagues greet this information,[1] establish the extent to which that blind-spot affects the scope of their visions. The outrage with which a parent grateful to the *Harry Potter* books for engaging their children greets an analytical (especially when not approbatory) remark about these books[2] also reveals the effects of that blind-spot.

A widely prevalent determination to keep something outside the sphere of social and political analysis is worrying for at least two reasons: (a) it makes one suspect that social and political implications are involved that are somehow embarrassing; and (b) it erects walls around human curiosity and reasoning (just as dogmatism, prejudice or ignorance do).

I know that *my* more erudite readers (who know their genres, and understand 'great' literature, and have touched their touchstones, and have interrogated the canon) would not be impressed by the above glibly generalizing statements. Out of respect for them particularly, but really also as a matter of interest and curiosity, I feel I should indicate after all why the *Harry Potter* books are *particularly* deserving of serious social and political analysis. There are three by now well-known observations about these books, or rather the *Harry Potter* phenomenon, that are worth noting here:

1 The *Harry Potter* books are *economically* the most successful of *all* literary books published in recent years. This hardly needs elaboration, but closer attention to the scale of this success is instructive. The *Harry Potter* books have engendered an economic phenomenon in publishing and related industries that is by all standards extraordinary; it is seldom that anything in the broad field of literature becomes so inextricably linked in such a short time to the discourses of market and finance. In March 2002 it was estimated that the *Harry Potter* books have had world-wide book sales of almost 140 million copies.

In the UK and the US, *Goblet* alone had an all-time record first print-run of 5.3 million copies, which were bought out so rapidly that second print-runs had to be ordered within a few days. *Publisher's Weekly* surveys of best seller lists across the world have shown that in 2001 the *Harry Potter* books (all four available at the time) were the number one international best sellers; and that all four of them were among the first twenty most sold children's books ever in the United States (among these *Goblet*, 2000, was fifth where the first four – J.S. Lowry's *Poly Little Puppy* [1942], Beatrix Potter's *Peter Rabbit* [1902], Gertrude Crampton's *Tootle* [1945], and Dr. Seuss's *Green Eggs and Ham* [1960] – had substantial time advantages in achieving their positions).[3] Not unnaturally this has made J.K. Rowling a very rich person: on 7 April 2002 Reuters reported that she had become the 147th richest person in the UK, with a personal wealth estimated at £226 million (well ahead of the pop-star Madonna, whose wealth was estimated at £200 million).[4] The effect of this on the UK publishers of the *Harry Potter* books, Bloomsbury, has been most satisfactory. Bloomsbury shares, *The Financial Times* reported on 9 March 2002,[5] which were below 100p in 1998 hit a peak of 972p in October 2001. Over two years to 1 March 2002 Bloomsbury had outperformed the FTSE All-Share Index by 380 per cent; pre-tax profits had grown from £1.58 million in 1998 to £5.46 million in 2000 and then to £8.75 million in 2001.[6] Of these figures, it is estimated that the *Harry Potter* books generated about half of the publisher's total turnover and an even greater percentage of profits.[7] *The Financial Times* piece also gave some details of the expansion of Bloomsbury activities in this buoyant position: they acquired the publishing company A & C Black which is best known for producing the *Who's Who* books; made an alliance with the Creative Artists Agency, aimed at getting more books into film; and agreed a business database deal with the *Economist*. The US publisher, Scholastic Children's Publishing Group's profits in fiscal year ending 1 May 2001 showed a 27.2 per cent leap over fiscal year 2000, with US$190 million being generated from the *Harry Potter* titles.[8] But it wasn't just the publishing industry which benefited from the Midas touch of these; the screen adaptation of *Stone* was a phenomenal success too: in February 2002 it was reported that it had become the second highest grossing film in history at US$926.1 million around the world, of which US$320 million came from the box office sales in US alone (the highest grossing film of all time at that point was *The Titanic* at US$1.8 billion globally).[9] But this phenomenon doesn't stop there either. The *Stone* film sound-track by John Williams became in February 2002 the eighth top-selling 'classical album' in the UK.[10] Numerous *Harry Potter*-related products industries found their share prices and profit margins boosted by the association: an audio-recording of *Goblet* by the actor and writer Stephen Fry attracted £1.8 million worth of advance bookings in the UK alone in April 2001;[11] in January 2002 Electronic Arts reported that it had earnings at US$1.03/share, whereas analysts had expected the company to report earnings at 89c/share, largely due to the strong sales of games related to the *Harry Potter* movie;[12] Mattel's Harry Potter Trivia Game, Mystery at Hogwarts and Quidditch Card Game showed satisfactory sales figures;[13] in March 2002 the computer games developer Argonaut reported stock rise by 8 per cent due to sales of hit products such as the *Harry Potter* game.[14] Charities tried to capitalize on the *Harry Potter* phenomenon: J.K. Rowling made something of a reputation for herself as an altruistic person after she gave £500,000 to the National Council for One-Parent Families (NCOPF) in October 2000 and made donations to cancer charities in December 2000;[15] in January 2001 it was reported that the comic writer Richard Curtis had persuaded Rowling to write two books which could have been found in the fictional Hogwarts Library, and was hoping to get £22 million for Comic Relief by selling 11 million copies of these.[16] Auction houses got in on the act too: in November 2000 it was reported that one of the 300 hard-back first editions of *Stone* had sold for over £6,000 in an auction in Wiltshire; and in February 2002 newspapers announced that a first edition of *Stone* had sold for £9,700 in London, and that a set of signed deluxe editions had fetched £3,000 for the Leukaemia Research Fund Charity.[17] This success story keeps going on but I don't think the point needs to be laboured here any further. Indeed, so inextricably entwined has the *Harry Potter* phenomenon become with market and financial issues that some of the more serious examinations of the *Harry Potter* texts have been undertaken from disciplinary perspectives that deal with those issues[18] (I discuss these later).

2   The *Harry Potter* books and their offspring have apparently transcended cultural boundaries more effortlessly than any other fictional work of recent years. By March 2002 it was reported that these have been translated into 47 languages and had sold well in most of the countries where available; 57 publishers covering different countries are involved. The second and third international best-sellers listed in March 2002 by *Publisher's Weekly* were significantly behind in the range of languages that they had been translated into: in the second

spot, John Grisham's *The Brethren* was at that time available in 29 languages, and in the third spot Umberto Eco's *Baudolino* in 32 languages.[19] The extraordinary sales in the US and the UK were accompanied by similarly healthy figures in most other European countries, and newspaper reports indicated that the phenomenon had extended to a range of countries in other continents. The film of *Stone* was also a substantial hit in each of these countries, as the status of being the second highest grossing film ever world-wide indicates. A November 2002 survey of the reception of the *Harry Potter* books and films in Germany, Japan, France, Indonesia, China, Spain, Australia, India, Mexico and Norway gives some indication of the success of both in all these contexts.[20] Giving more figures here would be tedious.

3   The *Harry Potter* books are the most challenged (i.e. where complaints are recorded by an institution about the appropriateness of the content of a book) and banned books of our time. According to the American Library Association's Office for Intellectual Freedom the *Harry Potter* books headed the top of their most challenged books list for three years running (from 1999 to 2001).[21] In 1999 itself it reached the top of that list in the US with 26 challenges to remove them from the shelves of libraries in 16 states – no mean achievement for a series the first of which was published in 1997. By 2000 it was placed among the top 100 most challenged books of the 1990s. In January 2001 it was reported that the number of complaints against the *Harry Potter* books in the US had tripled since 1999.[22] In 29 March 2000 Rev. George Bender of the Harvest Assembly of God Church in Pennsylvania led a ceremonial burning of pop items that were considered 'ungodly', including a *Harry Potter* book;[23] and in 30 December 2001 Rev. John Brock of the Christ Community Church of Alamogordo, New Mexico, led a book-burning service in which the *Harry Potter* and other books were thrown into the flames.[24] In March 2000 in the US eight groups including the American Booksellers Foundation for Free Expression, the Freedom to Read Foundation, the Association of American Publishers, the National Council of Teachers in English, the Children's Book Council, the Association of Booksellers for Children, the National Coalition Against Censorship, and PEN American Center formed a national association – initially called Muggles for Harry Potter and later renamed Kidspeak – to fight attempts to restrict access to the *Harry Potter* books. Their web-site ('http://www.mugglesforharrypotter.com') continues to provide information about the bannings of and complaints

against the *Harry Potter* books in the US. In November 2001 the United States Conference of Catholic Bishops issued a statement regarding the *Stone* film: 'Parents concerned about the film's sorcery element should know that it is unlikely to pose any threat to Catholic beliefs. *Harry Potter* is so obviously innocuous fantasy that its fiction is easily distinguishable from life.'[25] Attempted and implemented censorship of the above sort was also reported from several other countries: including the UK (St. Mary's School in Chatham, Kent), Australia (The Christian Outreach College in Queensland and about 60 Seventh Day Adventist schools), Canada (The Durham Region School Board and others), Germany (schools in the Muensingen-Reitheim district), the United Arab Emirates (all private schools) and Taiwan (the Ling-Leung Church).[26] There are probably other similar instances of denunciation and censorship that I haven't picked up. The above-mentioned cases are all at the instance of the religious right (primarily the Christian right), and are straightforwardly matters of attempted or implemented censorship. The phenomenon of censorship with regard to the *Harry Potter* books may therefore be regarded as a matter of religious bigotry and of little interest from an analytical critical perspective. It could be argued, and justifiably, that such bigotry is by definition outside the sphere of rationalistic discussion: banning is indicative of a desire not to engage with oppositional perspectives. There are several reasons for being cautious about such a dismissive attitude however. One, religious censorship on the scale that the *Harry Potter* books have attracted is undoubtedly a matter of critical interest for those who are interested in the reception of books, and responsive engagements with texts, as social phenomena. Such cases might not tell us much about the texts as such but they do reveal a good deal about the religious attitudes that attach to literature and direct much reading. As a symptom of religious bigotry in our world these cases are worthy of examination, and after 11 September 2001 it is transparent even in critical circles in the West that any careless and inattentive dismissal of religious bigotry, whatever the source and wherever, is unacceptable. Two, though it seems obvious that such a desire for making the oppositional disappear can only emanate from an uncritical perspective, there is some evidence that religious perspectives of *Harry Potter* haven't been entirely without the support of analysis and scholarship. Several studies questioning the ideological appropriateness of these books from Christian religious perspectives have appeared, including several substantial and reasonably well-researched books.[27] Three, these cases are not just about religious

bigotry, but especially about the location of children and the education of children (most of them have to do with schools and other
educational institutions, and the case for censorship has generally
been argued for in terms of protecting children) – these are, in other
words, revealing of the positioning of children as a category with
social and political effect within religious discourses. Four, though
religious perspectives provide the most obvious instances of disapprobation (all too easily falling in with calls for censorship), there simmers behind this a larger polarization of essentially unthinking
opinion about the *Harry Potter* books which is not unconnected with
the phenomenon of attempting to censor. Just as these books have
attracted a phenomenal amount of enthusiastic approval (much of
which is, I have maintained above, unthinking), these books have also
fuelled a noticeable quantity of (often equally unthinking) disapproval.
The kind of unthinking approval that the *Harry Potter* books have
drawn has been commented on already by some critics – especially
Jack Zipes and Christine Schoefer – who have expressed scepticism
about certain aspects of these books and found themselves beset by
outraged adults.[28] What is yet to be examined and analysed is the
kind of unthinking disapproval that is also being directed at these
books and not just from the Christian right. The NPD *Harry Potter*
popularity meter survey table given in Chapter 2 shows a more or
less balanced ratio of opinions between two extreme positions:
'Harry Potter is the best' and 'I can't stand Harry Potter'. These
extreme positions smell of unthinking sloganizing, of the chanting
of a cheering crowd or a lynch mob. What is noteworthy is both the
blind approval and the blind disapproval – the polarized opinions,
despite the indifferent middle ground (those who don't care). In
December 2001 it was reported that a Harry Potter 'hate-line' has
been established in Austria, a telephone service called the Anti-
Harry Potter Hotline, where those who wished could ring up and
rant about exactly what the title suggests.[29] A trawl through websites devoted to the *Harry Potter* phenomenon throws up several that
define themselves as anti-Harry Potter – notably, for example, that
of The Organization of People Against Potter (TOOPAP), 'http://
www.geocities.com/toopap/'. Though these are dominated by conservative Christian opinions, they are not entirely monopolized by
them.

These three points gesture towards the substantial social and political
effect of the *Harry Potter* books, and circumscribe the so-called *Harry Potter*

phenomenon. The manner in which the discourses of finance and markets mediate and moderate (immoderately in this case) the passage of books to readers, such that the reader's engagement rebounds back into financial and market discourses; the extent to which books get absorbed and accommodated in different cultures (drawing upon translated assumptions and cross-cultural perceptions); the extent to which different ideological positions seek to negate or silence oppositional perspectives, or (more importantly) *construct* certain subjects and objects in their own terms – all these are clearly matters of social and political concern. The picture that these observations gesture towards is undoubtedly a complex one (more complex than my schematic presentation of these has suggested) for there are probably significant links between the three points. The operations of markets and financial interests cannot be seen in isolation from their cross-cultural or international effects: in a vaunted age of globalization – a term that particularly applies to modes of economic organization – cross-cultural or international transmissions are determined to a large degree by such organization. The kind of unthinking enthusiasm and revulsion that was marked in point 3 above (whatever the ideological source thereof) may well have something to do with marketing and financial interests: with the manner in which books are advertised and promoted, and the manner in which consumers are acted upon and consuming desires created. The strength of religious opinion-forming and dogmatism in our world that is displayed in point 3 above also impinges upon prevailing understandings of the cultural locations from which they emanate. The fact that the *Harry Potter* books have been a focal point for religious denunciation in recent years may well be symptomatic of the larger growth of such ideologies in our world, which in turn could be regarded as a reaction to what passes for globalization. (This has been suggested in a plethora of political and sociological works.) There are, in other words, a set of fascinating questions of social and political import – a sense of underlying socially and politically effective patterns – that could, to say the least, be approached through a close examination of the *Harry Potter* phenomenon.

There are, it seems to me, two ways of approaching the task of elucidating such issues. One way, which may be regarded as a *world-to-text* approach, could be to address these patterns and questions at the level at which they are most ostensibly posed: to delineate them from the midst of an informed understanding of processes of globalization, financial and market discourses, religious and other ideologies, specific cultural formations and cross-cultural perspectives (with the underlying linguistic and political presumptions), and the linkages between these.

Two (I think of this as a *text-to-world* approach) follows from a conviction that one factor that connects all these social and political effects are obviously the *Harry Potter* books themselves, and close attention to these in the first instance is likely to provide some indication of how the effects in question emanate from them. The first (world-to-text) approach has a broad aim: *of examining how the condition of the world explains certain phenomena (in this instance the* Harry Potter *phenomenon could be regarded as one symptom of this condition among many).* Methodologically, this demands a primary understanding of the condition of the world in a broad sense. The contents of texts and their possible readings do not figure as being determinative in this approach; indeed these are more likely to be seen as being determined by extrinsic forces. The second (text-to-world) approach has a more specific objective: *to understand how specific texts and their readings lead outwards towards and devolve from the world they occur within.* Methodologically, this demands a primary focus on specific texts and how they may be read. It is more or less assumed in such an approach that the content of texts and their possible readings have something to do with their social and political effects, and indicate something of the social and political circumstances they derive from.

Ideally, of course, it may be hoped that some sort of balance is struck between both these approaches so that the world-to-text and the text-to-world directions converge at some point of lucid apprehension. The realization of this ideal critical situation is, it may be argued, often impeded by the contrary critical presumptions that underlie these two approaches. But I do not wish to go into that here. It is not my intention to examine the relative strengths and weaknesses of these two approaches at a theoretical level: I have simply outlined them briefly to enable a clear statement of my methodological prerogatives. An enormous amount of literary critical theory (arguably all literary critical theory) has revolved around this question. Let me simply say that I feel that both approaches are equally, albeit in different ways, valuable; and instead of trying to reconcile them, or choosing between them on reasoned grounds, or using both, for the sake of methodological clarity I more or less arbitrarily plunge for one of them in this study. Briefly then, *in this study I choose to approach the* Harry Potter *phenomenon with a text-to-world methodology.*

My essential questions are these: How are the considerable social and political effects of the *Harry Potter* books related to the content and possible readings of those books? To what extent could the latter be thought of as determining the former? What are the reasons that these particular texts and their possible readings have generated such effects, where many texts that are apparently similar to these in different ways, and subjected to similar market forces and ideological conditions, have not been able to do so?

These are serious matters and need to be treated as such.

4
Text-to-World Assumptions (Some General Definitions)

It may be useful at this point to recapitulate the critical decisions that I have taken so far, and to make explicit the connected questions that remain unanswered. There are three such critical decisions; the questions that arise from them are stated in italics:

(a) I have stated in Chapter 1 that this essay is devoted to examining the social and political effects of the *Harry Potter* books. *In stating this I haven't yet explained precisely what I mean by social and political effects.* That is what this chapter is devoted to.

(b) In Chapter 2 I have decided that this study would *not* try to analyse the *Harry Potter* books as being directed essentially towards or being consumed essentially by children. For critical purposes the books will be addressed here as any book directed at a fully critically aware and discerning audience normally is. *It might be felt that this decision needs further fleshing out and, in fact, I revisit the ground underlying this decision at some length in Chapter 7 below.*

(c) At the end of the previous chapter I have explained that I will adopt a text-to-world approach and methodology for this essay – with a view to a serious analysis of the books in question. Such an approach to the *Harry Potter* books would, I have tacitly assumed, counter the unthinking trend that much of the response to these has manifested so far. *However, I haven't yet clearly stated what makes an unthinking or misguided reading so, and what may characterize a serious thinking reading. And, in that connection, I also have not clarified what links serious thinking readings to an understanding of social and political effects – why I expect to be able to move from text-to-world if I approach the text in a serious thinking fashion. Is it not possible that in this case the content and readerly possibilities of the texts are such that they simply refuse our world*[1] *and location within our world?* Much of the remainder of this part is devoted to clearing up these issues.

The questions that remain are difficult ones, and yet it is necessary that for a rigorous and consistent consideration of the *Harry Potter* texts and phenomenon they should be answered. I can't help feeling that I have placed myself in a rather uncomfortable corner. When in doubt look for authorities has been the motto of my not unusual education; I am tempted to discharge a powerful stream of authoritative references at this point to wash away (or drown) any annoying scepticism about my position here. However, I am determined to resist this temptation. I do wish to be able to convey my arguments to readers who may be *seriously* interested in these matters but not necessarily expert in literary critical theories. Most importantly, I do not want to stray too far from my focus on the *Harry Potter* phenomenon – and this study is already in danger of turning into some sort of semi-philosophical musing with the *Harry Potter* books as an excuse. That will not do. So I proceed to some brief and to-the-point generalizations about political and social effects and different kinds of reading, unsupported by references to the numerous relevant works of literary theory, and open therefore to the interrogation of sceptics. Here we go then:

- As far as this essay goes, the social and the political are with regard to a collective, members of which understand that they are within that collective – a society or polity. Society refers to the constitution of a collective (with modes of subsistence, cultural forms, informal organizational structures, etc.); polity refers to the rules and values with which a collective is administered and conducted (with the aid of legal procedures, constitutions, executive and regulatory institutions, official organizational structures, etc.). Clearly, these terms are not independent: the same collective could be regarded as both a society and a polity; a society may have different polities within it; a polity may have a range of societies within it; societies and polities may overlap and yet be distinguished through a complex set of relations. Further, social matters would inevitably impinge on the functioning of a polity and political matters on that of a society. Social issues may comprehend issues that pertain to a significant part of a society or to a range of societies; just as political issues could pertain to some significant section of a polity or to a range of different polities. Some idea, event or phenomenon can be said to have social effect when it generates some form of activity or thinking that could be said to impact upon or have implications for, loosely, a society or a range of societies in general; and similarly political effect can be understood in terms of a polity or range of polities.[2]

- Every individual, group, institution, etc. is necessarily part of at least a society and a polity, and sometimes of several societies and polities. Every act of interpersonal or institutional or communal (or any other kind) expression and exchange (whether in daily life, through institutional forums, through the media, or through texts of any sort) is therefore determined to a significant extent by the social and political mores of the communicators–communicatees involved in complicated ways.

- Acts of communication do not necessarily have equal degrees of social and political effect: significant degrees of social and political effect would be such as would impact upon or have implications for significant quantities within/of collectives. Whether certain social and political effects could be regarded as significant or not is determined by the conventions surrounding the usage of such terms, or by what may be regarded as reasonable quantification of impact or implications entailed. Significant social and political effects are therefore either manifest and understood to be manifest among interested parties; or they have to be demonstrated as occurring by interested parties.

- Every text, of whatever kind, could be regarded as representing an act of communication, and therefore falling within a field (or more) of social and political mores, and possibly able to produce some degree of social and political effect. Since this essay is concerned with works of literary fiction, that is what I focus on. A work of literary fiction could be regarded as mediating communication between an author and readers,[3] between different readers, between different chronological and cultural locations, between different groups (say, reading and discussion groups devoted to particular kinds of texts), even within a reader (as in a reader thinking about a text, so to say, with herself), between different institutions (between say schools and publishers and the media, etc.), between different texts that already exist (in inevitably being associated with ideas, images, methods which occur elsewhere), and so on. At which of these levels a work of literary fiction is understood as mediating communication depends to a great degree on which level one chooses to focus (each of these has been discussed somewhere or the other). However, at each of these levels some kind of social and political relevance, some reflection of social and political mores, and some degree of social and political effect could be anticipated.

- Insofar as a work of literary fiction could be said to exercise a social or political effect on readers who belong to some society and polity (which all works of literary fiction could do to some extent), there are degrees to which readers may be involved in that process. Readers may passively or unthinkingly (similar to subconsciously, but without the psychoanalytical baggage that comes with that term) become participant in the exercising of the social and political effect; readers may be wilfully or unconsideringly indifferent to such social and political effects (which means that though such effects may be generated these readers have either chosen not to or happen not to be affected by them); readers may analyse and interrogate in an aware fashion what social and political implications and effects a work of literary fiction is generating and then situate themselves with regard to it. The first possibility I have called unthinking reading; the middle possibility is of no interest here; the final possibility has been thought of as thinking or analytical reading.
- It is generally recognized that a work of literary fiction does have some sort of social and political effect. *What* the degree of significance of such an effect is can be self-evident to all or discerned and understood through a thinking or analytical reading. *Why* a certain degree of such effect occurs can only be examined through readings that are thinking and analytical. Unthinking readings become part and parcel of that effect; unthinking participants in that effect; part of the *modus operandi* of that effect – their role is indistinguishable from that of the text in mediating the act of communication that leads to the social and political effect. The social and political implications of a work of literary fiction and the manner in which these impinge upon unthinking reading (which together forms the social and political effect) is what the analytical or thinking readings try to unravel and clarify. That, at any rate, is the key conviction of the text-to-world methodology that I have assumed here.
- Put in that fashion it might instinctively seem that analytical or unthinking readings are essentially what literary critics do or what literary interpretation does. To assume that there are hidden or non-explicit – but present and in some sense *true* – meanings and implications in works of literary fiction (any literary work), and to try and reveal them, seem to be what the institutionalized practice of literary study does. I am however not convinced that literary criticism or interpretation is necessarily the same as analytical and thinking reading. The former is primarily defined by the institutionalization of its practice, by the fact that those who engage with it have some

sort of institutional sanction and follow some sort of institutionally or communally agreed upon form. It is conceivable that analytical and thinking reading may occur outside those sanctions and forms. Let me put the situation as follows: analytical and thinking reading is *likely* to be close to literary criticism or interpretation (the institutional prerogatives are designed to encourage analysis and thought); but is not *necessarily* so. Literary criticism or interpretation may also be weak in analysis and thinkingness, may be constructed on questionable premises, may have contradictory or limited methodologies that dilute its analytical qualities. Such criticism or interpretation would be unthinking too, and therefore become unthinkingly participant in the social and political effect in question (thus transferring the institutional credentials to that effect, making it that much stronger). This, I argue soon, has actually been the case with regard to the *Harry Potter* books.

These, then, are clarifications of some of the terms I have used demonstratively so far.

5
A Thought about Open and Closed Texts

What sort of bearing the above definitions may have on a serious text-to-world reading of the *Harry Potter* books would naturally depend to some extent on the sort of presumptions that exist about the relationship of such books to readers *before* they are thinkingly read (an area that is connected to the book covers with which I began). This involves, in fact, the categorization of books vis-à-vis readers in a *general* sense: i.e. not in terms of descriptive (or broadly genre-based) categories according to form (fiction, drama, poetry), content (fantasy fiction, science fiction), authorship (women's writing, black writing), or type of reader (children's fiction); but categorization in terms of the *quality of general reading experience* that is offered (such as popular writing, pulp fiction, literary fiction, pot boiler, easy reading). I discuss the genre-based categorization or descriptive categorization at some length below; those can only be proffered, understood and accepted *after* some sort of thinking reading. Categories in terms of quality of general reading experience on offer do not lend themselves to discussion easily: they are somewhat arbitrary and off-the-cuff, and are usually *designedly* made unthinkingly for marketing purposes. If such categories are approached in a more analytical spirit, they can be dissected further only in descriptive terms or more analytically oriented generic terms – and then they lose their sense of being categories according to quality of general reading experience. For such categories to work they have to remain arbitrary, off-the-cuff, unthinking. Given that these are unanalysably such, however, these categories do undeniably play a determinative role in readers' attitudes and responses. The *Harry Potter* books are largely regarded as 'easy reading' or 'popular literature' (at any rate, no one would protest if I said that). That is, let's say, their category according to the quality of general reading experience. This has a clear effect on how they are regarded, responded to, and what sort of political and social effects may be attributed or may fail to get attributed to them. If I try to delve deeper into understanding why such a categorization attaches to the *Harry Potter* books, however, I will not be making the categorization clearer, but would be moving away to a somewhat different mode of categorization that is more amenable to critical thinking. I will have to start wondering (and indeed I soon do so) whether it has to do with the fantastic content, with being directed at children, with being written by a woman, with its linguistic form, etc. In doing so the category according to quality of general reading experience would have slipped out of my grasp, and I would be left talking about genre or descriptive categories. Given my commitment to serious, thinking, analytical reading there isn't much I can do about this, except: (a) recognize that there *are* such categories according to quality of general reading experience; (b) admit that these have a bearing on the social and political effects of texts; and (c) admit that this is a matter that I can't analyse further. This is an unsatisfactory state of affairs but there it is, and it is best to get it off my chest at this early stage.

Having said all that though, it occurs to me that there is at least one *analytical* attempt to categorize literary works in terms of quality of general reading experience that I could usefully refer to here and that could be brought to bear on the *Harry Potter* books' status as 'easy reading' or 'popular literature': categorization as 'open texts' and 'closed texts'. These terms come from Umberto Eco's reflections on reading and texts.[1] Simplistically put, Eco suggested that there are broadly two kinds of texts. There are those that can be read (interpreted) at a range of different levels, and engage a large number of different (and even contradictory) strategies and perspectives to make sense of them and derive pleasure from them – i.e. the pleasure derives to a large extent from the very act of negotiating between different and even contrary ways in which sense can be made from them. Such texts are *open texts. Closed texts* are those that can be read primarily and without much effort with one familiar strategy and develop coherently through a single uncomplicated perspective – i.e. the pleasure in reading these derive from the predictability of what the text presents and what the reader may find in it, the comfort and laziness of not having to negotiate with different and clashing perspectives and strategies. Eco's examples of closed texts include the James Bond novels and Superman comics; among open texts he counts James Joyce's works. It is reasonably clear that Eco didn't much approve of readers who prefer closed texts: they are seen as 'more or less precise empirical readers' who are themselves closed in categories: 'children, soap opera addicts, doctors, law-abiding citizens, swingers, Presbyterians, farmers, middle-class women, scuba divers, effete snobs or any other imaginable sociopsychological category'. The reader of open texts is a more alive and dynamic person, one who is 'able to master different codes and eager to deal with the text as a maze of many issues', and is only inevitably restrained by the physical limits of a text.[2] It is clear too that the closed texts are generally mass-market products, and the open texts would be regarded as up-market.

This is a rather unfair simplification of what is in actuality a complex exposition, but it would do for the present. It can be used to place the *Harry Potter* books as being closed and directed towards empirically precise readers who are (mainly) children – apparently an analytical category to do with the quality of general reading experience. This might not seem to be especially relevant to this essay on the social and political implications of the *Harry Potter* books and phenomenon. Obviously, Eco's interests are primarily with the aesthetics of reading, and mine more with the politics of reading. However, Eco's reflections do provide a particular insight that is relevant here. No matter how apparently politically or socially neutral, how pristinely aesthetic, such reflections and categorizations according to quality of general reading experience might appear to be, the fact is that the very act of *thinkingly* approaching them (Eco-like) inevitably brings to light a political and social backdrop. After all, thinking about anything entails an act of communication that would inevitably have social and political effects. This is worth remembering. What becomes explicit in Eco's thinking categorization according to quality of general reading experience is that it not only illuminates the literary works that are examined, it also throws his own socially and politically effective stance open to interrogation. The above summary easily raises questions: Doesn't that list of empirically precise categories as opposed to intellectually active persons have certain gender and class presumptions worked into it? Is not Eco committing himself to a particular ideological position by offering such schematic divisions between kinds of texts and kinds of readers? This is worth bearing in mind.

Finally, social and political effects cannot be assessed in terms of what is unthinking. Unthinking categorization of the *Harry Potter* books according to the quality of general reading experience may have recognizable social and political effects but they don't matter to my *thinking* reading of them. As soon as I am able, Eco-like, to give such categorization some sort of thinking structure, by dint of doing so itself social and political effects would come into play. It naturally follows that when I offer in these pages such categories as unthinking reading and thinking reading, and proceed to analyse the *Harry Potter* phenomenon with a text-to-world methodology, there is undoubtedly a social and political aspect to what I do as well. It is not my business to make *that* explicit, but to recognize that it is inevitably there.

6
The Irrelevance of J.K. Rowling

What about the author? I can see this question creeping up upon me from several directions. Did she intend that her books have the social and political effects that they have had? Is she responsible for those effects? There is a strong predisposition on the part of readers generally, in an obvious and natural fashion, to assume that if texts mediate communication, that communication must be from the author to readers. There is an undeniable logic about this: someone communicates to someone – if books are involved in communication why shouldn't we simply look to the source of that book as much as the audience to understand what is involved in the communication? J.K. Rowling wrote the *Harry Potter* books. She must be the person that communicates through these books to readers, and if there is a social and political effect from this book, it is surely as important to understand what she thought she was about as to comprehend what her readers thought they were about, and indeed as much as those other invisible creators who shape those books with Rowling (the cover designers, publishers, advertisers, etc.) might have known what they were about. The latter are in some sense peripheral, almost invisible, but Rowling's author-ity (a well-worn pun now) stares readers in the face on the cover of every one of the *Harry Potter* books, in every review, interview, every bit of media coverage. It is perverse not to take the author into account. Understandably, the *Harry Potter* phenomenon includes a perfect storm of interest in the author: admiring biographies of Rowling are cropping up steadily in book shops,[1] interviews are published in quantity,[2] she is honoured by several institutions,[3] her authorial status is quantified not just by prestige but by her financial worth,[4] hardly a review has failed to mention the circumstances in which the first *Harry Potter* books were produced (single mother on the dole, sums up the apparently not entirely accurate picture). Her statements on the *Harry Potter* books are taken as gospel; she is honoured by children and adults alike. The author has been incorporated into the *Harry Potter* phenomenon. Just as unthinking readers become participant in the *Harry Potter* phenomenon, are within the phenomenon rather than at any analytical distance, so too is Rowling as the author.

In becoming so, it seems to me, her intentions and responsibilities as author diminish and fade into irrelevance. She ceases to be the author of the phenomenon and simply becomes part of the phenomenon as author.

There is something familiarly perverse about saying that. It is reminiscent of the steady stream of pre-eminently thinking – thoughtful – writers and readers, recognized and canonized as being such, who have sought to take precisely this perverse position. It probably goes back to Gustave Flaubert's and other nineteenth-century realists' and naturalists' bid to achieve a recording of reality that is so objective that the author as a subject, a particular individual, leaves no trace in their writing.[5] It is found in the deliberate cultivation of an impersonal artist – impersonal to the point of disappearing – that reputed Modernists (Joyce, Eliot, Pound) cultivated.[6] The fallacy of constantly trying to retrieve the author's intention in the course of reading was explained by Wimsatt and Beardsley.[7] The death of the author was declared by Barthes.[8] A series of critics have chosen to look so closely at the forms, structures and linguistic nuances of texts, the relation of texts to other texts, the relation of texts to the historical circumstances out of which they devolve and into which they constantly get accommodated, the social discourses out of which texts emerge and into which texts are soaked up, that the author becomes apparently unimportant and fades into irrelevance and neglect – this could be seen as the substance of the development of literary critical theory. So imperious has this calculated disregard of the author grown through the 1970s and 1980s and since, that unconvinced voices have occasionally appeared, protesting against this new 'critical orthodoxy':

> Cogent as the reasons for [excluding the author] have often appeared, this talk of exclusion has done harm. It is better to think that all books have this doubtful person, and they also have in them the doubtful polity and community, whose claims he is praised for resisting and ignoring.[9]

Or again:

> A massive disjunction opens up between the theoretical statement of authorial disappearance and the project of reading without the

author. What [texts holding such a theoretical position] say about the author, and what they do with the author issue at such an express level of contradiction that the performative aspects utterly overwhelm the declaration of authorial disappearance.[10]

Such grumblings have, however, only had a limited impact.

But it is not the theoretical arguments about the relevance or irrelevance of the author that underlie my neglect of Rowling as author of the *Harry Potter* books in a consideration of their social and political effect. A somewhat different (and equally familiar) trajectory leads me in that direction. It does not have to do with what literary critical arguments have done with the idea of author-ship, it has more to do with unthinking constructions of author-ship when the natural and obvious presence of the author is taken for granted. It is the unthinking construction of the author that ultimately is the more powerful, occasionally disturbing careful critical arguments about author-ship and sometimes seeping into those arguments themselves against the current. It is evidenced through the defeat in the marketplace that cannot be ignored: literary biographies sell better than books of literary criticism. Apparently readers, even well-trained and professionally sceptical and analytical readers, seem to construct unthinkingly some sort of wraith of an author when reading books and feel some desire to give it flesh. This is revealed when their imagined constructions of authors are most gratingly challenged and they feel a need to admit that such constructions are at stake. This occurs, for example, when a highly regarded literary theorist (himself an advocate of the erasure of author-ity) is found also to have been the author of some articles which express sympathy with a Fascist position and this discovery somehow threatens to taint his writings;[11] when a widely admired set of poems are seen with different lenses because it is suspected that the poet may have been anti-Semite;[12] when the apparently autobiographical writing of one who presents himself as a Jewish child survivor of the Holocaust is discredited because it is discovered that he is not what he claimed to be;[13] when an initially sympathetically received novel about the travails of a South Asian family in Britain apparently written by an Asian woman loses credibility because the author is later revealed to be an English man[14]...Such events make good news, sensationally challenging the unthinking assumptions about authors that readers almost always entertain. Such events also raise critical controversies, causing unease because they subvert the unthinking constructions of authors that exist among the most blasé theorists and critics.

My point is that the 'author' who is talked about (like the 'children' who are mentioned in relation to understanding books for children) is primarily a construct that emerges from readers' engagement with texts. The biographical subject who is the author, that individual who tangibly personifies that construct, the author in flesh, may bear some resemblance to this construct, may try to live up to that construct, may become that construct or may prove to have no relation to that construct (which would be news to readers, and make even critics who deny author-ity uncomfortable). The fact that an especially subversive mismatch between the construct and the person causes consternation demonstrates that it is the *construct* who is allocated or attributed responsibility for the texts – it is the imagined author who, by proxy, bears responsibility for the texts, who comes to personify the commitments that the texts seem to present. The flesh-and-blood author is an inconvenience if she cannot live up to the author of the imagination. And *that* simply reveals that the former is *not* responsible for the texts (though indubitably having produced them), the former has always something – a uniquely subjective something – that can defy analysis as any occasionally inconsistent, often contradictory, sometimes unpredictable individual in the world that we inhabit can be.

So Rowling, the person who is interviewed and photographed and biographically charted, is irrelevant to an understanding of the social and political effects of the *Harry Potter* books. I don't care whether that Rowling can be held responsible for these effects, and I don't think it matters or can be determined. What matters for this essay is the con-structed author (a constructed persona with social and political effect), just as what matters for this study is children as a socially and politically effective category rather than real children: the constructed persona and the constructed category, like so much else, are integral aspects of the *Harry Potter* phenomenon.

Interestingly, the construction of the author in relation to the flesh and blood author is addressed in one of the *Harry Potter* books – in *Chamber*. Gilderoy Lockhart appears in *Chamber* as a famous wizard author, the hero of his own books, publicity-seeking and charismatic (at least to women). Lockhart the person takes full and deliberate responsibility for the author-construct who is so beloved in the wizard world: he *constructs* himself as the hero of his books so that to his read-ers the hero merges into their imagined author, who in turn merges into the real person; he *manages* his public encounters with the media and with his fans so that the imagined author and the real author can-not be distinguished. At the same time though, with fatal arrogance and magical ineptitude, Lockhart constantly gives the mismatch between the imagined author and the real author away to his students – at least to the male students – and of course to the readers of *Chamber*. There is a kind of inevitability about this mismatch: the author of the imagination is simply irreconcilable with the real author, the person who is author. To hope it would be otherwise is a deception, and Lockhart is seen as being culpable from the beginning as a deceiver, a conman. To some extent this inevitability is the result of Lockhart's characteristic duplicity and love of recognition; but, interestingly, when it comes to the final confrontation and Lockhart is forced to face up to his fraudulent practices he shifts the blame from himself. 'Books can be misleading,' he points out to Harry and Ron; and explains:

> My books wouldn't have sold half as well if people didn't think *I'd* done all those things. No one wants to read about some ugly Armenian warlock, even if he did save a village from werewolves. He'd look dreadful on the front cover. No dress sense at all. And the witch who banished the Bandon Banshee had a hare lip. I mean, come on...
> (*Chamber* 220)

Lockhart behaved as he did, in other words, because readers expected him to, and those who cater to readers therefore expected him to. Lockhart had simply fulfilled the desire for the author-hero that already existed, that the book industry could capitalize on, that the media could play to. He became the image (literally, someone who looks good on book covers, with the right dress sense) that readers wished to see: the imagined construction of author-ity in the minds of readers, helped along by the industry that deals in images. Not surprisingly, the most intrepid reader of Hogwarts School, Hermione, seems to be curiously blind to the flesh-and-blood Lockhart's inadequacies and clings most tenaciously to the author-image that she admires.

The unreliability of the constructed authors of books, who exist in the readers' imagination, is the *leitmotif* of *Chamber*. T.M. Riddle's Diary – a book too, but one in which authors become readers and readers authors, where authors and readers meet and change places – is the site of the ultimate violation of innocence. Through it the unscrupulous author and reader, Tom Marvolo Riddle (past incarnation of the evil Voldemort), exploits both the integrity of an author ('It took a very long time for stupid little Ginny to stop trusting her diary' [*Chamber* 229]), and the credulity of a reader ('I wrote back, I was sympathetic, I was kind. Ginny simply *loved* me' [*Chamber* 228]).

So the books of Magic world – like images within books, on posters, in paintings – have a life of their own (literally) which constantly thwart readers. In *Stone* when Harry sneaked into the Restricted Section of Hogwarts Library and opened a book: 'A piercing, blood-curdling shriek split the silence – the book was screaming! Harry snapped it shut, but the shriek went on and on, one high, unbroken, ear-splitting note' (*Stone* 151). In *Prisoner*, Hagrid's birthday present to Harry, *The Monster Book of Monsters*, is described as 'flip[ping] onto its edge', 'scuttl[ing] sideways along the bed like some weird crab', 'toppl[ing] off the bed' and 'shuffl[ing] rapidly across the room' (*Prisoner* 15). *The Monster Book of Monsters* later causes havoc in the bookshop of Diagon Alley, and in Hogwarts; obviously not only is *The Monster Book of Monsters* a large book about monsters, it is a monster itself.

This is an interesting theme, but what should readers of *Harry Potter* books make of it? Is it to be regarded as a message from Rowling? Is it Rowling warning her readers to be circumspect about how they construct the author, and simultaneously announcing that her subjective real space be left alone? Can she have deliberately and self-consciously intended such a message, and is she responsible for the consequences that it might have? These are questions of no interest in this essay. Irrespective of how Rowling may respond to these questions such observations are there to be inferred, and these inferences may have certain social and political effects, and an author persona would be constructed and dubbed Rowling by readers, and that construct may be held responsible for such effects as occur.

Those questions might become relevant if the real-life Rowling did or does anything to clash with the constructed author Rowling who already exists, who has been active in the exponential, indeed monstrous, growth of the *Harry Potter* phenomenon. The real-life Rowling has not been discovered doing anything that clashes with the constructed author who is spoken of. Both have, so far, merged seamlessly into a quiet and reassuring and conservative mythology of women writing (especially for children), that is not even as daring as the mythology of women writing and producing children observed satirically by Roland Barthes in *Mythologies* some time in the early 1950s:

Women, be therefore courageous, free; play at being men, write like them; but never get far from them; live under their gaze, compensate for your books by children; enjoy a free rein for a while, but quickly come back to your condition. One novel, one child, a little feminism, a little connubiality. Let us tie the adventure of art to the strong pillars of the home: both will profit a great deal from this combination: where myths are concerned, mutual help is always fruitful.[15]

The mythology of Rowling as the constructed author is a quieter one: it is that of a woman, a mother, a lover of children, a charitable person who is seen to write as such. She gives apartments to her friends, contributes to charities, marries, makes sure a British child plays Harry, and doesn't allow Coca-Cola to use Harry Potter too aggressively in marketing (protects children from becoming mindless consumers). It would take a very old-fashioned and hardened Thatcherite Tory[16] to find herself caught out by the mythologized author who was a single mother on the dole and made good and became one of the richest and most famous persons in Britain.

That's pretty much all I have to say about the author in this essay.

7
Children's Literature

[A]nalytical and thinking reading is *likely* to be close to literary criticism or interpretation (the institutional prerogatives are designed to encourage analysis and thought); but is not *necessarily* so. Literary criticism or interpretation may also be weak in analysis and thinkingness, may be constructed on questionable premises, may have contradictory or limited methodologies that dilute its analytical qualities. Such interpretation or criticism may be unthinking too, and become unthinkingly participant in the social and political effect in question (thus transferring the institutional credentials to that effect, making it that much stronger). This . . . has actually been the case with regard to the *Harry Potter* books.

I am quoting myself here – or rather repeating myself – from Chapter 4, where in the final point I had distinguished thinking and analytical reading from the institutional practice of literary criticism or interpretation. In an essay of this sort, which I know smells of institutional practice itself, it is necessary to explain why I feel literary criticism and interpretation of the *Harry Potter* books have to a large degree been unthinking too.

In the following I do not attempt to give a comprehensive literature survey of critical responses to the *Harry Potter* books, but rather a selective sampling that indicates characteristic positions. The choice of the selected examples allows me both to maintain a focus on the *Harry Potter* phenomenon, and to deal with broad areas without getting swamped by references to all the available theoretical and scholarly material. There are three broad areas, characteristic of three kinds of critical positioning pertinent to *Harry Potter* readings, which are covered here. These are, in the order in which they are discussed, those that understand the *Harry*

Potter books as belonging to the literary genre of 'children's literature', those that place these books as belonging to the literary genre of 'fantasy literature', and those that examine these from the perspective of religious values. My arguments with regard to the first two are primarily directed towards the assumptions implicit in making such genre placements; the third necessarily engages with specific kinds of religious evaluation. I have already glibly introduced terms that carry some considerable baggage of theoretical discussion. I don't mean terms like 'children's literature' and 'fantasy literature' (I am not being glib about *those*), I mean 'literary genre'. Using the term 'literary genre' as if it must be immediately clear to my readers – who, like me, have probably used it often, have a sense of the theoretical discussions that have surrounded it, and have experience of seeing it used – is a habit that characterizes the methods through which communities of literary critics and interpreters identify themselves as such, make themselves known to each other as belonging to such a community. It is the *raison d'être* of jargons. But doing so yet again, while being struck by this aspect of such usage, leads to an uncomfortable comprehension of the fuzziness of the term itself and therefore of the limitations of its usefulness (and applicability and comprehensibility). It is at some level simple enough: it connotes modes of categorizing the field of literature so that it becomes convenient (if not quite clear) to deal with that field for those who are interested in it (writers, readers, critics). But examples for clarifying what such categories are is a more slippery enterprise (poetry, novels, plays, lyric, epic, romance, children's literature, fantasy literature, realistic literature, etc.): they overlap, they are difficult to characterize so that specific works of literature can be unambiguously placed in them, they seem to derive from different descriptive principles (formal, according to readership, thematic, etc.). Every first-year literature undergraduate is faced with these difficulties, doesn't quite get used to it, but eventually gets accustomed to using the term and thus becomes part of the comunity to critics (becomes institutionalized). The attempt to give a general and inclusive definition itself reveals the fuzziness of the terms and ultimately the communal function that they serve. I might, for instance, have gone past this reflection on 'literary genres' with a quick reference to Tzvetan Todorov's rather suggestive and satisfying definition:

> Genres are . . . entities that can be described from two different viewpoints, that of empirical observation and that of abstract analysis. In a given society, the recurrence of certain discursive properties is institutionalized, and individual texts are produced and perceived in

relation to the norm constituted by that codification. A genre, whether literary or not, is nothing other than the codification of discursive properties.[1]

But there are obvious dangers in doing that: it almost immediately draws me, as it did Todorov, into a regression of further definitions (what do 'empirical analysis', 'institutionalization', 'codification', 'discursive properties' mean?), which in turn involves further references and discussions, which have no discernible end if pursued very rigorously and pertinaciously. I would probably just have to end this with the slightly careworn discontent that Todorov himself expressed at the end of a definitive and elaborative exercise regarding (not surprisingly) the term 'literary genre':

> The goal of knowledge is an approximative truth, not an absolute one. If descriptive science claimed to speak *the* truth, it would contradict its reason for being. ... Imperfection is, paradoxically, a guarantee of survival.[2]

Even when a critic tries to avoid jargonistic usage of terms she may not get very far from fuzziness. Since I have devoted some space to making this point here, I might as well add that this applies equally to 'children's literature' – and, for that matter, 'fantasy literature', to which I come later.

To simply assume that a particular text is self-evidently meant for children and should therefore be approached as such is a less agonized process. The idea that what is meant for whom is self-evident and doesn't need to be pondered too deeply is a relatively tranquil – and unthinking – part of literary criticism, which simply gets along with the job of analysing the immediate object of attention without worrying much about the assumptions at work. This idea of the self-evidence of what is 'children's literature' may follow some such untroubled argument as the following:

> [D]espite the flux of childhood, the children's book can be defined in terms of the implied reader. It will be clear, from a careful reading, who a book is designed for: whether the book is on the side of a child totally, whether it is for the developing child, or whether it is aiming somewhere over the child's head. Whether the text can then be given a value depends on the circumstances of use.[3]

The glib use of the phrase 'implied reader', which I have drawn attention to in Chapter 1, is one of those that announce the jargonizing of the professional critic. And yet it is slipped in so smoothly and unassumingly that it seems to make some immediate sense, and the rest follows as a monument of healthy, clear, unconfused (and equally unthinking) formulation. But start worrying about it and it all falls apart: Is the *construct* of the 'implied reader' (that is what Iser explicitly said the idea of the 'implied reader' is[4]) quite the same as real children reading? Who is doing the constructing? Does everyone construct the 'implied reader' in similar ways? If such constructions are going to be different (which may be anticipated if we think about how many different ideas are in circulation about what children should or shouldn't be exposed to) then aren't the evaluations going to be different too? – and so on. But if we don't worry about that sort of thing, we have more or less established a precedent of uncomplicated formulation and can move to ever more adventurous, apparently commonsensical but implicitly unthinking, further claims. A great many of the reviews and studies of the *Harry Potter* books coming from professional critics with the stamp of institutional authority behind them are such; it would be tedious to make a list of these here, so I illustrate the point by quickly mentioning two kinds of instances – one disapproving of the books and the other approving.

Consider a comment such as the following – this is from a review by George M. O'Har (actually a rather interesting one in some respects that I come to later) at the moment when he reflects on the appeal of *Harry Potters* as 'children's books' to adults:

> It is not so easy to understand why adults like these books. The writing is competent, but fails to rise to the level of art. The story itself is derivative, as are the characters that people it. Despite claims to the contrary, the Potter books do not belong on shelves alongside Robert Louis Stevenson, C.S. Lewis, Frances Hodgson Burnett, J.R.R. Tolkien, Lewis Carroll, and Madeleine L'Engle.[5]

I quote O'Har here mainly because of that list of names, which, he suggests, Rowling's could – but fails to – belong to. The names are, of course, of eminent 'children's book' writers and this is an act of fixing a genre in terms of which the *Harry Potter* books must be assessed aesthetically. It is not explained why this particular selection makes the best points of comparison, since the modes of evaluation of the *Harry Potter* books given there could apply to most conventional works of literary fiction. It is simply assumed that these would be appropriate objects of comparison because they are self-evidently known as 'children's books'. This unthinking convention of naming certain books as belonging to the genre of 'children's literature' and then evaluating them comparatively, though often the terms of evaluation have little to do with any feature that is peculiar to that collection of books, is a ploy that has been manifest in a large number of comparative views of the *Harry Potter* books from professional and institutionally approved pens.

A particularly gushing review of the *Potter* books by Roni Natov was published in the specialist 'children's literature' journal, *The Lion and the Unicorn*, in 2001, which provides another kind of institutionally sanctioned and unthinking approach. Here Natov starts by making some confident comments on what children feel and think, which have the character of someone with experience of these matters – not as an ex-child (everyone is that), but as someone who has studied these matters – such as:

> Harry embodies this state of injustice frequently experienced by children, often as inchoate fear and anger – and its other side, desire to possess extraordinary powers that will overcome such early and deep exile from the child's birthright of love and protection.[6]

And Natov ends with an equally confident assessment about the salutary effect that *Potter* books would have on children: 'The *Harry Potter* stories center on what children need to find internally – the strength to do the right thing, to establish a moral code.'[7]

I have no particular quibble with Natov's views, which many people would and obviously do agree with. But I am struck by the air of confidence with which the certainty of knowing how children feel and what children need is given, and by the even more overwhelming certainty that the *Harry Potter* books should be subjected to that frame of evaluation. What interests me is the unself-reflexive fashion in which Natov speaks both *on behalf* of children (how they feel) and *for* children (what they need), without interrogating the processes through which her conclusions are arrived at – that simple uncomplicated assertion of *knowing* about children. In fact, all the questions that have bothered me above would resurface if those processes of knowing were revealed or interrogated: the plain assertion of such knowledge seems to me to be another kind of unthinking critical stance.

I could carry on in that pernickety, complaining fashion, picking up a few lines here and a few lines there and holding them up fastidiously as examples of unthinking assessments of *Harry Potter* books as 'children's literature', but I suspect that may get tedious. I move on instead to a book that addresses the *Harry Potter* phenomenon in a usefully thoughtful fashion, from a reputed specialist in 'children's literature' – and therefore says/reveals (a bit of both) something substantial about the limitations of 'children's literature' as an area of study and a genre wherein certain books are located, in the context of the *Harry Potter* phenomenon (in fact this phrase is taken from this book). I have in mind Jack Zipes's *Sticks and Stones: The Troublesome Success of Children's Literature from Slovenly Peter to Harry Potter* (2001).

Jack Zipes's book has the great advantage of being written with the self-conscious commitment of a specialist in 'children's literature' and of being possessed of an analytical perspective that allows him to assess that commitment, and its underlying assumptions, in a reasonably clear fashion. The commitment is towards children as real persons in an all too material world, who are materially acted upon by a range of factors (corporations capitalizing on consumption by and for children, parents, schools and other institutions, and, through the channels provided by all of these as well as independently, i.e. books), and who have an independent space with their own perspectives and are capable of acting as independent agents. Zipes states this commitment early in the book with the informed understanding that the current condition of the world is such that the independent space and perspectives of children are being denied:

> I have always written with the hope that childhood might be redeemed, not innocent childhood, but a childhood rich in adventure and opportunities for self-exploration and self-determination. Instead, I witness a growing regulation and standardization of children's lives that undermine the very sincere concern that parents have for their young.[8]

The main culprits in this process of 'standardization of children's lives', for Zipes, are corporate capitalist processes which exercise so ubiquitous and encompassing a control on all aspects of the lives of parents and children that, even without their realizing it, every aspect of their lives and relations with each other become conditioned to corporate capitalist interests. Every realm of children's lives, even those that they feel are within their control, and those of their parents as parents, and even those that appear to be chosen for the good of children, are permeated by these interests in invidious and subtle ways. These interests are ultimately those that consolidate the material interests and power positions of those who control corporations and allied institutions (and what is not, in different ways, allied to corporations now?). Such interests perpetuate the dominant corporate capitalists' desires, fears, and perceptions of self-superiority (racial, cultural, sexual, etc.) in insidious ways. Parents and children are constantly sucked into unthinking collaboration with corporate capitalist processes, they think and act in ways which might appear to be free but are actually homogeneous and extrinsically directed ('one-dimensional thinking', Zipes calls it,[9] echoing the 1960s Herbert Marcuse[10]). In the course of presenting this overall argument Zipes also marks out specific observations and research that support these views and give some sense of children as independent agents who must be defended and, in some sense, liberated.

Within this grand perspective of children in the world he locates 'children's literature' as both a site that can be used (especially insofar as the production and dissemination of books are controlled by corporations) to perpetuate the 'standardization of children', and one that could be drawn into (in the writing and critical activity associated with it) enabling a different experience for children and subverting 'one-dimensional thinking'. The latter can be done, Zipes suggests, by the efforts of children's writers who actively challenge dominant and apparently obvious modes of thinking, though there is always the danger that their works would be appropriated by the corporations.[11] This can also be done by the kind of critical awareness that thinking critics of 'children's literature' may bring regarding such books, to which end he charts out a programme for critics of 'children's literature'.[12] The programme essentially lays out rules for careful analysis and greater awareness (thinkingness, in my terms).

All this is well argued and laudable (bar a small and unavoidable paradox which had been apparent to Marcuse too),[13] and it is certainly a position presented with sincerity and in a well-researched fashion. But with it we also need to take into account another strand of Zipes's argument regarding 'children's literature': one that finds it difficult to locate children except as adults' constructs in any sphere of 'children's literature' or critical interpretations thereof (a more sophisticated and academically resonant version of arguments given in Chapter 2 above). This is expressed in various ways. It appears in trying to make sense of the phrase 'children's literature':

If we take the genitive case literally and seriously, and if we assume ownership and possession are involved when we say 'children's literature' or the literature of children, then there is no such thing as children's literature, or for that matter children.[14]

Children are, of course, insofar as this phrase appears in any serious consideration of them by adults, what adults understand children to be; and children's literature is what adults write, publish, distribute, buy and even read or read aloud. Inevitably, in working through this and trying to understand how to characterize 'children's literature' then Zipes comes up with the notoriously useful 'implied reader', but with a much clearer sense of its constructedness than in the instance cited above in this chapter:

> The necessity and decision to find a narrative mode to which children might relate is what distinguishes the creative process that the children's book writer must undertake. In this process the writer conceptualizes what the child as implied reader is – the age, the background, the culture. The writer conceptualizes childhood, perhaps seeks to recapture childhood or the child in herself, or wants to define what childhood should be.[15]

These remain, however, indelibly the author's conception. Even in the 'children's literature' critic's programme (or manifesto) that Zipes presents, children appear only as constructs within socio-historical, political and institutional discourses.[16] And finally he locates 'children's literature' (logically enough in the context of the views summarized above) within the processes of corporate capitalism:

> We distinguish and misrecognize children's literature in its form of exchange value, as commodity. It is inevitable that we do this because its symbolic value in our institutional practice necessitates this. Just the very manner in which we think we are distinguishing children's literature from so-called adult literature belies the objective fact that there is no such thing as children's literature. On the other hand, there is a commodity that takes the form of a book, textbook, comic book, drawing book, religious book, gift book, and so on, that we use and children use and we use with children.[17]

What happens here is that Zipes removes 'children's literature' from the implicit assumption of literally involving the independent agents that are children (and therefore from making it his task to examine that involvement), and relocates it within terms of analysis that apply to markets and capitalist corporations. The latter terms are not those *given* by corporations, but terms that form the basis of examining such corporations and their overall organization in a capitalist system – terms that ultimately echo an original Marxist critique of capitalism (refracted through a Marcuse-like perspective). In the course of this relocation, children as independent persons become an incidental presence who are only acted upon, or only talked about in ways that essentially disregard them (they are 'misrecognized').

The two strands of Zipes's arguments do not sit comfortably with each other – they undercut each other. It may be argued that if 'children's literature', and 'children' generally, are constructed within the sphere of adult thinking, this may well be true of Zipes's own formulations about 'the standardization of childhood' and the need to 'redeem childhood'. If 'children's literature' as we are accustomed to speaking of it now contains political and institutional interests that inevitably involve a misrecognition, what guarantee is there that the 'children's literature' that Zipes champions and promotes as subverting or correcting that situation is not itself such a misrecognition too? After all, to try to negate or correct is still to think in terms of that which is being negated or corrected; that too is a construction that inevitably reflects political and institutional concerns that do not derive from an apprehension of children as independent persons. Further, if the whole sphere of 'children's literature' is indeed discussable and analysable only in terms of adult conceptualization and concerns, how can we be certain that this has any analysable impact on children at all? Even if we believe that such an impact must take place, how can we determine what sort of impact that is? In other words, if we accept Zipes's persuasive arguments about the manner in which 'children's literature' is inevitably within the embrace of adult systems, politics, ideologies, so that an understanding of children as such would always be intractable, then it is difficult to see how he hopes to achieve any impact (however well intentioned, redeeming or improving) on children as such through 'children's literature'. There would always exist some ambiguity about whether what the critic thinks 'children's literature' is communicating to children is indeed what is actually communicated to children. It must always be the case that children would have to be thought of as passive sponges absorbing hidden and explicit attitudes, predispositions, ideas, information, etc. (whether we like them or not) from the books they read, and this construction of children as 'implied readers' could always be thought of as some sort of 'standardization of children'. Only adult battles between different ideological positions, ideas, political beliefs, and so on can be fought on the terrain of 'children's literature': to try to 'redeem childhood' can be no more than a rhetorical flourish by Zipes in another adult battle.

The only alternative to that conclusion would be a more thorough and systematic examination of specific ways in which children do actually read, through some empirical methodology of ascertaining this (perhaps with the aid of rigorous socio-psychological or neuro-scientific experiments). As far as I am aware, this has seldom been the concern of specialists in 'children's literature'. The contradiction that Zipes talks about/reveals/is himself in the grip of in *Sticks and Stones* – i.e. the contradiction between recognizing the constructedness of 'children' in the context of 'children's literature' (and criticism regarding it), and hoping to impact in a material fashion on real children – is one that extends to the discipline of 'children's literature' in a larger sense. This is pondered in a lucid manner by, for example, Kárin Lesnik-Oberstein when she makes the three following points about 'children's literature' critics: (1) 'children's literature' critics set out to judge which books are good for children and why; (2) in each case this attempt depends on specific understandings of terms like 'children', 'children's literature', 'literature', and it appears that each of these terms can be understood in a wide variety of ways; (3) this variety of understandings in turn undercuts the 'children's literature' specialist's initial goal to prescribe for children, which is lost in the attempt to validate her essential views.[18]

With these clarifications about the background of Zipes's approach to 'children's literature' it becomes easier to understand the general tenor of his comments on the *Harry Potter* books. (I comment here briefly on the general tenor, and pick up matters of detail later when I get down to an analytical reading of these books myself.)

What Zipes does with the *Harry Potter* books is, in fact, *not* analyse them in terms of how children have responded to them or as the great mass of unthinking readers have pegged them as children's books, but see them as territory where the ideological proclivities of adults – a general readership – operate and where children are used with political and social effect. In analysing these, in other words, he calls for a thinking and analytical approach (which could be exercised by critics) to oppose the unthinking responses, and for a clarification of the manner in which adults construct and enclose children within their terms:

> I am not sure whether one can talk about a split between a minority of professional critics, who have misgivings about the Harry Potter books, and the great majority of readers, old and young, who are

mesmerized by the young magician's adventures. But I am certain that the phenomenal aspect of the reception of the Harry Potter books has blurred the focus for anyone who wants to take literature for young people seriously and who may be concerned about standards and taste that adults create for youth culture in the West.[19]

And a bit later:

> ... the only way to do Rowling and her Harry Potter books justice is to try to pierce the phenomenon and to examine her works as critically as possible, not with the intention of degrading them or her efforts, but with the intention of exploring why such a conventional work of fantasy has been fetishized so that all sort of magic powers are attributed to the very act of reading these works.[20]

It is readers' unthinkingness that clearly worries Zipes. Of course, there is within those words some inkling of the 'children's literature' critic's commitment to defend children from getting 'standardized'; but then that is an inevitable aspect of Zipes's disciplinary affiliation, which I applaud but do not think is especially functional in what he says about the *Harry Potter* books. There is also a valorization of the professional critic's clear-sightedness (an exaggeration) which we can probably put down as Zipes's effort to locate himself within a critical community and win at least their sympathy, and also assert something of a communal authority to his misgivings. But insofar as he addresses the *Harry Potter* books, he wishes to do so in a rigorous analytical spirit, and as reflecting ideological positions that pertain to the adult world wherein the children's world (insofar as it can be understood) is determined by 'standards and taste that adults create for youth culture'. It is also briefly suggested that real children, insofar as Zipes has interrogated them, are not as passionate about the *Harry Potter* books as their parents and other adults; he doubts how far it occupies the world of children at the level of peer interaction.

So, for Zipes, the appeal of the *Harry Potter* books is primarily as a marketing phenomenon and as a repository of ideological positions; the *Harry Potter* books exercise certain social and political effects, which include what their content conveys and the manner in which they are packaged and sold. As far as the content goes, Zipes notes that the *Harry Potter* books are conventional – they 'celebrate male dominance and blood rule'[21] and follow a thoroughly conventional form – and it is suspected that their success rests in the placating of conventional dominant groups and the ease with which they fall into corporate processes and endorse and further corporate interests. The details of Zipes's assessment of the conventionality of these books, and of their conservative attitudes to gender and race, are matters that I address in some detail later. Besides, in these details Zipes's engagement with the *Harry Potter* books is in fact cursory and superficial. He doesn't provide a substantial and serious textual reading of these books; he mainly recommends that such reading should occur and contents himself with making some provocative statements that might initiate such an effort. What is worth noting for the time being is that, despite his desire to approach children as independent persons and 'redeem childhood' as a 'children's literature' critic, what Zipes essentially does is recommend a serious and analytical reading of the *Harry Potter* books on the grounds that they are ideologically suspect – they may have questionable social and political effects (on young and old alike, *perhaps* more so on the young).

In this context, a somewhat more extended consideration of the *Harry Potter* books specifically, which follows a theoretical background that is in some ways similar to Zipes's, is Andrew Blake's *The Irresistible Rise of Harry Potter* (2002). The background similarity is not in affirming the commitments of a 'children's literature' specialist, but in assuming a similar ideological position and presumptively placing 'children' and 'children's literature' accordingly. Though Blake doesn't allow himself sufficient space to develop a systematic perspective of 'children' and 'children's literature', insofar as he implicitly deals with both he repeats many of the points made succinctly by Zipes. He places the *Harry Potter* books in comparison with other works of 'children's literature';[22] he analyses the impact of these particularly in terms of the experience of children and teachers in British schools in the 1990s;[23] he also dwells on the *Harry Potter* phenomenon as the product of corporations capitalizing on children's and teenage consumerism.[24] But these are embraced to a much larger degree in Blake's book by his ideological position (which he appears to share to an extent with Zipes) and political interests – a distrust of corporate capitalist industry and governance that draws every kind of cultural phenomenon (literature, music, art, media reportage, television programmes) and subject (children, parents, communities, countries) *into* a consumerist society and social organization. Like Zipes, Blake argues that the *Harry Potter* books manifest ambiguities regarding class, gender and race[25] that may be connected to an alignment with implicit superstructural prejudices in contemporary capitalist politics. But unlike Zipes, Blake airs his discontent not in terms of a primary focus on 'children' as a political category, but in terms of an overriding interest in specifically British politics and culture in the late 1990s, in the New Labour ethos of Britain. Blake concerns himself not so much with the consumerism and commodification of 'children', as with what he calls the 'retrolutionary' (a nostalgic invention of an idealized past in the present) nature of the *Harry Potter* novels, and the manner in which they are used for the magical New Labour 'branding' of Britishness.[26] Zipes concern with the condition of 'children' as a category in contemporary corporate capitalism gives his study a global air; Blake's view of 'children', *Potter* books and corporate capitalism is confined to a narrow view of British national politics (or in such interest in Britain as a brand name as may exist in the global marketplace). The similarities (including similar sorts of confusions) between Zipes's and Blake's comments of the *Potter* books are ultimately more in the details than in political overview, and these again I touch upon where appropriate in the next part.

Incidentally, despite being devoted (unlike *Sticks and Stones*) entirely to the *Harry Potter* books Blake also pays (like *Sticks and Stones*) only the most perfunctory attention to the texts. Some plot summaries and summaries of events are racily thrown in, with little attention to textual details or a holistic consideration of the books, to fit them into his British political perspective. Those in turn are connected to a sketch of the 1990s British cultural and political scene, which itself touches fleetingly on a plethora of relevant and not so relevant, but all peculiarly British (or American but sieved through British sensibilities), cultural and political phenomena.

I have, as I have mentioned, more to say about specific points in Zipes's and Blake's books in Part II. More immediately, the question that brings us to the close of this chapter: where do the above considerations of 'children's literature'-centred critics' positions with regard to the *Harry Potter* books leave me in my endeavour to conduct a text-to-world reading of these with a view to discerning their social and political effects? The following resolutions and clarifications delineate the position of this essay further:

- I reconfirm my earlier decision (Chapter 2) not to try to gauge how children have responded to the *Harry Potter* books, or to prescribe for children, or to try to improve the lot of children. Insofar as that is what 'children's literature' specialists do this essay is unlikely to be of much interest to them, and I do not count myself as a 'children's literature' specialist. If this essay does have any impact on the lives of children it would be an incidental impact which I have neither intended and nor tried to prevent.

- I also reconfirm my decision to address 'children' and 'children's literature', if at all, as categories that have social and political effect for and from adults. Insofar as 'children' are talked about with regard to *and* (I might as well add this here) appear in the *Harry Potter* books, I take that to be an adult's construction that reflects adult concerns and ideological positions, and have social and political effects in those terms.

- I realize that I need to be more precise about what I mean by terms like 'children' and 'children's literature' being used as adults' constructions with social and political effect. In this my views are similar to those of Zipes's that I have mentioned above. But several distinctions can be made here. (a) Insofar as 'children' are constructed as/assumed to be/shown to be passive persons (readers) who imbibe socially and politically pertinent positions tacitly through the medium of 'children's literature', those terms are a convenience. Such terms conveniently allow ideological positions to be presented with the least self-consciousness (as being obvious) and minimal rationalization (the reader is unlikely to interrogate). Also, any questioning of given ideological positions can itself be made to appear self-evident and obvious too. (b) Insofar as 'children' are understood as 'implied readers' *within* 'children's literature' books, they can be used as proxy for straightforward statements of commitments and convictions. Thus 'children's literature' books become sites where people do not have to take direct responsibility for their social and political claims, but can present these as claims being made by adults for and on behalf of children. The construction of 'children' as 'implied readers' absolves people from making certain aspects of their socially and politically effective positions clear, or dealing with the difficult connotations therein. (c) Insofar as 'children' are seen as the unique and preeminent consumers for 'children's literature' books (and other such products) they are the constructed targets that enable corporatons to mediate the movement of the book from author to reader. In this 'children' become a particular niche in the market, a particular channel of financial transactions that invisibly incorporate adults, a specific field of representation and innovation. To some extent this kind of construction (with slightly different prerogatives) also works for educational and other institutions devoted to children. (d) Underlying all the above there operates some such notion that 'children' represent a sort of modelling clay into which the condition of the future can be moulded, and 'children's literature' is one of the techniques involved in this moulding. Thus the social and political positions and effects available in 'children's literature' may be regarded as utopian blueprints – gesturing towards an ideal vision of the future – from different social and political perspectives. Whatever the role of 'children's literature' books in *actually* moulding children (something that I have decided not to worry about here), they reveal idealized aspirations of existing social and political positions (this does interest me).

As a conclusion for this chapter I feel I should mention the salutary example of Jacqueline Rose's careful and thought-provoking work on J.M. Barrie's *Peter Pan – The Case of Peter Pan, or, The Impossibility of Children's Fiction* (1984) – the attitude of which (though not the methods and themes) accords so closely to my own here that I cannot resist two final quotations from its introduction:

> Children's fiction is impossible, not in the sense that it cannot be written (that would be nonsense), but in that it hangs on an impossibility, one which it rarely ventures to speak. This is the impossible relation between adult and child. Children's fiction is clearly about that relation, but it has the remarkable characteristic of being about something which it hardly ever talks of. Children's fiction sets up a world in which the adult comes first (author, maker, giver) and the child comes after (reader, product, receiver), but where neither of them enter the space in between.[27]

And onwards:

> Let it be said from the start that it will be no part of this book's contention that what is good for the child can somehow be better defined, that we could, if we shifted the terms of the discussion, determine what it is that the child really wants. It will not be an issue here of what the child wants, but of what an adult desires – desires in the very act of construing the child as the object of its speech.[28]

Rose's curiosity is drawn primarily by the manner in which the child is construed *inside* texts of different sorts to do with *Peter Pan*. This essay isn't especially interested in the construing of children inside literary texts (the *Harry Potter* books). But this essay equally eschews any determination to discover what a child 'really wants'; and it is primarily concerned with adult readers, social and political effects which are primarily discernible among adults, and in the midst of which there must be, mustn't there, desire somewhere.

8
Fantasy Literature

Apart from the genre of 'children's literature', the *Harry Potter* books are also often located in the genre of 'fantasy literature'. Literary critics have been attentive to the nuances of 'fantasy literature' as a genre in two ways: either by attempting to describe its formal and thematic characteristics (there is a longish tradition of this), or by attempting to locate and understand 'fantasy literature' in terms of social and political environments and effects (a relative recent tendency). The latter is naturally of greater interest in this essay and this chapter is largely devoted to that. Only brief consideration is given here, therefore, to the status of the *Harry Potter* books as 'fantasy literature' in a formal or thematic fashion.

The only observation about the latter that is worth making here is that certain *rigorous* definitions of 'fantasy literature' – or of the 'fantastic' in literature – can effectively exclude such books as the *Harry Potter* series. This is noteworthy since it does seem wholly obvious that these are in fact aptly placed in 'fantasy literature'. But precise definitions of the 'fantastic' may entail reconsideration of the generic location of books, and dislocation of the seemingly obvious example of 'fantasy literature'. Such dislocations are useful in that they encourage a renewed awareness of that which had seemed obvious. In questioning unthinking assumptions with a view to developing an analytical perspective, dislocation of the seemingly obvious (evidently closely allied to the unthinking) is undoubtedly a crucial ploy. I say this in a somewhat oracular fashion, but safe in the familiarity of literary or philosophical pondering on concepts like 'alienation' and 'defamiliarization' (so familiar that I wouldn't venture a discussion, or even a footnote here). For the sake of such dislocation then, if nothing else, a questioning of the category of 'fantasy literature' is useful before the *Harry Potter* books are comfortably placed in its fold. Let's consider then the influential definition of the 'fantastic' as a literary genre (with a formal emphasis) by Todorov in 1970:

> The fantastic requires the fulfillment of three conditions. First, the text must oblige the reader to consider the world of the characters as a world of living persons and to hesitate between a natural and a supernatural explanation of the events described. Second, this hesitation may also be experienced by a character; thus the reader's role is so to speak entrusted to a character, and at the same time the hesitation is represented, it becomes one of the themes of the work – in the case of naïve reading, the actual reader identifies himself with the character. Third, the reader must adopt a certain attitude with regard to the text: he will reject allegorical as well as 'poetic' interpretations. These three requirements do not have an equal value. The first and the third actually constitute the genre; the second may not be fulfilled.[1]

What is interesting about the *Harry Potter* books is that the Magic world is so carefully distinguished from the Muggle world that any question of hesitating between a natural and a supernatural explanation is pretty much out of question. Ostensibly, the sphere of the natural and the sphere of the supernatural are held apart consistently all through, and distinct rules and modes of explanation attach to each. There isn't much space for hesitation here. But was there perhaps a moment of hesitation in the first transition from Muggle to Magic world in *Stone*, a hesitation that is perhaps re-enacted, and of which readers are reminded, at the beginning of each book in the series (each book is introduced through a re-enactment of Harry's passage from the Muggle household of the Dursleys to a Magic realm)? A closer examination of even that peripheral moment of the beginning (not the central feature of the series and therefore probably not enough for it to be located within the genre of the fantastic according to Todorov) is not designed to inspire hesitation. Both Harry and the Dursleys are, in fact, insurance against that: the Dursleys' overwhelming reaction to magic is irritation, not surprise, from the beginning; and Harry's preoccupation is more to hide his powers from them than to wonder at his having magical abilities. Apart from the Dursleys and Harry, the Muggle world at large is constructed to be curiously uncurious about the strange and unexpected, somehow constitutionally incapable of surprise and hesitation. Consider the Muggle television news report on unusual happenings in *Stone*:

'And finally, bird-watchers everywhere have reported that the nation's owls have been behaving very unusually today. Although owls normally hunt at night and are hardly ever seen in the daylight, there have been hundreds of sightings of these birds flying in every direction since sunrise. Experts are unable to explain why the owls have suddenly changed their sleeping pattern.' The newsreader allowed himself a grin. 'Most mysterious. And now, over to Jim McGuffin with the weather. Going to be any more shower of owls tonight, Jim?'

'Well, Ted,' said the weatherman, 'I don't know about that, but it's not only owls that have been acting oddly today. Viewers as far apart as Kent, Yorkshire and Dundee have been phoning in to tell me that instead of the rain I promised yesterday, they've a downpour of shooting stars! Perhaps people have been celebrating Bonfire Night early – it's not until next week, folks! But I can promise a wet night tonight.' (*Stone* 10–11)

What this description does is: (a) place the Muggle world that is presented as taking such events in their stride without surprise, and (b) rebounding into reflecting on the phenomenal real world of the reader, or our world. Those familiar with British television news broadcasts would recognize the general features of this exchange, would know that that kind of light-hearted banter between newscasters ('Going to be any more shower of owls tonight, Jim?') is considered rather smart on the BBC, would recognize that the location of these news items is on the periphery (the moment before the weather report, reserved for the relatively trivial on the BBC, and the weather bulletin itself, an unexciting but inevitable adjunct to the news). And with these recognitions comes the suspicion that instead of drawing the reader into the wondrous element of magic, the magical has pushed the reader into reflecting on the familiarity of news items. Does this passage perhaps playfully reflect on the manner in which the momentous and strange are rendered mundane and slight on the news media, by their very appearance in the media? Is this an ironic comment on the insensitivity and jokey lack of curiosity that pervades our culture? In these reflections there is a tendency to reach towards 'allegorical' explanations[2] – which of course is exactly what, according to Todorov, lies outside the genre of the fantastic in literature. And if we persist with Todorov, we do find a quite different category that might fit the *Harry Potter* books somewhat better than the fantastic: Todorov thinks of it as the 'marvelous', and comments more specifically (and pertinently insofar as *Harry Potter* books go) to fairy tales as a particular kind of the 'marvelous':

> In the case of the marvelous, supernatural elements provoke no particular reaction in either the characters or in the implicit reader. It is not an attitude toward the events described which characterizes the marvelous, but the nature of these events ...
>
> We generally link the genre of the marvelous to that of the fairy tale. But as a matter of fact the fairy tale is only one of the varieties of the marvelous, and the supernatural events in fairy tales provoke no surprise: neither a hundred years' sleep, nor a talking wolf, nor the magical gifts of the fairies (to cite only a few examples in Perrault's tales). What distinguishes a fairy tale is a certain kind of writing, not the status of the supernatural.[3]

This seems to fit the style of writing and placement of the supernatural in the *Harry Potter* books somewhat better than the fantastic.

Thinking in terms of rigorous formal/thematic reader-centred definitions such as Todorov's may jerk some readers out of unthinking assumptions in useful ways. More importantly, the effort allows for clarifications of the text that may impinge upon a text-to-world approach with a view to discerning social and political effects. However, despite the above, let me, along with many others, assume that the *Harry Potter* books do fall into a *loosely* (rather than *rigorously*) defined and *inclusive* category of 'fantasy literature' – something such as:

> Whatever the material, extravagant or seemingly commonplace, a narrative is a fantasy if it presents the persuasive establishment and development of an impossibility, an arbitrary construct of the mind with all under the control of logic and rhetoric.[4]

This bare skeleton of a definition would, of course, include something like the *Harry Potter* books.

As far as assessing the social and political effects of 'fantasy literature' goes, a fair amount of scholarly attention has been given to this since the 1980s. A determination to examine 'fantastic literature' squarely in terms of its social context resulted in the influential book by Rosemary Jackson, *Fantasy: The Literature of Subversion* (1981). As the title indicates, Jackson was interested in fantasy as a genre that questions existing dominant social and political positions (she also provided an excellent survey of formalistic and thematic considerations of 'fantasy literature' as a genre), and sometimes actually undermines them (which explains the radical sounding 'subversion'). Jackson made a crucial distinction right at the beginning of her book to show that fantasy, by presenting and playing with alternative, inverted, distorted, reversed, etc. perspectives, actually thereby expresses a certain disenchantment with dominant ideologies, brings to light certain desires that are repressed because of dominant ideologies. In the process of doing so 'fantasy literature' may have two kinds of outcome: it could through that process simply accord a subversive recognition and validity to those desires, or it could (in a therapeutic and conservative fashion) get rid of those desires:

> In expressing desire, fantasy can operate in two ways (according to the different meanings of 'express'): it can *tell of*, manifest or show desire (expression in the sense of portrayal, representation, manifestation, linguistic utterance, mention, description), or it can *expel* desire, when this desire is a disturbing element which threatens cultural order and continuity (expression in the sense of pressing out, squeezing, expulsion, getting rid of something by force).[5]

After making this distinction Jackson decided, for reasons best given in her own words, to focus her theoretical and textual analysis on the former sort of 'fantasy literature':

> Those texts which attempt to [recover desire] have been given most space in [my] book, for in them the fantastic is at its most uncompromising in its interrogation of the 'nature' of the 'real'.
>
> One consequence of this focus is that some of the better known authors of fantasy works (in the popular sense) are given less space than might be expected. For example, the best-selling fantasies by Kingsley, Lewis, Tolkien, Le Guin or Richard Adams are not discussed at great length. This is not simply through prejudice against their particular ideals, nor through an attempt to recommend other texts as more 'progressive' in any easy way, but because they belong to that realm of fantasy which is more properly defined as faery, or romance literature. The moral and religious allegories, parables and fables informing the stories of Kingsley and Tolkien move away from the unsettling implications which are found at the centre of the purely 'fantastic'. Their original impulse may be similar, but they move from it, expelling their desire and frequently displacing it into religious

longing and nostalgia. Thus they defuse potentially disturbing, anti-social drives and retreat from any profound confrontation with existential dis-ease.[6]

The long quotation is justified because of the clarity with which it lays out an influential critical choice in the criticism of 'fantasy literature'. It does two things: first, it marks out some 'popular' 'best-selling' fantasies (in a loose sense) as being conservative in temper and therefore (despite her protestations) not worthy of serious critical attention; second, it covers up the ideological proclivities that guide the decision to deliberately neglect the conservative, by *expelling* conservative fantasies from the realm of fantasy (rigorously defined Todorov-style, except that in his formalistic/ thematic terms Todorov *did* engage with the purely marvellous and uncanny) altogether. It also suggests implicitly that there is some sort of connection between popular and best-selling 'fantasy literature' and its conservativeness, without expressing too much analytical curiosity about this. Indeed, it represses any critical desire to examine the conservative-ness of expelling desire, the social and political effects of that expulsion of desire, the contexts in which these effects come to be popular and widely considered as desirable, etc. – all interesting issues.

This repression of critical curiosity has regretfully become characteris-tic of most serious analyses of 'fantasy literature' thereafter; unless, that is, literary texts which belong to the expelling-desire category of 'fantasy literature' can be deemed to have become historically important – revealing expelled subversive desires of some bygone period, anaesthetized by time. Thus a substantial amount of serious critical analysis has been devoted to popular Victorian fantasies (which, in Jackson's terms, could be thought of as 'expelling' rather than 'recovering' desire),[7] and some of the names that Jackson so blithely dismisses (Tolkien, Lewis) are rapidly entering the category of the historically relevant popular fantasy. Serious critical attention has also been drawn to *sub-categories* of what may be regarded as desire-expelling 'fantasy literature', especially where the sub-categorical qualifications are perceived as complicating (or even contradicting) the connotations of the fantastic. Thus, the so-called 'science fiction fantasies', where the calling of 'science' into the service of 'fantasy' leads to rather delicious tensions, has been food for some crit-ical debate;[8] as has 'children's fantasy literature' or 'fantasy literature by women', where consideration for children (I have already discussed the usual 'children's literature' specialist's commitments) and debates surround-ing gender give a particular piquancy to the subversive possibilities associated with fantasy.[9] But, apart from these, serious critics investigating the social and political effects of 'fantasy literature' in general have tended to make Jackson's choice their own, and pay attention primarily to subversive (rather than conservative and often therefore popular) 'fantasy literature' – in which it can always be suspected that apart from ideological inclination some notion of high and low taste also has a not inconsiderable (unthinking?) role to play. At any rate, such more recent overviews of the theory and practice of 'fantasy literature' as, for example, Lucie Armitt's *Theorizing the Fantastic* (1996), confidently assert:

> Now we can look at the fantastic as a form of writing which is about opening up subversive spaces within the mainstream rather than ghettoizing fantasy by encasing it within genres. In the process it also retains its important subversive properties without capitulating to classification.[10]

'Fantasy literature' has been withdrawn, it appears, from the enclosures of Todorov-style formalistic/thematic classification into genres (sub-categories notwithstanding); but equally it has been enclosed (in the name of being opened up) within some sort of political commitment to 'subversive spaces within the mainstream' (Armitt calls upon a range of highly regarded theorists to support this) that refuses to engage with the conservative effects of some popular 'fantasy literature' (unless tastily sub-categorized and thereby, perhaps and somehow, rendered subversive).

As a matter of symmetry I feel I should also mention Jacqueline Rose's innovative insertion of fantasy into explicitly political texts and discourses in *States of Fantasy* (1999).[11] That texts (literary to a large degree, but not just literary) that have explicit social and political content and effects, especially in the troubled contexts of our time (Israel–Palestine, South Africa), derive from and merge into the fantastic core of political desires, utopian imaginings of different sorts, and constructed communities, is not an unexpected observation – the specific contexts and texts Rose chooses to make her points, however, are uncharted territory from this perspective. But it is a matter of symmetry that reminds me of Rose's work here: the contexts and texts she deals with are as distant in their associations as it is possible to be from the *Harry Potter* books. Fantasy, as much as social and political effects, indeed through social and political effects and vice versa, evidently crosses the boundaries of associations and draws bridges across the apparently incompatible.

Critical discussions of *Harry Potter* books that have treated these as, simply, 'fantasy literature' rather than as 'children's fantasy literature' (with the emphasis on *children's* in all the senses outlined in the previous chapter) are few and far between. The status of the *Harry Potter* books as 'fantasy literature' has however been accepted widely as being self-evident and obvious, indeed so much so that it can merely (and unthinkingly) be mentioned as something that everyone in their right minds would simply know. Apart from explorations of rigorous definitions of genre (in Todorov-style), there is of course no need to interrogate such unthinking *inclusion* in a loosely defined genre (I have myself accepted the status of the *Harry Potter* books as 'fantasy literature' in that spirit above); but even so, and despite accepting the unthinking inclusion, there remain questions that may be thinkingly investigated. What are the social and political implications of such inclusion?

A useful critical paper which does approach the *Harry Potter* books more as 'fantasy literature' than as 'children's fantasy literature' (which, as with Zipes in Chapter 7, I treat as being representative of this kind of approach) is John Pennington's 'From Elfland to Hogwarts; or the Aesthetic Trouble with Harry Potter' (2002). As the title suggests, what the paper ostensibly does is question the *aesthetic* status of the *Harry Potter* books as 'fantasy literature'; and what I suggest below is that what Pennington thinks of as an aesthetic matter is actually a social and political matter. Pennington presents his agenda as an aesthetic one, and explicitly to do with fantasy, with admirable authority:

> My trepidation over the Harry Potter series is founded on the disconnect between *what* the books attempt to say ... and *how* Rowling says them, a disconnect between form and content. No matter how popular Harry Potter remains, I argue that on aesthetic grounds the series is fundamentally failed fantasy. ... The rule-bending/breaking in the Triwizard Tournament is a metaphor for Rowling's basic violation of fantasy literature ground-rules – she violates the integral rules of the fantasy game, never accepting the integrity of the very fantasy tradition that she is mining for riches. And thus the aesthetic trouble with Harry Potter.[12]

This is not as immediately clear as it sounds. What I think Pennington asserts here is that '*what* a book attempts to say' should be dictated by the *form* it uses (in this case that of 'fantasy literature') and '*how* it is said' constitutes the *content* of the product (the *Harry Potter* books as they stand) – and that in the case of the *Harry Potter* books, what the form used dictates ('fantasy literature ground-rules') is not what is actually delivered in the end-products (those rules are 'violated'). This is confusing because '*what* a book says' is usually associated with *content* (in the sense of referring to the particular story, the main themes, the characters and situations in question, etc.); while '*how* it is said' is generally associated with *form* (in the sense of referring to the use of or departure from stylistic and rhetorical conventions, narrative strategies, etc.). But let me accept the somewhat counterintuitive usage of terms here. Three questions arise from this assertion: (1) what exactly are the 'integral rules' that the form of 'fantasy literature' dictates? (2) why do the *Harry Potter* books *seem* to adhere to the form of 'fantasy literature', the rules of which they should obey?; and (3) how exactly do the *Harry Potter* books break those rules? Pennington's answers are, as far as I understand them, as follows. For one: the form of 'fantasy literature' demands that some notion of 'consensus reality' be changed, or that the reality which we take to be obvious and normal should be questioned (or, dare I make the connection, *subverted*?) by the presentation of a literary world where the obvious and the normal are no longer so. Pennington draws upon Kathryn Hume[13] to make this point:

> Kathryn Hume suggests that the two impulses that define literature are mimesis – the 'desire to imitate' – and fantasy – which 'desires to change givens and alter reality'. Consequently, Hume defines fantasy as 'any departure from consensus reality, an impulse native to literature and manifested in innumerable variations, from monster to metaphor.[14]

One may also note in passing that Pennington appears to be misreading Hume in using these quotations to define the *particular* form of 'fantasy literature' since these quotations appear to use fantasy in an abstract sense as a characteristic of *all* literature. Two: Pennington obviously thinks that the *Harry Potter* books adhere to the form of 'fantasy literature' by presenting a *superficial* alternative reality (the juxtaposition of Magic world and Muggle world) and through certain inter-textual resonances (there are covert and overt references to other 'fantasy literature' books and their alternative worlds). Three: Pennington argues that the alternative reality that the *Harry Potter* books present is only *superficial* (operating at the level of the textualized Magic and Muggle worlds), but at a *deep* level there is no alternative proposed (because the Magic world is actually just a version of the readers' or our world, following the rules of our 'consensus reality'):

> On a *fundamental* level, Rowling is unwilling – or unable – to depart from this consensus reality; her novels, for all their 'magical' trappings,

are *prefigured* in mundane reality, relying too wholly on the realm from which she simultaneously wants to escape.[15] [My emphases – the emphasized terms play out the superficial/deep opposition]

He gives a series of reasonably persuasive demonstrations of this that I do not need to go into at the moment. He also suggests that this makes the *Harry Potter* novels less effective than some of the fantasy books that are covertly or overtly referred in them, especially since the latter have managed to challenge a consensus reality successfully. Pennington more or less suggests that the inter-textual element in the *Harry Potter* books is a mode of claiming the success of other fantasy books without being in their league.

There are too many problems with Pennington's analysis if we try to understand it as an 'aesthetic' analysis. The distinction between content and form is not clear, between the 'what is said' and the 'how it is said'. All the points he makes are with reference to what is normally thought of as content, and usual expectations of formal analysis are actually hardly addressed. It is not clear why a fantasy *has* to be a deep questioning of 'consensus reality' and cannot be a superficial presentation of an alternative reality that is materially different in some ways to what we think of as our world. Why is it assumed that a fantasy that, for example, simply imagines that speedy travel can be achieved through magic rather than technology be any less of a fantasy than one that, for example, also imagines the deeper economic and psychological effects of such an possibility? Why, moreover, must we accept that certain accepted forms (pertinent to past experience of reading and writing 'fantasy literature') must dictate future works that are broadly understood as being affiliated to those forms (that the past experience cannot be tampered with)? To accept that would be to deny any progression in literary reading and writing. Most crucially, it is not clear why certain thematic and stylistic qualities are *better* (more successful) than others (which are failures) – what are the aesthetic evaluative criteria at work here?

Many of these problems however simply disappear if we do not press Pennington's emphasis on the aesthetic too far, and if we simply read his preferences and observations as matter of ideological critique or based on a social and political perspective. What happens above is that Pennington simply follows the tradition of thinking about 'fantasy literature' established with Rosemary Jackson, and assumes its prejudices. Pennington, like Jackson, is more drawn to what appears to be subversive fantasies, and tends to be dismissive of what he suspects to be conservative fantasies (quite possibly for the same reasons as Jackson's, as a political position). Also like Jackson, Pennington is inclined to justify this preference not by a straightforward acknowledgement of the political position from which it derives, but by simply labelling the conservative fantasy as not really fantasy at all (Jackson had glibly put it out of the fantasy genre into fairly-tale; Pennington calls it 'failed fantasy'). What Pennington effectively *means* is that he suspects that the *Harry Potter* books are conservative fantasies, and because he has more progressive or radical political convictions he doesn't like them. What he *says* to avoid having to own up to a particular political perspective is that conservative fantasies are failed fantasies on aesthetic grounds. What I think Pennington *means* is reasonably coherent (even if we do not agree with Pennington's politics); what I think Pennington *says* is, on close scrutiny, not coherent (it is difficult to understand Pennington's aesthetics). It is interesting that Pennington also (like Jackson) finds that his ideological proclivities are not necessarily popular ones (he speaks 'no matter how popular Harry Potter remains'), but he prefers to put this down with typical academic confidence in the inferior aesthetic discernment of the masses.

None of the arguments in this chapter, of course, actually demonstrates that the *Harry Potter* books should be regarded as conservative fantasies. I have not discussed that aspect of what I think Pennington means. I have addressed the structure and assumptions of his arguments, not the, often persuasive, demonstrations that he gives. I do address this squarely when I get down to a text-to-world reading of the *Harry Potter* books with a view to understanding their social and political effects.

So where does this discussion of 'fantasy literature' leave me insofar as I undertake such a text-to-world reading? The following points answer that question, and conclude this chapter:

- I do not try to place the *Harry Potter* books in terms of a rigorous definition of 'fantasy literature'.
- Insofar as the *Harry Potter* books are usually included in a loosely defined category of 'fantasy literature' this does not entail any presumption regarding their social and political implications or effects. In other words, I do not thereby base my analysis of the books on the expectation that some kind of interrogation or subversion of mainstream attitudes should be manifest or become desirable. It seems more reasonable to assume that what may be included in a loosely defined category of 'fantasy literature' may implicitly or explicitly espouse a range of different and even contradictory politically and

socially effective perspectives. The particular social and political effects of the *Harry Potter* books ultimately depend on their specific statements, contexts and readings, and not on their inclusion in 'fantasy literature' loosely defined.

- It is not especially useful to compare the *Harry Potter* books with other works of 'fantasy literature' (loosely defined) insofar as understanding social and political effects and implications go – at least no more useful than it may be to compare these to any work of literature. However, it may be worth making such comparisons in that there are broad formal and thematic similarities that form the basis of the loose definition of 'fantasy literature' and these may be usefully foregrounded for detailed analysis in a comparative fashion.

- Different rigorous understandings of 'fantasy literature' (and their sub-categories), and the inclusion or exclusion of certain texts from such rigorously defined categories, may *follow* from a discernment (or recognition) of the political and social implications and effects of those texts. In such cases, that rigorously defined understanding of 'fantasy literature' would have to be regarded as another social and political effect of those texts. So, for instance, if it can be demonstrated that a certain discernment of the social and political effects of the *Harry Potter* books have determined whether they have been included in or excluded from the category of 'fantasy literature', then it would have to be understood that the act of inclusion or exclusion was itself a social and political effect of the *Harry Potter* books. This sort of inclusion or exclusion can then be examined after the fact of the text-to-world analysis of the *Harry Potter* books. Naturally, insofar as this can be shown to have occurred with regard to the *Harry Potter* books this matter is of interest in this essay. Indeed the examination of Pennington's essay above was conducted on that basis.

- Insofar as exclusion of a loosely defined fantasy text from a rigorously defined category of 'fantasy literature' is understood as one of the social and political effects of that text, it might be possible to understand its popularity (which is also a social and political effect) with that background in mind. In other words, the fact that the *Harry Potter* books are immensely popular and the fact that they fit some modes of inclusion in 'fantasy literature' and not others, and that other books show a similar tendency – and that thereby there seems to emerge a distinctive category of 'popular fantasy literature' – all these observations *constitute* the social and political effects of these books, rather than *explain* them.

9
Religious Perspectives

Let me begin this chapter by acknowledging a personal difficulty (not, I feel certain, confined to me) in engaging with a particular kind of apparently serious critical analysis of the relationship between literature and religion. There are several kinds of analyses that could be mentioned here before I clarify what that *particular kind of analysis* is. Substantial critical effort has been devoted to examining the manner in which specific religious institutional forms and religious ideologies have impinged upon the production and reception of literary works in different cultures and historical periods. Insofar as it is *given* that the religious institutions and convictions are such as they are or are such as they have come to be, and the analysis *follows* from that background, these are generally illuminating and useful in various ways. Considerable critical attention has been devoted to clarifying how religious concerns and issues figure implicitly or explicitly *in* literary works, or genres, or the literature of certain periods and contexts. Sometimes texts that are allocated an extra-literary and ahistorical religious significance in some context or the other – those purporting to be divine revelations, for instance – may nevertheless be historicized and critically analysed as literature; and the very allocation of religious significance can be assessed as a peculiar variety of literary reception. Occasionally, serious analysis ponders analogues between processes that are familiar to a theologian (attempting to get to a mystical truth behind the surface of the world, for instance) and those that seem to attach to literary criticism itself (attempting to find a more or less hidden truth behind the surface of the literary text, for instance). Insofar as I am interested in the social and political effects of literary works, I have a great deal of sympathy with and interest in such analytical projects concerned with understading literature from a religious perspective and *vice versa*. All these are based on what no one can deny: that different kinds of religious ideologies and institutions are inextricably and deeply entwined in the histories and constitutions of a large number of societies and polities, and therefore in their cultural expressions, inevitably including literary works. As a matter of thinkingly engaging with social and political effects of literary works (or of societies and polities themselves) religion appears as an unavoidable – but not *subsuming* – matter.

It doesn't need much contemplation to grasp the social and political significance of religion even in our time. It can be observed that religious institutions and ideologies continue to play a salutary role (providing aid and charity where required, often championing emancipatory causes, occasionally providing necessary social services – education, for example – in a disinterested fashion, and so on) in some social and political contexts at the beginning of the twenty first century. It can also be observed that a range of different religious institutions and ideologies (none need be singled out, almost *all* the major world religions are implicated) play an enormously destructive social and political role in the twenty-first century – accounting to a great degree for such manifestations of xenophobia and prejudice, communal hatred and bloodshed, internecine and transnational conflict, unfreedom and narrow-mindedness as have been witnessed in the early twenty-first century. A discussion and analysis of the place of religious institutions and ideologies in our world is, however, no part of this study, and I don't take these comments any further. In passing though, it is material to this study that religious ideologies and institutions account for the majority of instances of book-banning and literary censorship in our time – not least with regard to the *Harry Potter* books.

But back to that particular kind of critical analysis that I have a problem with: let me give this in terms of examples. Two quotations (chosen, as before, as exemplifying a particular perspective) would serve to make my point here. Both belong to studies that examine the relationship between literature and religion in a reasonably recent (still relevant) context. The first is taken from the conclusion of David Jasper's *The Study of Literature and Religion* (1989/1992):

> The sense of the provisional, and of the possible, the sense of contradiction or, in better moments, of vitality, seems to me to be proper for anyone who is concerned with theology as a living enterprise. We need continually to be reminded that we undertake our task in the context of a journey and of change: but it is creative change, and it is above all the poet in the process of invention who illuminates for us the nature of God's mysterious creative redemptive activity.[1]

And the second is taken from the introduction to Graham Ward's *Theology and Contemporary Critical Theory* (1996/2000):

> This book is not intended...for the initiated. It is written for the interested enquirer; for those in the study of Christian theology interested in finding a place from which to survey, and appreciate, the relevance of contemporary critical theory to that study. The book is written from a standpoint from within the study of Christian theology itself.[2]

I cannot, despite my desire to engage with the issues that are addressed in these, actually do so because these declarations have excluded me, and I understand these declarations as excluding me. I need to explain that. I have a desire to engage with these books because both, in fact, do provide useful critical analytical insights along the lines delineated in the first paragraph of this chapter. I am excluded from such an engagement by the declarations of religious location made in these quotations; by the performative announcement that makes all the critical analysis that interests me therein *conditional* to that declaration. It is the assertion of that condition as *necessary* for understanding that foregoing analysis that excludes me, because if that must be considered *necessary* then I haven't understood the analysis. I can make my exclusion clearer than that. I do not feel excluded as someone who professes a different religious faith – though there may be just grounds for that sort of feeling of exclusion. Graham Ward's confining of his study and his audience to not only the field that is covered by 'an interest in Christian theology' (that could include an *extrinsic* interest in Christian theology) but that is '*within* the study of Christian theology itself' (which imposes restrictions as to faith and location) does exclude those of other faiths and locations than the (perhaps even including some of the manifold varieties of) Christian theology. Jasper's open-ended 'nature of God's mysterious creative redemptive activity' is perhaps less immediately exclusive in that sense, though persons of certain religious persuasions might feel alienated by the cultural baggage of monotheism and the specific linguistic associations of 'mystery', 'creation', 'redemption'. There are these exclusions; but there is an additional one that is more material to me. There is the exclusion of the entirely unreligious: those who refuse to espouse religious conviction or do not recognize any location in terms of religion or find any desire to be located in terms of religious positions. It is possible that those who feel excluded on the grounds of belonging to different religious persuasions may yet feel some affinity to the religious in any form (there is that familiar argument that all religions have certain essential common denominators – for example, in accepting some form of supernal intelligence and intent, or in allocating a certain centrality to faith). The exclusion of the unreligious is absolute.

The position of the unreligious is not dissimilar to that presented in certain philosophical expositions on atheism, agnosticism or freethinking,[3] but for the purposes of this essay I have used 'unreligious' in a deliberately distinct fashion. I do not wish to give my position here more content than is necessary – and those other more familiar terms affiliated to my position have a great deal more content (in terms of specific locations, histories and languages) than is desirable here. Here a briefer explanation of what my position is should do, an explanation that would be comprehensible to those who espouse a religious position (I have no desire to exclude). It consists in the following ideas:

(a) I do not *need* to justify why I am unreligious any more than I ask or expect anyone who is religious to justify why they are so. It should not be inferred from that statement that I am giving an unreligious perspective the same kind of validity as a religious perspective; that being unreligious is a kind of (admittedly inverse) religiosity too. All that statement indicates is that the same latitude that may be extended to people who claim to be, in whatever way, religious extends to those who claim to be, in whatever way, not religious. I *can*, in fact, justify why I am unreligious (and am convinced that an unreligious position is more valid than a religious one in every kind of way) but those who are religious may not accept my reasons; and equally I have not found myself accepting any justifications of religiosity that I have been presented with. It is not necessary or useful, therefore, in this essay to give an exposition of justifications and scepticisms.

(b) Insofar as I am interested here in the social and political effects of literary texts (on societies and polities generally) I can understand why it is imperative that the role of religious institutions and ideologies be taken into account, but I do not understand why I have to thereby espouse any religious conviction or location. I do not consider religious conviction or location to be a necessary background to political and social engagement, though I recognize that much social and political engagement has worked on that basis. My political and social engagement is not based on such a background (though it recognizes the institutional and ideological importance of religion); and, if questioned about it, I can come up with several plausible reasons why I consider such a background to be socially and politically undesirable.

(c) I am inevitably excluded by any position that makes analysis *conditional* to religious conviction and location; such conditionality excludes me before I can engage with the argument, makes what might otherwise be a perfectly comprehensible analysis immediately incomprehensible to me. This kind of exclusion cannot be argued with – it just *is* exclusion. Since it denies me entry, thought, argument by its very enunciation I have no choice but to consider such a demand for espousal of religious conviction or location, or such a presumptive expectation of religious conviction or location, as a particularly debilitating kind of unthinkingness – a kind that cannot be kept aside. An analysis, if it is to be that, cannot start by excluding: it can be disagreed with, argued against, or dispensed with after consideration, but it is recognizable as analysis by allowing for all those possibilities (and all of which are the opposite of exclusion). It is analysis (in this case of social and political effects of literary works) that my unreligious position enjoins on me.

That, I think, is all I need to declare of my position in this chapter, and these form the principles which guide my observations on the criticism of the *Harry Potter* books from a religious perspective that is available. As before, I take and treat a particular example as a representative or typical instance, in this case Richard Abanes's *Harry Potter and the Bible*. This is one of the more extensive treatments of the *Harry Potter* books from a religious perspective that is available at the time of writing this,[4] has a scholarly appearance, and expresses ostensible social and political concerns. Moreover, it has the advantage of being the most systematic and analytical presentation of the religious position (most contentiously associated with religious perspectives apropos the *Harry Potter* books now) from which some sort of censorship can be contemplated. I have not chosen a critical work that endorses the *Harry Potter* books from a religious perspective because: (a) I haven't found any that lay out the critical presumptions of the religious perspective rigorously or examine the *Harry Potter* books in those terms sufficiently; (b) because I am interested in the analytical justifications that are called upon in censoring the *Harry Potter* books as a matter of course (that is, I have observed above, one of the significant social and political effects of these books).

Abanes's book deliberately and systematically excludes certain perspectives (especially mine as outlined above) and therefore limits engagement with such analysis as it produces. In trying to retrieve an analytical or thinking perspective from within it, in trying to make some sense of it from my perspective, I necessarily have to read it against the grain of its expectations and rhetoric. In itself it is not just indifferent to any but a particular variety of Christian perspective for its analytical communication, it removes itself from any attempt at analytical communication to any but Christians. The emphasis on the conditionality of its arguments to its declarations of faith is absolute – in this it is characteristic of almost all critical examinations of the *Harry Potter* books from a religious perspective, approbatory or otherwise, that I have come across – and before I try an against-the-grain retrieval of its analytical procedures from an unreligious perspective, it is instructive to take note of Abanes's mode of expressing this conditionality. *The Bible* is not used simply as a normative *text* or the 'Biblical' as pertaining to perspectives that are laid out *in that text*: that does naturally happen, and on several counts textual quotation from *The Bible* are given law-like or norm-like validity to demonstrate, for instance and most extensively, that the occult is undesirable[5] or that certain moral positions are unacceptable.[6] More importantly though, the 'Biblical' is not just a textual referent, it is often used in an adjectival fashion that suggests that it is a self-expressive *quality*, as in 'patently unbiblical' or 'biblically speaking' (with the small 'b'). It is, in other words, normalized in language usage with the same kind of effect as terms like 'truthful', 'analytical', 'rational', 'speculative', 'optimistic', etc. might be. And, beyond the linguistic normalization of the Biblical by drawing it into the unthinking instrumental use of language, there are those explicit statements of faith. These are not merely moments when faith is declared which can be passed over without giving them too much attention; these are grating in their assertiveness, and are given as *a priori* to such historical perspective and logical inference as this critical work draws upon. This is especially true when Abanes introduces the second part of his book with a sweeping historical overview of Viking, Persian and Hebrew mythological representations of good and evil, and moves rapidly on to the following:

> This universal knowledge of explaining the presence of sin in the world dates back to the very beginning of time, to a place called the Garden of Eden. There, the Bible tells us, God created the first human; namely, Adam, who was made from the dust of the earth (Genesis 2:7), and Eve, who was fashioned by God from a portion of bone taken from Adam's side (2:21–2)...[7]

The manner in which the culturally-specific mythology becomes 'universal knowledge', and this universal knowledge is given through the Christian mythology without any awareness of the culture-specificity of the latter, and the manner in which the Christian mythology is given as not really mythological at all but as more or less historical (smacking of anti-evolutionary Creationism), all ensure that the conditionality from Abanes's faith is determinedly exclusionary.

Why bother to dwell on this then? Despite the taint of bigotry (behind all the apparent scholarship and critical logic) in this book – this sort of exclusionism amounts to bigotry – there is a valuable observation that an against-the-grain reading of this provides, which is relevant to much of the criticism of *Harry Potter* books from religious perspectives. The observation is straightforward: *to approach the* Harry Potter *novels seriously from a religious perspective these works of fiction have to be given an efficacy and relevance that is as 'real' and contingent as that which is found in religious texts and statements of religious doctrine*. For Abanes, the *Harry Potter* novels are worthy of censure because they derive from and present a world-view that is as 'real' and potent as the Christian world-view. It is because this is the case that the *Harry Potter* world-view can be construed as a substantial enemy of the Christian world-view; in some all too material sense it is dangerous to the truth of Christianity as Abanes understands it because it is as 'real' itself as Christianity is to believers. There is a competition for efficacy and territory, if Abanes's analysis is to be understood, between the world that devolves from believing *The Bible* and that which is inferred from the suspected beliefs that underlie *Harry Potter* books; and one can only win at the expense of the other (the logic of censorship is self-evident). What Abanes says in brief is: Christianity is the truly good; *Harry Potter* represents something that is equally truly bad. They belong to the same realm of convictions and effects. The equally 'real', but perniciously anti-Christian, potency of the *Harry Potter* books is presented by Abanes through a range of different arguments. It is suggested by the manner in which the alleged immorality of the *Harry Potter* novels is demonstrated by the normative enunciations of what is moral in *The Bible*. This effectively also suggests that the *Harry Potter* books are as definitively and normatively immoral as the Biblical statements are moral. A great deal of effort is expended by Abanes on demonstrating that some of the names in the *Potter* books are based on those of real historical personages; that some of the described events and phenomena are drawn from sources that attest to the 'reality' of such events and phenomena in the past; that there are some people involved in what they consider 'real' occult activity in our world who take the

Potter books seriously (such practices and practitioners are described with immense seriousness by Abanes); and that it is possible that Rowling believes in the occult herself (the ambiguity in several of her statements is dwelt upon). Abanes's argument as a whole is, therefore, two-fold: one, that the *Harry Potter* books are based on an occult world-view which is potentially as effective and certainly as much based on 'reality' as a Christian world-view is; and two, that the Christian world-view and the occult *Harry Potter* world-view consequently cannot coexist. There are here two more or less *equally* 'real' world-views in competition.

Other arguments which also draw upon religious texts and practices (such as those gestured towards in some parts of a book by Elizabeth D. Schafer,[8] for instance, which Abanes clearly dislikes intensely) could however be envisaged which present quite different possibilities. If it is argued, for example, that the *Harry Potter* books should be read as symbolically playing with the same concerns as, say, *The Bible* read also as a symbolic text, then the conditionality on faith becomes immaterial. To see *The Bible* as bearing symbolic meanings, and to make that the basis of assessing the symbolic meanings of other texts, is a process that may appeal especially to the religious but does not require any *a priori* and exclusionary faith. Such a method attests to no more than the 'reality' of symbolic connotations in any text, literary or religious, and recognizes the social and political significance that is allocated to texts in different contexts. In such a methodology the kind of excess of significance that some believers may attribute to a religious text, and the truth of the values that believers may discern within it, are no more than that religious text's social and political effect; at any rate those of other faiths, and even the unreligious, may engage with such a critical approach without being excluded. But there hasn't been much systematic criticism of the *Harry Potter* books along these lines.

Much of the criticism of the *Harry Potter* books from a religious perspective has been in an Abanes mould, presenting the practices of witchcraft and occult as some sort of competitive force which Christians must fight to determine who controls the terrain. Both exist and clash with each other at the same level of 'reality'. From an unreligious point of view, such critical efforts seem to throw religious texts and statements of doctrine as much into the realm of the fanciful and imaginary as the *Harry Potter* books; belief in a Christian world-view seems no more 'real' than belief in a magical world-view. Both seem equally ephemeral and removed from our world of understandable social and political effects.

10
Locations and Limitations

I have argued above that the *Harry Potter* books have had certain significant social and political effects, of which their enormous sales (to readers across age boundaries), their effortless reach across cultural and linguistic borders, and the unease they have aroused among certain (primarily religious) ideologically defined groups are symptoms. If these social and political effects haven't been seriously analysed and studied – if hesitation and doubt about the need for such analysis and study has been mooted – it is only because the reading of *Harry Potter* books has generally, sometimes deliberately, been unthinking. I have presented arguments against this sort of general readerly unthinkingness, and maintained that for the sake of analysis it is sensible to assume that the *Harry Potter* books exercise their social and political effects essentially on and through adults. I have also observed that it is possible for those who engage with any book with analytical rigour and critical seriousness as a matter of course, i.e. institutionally sanctioned literary critics and interpreters, are also capable of making unthinking decisions and judgements – and that this has been the case for those who have engaged with the *Harry Potter* books more often than not. I have enumerated the kind of unthinking decisions and judgements that critics have attached to the *Harry Potter* books by looking at four distinct critical ways of dealing with them: as reflecting the author's views, as 'children's literature', as 'fantasy literature', and in relation to religious perspectives. As against these approaches, I have delineated a critical methodology that would enable me to make a serious and analytical text-to-world study of the *Harry Potter* books with a view to discerning their social and political effects. With these observations and clarifications behind me it is now almost time for me to actually get down to that task – after a couple of final points to end this Part are made.

In going through the above it might occur to some careful readers that while I have said something about the kinds of unthinking and thinking, unconsidered and analytical, light-hearted and serious readings that are possible with regard to literary texts, I have not been precise about *where* in the process of reading these distinctions take place, or *how* in the course of readings do one or the other of these float up to the surface. In effect I have also not been clear about *where* and *how* in the process of reading do social and political effects intervene and emanate from. These are, of course, rather technical queries which are unlikely to make much of a difference to the above observations or to the text-to-world reading that I go on to; after all both these depend not on the *where* and the *how* of the reading process, but on the recognition that the reading process takes place with different nuances and discernments. It is not, therefore, necessary for me to dwell on the *how* and the *where* of the reading process in detail. However, curiosity is generally worth addressing, and this is the place to do so in a brief and indicative (rather than exhaustive and demonstrative) fashion. To do so then, let me first summarize three familiar models for understanding the process of reading, which, as the cognoscenti would know, are massive simplifications of the detailed and painstaking theories of Iser, Fish, and Wilson and Sperber respectively.[1] These are not necessarily compatible with each other (though there are obvious overlaps) and could be thought of as alternative models to understand the same process.

Model 1: Every literary text gives only a limited amount of linguistic information about the plot, characters, perspectives, scenes, events, ideas, emotions, etc. that it presents or addresses. This is inevitable – to give a *complete* account of these or to present any of these in an *exhaustive* fashion could be a very protracted, perhaps even inexhaustible, enterprise. Unavoidably, therefore, what the reader of a literary text faces are selected bits of information ordered in a particular fashion, in the midst of which there would necessarily exist certain gaps or blanks, certain contradictions and negations. Indeed, the literary quality of the text may depend on how these blanks and gaps, contradictions and negations are used to manipulate the reader, to make the reader aware of the text as being a text, an artefact. What the reader does when faced with these is to try to make coherent sense of these: she fills in the blanks or gaps, imagines certain ways in which the negations or contradictions may cease to be so, and so on; in other words she engages in trying to make the text consistent. In attempting this she would naturally draw upon her own understanding of how the world is ordered and lived, her own experiences and associations, her own sense of the conventions that attach to literary texts, perhaps her investigations into the context in which the text was produced and received, etc. Even if she is unable to resolve certain blanks and gaps or contradictions and negations in this fashion – so that she has to, say, conclude that these are simply part of the literary design of the text and have to be taken as such – this conclusion would still rest on her effort in the first instance to resolve them.

Model 2: All readers (all persons actually) inevitably belong to a number of communities. Thus all readers would, for instance, be part of a linguistic group (speaking a specific language), would adhere to certain cultural norms (therefore to a cultural group), be identified with a social class (in some sense belong to it), understood to be a member of certain employing institutions (be part of that institutional community), be part of an age-group, a gender-group, and so on. Each of these affiliations involve certain agreements with the group in question about how the world should be lived in and understood; or, in other words, each of these affiliations provide certain interpretive strategies which enable the reader to make sense of whatever she encounters and negotiates with. This is also the case when the reader encounters and negotiates with a literary text. In addition to all the above, the act of encountering and negotiating with a literary text may entail interpretive strategies which are agreed upon by communities which are devoted to reading (say, a group of professional literary critics, or students in literature classrooms, etc.). Such complexes of agreements, or interpretive strategies, enable the reader to start reading a literary text with some expectation of making sense of it, and would determine whatever sense she does make of it in the process of reading. It is therefore impossible to separate the text from all the interpretive strategies that the reader inevitably brings with her. The process of reading can happen only because of these, and texts exist *within*, so to say, such interpretive strategies and do not exist *without*. So all that can really be examined is the manner in which interpretive strategies work on certain texts, and it is pointless to try to figure out how texts direct reading by qualities that are innate to them (such as blanks, gaps, etc.).

Model 3: The process of reading is essentially a process of receiving a series of linguistic signals. Each bit of a literary text that is read, or the reception of each particular signal, could make sense and be understood in a wide variety of different ways. What the reader does at each moment of reading is make an assessment of the sense that is most relevant at that moment and accept that as the predominant sense of that bit of the text. This assessment consists in a determination of which shade of meaning, which sense, has the most contextual effects; i.e. can have an effect of some sort on the maximum number of different considerations and observations that happen to be in the reader's mind – or her field of perceptions – at that moment. What happens to be in the reader's mind at that moment depends on a range of different things: on who is the reader (what sort of experiences she has had, what sort of books she has read, what her memories are, etc.), where she is located, what is happening in the world around her, and also, of course, on what had happened in all the bits of text she had read before that particular bit, and how she had assessed their contextual effects. As she moves on to the next bit of text, the sense she had identified as being most relevant for the previous bit would become part of the context that would be in her mind, and in determining how this new bit of the text is relevant she would take that into account. Sometimes this might involve an adjustment of all her previous assessments; and in the process the determination of the most relevant sense of every subsequent bit of the text may become easier. So the process of reading involves essentially a constant series of assessments and determinations of relevance in terms of contextual effects, which may involve adjustments and readjustments of previous assessments and determinations, and in which the text itself, the reader, the world around her, and processes of linguistic communication, are all implicated.

What a cursory look at these models makes clear is that these cannot be considered to be processes that readers can be aware of in the act of reading. Reading is too quick for readers to be able to go through any of these processes in a well-considered and fully thought out fashion. We must assume that some such process occurs very quickly, almost spontaneously or unconsciously, when we read. In that sense all reading is unthinking, at least in the first instance. The best we can do is look back after an initial reading and consider how some such process has operated in that reading and resulted in certain effects, and then consider how we feel about those effects. A thinking reading could be thought of as this effort to reconstruct what had happened in the unthinking process of reading: *a thinking reading is a kind of retrospective reconstruction of the kind of things that might have happened in the initial unthinking reading.* The process of conducting this retrospective reconstruction could be thought of as a critical analysis of the reading of a particular text. The pertinacity with and detail in which we undertake such a retrospective reconstruction could determine the degree of thinkingness that is going into such analysis (reading can, I have already maintained, manifest different degrees of thinkingness and unthinkingness) – and the determination to carry out such a retrospective reconstruction can be thought of as a measure of our seriousness as readers with regard to a particular text.

It seems to me that the three models of understanding the process of reading outlined above are all equally plausible theoretical retrospective reconstructions of the general process of reading themselves, and are all therefore equally useful in retrospective reconstructions (serious critical analyses) of specific readings of specific literary texts. That is the strength of each of the models, and that no doubt is why it has proved difficult to decide which of these models is best or closest to the truth of the reading process, despite their apparent incompatibility with each other. Which model we might choose for such specific critical analysis (if not consciously, at least by implication) is therefore not guided so much by the superior strength of one model or the other (or our convictions in the truth of one or the other) as by convenience. I think it can be demonstrated that to some extent all these models come into play in critical analyses of specific readings of specific texts.

Whichever of the above models for understanding the process of reading one might feel attracted to there is an unavoidable common denominator: each of them involve the wider world in which the text (any text) and the reader (or readers) in question are located. In each case the process of reading is intricately interwoven with apprehensions of the world at various levels, certainly at levels that are larger than merely the purely subjective mind of the reader or any pristinely concrete location of a literary text. No apprehension of the world at some level can be a matter of complete indifference for critical analysis of specific readings and texts, though some critical analysts may chose as a matter of convenience not to address certain kinds of apprehension, or otherwise delimit the part of the world which they wish to be conscious of in their analyses. Reading, at any rate, however thinking or unthinking, unconsidered or analytical, light-hearted or serious, implicates a world-view – what matters in how determined we might be to be aware of that. It is here that the social and political effects intervene in and devolve from the reading of texts. Reading literary texts *involve* social and political effects; these social and political effects have degrees (as outlined in Chapter 4) and the degree can be gauged by certain symptoms (popularity, ideological unease, etc.); and these social and political effects can either simply be left at the level of effects, unconsciously absorbed and perpetuated, or they can be analysed by looking closely at the process through and from which they emerge – that of reading texts. Such an analysis is itself a retrospective reconstruction of reading that may use one or the other or any combination or all of the above models, with an awareness of the social and political world in which texts and readers are located and therefore with the expectation that some clarification of social and political effects will follow from such analysis. This is the *raison d'être* of my text-to-world reading of the *Harry Potter* books with a view to discerning their social and political effects. I don't think the above theoretical observations need have any further or more explicit bearing on the process of my attempting this.

These clarifications leave me with the final, but in many ways most crucial, consideration of this first Part. This is best broached in terms of a question. I have devoted considerable space to demonstrating the ways in which unthinkingness characterizes much of the obvious-sounding general responses to, and creeps even into apparently analytical and rigorous critical readings of, the *Harry Potter* books. I have developed these arguments in the course of charting out a methodology that, I hope, would help me guard against those particular kinds of unthinkingness, and produce a serious and analytical text-to-world reading of these books in Part II. Do I then believe that my reading is some sort of ideal and final understanding of the social and political effects of the *Harry Potter* books, and that my reading would be immune to any unthinking element itself, and embody the serious and the analytical?

It would be indefensibly and inexcusably arrogant of me to imply that. I don't at all wish to suggest anything of the kind. The kinds of unthinkingness that I have discussed above, and resolutions that I have made in view of my awareness of them, may help me to avoid those particular kinds of unthinkingness because I have brought them to awareness, so to say. But there probably are, inevitably must be, methodological and conceptual implications within my own method that I have not brought to awareness. Perhaps such manifestations of my own unthinkingness would suddenly dawn on me sometime in the future, perhaps the readers of this study would spot them and bring them to light. These may be relatively mild instances of unthinkingness that affect some of my observations and leave others unaffected; or these may be serious oversights that may undermine the whole argument (that would be failure). I do not know at the moment; I have not thought of them yet, otherwise I could avoid them. More pertinently though, even if the kinds of unthinkingness that may be discovered in my reading in Part II may not be too heinous, the resultant reading still cannot be considered to be in any way conclusive. The critical choices that underlie the retrospective reconstruction of my reading, that effectively forms my thinking analysis of the *Harry Potter* books, could be drawn from at least three plausible and consistent but mutually incompatible models of reading – and there may well be others. There would always be other critical choices possible, that may just make things look different, or draw unexpected attention to related material that I had not considered, and therefore bring new insights. Maybe my effort at a thinking reading is no more than an unthinking step in a long process that reaches towards an approximate and ever-shifting idea of a conclusive analysis. I don't expect any magical revelations.

Part II
Reading the *Harry Potter* Novels

11
Three Worlds

The *Harry Potter* books play deliberately and self-consciously with three worlds: the Magic world, the Muggle world, and (I qualify this soon) our world. I have mentioned this in Chapter 8. The manner in which the three worlds are juxtaposed against each other and give point to each other is worth teasing out further. Which of the three worlds, we might ask ourselves, is central, and why? It is an innocuous-sounding question, but the answer is not as obvious as it might initially appear to be.

The Magic and Muggle worlds are overtly presented in the books; our world is implied through both those worlds. It is clear that the Muggle world is in some mechanistic sense coextensive with our world (by and large the same laws of physics apply, for instance); the Muggle world and our world are immediately distinguished by the fact that the one is clearly presented within the books and the other is only implied (there are other more material distinctions which I clarify soon). The Magic world and our world are apparently different in the same way as the Muggle world and the Magic world are different, and yet there seem to exist preoccupations and systems in the Magic world which are so similar to our world (though not Muggle world) as to occasionally suggest that the Magic world is simply some sort of indirect commentary on our world. I examine these relations between our world and the Magic and Muggle worlds later in this chapter. As regards the juxtaposition of the Muggle world and the Magic world, the space given to the former in each of the books – usually a few chapters at the beginning of each and then intermittently at second hand – is obviously less than that given to the latter. By dint of quantity of attention given the Magic world certainly appears to be the focal point. It is possible to give more substance to that superficial quantitative observation. There are two ways in which the

Muggle world is presented: (a) substantively, or in terms of what it contains, which boils down mainly to the Dursley household; and (b) referentially, or in terms of its relation to various aspects of the Magic world. The substantive aspect of the Muggle world is presented in a contrary fashion to the referential aspect. Substantively, the Muggle world, reflected through the microcosm of the Dursley household, is *aware* of the Magic world but chooses to disregard or shun it; referentially, the Magic world deliberately locates itself in the interstices of the Muggle world, and works hard to ensure that the Muggle world is *not* *aware* of it. Quite a lot of the *Harry Potter* books are devoted to gleefully elaborating these relationships and exploiting the contradictions.

As the main substantive element of the Muggle world, the Dursley household is bound to appear to represent something general about the Muggle world at large, and whatever the Dursleys represent about the Muggle world is not pleasant. If I try to understand what the Dursleys represent about the Muggle world in general (and not at the moment in relation to our world) the following come to mind. The Dursleys represent a Muggle desire to reside in a causally explicable world, and simultaneously some sort of Muggle revulsion or fear at all that is not causally explicable. The Dursleys' reactions to Harry's unconscious magical feats early in *Stone* are instructive. When, for instance, Aunt Petunia fails in her efforts to keep Harry's hair short (it magically grows overnight when cut) he is punished: 'He had been given a week in the cupboard for this, even though he had tried to explain that he *couldn't* explain how it had grown back so quickly' (*Stone* 23). Similarly, when she attempts to get Harry to use one of Dudley's old jumpers and it magically shrinks: 'Aunt Petunia had decided it must have shrunk in the wash and, to his great relief, Harry wasn't punished' (*Stone* 23). In each of these instances the Dursleys' attempt to find a, patently misplaced, cause. Allocating blame is one way of finding the cause: the fact that such a discovery of the *cause* is not an *explanation* (as Harry protests) is, of course, self-evident – but then finding a cause itself is halfway there. To get rid of the inexplicable by extirpating the ostensible cause is not an entirely irrational idea if the inexplicable is considered unpalatable. That, for instance, can be the rationale for certain kinds of medical practice: if we can find certain bacteria causing a disease we don't necessarily have to explain how the bacteria does this (though it might become more feasible at that point to do so), we can concentrating on finding ways of getting rid of the bacteria. The Dursleys regard the inexplicable as unpalatable just by being inexplicable (for them Harry, like his mother, is a *freak* [*Stone* 44], an abnormality [*Chamber* 8]) – inexplicability is a disease. In the second instance both a cause and an explanation are found and Harry is left alone.

The desire to live in a causally explicable world and the revulsion of the inexplicable in themselves do not characterize the Dursleys as, let's say, the only Muggles of the Muggle world whom we have an opportunity to examine at any length. They suffer from two kinds of disadvantages in this context. One, the genuinely and unremittingly inexplicable – magical – simply exists and they *believe* it exists, so the best they can really do is either try to pretend it is not there or try to erase it, or alternatively to accept their own bafflement and impotence (it is not insignificant that the Dursleys also live in fear of Harry). Two, because they *believe* magic exists they do not have the conviction to deal with the inexplicable in any other way: Mr. Dursley cannot, for example, appeal to a scientist to investigate Harry's abilities and find an explanation. In this Muggle world nothing as mundane as scientific research and analysis exists, not even in the consciousness of Muggles. It is because they believe magic exists, and in fact magic does exist, that the Dursleys' desire for causal explanations and revulsion of the inexplicable becomes a kind of blindness, their attempts to extirpate the ostensible causes are perverse and brutal, their conception of normality appears arbitrary. The unpleasantness of the Dursleys is a condition of their world: their beliefs are unpleasant and oppressive because they patently don't fit into the Muggle world that they are made to inhabit. *The Muggle world that is presented exists as complementing the Magic world; in it magic can be manifested and causal explanations cannot always apply; magic is apparent as magic because it defeats the desires and sharpens the explanatory failures of Muggles; the Muggle world and the Magic world are mutually definitive.*

What sort of world is it where the desire for explanations and revulsion of the inexplicable are both undercut by a *belief* in the magical (and therefore, in some sense, the existence of the magical), devolving into arbitrary acts of brutality and helplessness that arise from that contradiction? In *Prisoner* the Muggle world of the Dursleys (or at least the Dursleys' view of it, but then what other view is there?) is characterized as 'medieval': '[The Dursleys] were Muggles, and they had a very medieval attitude towards magic' (*Prisoner* 8). Some reviewers had wondered whether this wasn't a slip-up; if the Dursleys represent those who don't accept magic then they shouldn't be thought of as medieval, since historically medieval people had accepted the possibility of magic. But this objection is entirely off the point: the Dursleys are correctly characterized as medieval because they do believe in magic and yet do not wish to entertain it, try to get rid of the ostensible causes in a brutal and exterminatory fashion, and actually the Muggle world they are in is medieval insofar as magic exists in it. That there is no slip-up here is evident because on the previous page what the medieval period characterizes is lucidly described in a quotation from one of Harry's textbooks, *A History of Magic*:

> *Non-magic people (more commonly known as Muggles) were particularly afraid of magic in medieval times, but not very good at recognising it. On the rare occasion that they did catch a real witch or wizard, burning had no effect whatsoever. The witch or wizard would perform a basic Flame-Freezing Charm and then pretend to shriek with pain while enjoying a gentle, tickling sensation. (Prisoner 7)*

This is interesting in all sorts of ways. If magic did really exist then the witch-burnings of the Spanish Inquisition or during the Salem witch-hunts could almost be justified. The quotation presents such acts of witch-burning as being laughably absurd, and focuses on the failure of recognition as the main problem here. Witch-burning (unless the victim was mistakenly not a witch) would be an understandable and quite possibly harmless exercise. From the medieval point of view the people's beliefs and fears and contradictory desires made the witch-burnings understandable insofar as they were convinced that witches were being burnt. The Dursleys are no more or less understandable than medieval people in that they do essentially believe in magic and wish it were not there and fear it; and as it happens their fears and beliefs are justified to some extent because they do live in a medieval world where magic can become manifest from a complementary Magic world. And magic is, of course, dangerous to Muggles – that, at any rate, is amply evidenced in the *Harry Potter* books and needs no demonstration.

Let me take a different tack and try to pin down something of the referential aspect of the Muggle world. A great deal of space is devoted in the *Harry Potter* books to making the Magic world exist in the interstices of the Muggle world so that it doesn't interfere in the Muggle world too blatantly. This conveys a different impression of the Muggle world from that which obtains from an examination of the Dursley household. The entry into the magical Diagon Alley is hidden behind an innocuous and unobtrusive pub, the Leaky Cauldron; the entry to the Hogwarts Express is precisely between platforms 9 and 10 of King's Cross Station (very precisely at nine and three-quarters); the Improper Use of Magic Office (from whom Harry gets a warning in *Chamber*) and Misuse of Muggle Artefacts Office (where Mr. Weasley is employed) in the Ministry of

Magic are devoted to ensuring that magical acts and objects do not intrude upon the Muggle world; memory-modifying spells are used on Muggles extensively for that end; large magical edifices like the Hogwarts School itself or the Quidditch World Cup Stadium are secreted away from Muggles by spells; Portkeys are created for mass entry into the Quidditch World Cup Stadium from unobtrusive Muggle objects; and so on. A great deal of effort is expended by the Magic world, in other words, to ensure that the illusion of what is normal and explicable in Muggle terms is maintained in the Muggle world. In fact, it probably won't be inaccurate to say that *what Muggles understand to be normal and explicable, and the norms and explanations in accordance with which Muggles conduct their lives, are to a very large extent the creation of the Magic world – it is not Muggles who determine the condition of their world but Magic people who do so in a benign and Muggle-friendly fashion, by making the Magic world invisible.*

The substantive and referential ways in which the Muggle world is *presented* in the *Harry Potter* books with regard to the Magic world leads to an inevitable conclusion. The Muggle world is presented within the embrace of the Magic world, and presented so as to draw the reader *away* from it and *into* the Magic world. Substantively, the Muggle world – mainly the Dursleys – is a marginal space from which the reality and pre-eminence of the Magic world *in Muggle terms* is affirmed. Referentially, the Muggle world is itself no more than a construction that exists (precariously) at the behest of Magic world. The Muggle world is, in brief, a kind of focalizing device that enables readers to bring the Magic world into sharper view; a knob on the readerly telescope that is directed at the Magic world.

But, the question remains, why should this focusing on the Magic world be of interest to readers who are squarely located in, let's say, our (or their, the distinction is immaterial at the moment) world, whose location and existence within our world impinges inevitably on their reading and engagement with the Magic world? It is, I hope, understood that by 'our world' I am referring to a phenomenal and a (despite the singular and abstract air of that phraseology) pluralistic world – a happening world, the world of political and social effects, the world out there (empirically apprehensible), all the different worlds that all the different readers experience and understand and live in, etc. (sociologists usefully call it the 'life-world'). Insofar as I refer to a particular reading (mine at the moment) and analysis of the *Harry Potter* books I can be more concrete about what I mean by 'our world': I mean something like the world in which political and social effects take place and

are perceived from the vantage point of being in Britain. I have a pragmatic understanding that the perception from Britain, while presenting
certain culturally specific aspects (usefully dwelt on by Andrew Blake), [1]
is such as can extend outside that domain and can be communicated to
other domains; and that those taking place in other domains can be
understood (with perhaps some limitations) in this. I do not emphasize
the British domain too much then (unlike Blake) and optimistically
address 'our world', but mention it nevertheless to be cognisant of my
limitations and specificities. Of what interest is the Magic world, conjoint with and focalized through the Muggle world, to readers in our
world? When I ask myself that question I naturally, given the specific
emphasis of this study, think of our world in terms of social and political
effects. So what I am really asking is, why does a series of books which
essentially present a Magic world appeal to readers in the world of social
and political effects, so much so as to become a significant socially and
politically effective phenomenon itself?

   It is possible to think of the Muggle world insofar as it is presented as
being relevant to our world (generally speaking) in certain ways by
itself. The following quotation from a review of the *Harry Potter* books
attempts this:

> Themes of personal and emotional security and the welfare of vulner-
> able groups and individuals – at the death knell of 'welfarism' and big
> government in a context where familiar institutions are under strain
> and are being reconstituted (often almost beyond recognition) – res-
> onate throughout the series. At a crude allegorical level, the Dursleys,
> Harry's Muggle guardians, his aunt, uncle, and cousin – stand in for
> the mean-spirited and small-minded neoliberal state with its minimal
> safety net and admonitions for personal responsibility enunciated from
> the moral high ground of the center right.[2]

This is suggestive but ultimately far-fetched. It is suggestive in that *if* we
impose such allegorical significance on the Dursleys and *if* that is how
we understand the neoliberal state, then there are certain moral evaluations available about both. But it is limited in that the grounds for
doing either are not self-evident and not given in the review: there is
little in the *Harry Potter* books to suggest that the Dursleys should be
understood in this fashion, and one needs a rigorous grasp of specific
political contexts (in our world) and political ideologies to take that
position on the neoliberal state. More importantly though, even if that
allegorical significance is imposed on the Dursleys (and therefore on

such of the Muggle world as is presented) then it must imply some allegorical significance on the Magic world, given the manner in which these worlds are related. The whole organization of the Muggle world with relation to the Magic world is such that any particular political or social significance given to the former would have to rebound in some fashion into the latter.

Insofar as the above question goes, I suppose it may be maintained that the Magic world that the *Harry Potter* books focus on appeal to readers in our world, and are the centre of a socially and politically effective phenomenon, *because* that Magic world is removed from our world, deliberately distanced from social and political aspects of our world. If that were true that itself would constitute a socially and politically effective position, and one curious enough to be ever more worthy of analysis. But I do not think it is true. I do not think (and I have argued this in Part I) that any literary work can be so removed from the social and political world, especially those that are at the centre of phenomena such as that brought about by the *Harry Potter* books. More specifically, it seems to me obvious that the Magic world that these books focus on is deliberately and self-consciously used to play with, allude to, comment on, interrogate and take positions with regard to social and political issues that are relevant to our world. It is very likely that that is why these books engage a wide variety of readers to such an extraordinary degree, however unthinking that engagement might be. It also seems to me to be likely that such engagement is often unthinking, in the senses delineated in Part I, because it is in the Magic world that our world is so self-consciously treated, and not in the Muggle world. The Muggle world *seems* to be akin to our world, and when the Muggle world is countered by the Magic world we may feel that we are withdrawing from our world. But the Muggle world is *not* akin to our world except in a shallow mechanistic way (I go into this at greater length later): the Muggle world is a 'medieval' world in Potter-speak, and only there to complement the Magic world, and our world does neither and we know it. The Magic world is the repository of reflections on our world that insidiously or overtly draws us in, makes us engage in it, while *seeming* not to.

There are several obvious areas in which the ongoing concerns of our social and political world are played out in the wizard world. Some of these are:

- The nature of kinship, and the social and political significance of bloodlines;
- The exercise of power between different social groups and individuals;

- The constructions of gender, and the characteristics of sexual desire;
- Consumerism and advertisement;
- The nature of human rationality.

There are, of course, other analogous features between our world and the Magic world that the *Harry Potter* books play with, but these are the ones that I focus on in this essay. In discussing each of these I chart out the precise ways in which the analogues between Magic world and our world are suggested, the manner in which the issue in question is dealt with in the presentation of Magic world, and the implications this mode of dealing with the issue in question has if it is assumed to operate similarly in our world. That forms the substance of my text-to-world analysis of the *Harry Potter* books to discern their social and political effects. I draw my observations regarding these issues together finally by dwelling on the underlying discreteness of the Magic world and our world, and returning to the unthinking quality of the *Harry Potter* phenomenon (squarely in our world).

That is my larger programme with regard to these books; and I get down to it as soon as I go through two relevant formal observations that occupy the next two (brief) chapters.

12
Repetition and Progression

It has been rightly observed by several critics that the *Harry Potter* books have a repetitive structure, and that each of them follows a similar sequence of events with a similar outcome. Schafer sums up the repetitive structure of each of the books as 'offering a happy ending complete with a vanquished archenemy, restoration of the status quo, and recognition of Harry's prowess'[1] and maintains that the repetitive structure is comforting to the reader. Zipes is also struck by the 'conventionality, predictability, and happy ends despite the clever turns of phrase and surprising twists in the intricate plots'[2] of the *Harry Potter* books, and also believes that this helps its popularity, but wonders belligerently why this utter predictability should be so universally admired. In broad structure Schafer's summary of what occurs in these books is, of course, accurate but it is also undoubtedly set off by the progression from one book and to the other. Interestingly the progression, which is woven *through* the repetition, is of a particular sort; and equally the repetition, which underlies the progression, has some peculiar features.

The repetition in the *Harry Potter* books is not simply the familiar variations-on-a-theme sort of repetition that is found in detective fiction series (all Agatha Christie's Hercule Poirot or Miss Marple books, for instance, or Simenon's Inspector Maigret stories) or spy fiction series (Ian Fleming's James Bond books, for example). In these some unchanging common denominators (usually a hero and his or her sidekicks) and the essentially similar structure of the series (a demonstration of the hero's abilities) are offset only by changes in the sequence of events, settings, characters, etc. in the constituent volumes so that little significant progression *between* them can be perceived. Each particular book of such a series is independent and complete in itself, and is linked to the others primarily by the unchanging common denominators and structural similarity. With growing familiarity with the series what the reader may look for in each new volume is how the predictable structure is varied and yet retained.

The progression in the *Harry Potter* books is also not merely of the familiar consequent-phases sort that is found in innumerable literary trilogies and quartets (and so on). In these generally certain common denominators (a particular setting, certain central characters) are developed in a linear or chronological fashion through each subsequent book of the series. In such series the sense of closure in each volume is diluted by the progression towards the next. With growing familiarity with the series the reader is unlikely to feel entitled to predict with any certainty how the subsequent volume will develop, and would hope to discover how the common denominators change and/or adapt as circumstances change. The emphasis is on the *progression* between constituent volumes in such series.

On the face of it, the variations-on-a-theme kind of repetition and the consequent-phases kind of progression do not seem to be compatible. It would appear to be a tricky act to both maintain a predictable structure involving certain common denominators (a particular setting, certain central characters) and yet also to have these common denominators change and/or adapt in consequent fashion as circumstances change. This would involve a series in which each constituent book is both sufficiently repetitively closed and yet progressively open, sufficiently repetitively predictable and yet progressively unpredictable. Tricky as this may appear, this is precisely what is attempted in the *Harry Potter* books. To be able to accommodate both repetition and progression, constraints common to both tendencies operate in all of them. Not only does each volume have similar structures which operate with regard to certain common denominators (roughly similar events are encountered by Harry in the Hogwarts environment in each volume, and culminate in similar results), but they also use the common denominators to demonstrate progressive development (the central characters – Harry, Ron, Hermione – are shown to grow; Harry's history – which is entwined with Voldemort's and Hogwarts' history – is gradually revealed). There is a sense of the independence of each subsequent volume after *Stone*, mainly maintained by repeating the background at the beginning and drawing each to a predictable conclusion. And yet each also leaves space for progressive development in the next volume beyond the variation-on-a-theme interest, primarily by leaving questions unanswered, by deferring information, by suggesting that time passes with each subsequent volume and the actions in one may have consequences in the next. But the charting out of these techniques still does't wholly explain *how* the contrary pull of repetition and progression is managed. It *is* clearly somehow pulled off in the *Harry Potter* books, and evidently with some success: the contrary expectations of readers do not seem to get cancelled out but appear to fuel each other toward, arguably, an ideal pitch of interest. Is there a technical key of some sort that allows this to be done across a series of more than a couple of volumes, something that applies equally to both repetition and progression which is singularly well exploited?

The technical key, so to say, seems to me to be a method of *elaboration*: both repeating and progressively delineating a finite number of situations and themes by adding ever greater degrees of complexity in their relationships. Elaboration in this sense necessarily involves both repetition and progressive delineation that are mutually dependent. To elaborate it is necessary to repeat that which is elaborated, and each elaboration leads to a series of consequences that mark progress. This occurs in matters of detail as well as in the unfolding of the overarching repetitive/developing plots of the *Harry Potter* novels. The manner in which the Muggle world is treated in referential terms to focus on the Magic world (that I have dwelt on in Chapter 11) is entirely a matter of repetitive and progressive elaboration. Each successive novel fills in details that clarify in a progressive fashion how the Magic world manages to exist within the interstices of the Muggle world without becoming visible therein. In *Stone* this is simply a matter of being hidden within or in-between obvious material objects, through the overlooked entrance to the Leaky Cauldron, through the wall that leads into Diagon Alley, through the midst of platforms 9 and 10 at King's Cross Station, through transformations into cats and other beasts. The Ministry of Magic is mentioned by Hagrid briefly in *Stone* ('their main job is to keep it from the Muggles that there's still witches an' wizard up an' down the country' 51), but it's mainly in *Chamber* that readers are introduced to the workings of the Ministry of Magic: mind-controlling spells come up, and manipulation of space (the insides of the Weasley's car and house are larger than they appear to be from outside) plays a role. In *Prisoner* the matter of transformations, which had only occurred in an off-hand magical fashion in the earlier books, is given flesh. In *Goblet* elaboration takes on grander proportions: the Magic world not only exists, the reader finds out, in the interstices of England but of the world at large. The manner in which large establishments like Hogwarts School, the Quidditch Stadium, or Hogsmeade Village (and others like these elsewhere in the world) are hidden from Muggle attention – something that readers may have been wondering about – is explained. Elaboration of the relationship between Muggle and Magic worlds occurs gradually. Past explanations are repeated and expanded as the reader progresses through subsequent volumes. The picture comes together as a painting comes together under the painter's brush (slowly acquiring definition and shades), becoming progressively more vivid and always retaining all the layers of past efforts. Over repeated observations new observations continuously accrue, and naturally as that happens what was initially simple becomes more complex, the previously naïve gradually grows sophisticated. The relation between Muggle and Magic worlds is obviously only one level of elaboration, a matter of detail. Similar details accrue *within* the Magic world: wizard relations with house-elves become more complex and elaborate as we move from *Chamber* to *Goblet*; the dragon that fleetingly appeared in *Stone* becomes a more concrete zoological phenomenon by the time we get to *Goblet*; the Quidditch matches develop from school games to an international event; and so on. But elaboration in this repetitive progressive fashion is not simply a matter of accruing detail, gradually adding layers to lie on top of previous layers, and making endlessly reiterated features (from whatever perspective) progressively sharper and more complex; it is also the deliberate technique which glues the repetitive plot structure of each volume to the progressive movement of successive volumes. Each successive encounter between Harry and Voldemort (or his agents) reveals something more of the past of both; and though every new revelation imparts to subsequent encounters an air of greater complexity and depth the outcome remains the same (the arch-enemy is vanquished, the status quo restored, and the hero's prowess recognized). It is elaboration in this fashion that allows for both repetition to occur and progression to take place. Elaboration and consequent increase in complexity gives the impression of Harry (and others) growing: the effect is of the central protagonist's and his friends' and the reader's acquiring greater degrees of awareness of essentially the same concerns, of moving from simple to complex apprehension (hence progression) of the same Magic-Muggle worlds (hence repetition), and therefore becoming capable of doing the same things (repetition) with more resounding effects (progression). Elaboration is, it seems to me, the key technique – no wonder each subsequent book threatens to grow more voluminous than the last.

13
Evasive Allusions

The *Harry Potter* novels constantly echo the faintly familiar. The names of magical characters, the motifs and rituals of magic, the stories and histories that give body to the Magic world appear often to refer back to a shimmering vista of folklore, fairy tale and myth drawn indiscriminately from a range of sources and contexts. The books do not perform self-conscious recreations and adjustments of self-evident fairy tales as Angela Carter did in some of her stories or as Anne Sexton did in some her poems,[1] and nor do they allude to the mythic or folkloric vista in any systematic fashion. Several studies have tried to chart out the various mythic and folkloric sources that are alluded to in the *Harry Potter* novels,[2] and the list of references are impressively wide and diverse. But these allusions do not coalesce into a considered transmission of any particular mythological or folkloric system, and the novels do not even discriminate sufficiently between the allusive moment (the particular name, the specific event that recalls a fairy tale or folklore or myth) and the cultural context that the allusion originates within. These are allusions of a different sort. They have some of the effects of fairy tales: some of the escape-effects and comfort-effects that Tolkien, amongst many others, squarely attributes to fairy tales.[3] But the *Harry Potter* allusions resist being fitted into patterns of transmission and negotiation (of social and political values, through the repetition and adjustment of cultural codes) that can be more or less unambiguously traced from a hazy source through myriad retellings and transmissions of myths, folklore and fairy tales. This observation may tickle the curiosity of mythologists, folklorists and fairy tale historians who have conscientiously and meticulously charted out such transmissions and negotiations,[4] but I doubt whether anything more significant can be done in this direction with the *Harry Potter* novels than the compiling of compendiums of allusions. Such compendiums only reveal the inconsistency and indiscriminateness of the allusive strategy of the *Harry Potter* novels. There is an implosion of discrete mythic, folkloric and fairy tale sources in these, which disperse into molecules that conglomerate with each other in reminiscent but new ways – something that is allusive but transformed. The closest anticipation of something like this by a folklorist that comes to mind is Vladimir Propp's, when he observed (not unnaturally given his location in the Soviet) that folklore is bound to be transformed in a socialist society and become remote from its origins:

> The question naturally arises: what is folklore in a classless society, under socialism? It would seem that folklore, which is a class phenomenon, should disappear. However, literature is also a class phenomenon, but it does not disappear. Under socialism, folklore loses its specific features as a product of the lower strata, since in a socialist society there are neither upper nor lower strata, just the people. Folklore indeed becomes *national* property. What is not in harmony with the people dies out; what remains is subjected to profound qualitative changes and comes closer to literature.[5]

Ironically, a similar transformation has been wrought on folklore, fairy tales and myths by the *Harry Potter* books, but from the midst of a capitalist society and through capitalist channels. The implosion that transforms these traditional forms and themes is that which brings them closer to – perhaps absorbs them within – popular literature or mass literature. But this is something to take up later, in considering consumerism in the context of the *Harry Potter* novels and the *Harry Potter* phenomenon. For the moment the following observation would do: the *Harry Potter* novels remind readers of almost familiar fairy tales, folklores, myths, but do not crystallize the relationship further. I am reasonably sure that after the compendiums of allusions are collated, critics would fail to find definite insights from them into these books. Certain general observations may become available: for example, that fairy tales, myths, folklore are alluded to in this way to encode modern values while retaining the traditional effect; or that this is a way of assuming and/or subverting the conventional authority of the story teller. But such observations, general as they are, are not really the province of research into original sources. They do not allude backwards to the past, but sideways from Magic world to our world.

14
Blood

The first time Harry actually sees Voldemort it is as a hooded figure in the forest feeding on a wounded Unicorn's blood (*Stone* 187). At that time Voldemort had usurped Quirrell's (the stammering teacher of Defence Against the Dark Arts) body, his face manifest on the other side of Quirrell's head. *Chamber* is about the opening of subterranean vaults and releasing the long dead (undead?) dark forces within. Harry hears the unleashed dark force (a Basilisk, it turns out eventually) slithering through the walls of Hogwarts and muttering: '. . . I smell blood . . . I SMELL BLOOD!' (*Chamber* 105). In *Prisoner* there are the Dementors, who, as Lupin (the new teacher of Defence Against Dark Arts) explains, *suck* – literally, it turns out, with their mouths – out human happiness and hope: 'If it can, the Dementor will feed on you long enough to reduce you to something like itself – soulless and evil. You'll be left with nothing but the worst experiences of your life' (*Prisoner* 140). The Dementors, who are spiritually akin to Voldemort, significantly make their victims like themselves. Near the culminating confrontation in *Goblet*, Voldemort brings himself to full strength from something like 'a crouched human child', almost helpless. To do this he gets his slave Wormtail to drop him in a cauldron, and add the 'Bone of thy father' (cemetery dust), the 'Flesh of the servant' (Wormwood's hand, chopped off), and 'Blood of the enemy' (a phial of Harry's blood) for a miraculous transformation into wholeness (*Goblet* 556–7).

These images of sucking, drawing life and soul out of persons, feeding on people, transforming physical form, gaining strength by imbibing blood, withdrawing into underground chambers (coffins) – the conventional associations of vampirism hardly need to be mentioned. Even in their crude and sensationalistic physicality these images may convey something of the social and political anxieties of our time, just as, for example, Nina Auerbach had discerned anxiety about 'demonic' New Women and social Darwinistic fears in Bram Stoker's *Dracula* and other late nineteenth-century vampires.[1] But I am not sure what sort of contemporary our-worldly significance can be attributed to these images yet; perhaps more time is needed to put our own social and political anxieties squarely into perspective. Or perhaps cannibalistic acts and monstrous transformations reach back somewhere deeper into 'our' unconscious.[2] However, that deeper delving into our minds is more likely than not to take me away from the matter at hand: text-to-world analysis with a view to discerning social and political effects. Let me, instead, take the crudely physical at its face value, so that there is at least this to infer: *in dark magic blood is an effective magical substance, not merely an organic component of wizard physiology but a powerful agent of magical transformations and the exercise of magical power.*

This crudely physical significance of blood to the wizard who delves in dark magic slips fluidly into another kind of relevance of blood, one that is also of particular interest to these wizards and one that unambiguously means something in our social and political world. This is how the matter develops. In *Stone* Draco Malfoy and his mates and family connections are presented as the unpleasant counter to Harry and his friends. In their first encounter in Diagon Alley and in the second encounter on the Hogwarts Express it is established that what makes Malfoy a potential villain is the sense of exclusiveness he draws from his family connections ('You'll soon find out some wizarding families are much better than others, Potter. You don't want to go making friends with the wrong sort.' [*Stone* 81]) and some sort of connection between Voldemort and allies and the Malfoys (Ron's father, reportedly, feels 'Malfoy's father didn't need an excuse to go over to the Dark Side' [*Stone* 82]). In *Stone* the connection between Malfoy and his family and Voldemort and the Dark Side is left unclear. Malfoy suffers from some sort of distasteful wizard snobbishness, it is suggested, rather than (here it is) prejudice about blood lineage (as it turns out later), and it is left at that. It is one of several kinds of evil – like the brutality of the Dursleys and the fear that Voldemort inspires. What Malfoy here mainly objects to, it seems, are Hagrid, a clumsy gamekeeper, and the Weasleys, who, despite being of sound wizard origins, are simply poor. In *Chamber* there is a sudden convergence between the presentation of Malfoy (and his family connections) and Voldemort (the Dark Side), and it has to do with prejudice against Muggle blood. What unites the Malfoys and Voldemort with the Dark Side is a certain ideological perspective, an explicitly fascist ideology that wishes to preserve the purity of Magic blood from any taint of Muggle blood. In fact, it gradually emerges that it is this fascist ideology that primarily characterizes the evil of the Dark Side. First Mr. Malfoy accuses Mr. Weasley of keeping the wrong kind of company because he was accompanied by Hermione's Muggle parents at the wizard bookshop, leading to a rather spectacular scuffle (*Chamber* 51). Then Hermione herself is spitefully called a 'filthy little Mudblood' by Draco Malfoy (*Chamber* 86), leading to even more spectacular confrontations. As Ron explains to Harry soon afterwards: "Mudblood's a really foul name for someone who was muggle-born – you know, non-magic parents. There are some wizards – like Malfoy's family – who think they're better than everyone else because they're what people call pure-blood' (*Chamber* 89). Soon after the Malfoys' fascism is thus revealed, notice is given by a written message on a wall in Hogwarts that 'THE CHAMBER OF SECRETS HAS BEEN OPENED. ENEMIES OF THE HEIR BEWARE', which is interpreted by Draco Malfoy immediately: 'Enemies of the heir, beware! You'll be next, Mudbloods!' (*Chamber* 106). The story behind the Chamber of Secrets is told in the following chapter by the ghostly History of Magic teacher, Binns, and it does seem to signify a long history of wizard fascism, going back to one of the founders of Hogwarts, Salazar Slytherin (*Chamber* 114). From here onwards the evil that Voldemort and the Dark Side personify, and with which the Malfoys remain consistently associated, has to do with this prejudice – hatred of Muggles and the desire to exterminate them and all who are contaminated by them, preservation of pure-blood wizards, presumably the desire to take over all worlds and rid them of Muggle blood altogether and populate them with wizard blood only. Against that alignment clearly stands the established order which is friendly to Muggles to the extent of taking the trouble of existing in the interstices of their world, and not interfering with them, and accepting those of the Muggle-born who have magical qualities (like Hermione, or Harry's mother) in their fold. Mr. Weasley represents this benign established order: a pure-blood wizard himself with very little direct contact with Muggles, but tirelessly working to maintain the invisibility of the Magic world, fascinated by all things of Muggle origin (a collector of all kinds of Muggle-made odds and ends, especially electric plugs), and most eager to know all about Muggles.

The theme of blood as lineage, analogous to race in our world, simmers away without being emphasized in *Prisoner* (where it becomes clear how effortlessly wizards can kill Muggles), but comes back squarely to the centre in *Goblet*. It starts with Voldemort killing a Muggle (18–19). This is followed by a remarkable scene of a kind of wizard lynch mob playing with a family of Muggles:

> A crowd of wizards, tightly packed and moving together with wands pointing straight upwards, was marching slowly across the field. Harry squinted at them . . . they didn't seem to have faces . . . then he realised that their heads were hooded and their faces masked. High above them, floating along in mid-air, four struggling figures were being contorted into grotesque shapes. It was as though the masked wizards on the ground were puppeteers, and the people above them were marionettes operated by invisible strings that rose from the wands into the air. Two of the figures were very small.
>
> More wizards were joining the marching group, laughing and pointing up at the floating bodies. Tents crumpled and fell as the marching crowd swelled. Once or twice Harry saw one of the marchers blast a tent out of his way with his wand. Several caught fire. The screaming grew louder.
>
> The floating people were suddenly illuminated as they passed over a burning tent, and Harry recognised one of them – Mr. Roberts, the campsite manager. The other three looked as though they might be his wife and children. One of the marchers below flipped Mrs. Roberts upside-down with his wand; her nightdress fell down to reveal voluminous drawers; she struggled to cover herself up as the crowd below her screeched and hooted with glee.
>
> 'That's sick,' Ron muttered, watching the smallest Muggle child, who had begun to spin like a top, sixty feet above the ground, his head flopping limply from side to side. (*Goblet* 108)

The manner in which the crowd grows and cheers marks this demonstration as a popular one, which the established order (the ministry) is hard-pressed to overcome. The image itself of Muggles as puppets being controlled by wizard puppeteers in reverse (not puppets hanging down from the puppeteer's hands, but being levitated above) is analogous to the situation that obtains in the existing Muggle–Magic worlds: wizards do control the Muggle world by, as I have argued above, not revealing themselves – by creating a sense of its independence (Muggles seem to be and feel on top of things but are controlled secretly from below, from the invisible interstices). But in this image the existing situation, which is generally designed to be benign to Muggles, has suddenly taken on a nasty turn: Muggles become the cogs in wizard spectator sports; the demonstration is imbued with the perversion of a molester's or rapist's desire (flipping Mrs. Roberts upside-down); it teeters on the annihilation of the most vulnerable (the smallest Muggle child), conjuring up all the horror of children being abused and shaken to death ('his head flopping limply from side to side'). The impact of this scene on Harry and his friends (even Ron, who expresses disgust at the moment) is, however, fleeting, and the whole thing is quickly forgotten after a few memory-modifying spells return the Roberts to their world. Hermione, who has affectionate and supportive Muggle parents, gives it little time. Harry doesn't much dwell on it – after all, his Muggle guardians, the Dursleys, are not especially splendid representatives of Muggledom. But perhaps some readers may begin to sympathize with something of the Dursleys' medieval attitude to magic in a medieval world?

The theme of the fascist obsession with blood grows more complex in *Goblet* thereafter. More dimensions of prejudice are added in. Another strain of blood, another magical race, is inserted in the picture – the giants, from whom it appears both Hagrid and the Beauxbatonians' Headmistress Madame Maxime have partly descended. Ron, generally well informed of blood-lines, explains the problem with giants to Harry: 'Harry, they're just vicious, giants. It's like Hagrid said, it's in their natures, they're like trolls…they just like killing, everyone knows that' (*Chamber* 374). Greater degrees of complexity come in. Ron's assertion that the giants are vicious is, of course, undercut by the fact that Hagrid's wizard father and a giantess had had an affectionate relationship. The Aurors, who protect the established and apparently benign (at least to Muggles) order from the fascist Dark Side, have apparently done some exterminating of their own. The unscrupulous journalist Rita Skeeter's story gives an interpretation of the background of the giants (*Chamber* 381–2), mainly claiming that the giants were killers by nature and had joined the Dark Side. It is however indicated that Hagrid's father and Dumbledore had a different view of giants (*Chamber* 395–6). Yet other magical races seem to lurk in the background. There are the enticing Bulgarian Veelas, for instance, and it turns out that the Beauxbatonian Fleur Delacour was part Veela.

The preoccupation with blood as a signification of magical races, and the identifiably fascist politics of the Magic world associated with that, cannot but resonate with the politics of race in our world. I do not need to give a survey of what the politics of race in our world consists in: in many different contexts and with various connotations the politics of race (from far right fascist politics, to left-leaning anti-racist movements and liberal multiethnic policy-making, to racial supremacism that opposes certain racist alignments in mirror images) in various forms (in terms of immigration policies, with regard to nationalism and religious fundamentalism, through imperialist and anti-imperialist processes, in the context of positive discrimination legislation, etc.) has subsumed and continues to subsume our world. Even as I write this (summer 2002) in London, the newspapers I read are occupied with the so-called immigration 'problem' in Europe, the rise of the far right in a range of Western European countries in local and national elections (Austria, Denmark, France, Holland, Italy, Germany, Britain), the fall-out of the terrorist attacks of 11 September in the US, the terrible bloodshed between Israelis and Palestinians – and all of these are at the root to do with the politics of race. In Britain the heightened awareness of institutional racism following the Stephen Lawrence murder (April 1993) case; a continuous bubbling of hysteria directed against allegedly vast numbers of asylum seekers who are targeting Britain; a series of racial riots in Oldham, Burnley and Bradford in summer 2001; Britain's delicate role of chief instigator of the 'war against international terrorism' after the US following the terrorist attacks of 11 September; the gains made by the far right British Nationalist Party in local elections in May 2002 – all these have kept the politics of race on the forefront. Lurking behind these immediate manifestations, a long history of imperialism and discriminatory politics, as well as hard-fought emancipatory battles, stretches backward. In our world the pervasiveness of the politics of race is difficult to evade; unthinkingly or otherwise the presentation of magical races and the wizard politics that devolves from the conflict between them is bound to become a gesture made in the politics of race in our world.

Insofar as the *Harry Potter* novels are a gesture made in the politics of race in our world, they appear to be fairly unambiguously against intolerant and extremist ideologies; against violent demands for racial purity, and in favour of tolerance and the widest ambit of personal relationships between people.[3] At the very least these make a liberal gesture, in keeping with the quest for a 'multicultural society' that New Labour policy-makers have made their ostensible task in the United Kingdom in the midst of devolution and the immigration 'problem' (wherein these books were produced and first received). Fascism, with its demands for racial purity and conviction in the insurmountable difference between racial groups, and with its violent exterminative mentality, becomes the embodiment of absolute evil, Voldemort and the Dark Side, when translated to the Magic world. Just as people of different races are ultimately drawn together by the possibility of love, desire and procreation that transcend racial boundaries, those of different magical races are shown to be similarly drawn together: Muggles and wizards, wizards and giants, wizards and Veela are attracted to each other, love and procreate. Just as racial boundaries sometimes are almost invisible in any culturally effective sense (the Jews in Europe, second- and third-generation ethnic minorities in a range of contexts), so too the magical races can become effectively invisible (which allows the Muggle-born to merge seamlessly into the Magic world, and the part-giants to become – despite their obvious size – invisible as such). Just as racism in our world is associated with arbitrary and irrational violence and brutality, so too in the Magic world the cruelty and violence of the Dark Side is indelibly associated with blood-prejudice.

And yet in the midst of that on the whole liberal gesture there are little fissures that have worried some critics, so much so that Jack Zipes, for instance, felt (unpopularly at the time) that:

> The scheme of things [in the *Harry Potter* novels] is very similar to the Disney corporation's *The Lion King*, which celebrates male dominance and blood rule. In fact, here people are 'chosen' for the task of leadership because they have the right magical skills and good genes. It doesn't matter that they happen to be all white, all British, all from good homes, and that the men and boys call the shots. What matters is the feeling of security that we gain after reading one or more of Rowling's novels.[4]

A more considered view of the matter is in Andrew Blake's observations on the place of Muggles in the Magic world-view, which clearly impinge on the liberal gesture regarding racial politics that is made:

> Consider the pervasive peripheral presence of an inferior species, the Muggles. They can give birth to wizards...; doubtless this works through some set of recessive genes. Harry's own Muggle ancestry should not blind us to the ways in which Muggles are represented as different from wizards – and that difference, let's be clear, is constituted by lack of ability. ...In these Roald Dahlesque portrayals Muggles are *disabled*; constrained by their lack to rely on technology, while hopelessly unaware of the parallel world around them. Popular etymology has already adopted 'Muggle' as a term of abuse. ...The books do their best to raise awareness of racism, and they consistently attack ideas about purity, blood and race, but at the heart of all the stories is a semi-parallel magical world whose inhabitants are superior to ordinary humans, and that's that.[5]

The criticism about the attitude to race (blood) in what is apparently a liberal gesture is worth teasing out further. It may be worrying that the established order that opposes the absolute evil of Voldemort's fascism is not entirely free of its own kind of fascist proclivities. There is, after all, no Muggle representative in Magic political institutions that have so much to do with Muggles (there is though a course on Muggles offered at Hogwarts); the most well disposed towards Muggles of wizard officials (Mr. Weasley) has little or no contact with Muggles, has something of an air of an entomologist studying insects as far as Muggles go, and could be thought of as rather patronizing towards Muggles like Hermione's parents and the Dursleys; the established order has a dubious role in tolerating the Malfoys and other obviously fascist elements within itself; the established order has also carried out its own dodgy extermination-of-giants agenda sometime in the past; such Muggles as are presented (the Dursleys) are not good specimens of the race; wizard children, even those with Muggle parents, seem to worry little about the dangers that Muggles face. These or such observations are, naturally, not a little worrying; but against that it could be argued that these do *describe* something like the truth of our world. It is arguably not the job of the fictional world to correct the unpalatable facts of our world but to reflect them and raise them to awareness, and certainly such ambiguities are amply manifested even amongst the well-meaning and more tolerant institutions and people of our world. On the other hand, it is not so much that Zipes and Blake above question that such ambiguities exist in our world and could therefore exist in the fictional Magic world, but that these are presented in a fashion that *doesn't* bring them to awareness: these are presented as being natural and comfortable. If that is the case these worries are not entirely off the point.

Zipes's comment about the manner in which the races of our world (white, black, brown) are positioned in the wizard world is an interesting crossover observation. A similar comment is made by Blake, though with a contrary emphasis. For Blake the races of our world are presented in the *Harry Potter* books as being a matter of complete indifference to Magic world fascism, and yet as significantly being there. Blake observes that the fact that what in our world would be considered 'mixed-race relationships' are so happily accepted in Magic world is bound to make an impression on our world readers: in brief, 'The idea of pure-blood is...undermined by the ways in which different ethnic groups interact'.[6] In these observations about the relationship between the races of our world and Magic races both Zipes and Blake make equally valid though contrary observations. In the Magic world the races of our world are obviously not deliberately discriminated against (indeed, the contrary), and yet it is the white characters who are centre-stage while the others are tokenistic marginal characters. But so what? That contrary positions in such crossover (between Magic and our worlds) can both seem equally persuasive is due to the complexities of race politics in our world.

In practice, it has often been found that legislation on the basis of a liberal multiculturalist or ethnically pluralist idea has been received with trepidation not only by those with nationalist or far right sympathies but also by the minorities it was meant to protect. It is hardly surprising that the ambiguities of our world could be transferred to our reading of any treatment of such issues.

The more obvious and far more worrying matter at the bottom of the apparently liberal and no doubt well-meant gesture that the *Harry Potter* books make is that which Blake touches upon without fully elucidating the consequences, in remarking the insurmountable 'disability' of Muggles compared to Magic people. This is not simply a 'caveat' in a liberal gesture (as Blake says), it is ideologically central with ripples of overt and covert effects that spread out in concentric circles across the entire treatment of race politics in the *Harry Potter* books. Those who have opposed racism and explicitly or implicitly racist ideologies have generally done so on the understanding that despite some physiognomic and physiological differences the people of different races are essentially equal in intellectual and physical terms, and therefore should be offered equal recognition and opportunities in social and political spheres. There are obviously a few exceptions to this: for example, a fight against racism can take the form of political representatives of an oppressed and dominated race asserting the supremacy of that race over that of the oppressor's. Certain strands of the black civil liberties movement in the US had, for instance, asserted the (at least) moral superiority of oppressed black people over oppressive and racist white people in racial terms.[7] This could be thought of as a pragmatic oppositional stance, or as reverse racism. But by and large anti-racist positions have almost always been assumed and argued for on the understanding of an essential equality of people irrespective of racial categories, whether this equality is argued for on religious grounds ('equality in the eyes of God'), or in common-sense symbolic terms ('beneath the skin everyone's blood is the same colour'), or in terms of contribution to society, or in terms of intellectual and physical capacity. The social and political connotations of equality and their practical consequences are fraught with several complicated considerations (such as the need to make distinctions between absolute equality, complex equality and basic equality) that I have examined elsewhere[8] and do not go into here. But, this is worth emphasizing again, irrespective of the exceptions and the theoretical complexities that intervene, there can be little doubt that the spirit of resistance to fascist ideologies and proclivities have derived overwhelmingly from some understanding of the essential equality of people irrespective of race; or, in other words, on the understanding that racial distinctions do not provide rational grounds for explaining such differences as are apparent between different groups of people, not to speak of individuals.

With this in mind it becomes apparent that as a liberal gesture within the politics of race in our world the *Harry Potter* books inevitably fail. They don't fail because they (probably unthinkingly) countenance prejudice themselves (as Zipes suggests); they fail because the apparent analogue of Magic racism with racism in our world is misleading; there is, despite appearances, nothing analogous. The thing is that the wizards as a magical race *are* in some significant and unquestionable ways *superior* to the Muggles (as Blake notes). The wizards simply have magic, and Muggles don't. This makes Muggles slow (in covering distances, making things, etc.) and wizards fast. This makes Muggles weak and wizards strong. Muggles are limited to their given physical forms, wizards can transform themselves in various ways. Most importantly, in relation to wizards Muggles are inevitably and uncontrollably passive – as puppets to puppeteers. If Muggles are left free and in control of their world it is because wizards have kind-heartedly and charitably chosen that it should be so; it is always possible that if wizards who are otherwise disposed come to power all that would change and Muggles would have little choice in the matter. The Muggle–Magic worlds of the *Harry Potter* books are after all part of a medieval world, and here medieval conceptions – even of difference – apply. Not insignificantly, as I observed at the beginning of this chapter, in the Muggle–Magic worlds blood is not simply a passive organic substance, it does have magical properties. To the wizard fascist blood is not simply a symbolic signifier of race that acquires irrational and arbitrary significance (as it does to fascists in our world); in the Dark Arts blood all too materially *matters*. A preoccupation with blood is not a kind of obsessive disorder in the wizard fascist's mind; it is a potent and magically real agent. The presentation of magical races and consequent ideologies might seem to make for a liberal gesture that is relevant to our world, but actually there is no gesture (liberal or otherwise) that can be understood in our world. A liberal gesture is generally understood as implying that all races are essentially equal; but where such a gesture *seems* to be located in the *Harry Potter* books, only magical races that are unequal are presented. This can't apply to our world as a liberal gesture. And yet it would be incorrect to think of the *Harry Potter* books as therefore countenancing and perhaps even supporting racial prejudice: that sort of prejudice is unambiguously placed *within* the magical world (and therefore insofar as it can apply to our world therein too) as the absolute evil. There is no doubt that the possibility of transcending magical racial boundaries through interpersonal relationships and desire is presented in a favourable light. It is probably best to consider the misplaced analogue as one that is unthinkingly made. However, if this misguided analogue is *not* taken as a manifestation of unthinkingness, then the only coherent inference of social and political effect (in this regard) in our world from the *Harry Potter* books that remains is a disturbing and paradoxical one. This would be more or less as follows: the anti-racism and tolerance that exists in our world is essentially due to the charity and altruism of those belonging to super= ior races. There are superior and inferior races, and the latter are necessarily at the mercy of the former. It behoves the superior races to *choose* to be benign to the inferior races, to leave the inferior races free and in control of their spaces (however defined), as a moral obligation. That superior races are able to do so may be enlisted as another attribute of their racial superiority. It is out of the goodness of his heart, after all, that Mr. Weasley is so friendly to Muggles and that Dumbledore is inclined to accept the Muggle-born in Hogwarts and that the Ministry of Magic chooses to keep the Magic world in the interstices of Muggle world – none of this occurs because any one in Magic world is convinced that Muggles are equal to them. At best, Muggles are useful (as Ron says in *Chamber*) because they can be non-interfering vessels for accommodating and perpetuating wizard blood. All that this demonstrates is that the established order is controlled by good wizards, not that wizards and Muggles can be considered equal. Voldemort and the Dark Side are not wrong in considering themselves superior to Muggles, or in their assessment of the power of blood, but they are misguided in thinking that wizards with Muggle blood are weaker and they are simply bad in choosing to exterminate Muggles and Muggle-born wizards.

This position is, of course, racist too in the same way that Kiplingesque ideas like 'the white man's burden' or the 'imperial mission', used to justify European colonialism in the nineteenth century, were racist. I doubt whether it was intended thinkingly and deliberately in the *Harry Potter* books. But equally I don't (and I have explained already why I don't) think it matters whether it was intended. Most probably it crept in unthinkingly despite well-meaning liberal intentions. But it can certainly be inferred. Perhaps *unthinkingly* none of this would be inferred; perhaps it requires careful analysis for such a position to emerge from the *Harry Potter* books. But then again, perhaps precisely this position can be unthinkingly inferred and absorbed without any interrogation, perhaps without even being aware enough of its implications to know that it has quietly been inferred and absorbed. It is possible that the fact that such a position can be unthinkingly inferred and absorbed from the *Harry Potter* books has some role to play behind the *Harry Potter* phenomenon – is part and parcel of the social and political effects of the *Harry Potter* books. It is conceivable that even if a prodigious number of readers have inferred and absorbed such a position through reading *Harry Potter* books they may not be fully aware of it. It is perfectly possible that the *Harry Potter* books appeal to some readers because such a position is available within it and it chimes in, unthinkingly, with their existing unthinking ideological attitudes. Perhaps such a position is not really inferred but constructed under the guise of being inferred by those who have it in mind already. But then is my analysis above no more than a product of my own ideological tendencies and preoccupations?

And yet the nineteenth-century 'colonial mission' kind of thinking is not inconsequential to our social and political world. It has reappeared, has it not, after the terrorist attacks in the US? Robert Cooper's (one of British Prime Minister Tony Blair's advisers) call for a 'new kind of imperialism' (from the West) that would render 'rogue states' and fundamentalist political alignments more pliant to the current world order received considerable media attention.[9]

Plenty of perhapses and plenty of open questions there. I do not undertake to resolve these; I do not think they can all be conclusively answered anyway. But my text-to-world analysis, even in this regard, is not done. This leads on to further considerations. I come to that gradually. There are other analytical directions to follow up which can be tied to this later.

15
Servants and Slaves

At the beginning of *Stone* Harry appears to be a sort of boy Cinderella in the Dursleys' home, being maltreated and made to do all the housework (he is set to fry bacon and eggs pretty much as soon as he is properly introduced to the reader), while his cousin Dudley is showered with presents and spoiled. He lives in a cupboard under the stairs, a space that serves as both bedroom and punishment chamber. Cousin Dudley and his friends bully Harry constantly, his Aunt and Uncle shout abuse at him as often as they set eyes on him and otherwise neglect him. When the move to secondary school is imminent, the reader is informed that Dudley will go to Vernon's old school while Harry will go to Stonewall High, the local comprehensive (*Stone* 28). In being transported to Magic world Harry's lot in life changes substantially. Instead of being abused and put to work he finds himself in an environment where he is particularly favoured (he is famous already), and where work is apparently not an issue. At Hogwarts the food seems to appear spontaneously on the plate, and no one mentions the need to dust or clean the sumptuous apartments that the students occupy – at least in *Stone*. Domestic chores in Magic households, judging from the Weasleys' Burrow, also seem to be relatively painless: while Mrs. Weasley does take the trouble to fry sausages and sends her sons off to 'de-gnome' the garden, cleaning is automatic with the use of a wand (*Chamber* 31), and there is even magical help with cooking (books in the kitchen have titles like *Charm Your Own Cheese, Enchantment in Baking* and *One Minute Feasts – It's Magic*, all literally meant no doubt [*Chamber* 31]). Hogwarts itself has the air of an elite English public school; the prevailing codes of conduct, the hierarchies among students, the sumptuousness of the surroundings and sense of tradition are all reminiscent of an establishment from the past when mainly the elite were entitled to an education, rather than an establishment of the welfare state where all are entitled to an education. The redeeming feature is that in fact Hogwarts appears to be the only school in British Magic world, accommodating all wizards of whatever class (whether rich Malfoys or poor Weasleys or Muggle-blood Potters and Grangers). The only condition for admission into Hogwarts seems to be magical ability (however little, even Neville gets admission), and an ability to at least provide school texts and equipment.

In other words, in being transported from Muggle world to Magic world Harry escapes servitude in at least two senses. He escapes the kind of servitude that Muggles impose on each other (as the Dursleys impose their demands for help in the house on Harry), which in the broader picture results in class distinctions and hierarchies (marked by the distinction between those who have access to, say, elite public schools and democratic comprehensive schools). He also escapes the kind of servitude that is, so to say, the Muggle-condition compared to the Magic-condition: Muggles just have to labour more for survival and further attainment (in serving themselves) than wizards, who can achieve much by magic. The distinction in terms of labour between Muggle and Magic worlds that is suggested by *Stone* is, however, not maintained much further. With the introduction of Dobby, and therefore house-elves in general, from *Chamber* onwards the concept and practicalities of servitude are introduced into Magic world in a manner that is clearly resonant with our world, if not Muggle world.

A preliminary observation about house-elves like Dobby: there is no evidence that house-elves constitute another magical race like giants or Veelas. If the comparison with human races in our world is to be maintained, what marks humanity across races is the ability to procreate with each other.[1] Despite apparent physical differences the fact that wizards and Muggles, wizards and giants, wizards and Veelas can have intercourse with each other and have progeny marks them as all members of one species. House-elves are magical, but there is no evidence that they can procreate with wizards; it is likely that house-elves simply belong to a different magical species. The only thing that delineates house-elves as a magical group apart from their distinctive appearance and verbal ticks (that habit of speaking of themselves in the third person), is their absolute servitude. Their situation is explained by Dobby when he introduces himself to Harry: 'Dobby is a house-elf – bound to serve one house and one family for ever', 'A house-elf must be set free, sir', they can't escape (*Chamber* 16); and admirably summed up by Fred Weasley, Ron's brother: 'house-elves have got powerful magic of their own, but they can't usually use it without their master's permission' (*Chamber* 27).

The conditions that attach to magical races therefore are not relevant to Dobby; with Dobby the reader is introduced to the conditions of servitude in Magic world that may be considered to be analogous to those that pertain to our world, quite distinct from the matter of blood-prejudice.

It is immediately evident in *Chamber* that the conditions of servitude that attach to Magic world apropos Dobby split into two considerations, both of which are suggestive given experience of our world (or to servitude in Muggle world that Harry escapes). Dobby is the representative of a condition of wizard servitude that is peculiar to his species, and before long (primarily in *Goblet*) the entire condition of servitude as a kind of species-specific characteristic is taken up. Dobby also gives insight into particularly negative manifestations of Magic master–servant power relations – he is the abused servant. The manner in which an individual will is brutally used to command service from another individual even against the latter's will, or the dark side of master–servant relations, is taken up as an aspect of the magical Dark Side in both *Prisoner* and *Goblet*. In many ways Dobby in the Magic world is obviously not unlike Harry in the Muggle world.

Dobby's plight as a house-elf of the Malfoys is essentially the result of poor treatment rather than being caused by his sense of injustice about his species-condition. Dobby's will is cruelly subjugated against his judgement and desire *despite* his species-conditioned inclination to be a faithful server. It is the cruelty of this situation, the constant and painful suffering that Dobby has to endure, that makes the master–servant relationship in this specific case an undesirable one, and aligns it with the Dark Side (with which the Malfoys are clearly associated, and to aid which the Malfoys use Dobby). The alignment with the Dark Side, and the kind of master–servant relationship that it entails, is Dobby's complaint to Harry:

> 'Dobby remembers how it was when He Who Must Not Be Named was at the height of his powers, sir! We house-elves were treated like vermin, sir! Of course, Dobby is still treated like that, sir,' he admitted, drying his face on the pillowcase. 'But mostly, sir, life has improved for my kind since you triumphed over He Who Must Not Be Named. . . . '
> (*Chamber* 133–4)

Any pity, then, that Dobby's condition deserves is not because he is bound to a species-condition of servitude (Dobby doesn't complain about *being* a house-elf), but because of the particular kind of master–servant relationship he suffers from (he complains about the *treatment* he receives under specific conditions and from specific quarters). It is essentially that that Harry ultimately releases Dobby from. In the process he also releases Dobby from his species-condition of servitude, but the consequences of that doesn't become evident till *Goblet*.

The kind of oppressive master–servant relationships that are associated with the Dark Side is developed elsewhere in the depiction of that between Voldemort and his servant – known variously as Scabbers, Peter Pettigrew or Wormtail. Chapter 19 of *Chamber* ('The Servant of Lord Voldemort') gives a quite different sort of depiction of the servant, one that is not bound by a species-condition but by a particular bent of character. Sirius Black, Harry's parents' friend and his Godfather, sums up the driving force of Wormtail's character when he says: '...you never did anything for anyone unless you could see what was in it for you' (*Prisoner* 271). Combined with that is Wormtail's lack of self-confidence, his innate dependence on others to protect himself, apparent even at that moment of crisis when he is faced with his crimes by his former friends and now deadly enemies, Lupin and Black. The pathetic appeals that Wormtail makes, first to Ron ('"Kind boy...kind master..." Pettigrew crawled towards Ron, "you won't let them do it...I was your rat...I was a good pet"' [*Prisoner* 274]) and then to Harry ('"Harry!" gasped Pettigrew, and he flung his arms around Harry's knees, "You – thank you – it's more than I deserve – thank you – "' [*Prisoner* 274]) – reveal a character that is ready to serve his interests at any cost to his dignity and independence, a weak and dependent personality. Self-seeking combined with weakness and dependence makes Wormtail endlessly manipulable, either by threats of violence or promises of reward; he becomes naturally the ideal servant of Voldemort, who is ready to exploit both. In *Goblet* the reader finds Wormtail serving Voldemort with fear and reverence, the absolute pawn of the brutal master: he is repulsed by Voldemort's monstrous appearance but kept subservient by his fear of Voldemort's power; he sacrifices his hand finally in expectation of a reward from Voldemort and gets it, a magical hand, in return. And fear too is what all the other followers of Voldemort, the Death Eaters, feel for him – and it is fear too that makes them all serve him: when Voldemort comes back to full-blown life at the end of *Goblet* and faces his loyal Death Eaters, they all address him as 'master' and all bow to his power in fear. In some sense they all prove to be not unlike Wormtail. It is the brutal master–servant relationship (of a dominating will that overcomes others and exploits self-seeking and unconfident desires) that cements followers of the Dark Side under their leader, their Führer. The alignment of absolute evil that is Voldemort and the Dark Side has the fascist desire for pure-blood as its ideological characteristic, and master–servant bonding as its organizational mode.

The master–servant relationship as brutal, punitive and consuming manipulation is that aspect of wizard servitude that is clearly aligned with the Dark Side – with evil – through the depiction of Dobby's plight as well as through the description of Voldemort's servants (primarily Wormtail, but to some extent all Death Eaters). But that, I have observed above, is a *particular* kind of master–servant relationship, and its association with the Dark Side cannot therefore be read as a mode of expressing reservations about master–servant relationships *per se*.

Though it is explicitly the oppressive and exploitative master–servant relationship that Dobby abhors, there is in the quotation of Dobby's speech above just a whiff of a larger discontentment: discontentment with his species-condition of servitude itself. While recalling with horror the kind of treatment house-elves had received when Voldemort was in power, and admitting the improvement in house-elf service conditions under the present dispensation, Dobby speaks in the name of all house-elves: 'us, ... the lowly, the enslaved, us dregs of the magical world'. This designation of house-elves may be read as demonstrating, irrespective of conditions of service, a clear and unhappy apprehension of the very condition of inevitably being a subject-species, the 'dregs of the magical world'. There is, irrespective of how well or badly house-elves are treated, some undeniable justice in this disgruntlement: after all, how well or badly house-elves are treated is, in the final count, not under the control of house-elves; it is always something that is decided from above, so to say. And clearly there exists no mechanism in the Magic world to rectify this situation. Even if we are assured that in general wizards tend to be benign and considerate masters, it must be admitted that being a house-elf (inevitably bound by a species-defined servitude) is a pretty uncomfortable condition. This is so *especially if house-elves prove to be or prove capable of being aware of the condition as such*, which Dobby certainly is.

In *Chamber* this was a fleeting and insubstantial consideration, which could be thoughtlessly neglected, but which could equally make some sort of passing impression on some readers – accustomed as most readers in our world are to sorting out what constitutes fair conditions in matters of service (for, say, an employee), and what constitutes unfair conditions of service. Being inevitably in a situation where one has no choice about how one may be used and no mode of redress if one is used badly would, I think, strike most in our world as being unjust. This might well be a key criterion in the distinction between slavery and being in service (or being a servant in the broadest sense). The other obvious criterion in distinguishing between slavery and service is, of course, the matter of payment: the status of the slave as possession of the master is made clear by not making service conditional to any necessary payment; the independence of the servant (in the broadest sense) is acknowledged in the payment that is contractually made for her services. Interestingly, in *Goblet* the reader is presented with a consideration of these issues (both in terms of discomfort at the notion of a species-conditionality of servitude, and in addressing the question of pay for services) beyond the issue of masters mistreating their servants.

A series of interesting reversals from impressions conveyed in *Chamber* are set in motion with the introduction of another house-elf in *Goblet*. A female house-elf called Winky, who is in the service of Mr. Crouch of the Ministry of Magic and turns out to be Dobby's friend, is accidentally befriended by Harry at the Quidditch World Cup stadium. On being questioned about Dobby's welfare she too (reminiscent of Dobby) speaks with a sense of what is expected of house-elves as a species, but in a quite different tenor from Dobby's impassioned and agonized pronouncements. She regrets that Harry had set Dobby free because he is getting, 'Ideas above his station, sir'; denounces him because '*He is wanting paying for his work, sir*'; and states with conviction what is apparently understood as *a priori* for house-elves, 'House-elves is not paid, sir!' (*Goblet* 89). Now, here's clear confirmation of something that could have been suspected before but not confirmed: house-elves are, as a species, slaves and not servants. They are not paid. As a species also, house-elves (quite unlike the impression Dobby had made in *Chamber*) are actually quite happy to be slaves, content with that lot in life and expecting nothing else. And, house-elves are not merely kept by wizards associated with the Dark Side, but also by wizards at the heart of the establishment, like Mr. Crouch of the Ministry of Magic. When, a little later, Winky is suspected by Mr. Crouch of conjuring up the Dark Mark of Voldemort and dismissed her reaction is very different from Dobby's when he was released. She is clearly shattered and remains inconsolable for the rest of the novel despite finding employment eventually at Hogwarts along with Dobby. That house-elves occupy the nether territories of Hogwarts itself comes as a revelation: the cooking and cleaning of Hogwarts isn't done magically after all, and house-elves are not only possessed by the occasional snobbish family, but are at the heart of wizard institutions, including the most upright of them. As this realization dawns on the reader, so gradually does the understanding that Dobby was in fact the odd one out among house-elves, and Winky the normal one. When Harry, Hermione and Ron find their way to the domain of house-elves in Hogwarts, the kitchens where Dobby and Winky are now employed, they discover that Dobby is looked upon as an embarrassment by Winky and *all* the other elves. The more proudly Dobby speaks of his freedom and his desire for getting paid, the more the other house-elves behave as though Dobby had behaved embarrassingly (*Goblet* 329–30). It is soon revealed that Dobby's desire for payment is itself more than modest, for though Dumbledore had apparently offered him ten galleons he had accepted only one as adequate payment. But that itself is considered stooping too low for a house-elf by Winky, who scornfully announces that getting paid is beneath her, that she is ashamed of having been set free, and expresses her deepest loyalty to Mr. Crouch (*Goblet* 331). Dobby's sense of outrage at his former master, his dissatisfaction with his status as a house-elf, his joy at being released from slavery in *Chamber* – all these turn out to be *uncharacteristic* of house-elves, a sort of aberration. Everything that the reader may have gleaned about house-elves from *Chamber* is reversed in *Goblet*. House-elves, all those in the know (Hagrid, Ron) firmly affirm, are 'natural' slaves, it simply *is* their species-condition.

The only character in *Goblet* who is uneasy with these revelations is Hermione. Hermione's reservations spring not so much from her knowledge of Dobby's treatment by the Malfoys (villainous at the best of times, nothing better could be expected of them), but as a witness of Winky's treatment by Mr. Crouch (a stalwart of the prevailing order and at the heart of the establishment) and Mr. Diggory. Mr. Crouch's dismissal of Winky and Winky's humiliation enfuriate Hermione (*Goblet* 125). As a result Hermione tries to set up a Society for the Promotion of Elfish Welfare (with the unfortunate acronym S.P.E.W.), to secure fair wages and working conditions, and in the longer term to change the law and get an elf into the Department for the Regulation and Control of Magical Creatures (*Goblet* 198). S.P.E.W. however doesn't find any followers and Hermione's efforts in this direction make her the butt of her friends' jokes (*Goblet* 320, for example). Clearly, all except Hermione are comfortable with the 'natural' slavery of the house-elves.

How do these developments in the delineation of house-elves and their place in Magic society impinge upon, if at all, concerns of readers in our world? The presentation of Dobby's plight in *Chamber* (and Wormwood's character in *Prisoner*) could be extrapolated from the Magic world context to make sense in our (social and political) world in ways that are outlined above. But how may readers in our world respond to the reversals that are made in the depiction of house-elves in

Goblet? These appear to touch upon matters (servitude, slavery, domination, natural proclivities) that should have social and political relevance in our world, and that ought to be socially and politically suggestive in our world and enable readers to respond accordingly. This however does not happen quite as smoothly as might be expected. There are, it seems to me, two different and equally unsatisfactory responses to this that are likely:

1   That in fact the house-elves as described in *Goblet* are within an area of the purely imaginary without any social and political equivalence in our world. For reasons that I have outlined in Part I, this seems to be a most unlikely possibility – but that is one unsatisfactory way of dealing with the presentation of house-elves in *Goblet*. There are, of course, historical phases in almost all societies when slavery had been institutionalized and experienced; but it is a reasonable consensus of our time that there are no 'natural' slaves, and if bonded labour continues to occur anywhere (as it does) it is a reprehensible social malaise rather than a naturally determined affair. To speculate about any group that is predeterminedly born to slavery through the course of nature is to speculate about something for which there is no social and political analogue in our world – it is merely a matter of remote theoretical and (in this case) fictional interest, and no more. The house-elves may recall another rather more obviously serious (in a social and political sense) literary speculation of this sort in Aldous Huxley's *Brave New World*. In the Brave New World different classes are genetically selected, cloned and then brainwashed to serve certain preordained roles in society. These classes are categorized from Alpha to Epsilon, where Alpha and Beta are the brightest and meant for intellectual labour and the Delta, Gamma and Epsilon are the dimmest and directed towards routine menial work. It so happens that the Alpha and Beta are almost invariably white, and all the Alpha are male, and the Gamma and Epsilon are predominantly black – but that's a different strand from the one that I am interested in here, not to be pursued now. Anyway, the position of the Delta, Gamma and Epsilon are not unlike that of the house-elves in Magic world; and like Hermione in *Goblet*, the Savage (a main protagonist) in *Brave New World* tries to arouse a group of Deltas to higher aspirations and fails miserably.[2] There may be some resemblance here, but the difference is far more material. The Deltas, etc. of the Brave New World are *engineered* to be what they are; the speculation about their preordained role becomes effectively a socially and politically relevant

(to our world) consideration of the dystopic possibilities of unconsidered technological development. The house-elves of the *Harry Potter* novels are, on the other hand, *naturally* such as they are – as a species – and do not quite fit into that variety of futuristic reflection on the condition of our world.

2   That the house-elves are an obviously exaggerated aspect of something that does pertain to our world – namely, natural inequality – maybe another way of coming to grips with their appearance in *Goblet*. The house-elves are clearly exaggerated: they have caricature appearances (enormous eyes, mismatched socks, bouncing around and bashing themselves up like any Disney animated character), and they speak in clichés (with an enormous density of 'sirs', and those childish verbal tics or upper-class-view-of-working-class syntax). So too their condition of being natural slaves is an exaggerated one, just another way of heightening interest or bringing the obvious to attention by making it appear strange. What they do help us think about despite the exaggerations are the implications of natural inequalities that are amply in evidence in our world (some people are born stronger and others weaker, some people are more or less intelligent than others, different people have different genetically ingrained aptitudes, etc.). But having drawn the argument plausibly this far I must confess that I can't see how to take it any further. Natural inequalities undoubtedly are a condition of our world but it is not incumbent on us to accept these if they prove to be disadvantageous. By and large in our world nurture and determination can overcome natural inequalities which are disadvantageous; clearly in our world people do not necessarily give in to or accept naturally preordained roles – even when there may be some social or political predisposition to doing so. The house-elves are presented as *too* restrictively bound by their species-condition of servitude. Also the house-elves are strongly bound to their nature-given collective identity, whereas nature-given human differences can primarily be sensibly and unambiguously discerned among individuals. The approach that, in other words, may try to find this sort of our world relevance in the house-elves in *Goblet* is unlikely to get very far.

These unsatisfactory responses from the perspective of our world to the presentation of house-elves, especially in *Goblet*, actually derive from a deep-seated contradiction within that presentation itself. Ultimately, readers are unlikely to be able to find any social and political relevance apropos the house-elves in *Goblet* – despite apparent promise – because they cannot really be understood at all in our world: there are unresolvable problems with the manner in which nature and ability are played against each other in the presentation of house-elves. That Hermione momentarily thinks of Winky as 'human' is no accident: apart from their naturally determined role of being slaves as a species there is little to distinguish them from humans. Both Dobby and Winky show moral discrimination, rational ability, emotional attachments, strong feelings, an extraordinary sense of responsibility, an ability to express themselves adequately – and insofar as having magical power is human too in the Magic world, house-elves also have magical ability. It is simply irrational that with these characteristics house-elves can be so different from humans in only that one respect, in accepting unconditional slavery without resentment. *To resent unconditional servitude, to wish for fairness, to aspire for independence of action and thought, to strive for recognition are the rational outcomes of the condition of being human in exactly the ways that the house-elves are.* If all those human qualities exist in house-elves then the desire for fairness, independence, recognition, etc. would have to rationally follow. I hardly need to site the prodigious amount of political thinking starting from Plato's *Republic* that rests on this understanding. And here is the crux of the matter: house-elves can use their humanness to reach rational human conclusions (how can they not? they are rational); not only are they human, they are aware of being human. This was the impression readers are likely to have gleaned from the presentation of Dobby in *Chamber*, and it made Dobby understandable. The reversal in the presentation of house-elves in *Goblet* makes both the house-elves incomprehensible as a species and Dobby incomprehensible as an individual house-elf. The natural predetermination to servitude is so completely arbitrary, so completely at odds with the human characteristics of the house-elves, so contradictory to the possibilities that Dobby's character had revealed, that it is impossible to reconcile all these elements into a satisfactory whole. Hermione's is in fact the only understandable reaction within Magic world that is imaginable, and that it is presented as an eccentricity and taken as an eccentricity by all around her either shows that the Magic world is incomprehensibly irrational from any our world perspective, or that the picture is flawed in its presentation.

I do not think these contradictions can be removed or reconciled, but I do think they can be explained further.

16
The Question of Class

I have been edging towards the issue of social class – one that, in the context of the *Harry Potter* books, has attracted some attention – for a while now. In the previous chapter I have noted that the educational experience of Magic world is apt to be viewed in our world as being specific to a certain social class. This has in fact been the main thrust of observations about class attitudes in the *Harry Potter* novels, and to this I return later in this chapter. In the previous chapter I have also commented on the manner in which the house-elves' class characteristics (being servants, the kind of treatment they receive, the spaces they inhabit, their way of speaking, etc.) is made uneasily coextensive with their species-condition of servility. This latter observation arguably has a bearing both on prevailing conceptualizations of class in our world and (to some extent) on the social and political implications of the reception accorded to the *Harry Potter* novels.

The analytical efficacy of the concept of social class is naturally indelibly associated with Marxist theory. For classical Marxists, the manner in which the productive and economic relations in different societies are organized both devolve into and derive from the relations between different social classes; changes in such organization (different phases of societal development from division of labour to capitalism) are primarily explicable in terms of conflicts between classes and the attempt of dominant classes to preserve their position; social upheavals (crises in capitalism) and transformations (proletariat revolutions) become universally imminent because of class conflicts; every aspect of human culture and expression that is there to be examined has an explanation in implicit or explicit class attitudes; and the final endeavour of societal development should be towards classlessness. In effect, class becomes a central and universal analytical category in Marxist thinking. Not unnaturally, those who disagreed with Marxist analysis, and also those who have sought to reform Marxist theory to keep up with seismic changes that early Marxists couldn't have anticipated, have eventually diluted the analytical efficacy of the category of social class. Gradually, now that Marxist thinking has either been modified to the extent of becoming transformed itself or has been superseded by a plethora of other modes of sociological analysis, the universal air and analytical efficacy of the idea of social class has almost disappeared. To a large extent social class is now regarded as only one social category (to do with economic and culturally differentiated strata) amongst others (to which they may or may not be necessarily related), like ethnicity, caste, gender or sexuality-based categories. Some have even declared the demise of class analysis as a useful category.[1] If social class lingers in academic research, it is mainly in terms of its ambiguities: for example, the problems of negotiating between the analysis of gender and class perception, the ambiguities in assessing class position and individual position, the difficulties of using class analysis to explain social mobility.[2] And yet, in the midst of all that, the effects of the Marxist legacy lingers; so profound and powerful has the impact of Marxism been on every aspect of social and political life that the sense of universality of social classes is unthinkingly retained, the language of class analysis has become an unthinking part of language itself, the unthinking evocation of social classes always equally unthinkingly seems meaningful. But the unthinking persistence of the idea of class, compounded by a thinking proclivity to focus on its ambiguities, means that there is often a great deal of fuzziness and confusion when it appears.

Insofar as social class is treated in the *Harry Potter* books, and also often insofar as readers of these talk about social classes, it seems to me that such fuzziness and confusion is manifested. It seems to me that the fact that the class characteristics (pertinent to that part of the working class which is involved in domestic labour) of house-elves is given as a species characteristic is due to this confusion. Servitude makes sense in our world primarily as a matter of class-based social organization (which is related, however remotely, to the classical Marxist approach): it involves stratifications (often provisional and fluid) in society according to labour and economic relations, it entails formal social agreements (responsibility and limitations of authority, for instance, and fairness of compensation) and informal social understanding (privileges of behaviour and status) in accordance with that. As we have seen in the previous chapter, the *Harry Potter* books do two things of interest in this context. One, some kinds of unfair consequences of such class divisions (such as the ill-treatment of servants) is dislocated from class analysis and turned into matters of individual morality. Thus, house-elves are treated badly not because they are particularly vulnerable to bad treatment by dint of their class location, but because some people are bad. Two, the symptoms of class standing, which in our world can be explained in terms of the material social factors underlying class division, are dislocated from the concept of class and turned into endemic or inborn characteristics. Thus house-elves are not servile because of the way society is organized, they are born servile. These dislocations effectively mean that, in fact, the *Harry Potter* books have not presented the house-elves as in any understandable way anything to do with social classes at all. Yet, unquestionably, to any reader the house-elves would inevitably appear to be evocative of class divisions. The contradiction is irreparable.

As I have observed already, it is impossible to make any political and social sense in our world of the house-elves' position in Magic world. But – and here's the point of the above argument – *we are tempted to*, because in a symptomatic fashion the house-elves are recognizably very like servants in certain exploitative class-dominated societies of our time. However, if we did we would, like Hermione, inevitably be making fools of ourselves in Magic world. How is this temptation that is so alluringly held out to and yet so precipitately withdrawn from those who object to exploitative forms of class inequality to be interpreted? I don't know – but I can hazard a guess at how it may be unthinkingly received. Don't meddle with what appears to you to be a matter of inequality between and exploitation among social classes, may be a reasonable unthinking inference. However counter-intuitively, it appears to be implied, what you think of as social class characteristics may be bio-genetic. And related to that, political resistance to perceived inequalities is best conducted without any hope of social reconstruction or change, but as a matter of moral virtue (this is what Hermione needs to learn). It should be conducted as Mr. Weasley, despite his unquestionable superiority, resists any desire to put down Muggles (or broadly, as liberal race politics is understood in the *Harry Potter* books). Or perhaps, given that the house-elves are bound by a species-condition of servility (despite everything no evidence of reproduction with humans, but that's enough), as some sort of animal rights campaign.

To take such an inference seriously would, I feel, be patently absurd – but then, given the prevailing confusions about the category of social class itself, and given the manner in which even thinking sociological approaches have obfuscated the distinctions between class analysis and gender or race or ethnicity based analyses, consent for such an inference from the *Harry Potter* books would probably not be too outlandish in our world. The fact that there has been so little mention of the curious phenomenon of the house-elves in the *Harry Potter* books, that this clearly disruptive imagining has passed by readers so smoothly, suggests that there has at least been tacit consent for it. There has at least been consent enough for the disruptive nature of the house-elves presentation not to have made a sufficient impact. That is a disquieting thought.

If house-elves have not made much of an impact vis-à-vis the implications for social classes, the presentation of Hogwarts as an educational institution has. A tiny comment about schooling arrangements for Dudley and Harry in *Stone* showed that if not in Magic world at least in Muggle world some symptoms of class divisions are apparent with regard to educational affiliations. Though it is clear that all schools in Magic world, not least Hogwarts, are only apparently very similar to old-fashioned English boarding schools, and do not discriminate according to class, critical unease about the impact of such imagined institutions on the class-ridden societies of our world (certainly Britain) has been consistently expressed. Here's such a characteristic comment, in this instance by Karl Miller:

> Why should the Potter stories not be about English boarding schools, or seem so little Scottish or so exclusive of the poor? This too, after all, has been familiar ground in children's literature, and I am not attempting to deplore what happens in J.K. Rowling's academy. But there is a bitter irony in the thought of her stories being, as they are, eagerly read in the state educational system, currently underfunded and in trouble. A recruitment crisis of unprecedented dimensions has hit state schools, whose teachers have been demonized by a Labour government unmoved by the two-tier schooling which must count as one of the chief sources of contemporary class division and social desolation. Public-school teachers are paid more, and have, as Hogwarts indicates, more time to devote to the children whom they are grooming for stardom. State-school readers of Harry Potter are looking at a place which must seem very like and very unlike the schools they attend.[3]

This statement, in itself, of course simply uses the *Harry Potter* books as an excuse to air some well-founded discontent with the educational system in Britain. But it echoes the sort of thing that has been said most often about these book in relation to concern about class division. The thing that interests me is not that such (perfectly justified) class concerns about education are expressed in the context of reading the *Harry Potter* books, but that this seems to be almost the *only* kind of class-related concern that is routinely expressed in this context. The reasons for that also, it seems to me, lie in the background of class analysis and the prevailing attitudes to social class that I have outlined above.

To relate a concern with social class unthinkingly and single-mindedly to the British boarding school (which is what occurs in most such readings of the *Harry Potter* books) is to reduce it from a broad-based (if not universal) analytical category to a particular cultural symptom. This suits the prevailing dilution of the social class as an analytically efficacious category that I have described above. Most critics who deplore the class attitudes that are intentionally or otherwise conveyed in the depiction of Hogwarts, assume that they are talking about a specifically British – or rather English – cultural phenomenon. Their criticisms therefore cannot be regarded as directed against inequality in social classes *per se*, but against the particular English kind of class-consciousness that is rooted in the public school/state school divide. Social class thus reduced to a specific cultural symptom is a far less politically worrying phenomenon, a narrowly circumscribed matter. Of the critics who have commented on class vis-à-vis the *Harry Potter* books the one who seems to do this in the most self-conscious (and therefore the most productive) fashion is Andrew Blake. Since Blake's analysis is, as I have observed, essentially a fitting of the *Harry Potter* phenomenon into an English cultural landscape in the 1990s, his reduction of social class to a peculiarly English cultural phenomenon is a natural consequence:

> Inheritance is explored at Hogwarts in another, very English, way – the stories feature class differences and snobberies. Not all children at Hogwarts are social equals, and neither are their parents (which is one reason why this is *not* just another public school story). Many people have noticed that the school houses map on to the class system, with the worthy workers (Hufflepuff), the brave, stolidly reliable lower middle class (Gryffindor), and the professional and intellectual middle class (Ravenclaw). At the top of the tree, on Harry's arrival, we have Slytherin, where we find wicked aristocrats, those stock baddies of the public school stories.[4]

The full import of Blake's discernment of a peculiarly English class organization in Hogwarts can be understood if his placement (again in a typically English cultural code related to class) of Harry as a 'Home Counties suburban child'[5] is inserted into the picture. For Blake, therefore, the English class-consciousness that is particularly encoded in the presentation of Hogwarts becomes a cultural commodity, a New Labour branding of Englishness, for global consumption.

Blake's is an attractive argument, but it is confined to his focus. As far as this text-to-world analysis goes it is difficult to affirm that the global euphoria about the *Harry Potter* books, in many different languages and vastly different social and cultural contexts, occurs because a well-packaged brand of Englishness is discerned in them. Insofar as it has been consumed as such, it must be primarily in Britain where such cultural codifications are received most intelligently, perhaps in the US and other past colonies (only to an aware elite). Some critics, including Zipes, have suggested that in fact in the United States *Harry Potter* enthusiasts are primarily from such an elite background,[6] but there isn't enough evidence to support this, and the extensive sales figures there and elsewhere belie the argument. It seems to me very likely that if such commodification of English class-consciousness through Hogwarts has played a role in the books' success it is because *some* readers were predisposed to perceiving it. That is one social and political effect to do with reading *Harry Potter* books with an awareness of social class. But there must be others.

Ultimately, the onus of class-sensitive reading is squarely located in specifically culturally ensconced readers, who can discern class codes according to their proclivities. As far as the text-to-world methodology goes this much can be affirmed: the *Harry Potter* books evidence several different class related themes that are confused and inconsistent. Of these I have touched upon two here – in the presentation of house-elves (which has wider theoretical implications apropos understanding social class) and in the description of Hogwarts (at best a superficial association with the specifically English cultural phenomenon of class consciousness). If the former has been disregarded and the latter extensively discussed, it is because readers have unthinkingly brought our world perspectives into play.

17
Desire

An article by Christine Schoefer, 'Harry Potter's Girl Trouble', in *Salon Magazine* had argued plausibly that the *Harry Potter* novels uncritically present a male-dominated society with conventional assumptions regarding women. The basic argument is best given in her introductory statement:

> Harry's fictional realm of magic and wizardry perfectly mirrors the conventional assumption that men do and should run the world. From the beginning of the first Potter book, it is men and boys, wizards and sorcerers, who catch our attention by dominating the scenes and the action. Harry, of course, plays the lead. In his epic struggle with the forces of darkness – the evil wizard Voldemort and his male supporters – Harry is supported by the dignified wizard Dumbledore and a colorful cast of male characters. Girls, when they are not downright silly or unlikable, are helpers, enablers and instruments. No girl is brilliantly heroic the way Harry is, no woman is experienced and wise like Professor Dumbledore. In fact, the range of female personalities is so limited that neither women nor girls play on the side of evil.[1]

This view was broadly supported by Zipes,[2] as I have indicated above, but the general reaction at the time was that this was a rather fussy feminist stance.[3] It was pointed out that the author of the *Harry Potter* books is a woman and is surely cognisant of the situation of women, that there are various significant roles that are in fact given to women (including being head of a Hogwarts house, and being a Quidditch Seeker), that this is no more than a reflection of the sad reality that attaches to our world, that this has no effect on children's perceptions of gender relations and there is no evidence that it makes girl readers uncomfortable (indeed more girls and women read *Harry Potters* than boys and men), that giving central roles to women in fiction is hardly a panacea for the gender inequalities that dog our world, and that this is taking the novels too seriously when they are actually just good fun for young readers. I have discussed the unthinkingness that is manifest in most of such reactions already, and I do think that Christine Schoefer's arguments are significantly stronger than those of her retractors. However, I do not intend to revisit those arguments here again, or dwell particularly on gender representation. I mention this mainly to lead on to a related issue – not to dwell on gender representation but to discuss briefly the representation of relations and desire between men and women (desire in the *Harry Potter* novels is uncontroversially heterosexual).

A focus on two thematic strains in *Chamber* and *Goblet* respectively helps both to delimit this discussion and present an indicative point of comparison. Gilderoy Lockhardt in *Chamber* is presented as being pretty much universally appealing to girls and women (and quite the opposite to boys and men); and the Veela in *Goblet*, especially the part-Veela Fleur Delacour, embody the universally appealing to men. The appeal in both cases is sexual (heterosexual); they embody something *essential* to female desire and male desire – something that is not pertinent to particular individuals, but applies to men and women irrespective of individual personalities. There are also, of course, several individual male–female relationships depicted in the *Harry Potter* novels: Ginny's affection for Harry, Harry's crush on Cho Chang, Cho Chang's attraction to Diggory, Percy's affair with Penelope, Hermione's and Krum's affection for each other, Hagrid's passion for Madame Maxime, and Ron's growing love–hate relationship with Hermione. These are predictably developed, with all the expected intractability and yet familiarity of individual romances. But the essential sexual appeal embodied in Lockhart and the Veela (Fleur) is food for contemplation because it is presented as *essential*, something that none of the characters mentioned can escape from – including Hermione (the most discerning and intelligent) and Mrs. Weasley (the most matronly) with regard to Lockhart, and absolutely all the boys and men with regard to the Veela.

That almost universally desirable gendered objects can be construed obviously suggests that heterosexual desire can be dislocated from the bonds of individual relationships and personalities. Heterosexual desire is given as a common denominator in all men and women that can be triggered by certain qualities rather than certain personalities, qualities that can be isolated and concentrated or embodied in Lockhart and the

Veela. What precise relationship this common denominator has on specific individual relationships (how come certain men feel greater sexual desire for certain women and vice versa and none at all for others?) is left unclear. Concentrating heterosexual desire in certain universally appealing objects has, in the *Harry Potter* novels, the effect of removing that element from individual relationships. However Harry may feel about Cho Chang, or other boys about specific girls, they would inevitably be drawn to the universal appeal and desirability of the Veela. This has the effect of diminishing the sexual content of Harry's attraction to Cho Chang, and it is not unremarkable that all the individual relationships that are developed studiously avoid physical contact or any evidence of *sexual* attraction. There are individual affinities (physical stature for Hagrid and Madame Maxime, in spirit among seekers like Cho Chang and Harry, in combativeness between Hermione and Ron or Krum, and so on) but sexual desire is something else.

It is more Gilderoy Lockhart's image, carefully constructed and relentlessly advertised by him, than his person that appeals to women. The image (his alleged exploits in his books, his photograph on the cover) makes Mrs. Weasley a blushing admirer (*Chamber* 32), brings a large number of witches to his book signings (*Chamber* 48–9), keeps Hermione glued to his most extravagant narcissistic displays. So when Lockhart sets his class a quiz of 54 questions on himself and proceeds to comment on their answers Ron stares at Lockhart in disbelief; Seamus Finnigan and Dean Thomas shake with silent laughter; but Hermione listens to him intensely, and starts when he mentions her name (*Chamber* 78). Even when Lockhart messes up with the Cornish Pixies and leaves Hermione, Harry and Ron to clear up after him, Hermione is inclined to defend him against the others' mockery (*Chamber* 80). It is the image – the hero of his books juxtaposed on to his own confident and undeterred (despite continuous blunders) appearance – that attracts women. This is consistent with other observations in the *Harry Potter* books. The idea of heroism seems to be one of the qualities that appeal to women generally: Harry (a true hero) has his own little flock of female admirers (Ginny, and those who ask him to the Yule Ball, for instance [*Goblet* 339]); and Krum (a Quidditch hero) is almost continuously followed around by an admiring gaggle of girls. What Lockhart had managed was to concentrate the quality of heroism – a lot of different heroes' heroism (*Chamber* 220) – into his own image, and the result is the sexual irresistibility of that image to women. But Lockhart is also a salutary reminder that images are insubstantial, and that rather makes female desire insubstantial and manipulable too.

The Veela are a somewhat different and more immediately effective trigger of sexual desire for men than Gilderoy Lockhart the fictional hero is for women. When Harry (this once simply the quintessential male and no more) first sees them on the Quidditch World Cup pitch he thinks they are most beautiful women he had ever seen. The sight subsumes his awareness of the world: 'Harry's mind had gone completely and blissfully blank. All that mattered in the world was that he kept watching the Veela.' Gradually this loss of awareness is complemented by a desire for self-promotion that reaches the point where Harry begins to contemplate suicide by jumping from the box into the stadium as a grand attention-grabbing gesture (*Goblet* 93–4). Fortunately he is brought back to his senses by an unimpressed Hermione (just as boys aren't affected by Lockhardt, girls are immune to the Veela – the charm doesn't work on the same sex). In brief, the Veela are purely physical manifestations of ideally beautiful women – they are seen and watched. The desire they trigger among men is one of a complete suspension of awareness of others, and an absolute need to assert oneself (to be seen in return). The pure physical manifestation that inevitably grips the male gaze and erases every other presence in the vicinity – the completely crystallized object that puts everything else out of focus – is the trigger of male sexual desire. This too is consistent with other episodes in *Goblet*, such as Ron's asking Fleur to accompany him to the Yule Ball:

> 'I don't know what made me do it!' Ron gasped again, 'What was I playing at? There were people – all around – I've gone mad – everyone watching! I was just walking past her in the Entrance Hall – she was standing there talking to Diggory – and it sort of came over me – and I asked her!' (*Goblet* 347)

The appeal of the purely crystallized physical sight of the Veela is evidently just as insubstantial as that of (on a lower key of intensity) Lockhart on women. It is transient. The suspended awareness of others and surroundings, the period for which the mind grows blank and blissful, is finite. When the larger reality reinserts itself there is always an awakening, and male sexual desire becomes no more than a transitory madness.

The relegation of sexual desire – whether male or female – into the realm of the insubstantial but effective, where automatic and implicitly irrational or thoughtless reaction is ensconced, in Magic world rebounds into and bounces away from attitudes towards sexual desire in our world. In Magic world the essentiality of sexual desire, as well as its transience and insubstantiality, can be *confirmed* in magical fashion by the concretization of the Veela and by the complete dissociation between Lockhart the hero and Lockhart the incompetent wizard. In Magic world this essential quality of sexual desire can itself be shown to be universal and unambiguously effective. The Magic world confirms that *that* is just the way sexual desire is: it is *manifestly* so, it does not need to be agonized over further, or examined more closely. In our world sexual desire has a more troubled and ambiguous history. Several cultures (especially in the West) in our world have a long history of *assuming* an attitude towards sexual desire that chimes in with what seems to be unambiguously true and magically manifest in Magic world: sexual desire as insubstantial and transitory, effective in an undesirable manner, to be more or less excluded from our understanding of individual relationships except in a functional or instrumental fashion, and certainly to be smothered out of sight as far as institutional social and political concerns go. There is now also a fairly substantial understanding of the fact that sexual desire does not unambiguously fall in with this attitude; that in reality sexual desire seeps into pretty much every aspect of human existence, including social and political domains. Literary expressions that have both encompassed and subverted the social and political attitudes of the times they were concerned with most effectively from *Satyricon* to *Gargantua and Pantagruel* to Restoration Comedies to *Ulysses* and onwards have mined into the quirks of sexual desire gleefully. One of Freud's controversial achievements was the demonstration that sexual desire could lie underneath almost every kind of human expression and relationship, from those to do with infants and their development, to those to do with societal and political organization, to daily slippages and dreams and high art. Michel Foucault's *History of Sexuality* influentially demonstrated how sexual desire lies at the heart of social discourses and the body-politic of a range of historical contexts; and since then one of the apparently most ostentatiously strait-laced historical periods in Britain (the Victorian) has been intensively researched to reveal a perfect morass of garrulity and power-play explicitly connected to sexual desire.[4] Several strands of the women's movement especially after second-wave feminism, and the gay movement after the Stonewall riots, have brought sexual desire squarely and explicitly and persuasively into the mainstream of political activism. The unambiguously manifest and confirmable essentiality and insubstantiality and transience of sexual desire in the Magic world may unthinkingly appear to chime in with attitudes that have been and still are widely prevalent in our world; but in our world these are neither unambiguously manifest nor confirmable. On the contrary, it is steadily becoming clearer and better understood that there is no *essential form* to sexual desire (sexual desire is culturally as well as biologically located), that sexual desire is ubiquitous and permanent in different forms, that it is substantially in the sphere of social and political effects rather than being a sort of blind madness.

18
The Magic System of Advertising

Advertising, in its modern forms...operates to preserve the consumption ideal from the criticism inexorably made of it by experience. If the consumption of individual goods leaves that whole area of human need unsatisfied, the attempt is made, by magic, to associate this consumption with human desires to which it has no real reference. You do not only buy an object: you buy social respect, discrimination, health, beauty, success, power to control your environment. The magic obscures the real sources of general satisfaction because their discovery would involve radical change in the whole common way of life.

Of course, when a magical pattern has become established in a society, it is capable of some real if limited success. Many people will indeed look twice at you, upgrade you, upmarket you, respond to your displayed signals, if you made the right purchases within a system of meanings to which you are all trained. Thus the fantasy seems to be validated, at a personal level, but only at the cost of preserving the general unreality which it obscures: the real failures of the society which however are not easily traced to this pattern.[1]

The quotation, making an observation the truth of which is largely self-evident in our world, is from Raymond Williams's essay 'Advertising: The Magic System'. In the literally magical Magic world of the *Harry Potter* novels advertising plays a significant role that seems to gesture towards the market phenomenon that these novels have engendered. The link drawn here from the fictional Magic world (presented *in* the *Harry Potter* novels) to our world (where the *Harry Potter* phenomenon takes place) may seem tenuous – but the temptation to make it is itself worthy of discussion.

The *Harry Potter* phenomenon has naturally been understood primarily in terms of the hype culture of our world,[2] in which the content and utility of the product is drowned in precisely what Williams sees as the magic of advertising – a surfeit of lifestyle associations and codes. But the connection between the content of the *Harry Potter* novels and the hype-induced phenomenon has been made, notably in a review by Stephen Brown for, interestingly, the *Journal of Marketing*:

> Although many readers might be tempted to dismiss Harry Potter as a passing marketing fad, yet another in a long line of preteen obsessions, it is precipitate so to do. Apart from the inspiration that many cutting-edge management commentators are drawing from kiddie culture, Harry Potter is particularly pertinent to the contemporary marketing condition. The books, after all, are as much about marketing as the outcome of marketing. They deal with marketing matters, they are replete with marketing artifacts, they contain analyses of marketplace phenomena, and they hold the solution to an ancient marketing mystery. The books are not merely a marketing masterpiece, they are a marketing master class.[3]

The review goes on to comment on the glee with which magical consumables (sweets, books, pets, broomsticks, and other objects) – often displayed in different magical shop windows – are described in the *Harry Potter* books; draw attention to the large number of catchy, advertisement-inspired names and phrases that are rattled off when ever the opportunity presents itself; and observe the manner in which some of these have flowed smoothly into the methods through which the *Harry Potter* books were marketed and *Harry Potter*-inspired consumables were realized in our world. The 'solution to an ancient marketing mystery' that Brown mentions above I come back to soon.

A close examination of some of the more memorable and detailed advertisement-related motifs in the *Harry Potter* books may give some indication of the effect with which advertisements are used there. I lead up to this after setting the scene, so to say.

Harry's introduction to the Magic world is also an introduction to the Magic marketplace of Diagon Alley and the wizard Gringotts bank. He glimpses the cauldron shop and the owl emporium fleetingly before being taken to the bank by Hagrid where there's an inheritance of coins stashed away for him (*Stone* 58). Harry grabs some and goes shopping. The bank and the marketplace mark the Magic world, much like our world, as one that subscribes to recognizable political-economic principles. The details of the political-economy of Magic world – the relations between labour (however magically underpinned), management/ ownership of means of production, production, distribution, demand, consumption, and the regulations that pertain to Magic production-consumption – are however obscured by the focus on Harry's experiences. There is a vague sense of the Magic world being a pre-industrial society where hard money lies in vaults, small retailers hold sway in the marketplace, and products seem to be largely locally produced (there is no evidence of international wizard trading). But that is but a hazy view of the matter. The focus on Harry ensures that every kind of detail about the political economy of Magic world is obscured because he is simply and carelessly removed from them. Harry inherits a fortune. He can buy, without a worry, pretty much anything he wants. As it happens he doesn't even have to do that, because he just keeps being given the most desirable things without having to lift a finger (the best broomsticks in the market, an invisibility cloak, the Marauder's Map, useful birthday presents from his not too well-off friends). Harry is the consumer's dream: he can buy and buy and take and take without having to work or fret about financial resources. Harry is also the capitalist's dream: someone whose entire sense of the world – the Magic world – is sieved through impressions gathered in the marketplace while having plenty of money in his pocket. Harry enters the market of Diagon Alley with a clean slate as far as impressions of the Magic world go; he leaves the market with a formative impression of the Magic world which all comes from the bank and the shops. Some of his friends are not so fortunate. The Weasleys are clearly not as well off (the butt of the Malfoys' snobbery for that reason) and the Weasley children often have to do with second-hand things; the Weasleys have to think twice before buying things. Hermione's parents are Muggles and have to exchange Muggle-money for wizard-money: details of these transactions might have given readers in our world a clear sense of the relative worth of things. Dobby's pay and life-style at Hogwarts are frugal: but we don't really know what unemployment may mean for a house-elf (starvation? homelessness?). More attention to such details may have revealed more of the political-economical relations of Magic world. Harry is ideally placed not to have to dwell on these. However, it is reasonably clear that the political-economic arrangement of Magic world is such that it is recognizable in our world: its principles might have been unravelled and turned out to be the same as those that have pertained or sometimes still pertain in our world. In political-economic terms Magic world is simply a magically enhanced version of some context of our world, probably a pre-industrial context.

One of the points that Williams makes in the essay quoted above is that advertising developed to its modern level, acquiring those magical qualities (of associating consumer items with life-styles, for instance) only as industrial and post-industrial capitalism developed. Under less complex political-economic conditions advertising tended to be simply declarative and descriptive. What may strike the reader about the advertisements of Magic world is that they are highly developed and sophisticated examples of their kind, not really in keeping with the pre-industrial environment of the marketplace and bank. These advertisements are given in unusual detail: while every other insight into the political economy of Magic world is carefully obscured, the high development of advertising is emphatically brought to attention by complete quotations from several of these. Again, it is the focus on Harry that enables this even while obscuring Magic economic relations: since Harry's approach to the Magic world is mediated by his exposure to the bank and market, since Harry is the ideal consumer in several senses, his magical sensibilities seem to be especially honed to Magic advertisements. He notices them and absorbs them, just as he notices the brand names of things. To the blasé consumers of our world advertisements are so familiar that we absorb their impact without quite noticing it; to Harry advertisements are an entry into Magic world, he studies them and absorbs them with care. What may readers infer from the Magic world advertisements that are given in the *Harry Potter* books?

Broomsticks figure significantly in Harry's entry into and establishment within Magic world (virtuoso broomstick rider and the youngest Quidditch Seeker ever at Hogwarts), and broomsticks naturally are the centre of the language of advertising in the *Harry Potter* books. In *Stone* it is the possession of the Nimbus Two Thousand broomstick that magically endows on Harry an enviable status at Hogwarts (even Malfoy is impressed). The status clearly comes because the Nimbus Two Thousand is a status symbol; all the students at Hogwarts know of it by reputation, the reputation has something to do with advertisements. The very way in which they think about it and talk about its packaging and performance is reminiscent of advertisements, and replete with advertisement-induced desires. There is the association with status involved: '"It's not any old broomstick," [Ron] said, "it's a Nimbus Two Thousand. .... Comets looks flashy, but they're not in the same league as the Nimbus"' (*Stone* 122). The fetishistic satisfaction of possessiveness is described: 'Even Harry, who knew nothing about the different brooms, thought it looked wonderful. Sleek and shiny, with a mahogany handle, it had a long tail of neat, straight twigs and *Nimbus Two Thousand* written in gold near the top' (*Stone* 123). There is the association with being in control: 'What a feeling – he swooped in and out of goalposts and then sped up and down the pitch. The Nimbus Two Thousand turned wherever he wanted at his lightest touch' (*Stone* 123). By *Chamber* however Harry's Nimbus Two Thousand has been superseded by a superior model – the Nimbus Two Thousand and One. The entire Slytherin team acquires these thanks to Mr. Malfoy's generosity, and the Slytherin captain, Flint, gloats about these in recognizably advertising terms (playing with words and throwing in advertising clichés): 'Very latest model. Only came out last month,' said Flint carelessly, flicking a speck of dust from the end of his own. 'I believe it outstrips the old Two Thousand series by a considerable amount. As for the old Cleansweeps,' he smiled nastily at Fred and George, who were both clutching Cleansweep Fives, 'sweeps the board with them.' (*Chamber* 86). Luckily it is not long before, in *Prisoner*, a superior model makes its appearance in the market – *The Firebolt* – and here the advertisement is given verbatim:

> *This state-of-the-art racing broom sports a streamlined, superfine handle of ash, treated with a diamond-hard polish, and hand-numbered with its own registration number. Each individually selected birch twig in the broomtail has been honed to aerodynamic perfection, giving the Firebolt unsurpassable balance and pinpoint precision. The Firebolt has an acceleration of 0–150 miles an hour in ten seconds and incorporates an unbreakable braking charm. Price on request.* (*Prisoner* 43)

This is replete with advertising motifs, which I come back to below. Harry wants it and mysteriously but typically Harry gets it (*Prisoner* 165). It is, as Ron says, 'an *international*-standard broom' (*Prisoner* 166), 'the best broom there is' (*Prisoner* 167) – so naturally it is unlikely to be surpassed in a hurry. In *Goblet* the quality of the Firebolt is confirmed when it turns out that all the players in the Quidditch World Cup have one (*Goblet* 96). But broomstick advertisements still draw Harry effortlessly, and while he waits to see the Quidditch World Cup match an advertisement blackboard catches his eye: '*The Bluebottle: A Broom for All the Family – safe, reliable, and with In-built Anti-Burglar Buzzer*' (*Goblet* 88).

Broomsticks provide the single advertisement-motif that is developed most systematically through the *Harry Potter* novels. But there are other advertisements that are described in detail, notably one for Kwikspell, A Correspondence Course in Beginner's Magic, which is given at such length that it is worth checking out in the book (*Chamber* 97–8). It uses the customary advertising ploys of targeting the audience by asking questions ('*Feel out of step in the world of modern magic? Find yourself making excuses not to perform simple spells? Ever been taunted for your woeful wandwork?*'); presenting quality claims through conjoint words ('*Kwikspell is an all-new, fail-safe, quick-result, easy-learn course*'); and giving customer endorsements with a touch of humour ('*Warlock D.J. Prod of Didsbury says: 'My wife used to sneer at my feeble charms but one month into your fabulous Kwikspell course I succeeded in turning her into a yak! Thank you, Kwikspell!''*'). A strikingly familiar format for anyone who has seen an advertisement for a correspondence course in any newspaper or magazine.

A cursory look at those advertisements (this is merely a small selection of the advertisement-related motifs that appear in the *Harry Potter* books) makes it clear that almost every aspect of modern advertisement has been covered there. There is a range of linguistic gimmicks typical of advertisements[4] in there: the calculated misspelling ('kwik'); the pat brand name (Nimbus, Comet, Cleansweep, Firebolt); alliterations ('simple spells', 'woeful wandwork', 'magical mess-remover', 'unbreakable braking'); brief declarative statements ('No Pain, No Stain!'); excessive adjective usage and conjoined words ('all-new, fail-safe, quick-result, easy-learn course', 'streamlined, superfine handle'). There are the familiar advertisement techniques:[5] endorsements (Madam Z. Nettles and Warlock D.J. Prod for Kwikspell); description of product and performance (especially for the Firebolt); description of accessories ('In-built Anti-Burglar Buzzer'); guarantee of performance ('unbreakable braking charms', 'fail-safe ... course'); humour ('I succeeded in turning her into a yak!'); indication of exclusiveness ('hand-numbered with its own registration number'). There is discussion of the effects of product enhancement (from Nimbus Two Thousand to Nimbus Two Thousand and One to Firebolt); and there is demonstration of the manner in which the language and perspectives provided by advertisements enter everyday usage (see Ron on the Nimbus Two Thousand or Flint on the Nimbus Two Thousand and One above), and gradually take over modes of self-appraisal and evaluation and the estimation of others, and set measures for aspiration and success.

But there is more to Magic world advertisements that just a demonstration of what advertisements do. In terms of what they do obviously Magic world advertisements are no different from advertisements in our world. Those broomstick advertisements and descriptions cannot but bring to mind innumerable car and scooter or motorbike advertisements in our world. The Kwikspell correspondence course is similarly reminiscent of advertisements that we frequently come across in newspapers and magazines. Indeed, every advertisement that is mentioned in Magic world, every Magic product brand name, closely resembles those that attach to consumer items in our world. The resemblance is so close that in his essay Pennington felt that these advertisements merely give evidence of the failure of *Harry Potter* books as fantasy; these advertisement motifs merely replicate experiences of our mundane world rather than allow any escape into a fantastical world.[6] But there is in fact one immensely significant way in which the experience of advertising in Magic world is somewhat different from our world, and it has to do with magic.

In Magic world advertisements never disappoint. The magical claims made on behalf of certain products are literally magical. Each broomstick that Harry gets leads to a greater level of satisfaction than the one before. Each magical sweet that Harry tastes, each drink he drinks, every book he acquires give exactly the level of delight and pleasure that the brand names and advertisements promise. In our world advertisements often make magical claims: detergents that can make stains simply vanish, washing liquids that cut through grease in a wondrous fashion, cars that are unbelievably safe and smooth and soundless and fleet, food that is unfailingly delicious, shaving lotions and underwear that act as aphrodisiacs, correspondence courses that give the gift of tongues in a matter of days, etc. are the stuff of advertising in our world. We know these are mostly exaggerations, we are prepared for failure and disappointment, we tone down our expectations according to the condition of our world. But if taken literally, advertisements in our world gesture towards a world that is not at all unlike Magic world. In our world advertisements claiming magical properties for products are exaggerations, in Magic world advertisements making similar magical claims for products are generally literally trustworthy. *Magic world is in a literal sense the concretization of the magic world of advertising in our world as a place in-itself*; it is no accident that Harry is introduced to it through the bank and the marketplace.

Another way of looking at that would be to turn Williams's observations about the magic system that is advertising inside out: in our world advertisements are in our terms magical and make extraordinary and obviously figurative associations; in the Magic world of the *Harry Potter* books advertisements are actually simple declarative statements which, while still seeming magical in our world, are no more than ordinary statements of fact where everything is literally magical. Insofar, therefore, as advertisements of the Magic world are directed at readers in our world, who would recognize them as pretty much the same as our-world advertisements but nevertheless no more than literal statements of fact in a Magic world context, who would be aware of both their familiarity from an our world perspective and their literality in Magic world, they have a predictable effect. *To readers of our world the advertisements described in the* Harry Potter *books are advertisements – but not of the specific products that they announce in Magic world. They are, in some sense, advertisements of advertising itself; they are advertisements that conjure up and concretize and draw us into the Magic world that is closely associated with advertising itself in our world. They advertise magic for us.* And naturally, in making the Magic world of advertising come to life, they draw attention away from an awareness of political economy: it is pushed into the background, magically made to vanish into marginality (no one worries about the not particularly serious poverty of the Weasleys or house-elves).

The *Harry Potter* phenomenon emanates from amongst those who receive the advertisement for magic from within the pages of the *Harry Potter* books. When Brown in the review that I have quoted above claims that the *Harry Potter* books 'hold the solution to an ancient marketing mystery' this is precisely what he is (a tiny bit unthinkingly but nevertheless obviously) referring to. Brown clarifies that claim later in the review in the following words:

> More than 20 years ago, Jagdish Sheth (1979) pointed out that marketing fads are a mystery, and they are no less mysterious today. Despite recent attempts to map the fadscape ... fads remain as inexplicably enigmatic as ever. Although I am hesitant to draw lessons from a single case study, let alone a purported passing fad, the Harry Potter megafad suggests that the answer to this marketing mystery is mysteriousness itself.[7]

Brown correctly suggests that the mystery (we can call it magic) *in* the books is continuous with their mysterious (call it magical) growth into a fad themselves. Brown is unclear about what he means by 'mystery': he takes it as something that is simply unanalysable. That, it seems to me, is actually beside the point insofar as the *Harry Potter* books themselves deal with advertising. Insofar as these books do that, they simply advertise and concretize the magic of advertising itself; the books are extraordinarily deftly designed to advertise themselves, their magic world creation, even as they are read.

19
Movie Magic

The subtle interplay between our world and Magic world presented through the depiction of advertisements in the *Harry Potter* books is given a further turn by our world renderings of the books on screen. The advertisements in the *Harry Potter* books in some sense become advertisements for advertisement itself in our world (the magic of advertising); the screen versions of the *Harry Potter* books are, in a similar fashion, larger than themselves. They draw attention to the illusionary qualities of films generally, and the manipulations that underlie them, in our world. This is so because the phenomenon arising from the *Harry Potter* books has been so spectacular that the film versions could not but be deliberately phenomenal; the filmic replication of the texts *and* of the phenomenon arising from them necessarily becomes a process that interrogates the film medium. That the market conditions which brought about this particular situation also, almost simultaneously, generated the film version of J.R.R. Tolkien's *The Lord of the Rings* is noteworthy too. This calculated coincidence probably indicates the degree to which the *Harry Potter* phenomenon, with the implicit social and political effects, has impacted on the field of filmic reproduction generally. The market manipulators of our world have arguably abstracted certain magical qualities of the *Harry Potter* phenomenon that can be transferred to other media, and turned it into a producing and consuming frenzy of magic (and fantasy). How magic may be extrapolated from the *Harry Potter* books as a matter of social and political effect is the subject of the next and final chapter of this study.

The institutional nature of film production and spectatorship has been discussed widely by film theorists. The planning, production, advertising and distribution of films involve collective and coordinated processes that bring together various strands of an international industry. The manner in which spectators are made aware of and brought to view films, the ways in which they employ certain conventions of interpretation, and the degree to which they finally engage with particular films are also part of collective and often carefully coordinated processes. These institutional processes have been examined extensively. In the following brief discussion of the *Harry Potter* films I mainly address the latter (the matter of spectatorship), with the understanding that that, to some degree, must reflect the calculations of the former (the prerogatives of productive processes). My focus on spectatorship here is consistent with the patterns established for a text-to-world approach, which emphasizes the prerogatives of reading.

By their very nature the medium of films involve what John Ellis calls: 'The predominant myth of cinema, fostered by cinema itself... that its images and sounds represent reality'.[1] Films usually produce an *illusion* of reality. They use wholly artificial devices to convey the impression that what is observed on screen by a spectator is in some sense *really* happening. Even if what occurs is fantastic, as in the *Harry Potter* films, spectators can engage with and immerse themselves in depicted events *as if* they are, so to say, really happening. Ellis also pertinently observes that every particular illusion of reality is inevitably predetermined by the targeted audience; all films in some sense anticipate their spectators' expectations in specific ways, even if the expected spectatorship is very large:

> Cinema habitually proposes a particular enigma to its spectators through the operation of the narrative image which offers scrambled meanings to be sorted out by the film itself. These meanings are always particular and specific. The spectator is therefore always specified in her or his turn: a spectator who is curious or expectant about the particular problem with which the film promises to concern itself. Such a specification can be highly defined (as with an anthropological documentary for example), or it can be of the vaguest kind. With entertainment cinema, it is usually vague because of the institutional demands of a cinema that conceives of itself as a mass medium. To get twelve million or more people to see a film dictates that the narrative image should produce the most general possible specification of the audience. However, this general spectator specification still has to be specific, it still has to provide something that will produce curiosity or expectancy.[2]

Few would argue with the assertion that the particular specifications of the projected mass spectatorship for the *Harry Potter* films has to do with a desire to see the Magic world of the books brought to *life*, as it were – or given a filmic illusion of reality. This desire, happily already a mass desire before the films were even conceived, was pre-eminently worth tapping into because of the scale of the *Harry Potter* phenomenon as engendered by the books. Very seldom have films been so preordained to be blockbusters, received so much media attention before they appeared (pondering how faithful they are likely to be to the books, to what extent author Rowling intervened in their making, how well those cast match readers' expectations), been anticipated with so much *informed* readiness. I have given some indicative figures in this regard in Chapter 3. In this instance the (mass) spectator specifications of the films were predetermined by the books (the phenomenon of the books). The films were from their inception with reference to the books rather than independent filmic texts. The precondition of the making and reception of the *Harry Potter* films was their ability to provide a convincing *illusion of the reality* of the Magic world, and they were to be tested and judged accordingly. Let's be clear about this expectation: no one was seriously going to believe that magic *happened* in the films, everyone was going to see whether the films had succeeded in making the unbelievable believable. This was going to be, in other words, a test of the skill of film-making, an assessment of the art of filmic illusion-building itself. Spectators were going to receive the *Harry Potter* films to an extraordinary degree not straightforwardly as simply a story or simply entertainment (if successful that would follow, but one has to wait and see whether it is successful enough to be entertaining) but as films. Those involved in the production of the film undoubtedly knew that this would be the case and it cannot be surprising if their awareness of this expectation happened to be reflected within the films.

This illusion of reality, within certain limits and within defined degrees of control, can occur in other media too – in literature and painting, for instance. I have already discussed Iser's notion of illusion-building in the context of reading literary texts in this connection. But there are arguably different kinds of awareness of *illusoriness* involved in the illusory effects of, say, painting and those of film. This is not a matter of the deliberation with which artifice may be deployed, but of the technical content of the media in question. The point is made neatly by Richard Allen in a comparison between trompe l'oeil painting and what he calls 'reproductive illusion' (film) – the specific nuances of these terms and the distinction I wish to highlight are clear in the following quotation:

> In a trompe l'oeil painting I see the painting as if it were an object and not a pictorial representation at all; the trompe l'oeil thus entails a loss of medium awareness. ... In a reproductive illusion – so named because it is created by forms of mechanical or electronic reproduction (photography, film, video) – I mistake the fictional referent of a pictorial representation for an actual one. Reproductive illusion may be considered a form of trompe l'oeil in the sense that it entails a fictional object taken for a real object; but I wish to emphasize its difference from the trompe l'oeil illusion as I have defined it. The difference lies in the fact that the spectator of a reproductive illusion remains medium aware. In projective illusion I experience a pictorial or dramatic representation as if it were a fully realized world of experience and not a representation. Projective illusion is not a form of trompe l'oeil: The reality is a 'virtual' one. Yet, like the trompe l'oeil, it entails a loss of medium awareness.[3]

So, there is always in filmic representation (from this perspective a particularly potent kind of reproductive projective illusion) a certain degree of awareness of illusory quality, not in terms of medium awareness but in terms of the *virtual* nature of the reality (where the medium seems to disappear) that is presented. Insofar as the *Harry Potter* films go, this allows us to hone our understanding of the precise kind of spectatorship specifications that these are constructed to. The audience in this case, informed and aware of the *Harry Potter* texts and phenomenon as it is, looks to assess the success of the *virtual reality* (as virtual – and therefore able to accommodate the magical easily – and yet appearing to be real to the senses) of the illusion, without compromising the medium invisibility (without having to become aware of *how* the medium was used to achieve this). If, for instance, there are special effects to be seen (as there must be in representations of the magical) the audience wouldn't want the fact that these are special effects, technologically manoeuvred, to be visible on the screen, it would want them to appear as *virtually* real – it would like to experience them as virtually real. But it would know all the time that they are virtual.

The expectation of a convincing virtual reality in the presentation of *Harry Potter* Magic world is what the mass spectators naturally expect (conditional on the determination of the *Harry Potter* phenomenon), what the producers know the mass spectators expect, and what therefore they try to produce. To do so, they fall back on filmic techniques of fantastic illusion creation that are tried and tested. These can be elucidated for the *Harry Potter* films by using distinctions offered in the classic work of Siegfried Kracauer, *Theory of Film*, in which a section is devoted to outlining how fantasy is established from/for the cinematic viewpoint. According to Kracauer this could be done through three techniques: one, in a stagey manner (by using bizarre settings, make-up, gestures, etc.), where the stagey fantasy can either be allocated the same aesthetic legitimacy as actuality or assigned a lesser validity than physical reality; two, through cinematic techniques (multiple exposures, superimpositions, distortions, editing, computer generated special effects, etc.), and again with at least two alternative levels of relation with physical reality; and three, in terms of physical reality itself (i.e. not by staged or cinematic effects but by the defamiliarization of shifting perspectives).[4] The first two of these are particularly relevant to the film versions of the *Harry Potter* books. The manner in which these are deployed also reveal interpretive acts that occur between the texts and the films – especially (given Kracauer's sensitivity to the relation between fantasy depiction and depiction of 'actuality') in the negotiations between Muggle and Magic worlds.

The staged elements in the *Harry Potter* films provide the most effective extraneous (in the sense of not deriving directly from the books) threads of continuity. In the books the description of Muggle and Magic worlds, and events therein, are primarily held together by devices of narrative continuity. So, the different described episodes and images – what Privet Close looks like, what impression the characters of Dursley and Harry and Hagrid and others make, what happens in Diagon Alley or Gringotts Bank or Hogwarts, the different magical episodes, the final confrontations with Voldemort in different guises – are all held together primarily by the internal logic of the story. This internal logic can be read in different ways. For instance, as a reader I might choose to link all the episodes and images together in terms of my understanding and expectations of the central protagonist Harry, of the manner in which his character is developed through exposure to other persons and situations. Or, alternatively, I might choose to link the different episodes and images in terms of the consistency of the rules that govern magic, the manner in which these are revealed and elaborated as the story progresses. These or such strands of internal logic and continuity have been the *raison d'être* of my text-to-world reading so far. In the *Harry Potter* films the absence of the expository pace of the novels, the immediacy and abundance of the images (compellingly fantastic) diverts attention away from the more leisurely narrative strains of continuity. In the films therefore the sense of continuity has to be established through compensatory means, preferably such as are manifested *through* the abundance and immediacy of the images themselves. This is primarily where the stagey effects come in. John Williams's *Harry Potter* music plays a crucial role here. Some suspenseful episodes are linked together by the somewhat portentous slow movement of the theme music, which chimes in the background as Harry is gradually drawn into Magic world from the Dursley household, and as the mystery of his heritage is gradually revealed thereafter. It comes full blast at times (say when Harry flies for the first time in the *Stone* film), and is occasionally played with quiet pathos (when Hagrid plays it on the flute in the *Stone* film). Some wondrous magical moments are connected by the crescendo of the *Harry Potter* theme music (as when Harry walks into Diagon Alley for the first time, or when Harry and friends enter the Hogwarts dining hall for the first time). Along with the music the visual effect of the Hogwarts environment provides a sense of continuity that is not wholly due to the descriptions in the books. The dark (always shadowy) cavernous Gothic environment of Hogwarts pervades the films and lingers in the spectators' minds. Fantastic costumes play their role too: those black academic cloaks that students and teachers are always enveloped in Hogwarts' classrooms, the vividly coloured cloaks of Quidditch players. Extraneous staged effects such as these, more than the internal logic of the narratives, it seems to me, give coherence to the fantastical audio-visual abundance of the films. All the magical, fantastical, surreal happenings and effects, which draw and fill the senses immediately in the films, fall into a whole primarily because of such staged effects.

Interestingly, the relation of Muggle and Magic worlds is given a more definite sense of *continuity* than might be inferred from the books. I have discussed the implicit continuities between these already in Chapter 11, but against the unthinking presumption that these reflect opposed realms of Magic-ness and Muggle-ness, the latter superficially akin to our world. In the films the sense of continuity is more immediate, not even unthinkingly mistakable – the Dursleys and Privet Close are themselves depicted as fantastical in the same way as Magic world, as belonging to the same carefully staged environment. The characters in both worlds are presented as possessed of similar sorts of physical and behavioural quirkiness. A similar sense of vivid colours alternating with dark shadows (especially in the sweep from Privet Close to the Dursleys' tower in the *Stone* film), a continuity of frenetic action, a similar audio-visual abundance holds Muggle and Magic worlds together.

Unsurprisingly, in the films of *Stone* and *Chamber* there is no transition from Muggle world (a bit like our world) to Magic world. It begins with magic, and from the first scene and onwards Muggle and Magic worlds are equally drawn into fantastical staginess. In both the books *Stone* and *Chamber* Harry is returned at the end to the Dursleys into Muggle world; the film versions end at Hogwarts (at the Hogwarts train station in *Stone*, with an aerial view of the school building in *Chamber*). If Muggle world is the nearest representation of physical reality in Kracauer's sense in the *Harry Potter* films, it has equal aesthetic validity as the fantastical Magic world.

The audio-visual abundance of the stagey effects in the *Harry Potter* films is consolidated, as it would be expected to be by spectators seeking a realization of magic in virtual reality, by the use of cinematic techniques. Some are subtle matters of editing. Harry's point of view is often, for instance, suggested by the manner in which the direction of gaze is directed. When Hagrid confronts the Dursleys and Harry for the first time in the tower in the *Stone* film, for instance, all the exchanges are seen from particular points of view: all the characters gaze (through the camera) *down* overbearingly on Harry, Harry looks (through the camera) *up* at the threatening Dursleys, and both the Dursleys and Harry look (through the camera) *up* at the awe-inspiring Hagrid. When it comes to true evocations of the wondrous, scenes unfold, in time-honoured fashion, from above – the audience has a belittling eye-view of, for example, Diagon Alley, Hogwarts' dining room, the Quidditch stadium. Ultimately, however, these commonplace editing techniques for evoking empathy or wonder by determining the direction of gaze are overshadowed by the feast of special effects that the films naturally, and to the spectator's full satisfaction, present.

I hardly need to dwell on the special effects – these are so abundantly and sensationally used that they do their job perfectly. It is worth noting though that the use of special effects allow for a kind of visual imagining that has well-established cinematic conventions but do not originate directly from the texts. This is where the autonomy of the filmic medium from the *Harry Potter* books is most evident, used however with the effect of enhancing what is implicit in the books while departing from the strict law of the written word. Thus, for instance, in *Stone* the book in the Hogwarts Library Restricted Section that screamed when Harry opened it (the scream is described at some length in *Stone* 151–2), is shown as not only screaming in the film version but with a screaming face that suddenly materializes out of the pages of the book. The convention of having creepy faces suddenly materializing out of all kinds of surfaces is a familiar feature of a large number of horror films and supernatural thrillers. In a similar vein, the exciting description of Ron and Harry in the flying Weasley car on their way to Hogwarts after missing the train in *Chamber*, becomes in the film version a good place to put in a whole slew of special effects conventions. The car is shown dodging under arches, becoming invisible and visible by turns, almost crashing into the Hogwarts Express, and getting terrifyingly bashed up (the whole experience shown from Harry's and Ron's point of view inside the car) by the Whomping Willow. Most predictably, it allows for a sequence in which Harry falls out of the car and hangs on by the tips of his fingers in mid-air in typical 'cliff-hanger' fashion. Much of these don't happen in quite these ways or don't happen at all in the *Chamber* book. But the film still appears to be close to the spirit of the book; cinematic conventions are used with similar effect in the *Harry Potter* films as fiction conventions are used in the *Harry Potter* books.

As I have observed above, the audience of the *Harry Potter* films, informed and aware of the *Harry Potter* texts and phenomenon as they are, look to assess the success of the *virtual reality* of the illusion, without compromising the medium invisibility. And in every way, every filmic device, whether in terms of staginess or cinematic technique, is used by the producers to fulfil that particular spectator specification. The result, in the *Harry Potter* films, is a meeting of spectator desires and producer awareness to produce an audio-visual abundance, an assault on the senses. From the midst of this surfeit there emerges a joint (producer-spectator) awareness of the filmic medium in general. I have anticipated this already. This joint awareness is well worth emphasizing as another element in the *Harry Potter* phenomenon. It is an awareness that has to do with a joint apprehension, never harshly exposed but always there, of the place of cinema in our world. In some sense, in this joint (or to give it its wider implications, institutional) apprehension there is a grasp of what films provide and spectators receive: a magical vision (the virtual reality) based on invisible technology (the medium itself) possible only because spectacle providers (producers) and spectacle consumers (spectators) knowingly collude with each other. This happens to some degree in all films, every would-be blockbuster depends on it. But the enormity of the *Harry Potter* phenomenon engendered by the books lays bare, it seems to me, the bones of this collusion in the filmic reproductions through the *Harry Potter* films. The field where this complicity of producer and audience is concretized is the virtual reality market. The enormity of the *Harry Potter* phenomenon *before* the films appeared means that the spectator specifications for the films are more easily determinable, the collusion between producer and consumer more starkly evident, the conditions of the market more clearly manifest, than is usual. All that needs to be done, and that is what I have been gesturing towards above, is to see how it operates in practice in the particular instance of the *Harry Potter* films.

Interestingly, it seems to me, that the producers' awareness of this collusion is encoded *within* the *Harry Potter* films. The *Harry Potter* books allow discussion of the implications of technology vis-à-vis magic (an issue that several critics have commented on) – I discuss this in the next and final chapter. As far as the films go, this feature of the books allow the producers of the films to encode their awareness of precisely what spectators expect of them within the films. Here's how the situation stands. Spectators expect the *Harry Potter* films to make virtually *real* the Magic world that defeats rationalistic and technological enterprise. Ironically, the means through which this can be done is through the technologically manipulable medium of the film: largely by the use of technology-intensive devices (such as computer-generated special effects) and technology-enhanced staginess. The thematics of the *Harry Potter* books therefore impinge with a peculiar irony on the pragmatics of the *Harry Potter* films. That this is so appears to be (deliberately?) indicated in some of the obvious slippages between the narrative of the books and the films. The most obvious of these are in the beginning and ending of the *Stone* book and film. The book *Stone* begins and ends squarely in Muggle world, with the Dursleys. The substance of the book is the apparent inversion of the our-world-like Muggle world (constrained by mechanical laws) to present a Magic world (rendered free of those constraints with magical ease). The film *Stone* however begins and ends with Magic world. In the first scene of the book we have Mr. Dursley having some unpleasant experiences. In the first scene of the film Dumbledore appears in Privet Close, takes out a black sceptre-like instrument, opens it so that a small industrial claw seems to emerge, and with it *sucks in* the light from the street lamps. This could be some sort of technical instrument, albeit an unusual one. It is very different from the one described in the book *after* Mr. Dursley's day is done: 'It seemed to be a silver cigarette lighter. He flicked it open, held it up in the air and clicked it. The nearest street lamp went out with a pop' (*Stone* 12). This too is an instrument of some sort, but it looks like one that is familiar in our world (and Muggle world) though it serves an unexpected function (the opposite of the expected in fact). It appears and is used with a thoughtless ease that the reader may or may not be struck by. In the film it is an instrument that is clearly mechanical, but more sophisticated in appearance than a lighter. It is pretty much the first thing the spectator is struck by. Immediately after McGonagall performs her favourite transformation from cat to witch (seen in shadow), and the spectator knows that magic is in the air. This resequencing of the beginning in the *Stone* film has the effect of, one, briefly but effectively exorcising the expectations of technology at large (not simple technology like a cigarette lighter but sophisticated technology), and two, plunging the spectator straight into magical happenings. That brief exorcism of technological expectations could also be read as a gesture to the spectator to suspend her penchant for looking on the film as a technologically manipulated medium, to take it on the surface as the virtual presentation of a magic world.

At the end of the *Stone* book Harry is returned to the Dursleys for the holidays, happy in the knowledge that though he was not allowed to use magic in Muggle world the Dursleys didn't know that and could be threatened with the use of magic. The books ends, in other words, with a reassertion of the Muggle world where magic can only be wish-fulfilment. In the *Stone* film it is Hagrid who sees Harry off at the station, tells him that he could threaten the Dursleys with magic because they didn't know that he wasn't allowed to use it, and gives him a magical photograph album of his parents (with which Harry could no doubt find solace even in the company of the Dursleys). In the *Stone* book there is an inversion, in the *Stone* film there isn't. Right at the beginning there is brief injunction to overcome technology-oriented expectations and get absorbed into the audio-visual surfeit of virtual reality – and the rest, to the happy end, is a straightforward consumer-satisfying display of movie magic. In the *Chamber* books that inversion is repeated – it opens in the grim Dursley household with Harry having a miserable time, and an authorial voice chimes in and gives the reader all the background. In the *Chamber* film the spectator is just plunged in where she had left off in the *Stone* film. Here the spectator's gaze homes in on Harry, still squarely in Magic world (albeit in Privet Close), looking at that magical photo album which Hagrid had given him in the previous film.

The *Harry Potter* books conduct a complex negotiation and renegotiation – repetitive and progressive – between Magic and Muggle and our worlds. The *Harry Potter* films simply, straightforwardly, do what the spectator specifications demand with full medium awareness – the audio-visual realization of Magic world as virtually real *in* our world.

20
The Beginning

Through most of this text-to-world analysis of the *Harry Potter* books I have suggested that there is an underlying theme that connects up observations about races, servitude, sexual desire, class, advertisements made above; and that this underlying theme would take me back to the preoccupation with unthinkingness with which this essay started. It also leads to a possible explanation of the *Harry Potter* phenomenon. In this chapter I attempt finally to place this essay as a whole where it belongs – in our world. This concluding chapter is the place to make that underlying theme explicit, and to weave the various threads drawn out in the above analysis together. I begin this chapter therefore with a straight-forward statement of that underlying theme.

The creation of the Magic world – i.e. the construction of an institutional structure for it, the detailing of the environment and people within it, the focusing on it through the Muggle world, the systematization of magical processes within it, the invention of a history and mythology behind it, etc. – is such that it is fundamentally antithetical to our world. This is so despite its being used (generally unsuccessfully or in an unsatisfactory manner) to ostensibly reflect and comment on concerns in our world. Indeed, it is *because* there is an attempt to use the Magic world to illuminate certain preoccupations of our world, to strike mark-edly familiar chords of our world, that its antithetical nature becomes all the clearer. Briefly, in being constructed around a notion of magic the Magic world is necessarily, and quite deliberately, presented as being essentially anti-rational. There are strong limits to the questioning that is possible and the explanations that are available in the Magic world. In the Magic world things and qualities are simply manifest – they just are so – there is no need, no ability, no desire, no will to explain *why* they are so. The self-evidently manifest is simply accepted as the generally unambiguous and unequivocal truth. That is why things and events are magical in Magic world. It is also therefore essentially a ritualistic world: spells are learnt and used, their effectiveness and process is not explained and nor is there any evidence that it can be explained; the proclivities of sentient beings are predetermined (Voldemort is bad, Dumbledore is good, house-elves are slavish, Trolls are stupid, a Veela is a *femme fatale*, Slytherins are Slytherins and Griffindors are Griffindors), they are not significantly moulded by experience and education; learning is a matter of constantly acquiring greater and greater levels of information and memorizing facts, it has little to do with understanding the principles underlying different ranges of information and being able to synthesize or collate facts; humans either have magic or they don't, they are either Magic or Muggle, and there is no point questioning why this is so (it might have something to do with blood). The Magic world is one where questioning cannot be imagined except to discover facts, to uncover what has happened. Evidently therefore, our ordinary sense of mystery, and curiosity about the mysterious, does not exist in Magic world; the only kind of curiosity that can exist (and one that drives Harry and some of his friends) is one that tries to uncover a sequence of events that have happened – to uncover the facts of the past that are relevant for whatever reason. That is no more mysterious than history is mysterious. *The only sense of mystery that can be brought to the Magic world has to be brought by the readers of the* Harry Potter *books of our world: the magical beings and happenings are mysterious to readers of our world because we are accustomed to trying to explain things, to understanding principles, to trying to rationalize, and the magical is definitively inexplicable.* It is because we are rational and can hope to explain phenomena and look for deep principles, that we recognize that which resists explanation and understand its mysteriousness. Understanding its mysteriousness is also a powerful motive to try to explain it. In our use of language, in our engagement with the world, in our institutional structures, in our technological abilities, in every aspect of our present lives and that of our past the binding thread has been the desire, ability, will to rationalize. The comfort of faith (along with which comes religious acceptance, or reconciliation with the miraculous or magical) is constantly complemented by the desire to understand and explain. The institutional forms of faith (religions) themselves provide ways of explaining the apparently inexplicable. And when those explanations refuse to satisfy, more rational explanations emerge from within faith and defying faith; so that theology may lead on to philosophy and philosophy to science, and they can also lead back to or across each other in a variety of different ways. Our world is constantly, and both universally and at the same time pluralistically, predicated on the possibility, desire, ability, will to rationalize. This is so even when it becomes evident that rationalism is limited or can be devastatingly wrong-headed. End of catechism.

The Magic world is not predicated on rationality. It is based on the unquestioning acceptance of what is manifest or can be or comes to be manifested; on the acceptance of the way things just magically are. The Magic world is definitively anti-rational.

Several reviews of the *Harry Potter* books have tried to understand the appeal of the Magic world in terms of its relation to the most hard-headedly rationalistic aspect of our world: the large-scale development of technology and scientific method. The *Harry Potter* books do perform their own putting of magic into perspective in terms of Muggle technology. So images of Dumbledore putting out the streetlights of Privet Close, the Weasleys' car flying and finally going wild in the Forbidden Forest, Mr. Weasley obsessively collecting Muggle electric plugs which have no function in Magic world, the Weasleys struggling with the telephone, various Muggle-produced objects behaving strangely in the hands of wizards – these are all images of technology being superseded by magic. So much so that various technological appliances seem to obstruct wizards, appear quite unfamiliar and strange in the Magic world. What Muggles (in this respect like us) can do slowly and laboriously by working out scientific principles of mechanics, optics, electricity, etc. which can then be used to create instruments and equipment to extend natural human abilities, the wizards are gifted with as natural magical ability. Wizards, in other words, supersede the need for science and technology by having at their disposal natural magical abilities that render scientific investigation and technological innovation unnecessary. But, why dwell on this relationship between magic and technology? Some reviewers, Lankshear and Knobel, for instance, feel that this is done to show that there is something intractable and inconclusive *within* technology itself, since magic as presented in the *Harry Potter* books is itself a kind of technology:

> The books also purvey a philosophy of technology that provides a timely corrective to the championing of contemporary information and nano and bio technologies as the defining force of the future. Daniel Bell's definition of technology as ways of doing things in a reproducible manner … extends here to casting spells and using wands. Against the tendency of positivistic scientism to explain all cause and effect relations in quantifiable and observable terms,

Rowling promotes mystery and inexplicability within her techno-logical universe. Moreover, she reminds us constantly that technologies are never neutral, self-evident, or 'essentialized.' What they are depends on how they are used.[1]

Unfortunately, Lankshear and Knobel in this instance are simply wrong about technology. Technology is not about doing things in a reprodu-cible fashion but about extending human ability by inventions that 'involve ... the use of systematic and scientific knowledge'.[2] Magic does not involve an extension of wizard ability (magic is innate), and it doesn't involve systematic and scientific knowledge (it involves going through certain inexplicable, but effective judging from past experience, processes of concentration, thought, gesture and enunciation). Technology needs rationalistic thinking; if the magical ability exists innately it can be controlled by learning spells, etc. more or less by rote and some practice. Lankshear and Knobel are mistaken in thinking that technology is uniquely associated with 'positivistic scientism', or that science is simplistically 'positivistic' in some sort of nineteenth-century Comtean or Machian sense (dealing with 'cause and effect' alone and especially concerned with 'quantification'). Consequently, the *Harry Potter* books cannot be seen as the repository of any 'philosophy of technology'. There may be some similarity between the manner in which wizards use their powers (for both good and bad) and in which humans use technology (also for good and bad), but I do not see how it follows that: 'What they [magic, technology] *are* depends on how they are used'. The *Harry Potter* books definitely don't suggest that magic is itself good or bad according to usage (it *is* neutral, as technology may be thought to be), it is used for good or bad purposes by wizards and witches. Lanks-hear and Knobel were, clearly, rather confused when they wrote this – but there is a sensible connection between *Harry Potter* magic and tech-nology in our world that they were trying to grasp (and thoughtlessly missing), and which has been grasped better elsewhere, by O'Har, for instance. The relationship is one of exclusion: magic and science-technology are contrary to each other. Both are attempts to understand the world and do things within it. Magic had been the predominant way of apprehending the world and trying to get control over it before science-technology replaced magic by its greater effectiveness and persuasiveness, especially effectiveness in doing things. But science-technology wasn't able to satisfy everyone insofar as understanding the world goes (probably because science-technology limits itself by its own rigorous methods) whereas magic was able to do so (mainly by making entirely unsubstantiated but attractive and reassuring claims) in the past. So, even in our world, dominated by the effectiveness and persuasiveness of science-technology as it is, there is still some longing for the reassurance and comfort that magic had provided in the past, and this is where the Magic world and the *Harry Potter* phenomenon come in. In O'Har's words:

> When science and technology replaced magic, what was removed was that physical-mechanical part of the magical system that simply could not compete in a new world based on scientific method and technological efficiency. The part of magic which functioned for the adherents in the spiritual realm was never replaced. Machines cannot do the work of gods. Machines cannot calm fears and provide answers to our deepest fears. ... The Potter books provide an alternative reality where magic retains its hold on the world.[3]

This makes more sense than the former argument about science-technology and magic. This also hints at an explanation of the *Harry Potter* phenomenon, but in an unclear and abstract fashion which is not placed firmly enough amidst the concerns of our social and political world. But there are further clarifications to be made before I can state firmly what I think lies behind the *Harry Potter* phenomenon.

It is not enough simply to delineate what the distinction between the magic of the Magic world and the unavoidable rationalism of our world is. As far as the *Harry Potter* books play on that distinction there are two significant inter-linked effects (of significant social and political import) that need to be laid bare: the deliberate anti-rationalism of the books; and the idea of *chosen* people that is simultaneously conveyed in them.

One of the happy circumstances of Harry Potter's entry into the Magic world in *Stone* is that he seems to be famous there already without his quite knowing why. He enjoys a celebrity status without apparently having done anything to deserve it. It gradually emerges that his fame is due to the conviction among wizards that he was responsible for Voldemort's fall from power. Voldemort had apparently killed his parents and cast a spell to kill him too, a mere infant at the time, but unsuccessfully. Voldemort's spell had left a lightning mark on Harry's forehead but no other visible effect, and had at the same time rendered Voldemort himself powerless. It is possible that Voldemort's failure in this regard was due to the extraordinary love that Harry's mother bore him (*Stone* 216; *Chamber* 233); it must have been extraordinary love since the affection that other victims of Voldemort must have enjoyed hadn't protected them as effectively. At any rate, it is clear that the happy circumstance of Harry's celebrity status does confer on him certain advantages. He is the object of envy and interest among his schoolmates, and has to do little to make friends and, for that matter, enemies. It gets him a most interesting and loyal friend in Hagrid from the beginning. All his teachers are aware of his special status and respond accordingly – Snape with malice, and most of the others with indulgence (especially the all-knowing Dumbledore). Harry is from the beginning a kind of chosen person in the Magic world, who has acquired fame, friends and enemies, a peculiarly attractive status and great expectations without having made any conscious effort to deserve them. No one has any doubts that his innate abilities would be equal to his reputation – except naturally Harry himself.

Fortunately for Harry, his innate abilities do turn out to be more than adequate to his reputation: he is not mistakenly thought of as a chosen person, he *is* one. He appears to have a natural ability to fly on a broomstick, which lands him one of the most enviable roles possible in Hogwarts: that of a Quidditch Seeker (the youngest ever). Now Quidditch is an odd game[4] that, though apparently a team sport, is heavily dependent on one player alone to decide victory or defeat – the Seeker. This is how it works. There is something like a football or rugby field with goalposts on either side, and seven players in each team. There are three kinds of balls in the game: a Quaffle, Bludgers and a Snitch. From each team there is a goal keeper, or Keeper. Three players in each team, called Chasers, try to score goals with the Quaffle; each Quaffle-goal is worth ten points. The Bludgers constantly try to knock out team members, and two members of each team, called Beaters, are devoted to keeping the Bludgers at bay by hitting them whenever they appear to threaten anyone. That leaves the Snitch – a fleet, small, golden ball – that flies around randomly. The Seeker in each team has only one job: they have to catch the Snitch, which effectively ends the game *and* gives the successful Seeker's team an extra 150 points. Quidditch, in other words, seems to be designed to give an extraordinarily important role to the Seeker. The Seeker's efforts are worth precisely fifteen times the efforts of the Chasers. So exclusive is the Seeker's role that it does not intersect at all with that of the larger part of the team: the Chasers and Keepers play their own game and cannot influence the Seeker in any way. Only the Beaters have a role that influences the Seeker, and it is that of protecting him. It might seem like a team sport, but it is one in which team-effort has no particular role to play; it is a team sport in which the rest of the team is *below* one person, pretty much entirely dependent on one person, by the rules of the game. That Harry's innate abilities makes him a natural Seeker is about as much confirmation of being a chosen person in the order of Magic things as could have been needed. Harry's natural abilities as a Seeker appear to be true in that in his first few Quidditch games he overcomes odds that have nothing to do with the game itself (a hexed broomstick in *Stone*, a Bludger that particularly targets Harry in *Chamber*) to decide victory. He never loses through a fair game, and usually wins despite unfair disadvantages. And it all comes naturally.

In the spirit of complicating matters, in *Goblet* a Quidditch World Cup game is described where victory goes to the team the Seeker of which didn't catch the Snitch. All that manages to demonstrate though is how important the Seeker really is: the glory of the moment goes to the Seeker of the losing team who does get the Snitch, Krum. It also proves how poor the rest of the losing team is.

The team game that is designed to depend largely on one person is used to bring out the chosen-ness of Harry. This quality of being chosen is then magnified, taken to heroic proportions, in the more deadly games (each involving rules, each involving adversaries, each involving victory or defeat) that Harry has to play with Voldemort in each of the novels. Harry keeps winning despite himself. More interestingly, in these serious life-or-death games Harry wins against rational odds – and in each of these victory is literally beyond reason (one can't win by being rational, rationality plays a role but never a winning role, winning ultimately depends on being chosen to win or on being the chosen person). That is where the more explicit anti-rationality of the *Harry Potter* books kick in.

Harry Potter's victories in the life-or-death games are won through two means: by the shakiness of the rules of the game (these can be broken or superseded according to convenience at any time), and by the help of friends who deal with those aspects of the games that can be rationally dealt with so that Harry can finally win. The rational aspects of the game are seldom those that Harry deals with himself, and rationality is always secondary to the final stage where Harry's natural abilities – his chosen-ness (in terms of gifts unknown to himself, and courage which he seems to be born with) – shine through. The endgame of *Stone* sets the tone for these contests. Harry, Ron and Hermione go through the trapdoor to face the man with two faces (one Voldemort's), and encounter a series of obstacles. Hermione works out how to get through the Devil's Snare plant because she had read about it (she had prepared herself for it and reasoned her way through a tough situation). Harry catches the key to the door by using those innate flying skills that made him a Seeker. Ron gets Harry and Hermione through the deadly chess-game at his own expense by working out the moves that would enable that to happen (he also reasoned his way through a tricky situation). Hermione solves the riddle that gets Harry into the final stage – Hermione's reaction on seeing the riddle speaks for itself:

> Hermione let out a great sigh and Harry, amazed, saw that she was smiling, the very last thing he felt like doing.
> '*Brilliant*,' said Hermione. 'This isn't magic – it's logic – a puzzle. A lot of the greatest wizards haven't got an ounce of logic, they'd be stuck in here for ever.' (*Stone* 207)

Hermione lets Harry go unprotestingly into the final stage because she now knows the truth of the Magic world: that Harry is the chosen person – 'Harry – you're a great wizard, you know' – and that that is more important than her 'Books! And cleverness!' (*Stone* 208). And there Harry, with some courage and not a little serendipity, wins against Voldemort. The pattern carries on in *Chamber*. Hermione makes the Polyjuice Potion and solves the problem of what's in the walls of Hogwarts, but all that doesn't matter ultimately. Ron and Harry finally go to the Chamber of Secrets, Ron is put out of action, Harry faces the past incarnation of Lord Voldemort alone, and asks for help and magically gets it from Dumbledore. The sorting hat with a sword and a phoenix named Fawkes turn up and sort things out for Harry. And the pattern carries on in *Prisoner* – reasonable counter-moves getting ever less useful, luck and courage and help from friends (it is Hermione who turns the clock back at Dumbledore's suggestion for a happy denouement) serving Harry as well as before. Then, of course, there's the Triwizard Tournament in *Goblet*. Since this occupies most of that novel, and conflates the sporting wizard game with the life-and-death game against Voldemort, it is worth dwelling on this for a bit.

If Quidditch is a team sport that seems to be designed to depend on one person, the Triwizard Tournament is a game that appears to thrive on the breaking of rules that define it – thus defeating all *reasonable* moves and counter-moves that are possible since these must depend on accepting the rules. That Harry finds entry in it at all demonstrates how central to it – at least insofar as it is conducted in this instance – rule-breaking would be. Harry's being chosen by the Goblet of Fire as the *fourth* contestant undermines the name of the tournament itself. And that Harry finds entry in it at the expense of all the rules that define the tournament is undoubtedly a clear indication of his chosen-ness: it would have been clear to all readers that Harry would win, as indeed he does (though strictly speaking it is a gift from Cedric, but that is only because Cedric felt – as most readers probably do too – that Harry was the real winner). There is of course an explanation other than Harry's chosen-ness for his participation: the whole thing is engineered by Voldemort to lure Harry to the graveyard where Voldemort's rejuvenation was to take place. But that actually merely emphasizes Harry's chosen-ness all the more. For Voldemort's plan to work he must have been reasonably sure from the beginning that, with only slight assistance from his spy, the fake Mad-Eyed Moody, Harry would win the tournament. Besides, at least Voldemort recognizes Harry's chosen-ness just as he believes in his own; Harry is to Voldemort himself, who is the Dark Arts personified, undoubtedly the arch-adversary – the enemy. It is not Dumbledore, for example. It may also be noted that Voldemort's scheme to get hold of Harry appears to be extraordinarily elaborate. Someone who is capable of placing a spy in Hogwarts, tampering with the Goblet of Fire and turning an object as secure as the Triwizard Cup into a Portkey could have chosen a simpler way to achieve the same end. He could, for instance, have arranged for a potato chip to be a Portkey. As for the Triwizard Tournament, Harry – like all the other contestants – freely breaks the rules, and in by now time-honoured fashion, gets selfless help from his friends on most things that required some elementary reasoning. For the first task (getting past a dragon) Hagrid helps him find out in advance what the challenge would be and Hermione spends a whole night teaching him what to her was a simple Summoning Charm. For the second task Cedric tells Harry how to unravel the mystery of the egg and Dobby informs him of the crucial properties of Gillyweed. For the third task Harry uses all his own gifts, courage and determination, and some of the things he had been taught by friends (Mr. Lupin's instructions on getting rid of Dementors and Bogarts in *Prisoner*, Hermione's confidence in solving riddles in *Stone*) – and readers might begin to think that here at last is a victory that is being more or less fairly won (where the brain wasn't being entirely left out, where obstacles were being thoughtfully overcome, where no outside help was being offered) when, lo and behold, the rules of the game change again and the whole thing dissolves into a different and deadlier game against Voldemort. This is where Harry's chosen-ness comes into its own, and all his attempts at thinking himself (almost rationally) through the maze become yet another stepping-stone to be left behind.

The ultimate and, really, only weapon that Harry needs and that works in Magic world is that Harry is Harry, chosen adversary of Voldemort from infancy. When the awe-inspiringly powerful Voldemort and the novice Harry (who could scarcely do elementary spells without Hermione's instructions) duel with each other incredibly they appear to be evenly matched.

The inference seems to me to be inevitable: all the *Harry Potter* books centre on the fact that Harry is *chosen* to be Voldemort's adversary in advance and *chosen* to win; innate abilities account for this victory far more than any rational ability or anything that Harry can think his way through and work out; indeed Harry's chosen-ness is a function of his innateness; rationality is only useful along the way, but ultimately doesn't matter and shouldn't be taken too seriously; innate abilities are best exercised in an ignorant and *unthinking* fashion. Who chooses Harry? one may ask. It doesn't matter. There is no answer – whoever gives magical abilities and innate powers, could be the answer. What does matter is this: the *Harry Potter* books are an extended celebration of unthinking courage and luck; to make this celebration possible an unthinking hero is placed in a Magic world that is definitively unthinking to be the chosen victor; and all this is largely deliberately presented at the expense of seeking explanations and using rational principles – which inevitably, and despite numerous failures and shortcomings, underlie our engagement with our world.

The anti-rationality and the deeply ingrained centrality of chosen-ness in the *Harry Potter* books is the reason why the various apparently obvious and well-meaning gestures towards our world made therein either fail or reach unsatisfactory resolutions on closer inspection. The liberal and well-meaning and anti-fascist veneer in the presentation of magical races as analogous to human races, and wizard racism to human racism, is undercut under closer scrutiny by an endorsement of a deeper form of racism in the Magic world – equivalent to the patronizing, imperial-mission variety of racism of our world. This deep racism in the Magic world is not a purely invidious construction; it is a condition of the manner in which the Magic world is conceived. The inequality of races is close in spirit to the rule of innate abilities that can't be explained and the centrality of chosen-ness that is *a priori*. Anti-racist and anti-discriminatory ideologies in our world depend on rational arguments that are based on a fundamental equality of humans for social and political purposes. This equality has nothing to do with innate qualities and natural abilities; this equality devolves from any sane attempt to employ rational principles with social and political effect. It is the anti-rationality and centrality of chosen-ness too that underlies the peculiarly unsatisfactory account of servitude and slavery given for the house-elves. Here again, the *Harry Potter* books appear to say something relevant about servitude and class-attitudes in our world. But, in fact, the deeper the reader goes into the presentation of house-elves the more unconvincing is their species-conditional servitude likely to appear. Whatever possible relevance the treatment of servants/ slaves might have had is entirely lost under the conceptual necessity to accommodate house-elves in the anti-rational magical domain where innate abilities and chosen-ness reign. Servitude is thus made not a matter of social injustice but a matter of natural disposition, and in the presentation of this any equivalence that the house-elves might have had with situations in our world is lost. Inexplicable innateness, chosen-ness, magical manifestness also influence the delineation of sexual desire: what is ambiguously poised in our world between biological determination and social constructedness, is turned into a simple and essentialist distillation of biological proclivities. The result (images like that of the Veela) might have a hint of our-worldness about them, but almost inevitably fall apart if they are compared closely with sexual desire in our world. They appear to be reductionist, conventional, trivial versions of something that looks very remotely like the ambiguous, ubiquitous, vibrant our-world affair. Since everything significant in the *Harry Potter* books is innate, inborn, essential, simply manifest, definitively inexplicable in terms of rational principles and processes, the wizard racial traits and house-elf servitude and wizard heterosexual desire have to be so too. And naturally then they have only tangential, unsatisfactory, contradictory and, often, ominous implications in our world. But all this is nevertheless attractive, nevertheless apparently suggestive in our world, because the possible – the failing – analogues are carefully deployed, nowhere more effectively than in the use of advertisements and advertising techniques, or in cinematic renderings. In our world we are accustomed to being lured by the magic of advertisements; in the *Harry Potter* books advertisement magic becomes real and draws us into what is effectively a massive advertisement for magic, for the magicality in advertising, itself. The *Harry Potter* films in our world are pre-determinedly satisfactory concretizations of agreements that are the *raison d'être* of the virtual reality market itself.

The effect of these carefully posed juxtapositions and separations between the Magic world and our world is that we tend to accept magic in its own terms, i.e. unthinkingly – with little analysis and a great deal of acceptance, being light-heartedly lured by the manifest rather than

being seriously concerned with the not-too-immediately-obvious implications. It is possible that in the process some of those distinctly unsatisfactory, contradictory, even ominous social and political connotations
of the *Harry Potter* books would unthinkingly convey themselves along
with the superficial and comforting liberal morally correct gestures and
the pleasure of being lured into an unthinking world. Or perhaps it is
precisely all those qualities – the superficial unthinking qualities as well
as those insidiously underlying them – that actually agree with what
a very large readership in our world (those who have made the *Harry
Potter* phenomenon a phenomenon) already inclines towards. Perhaps
the current social and political condition of our world is gradually
inclining us away from the rationality that is (often inadequately but
nevertheless inescapably) constituted within it, towards a desire for the
unthinking *with* some of the implications that follow. Perhaps, in other
words, the *Harry Potter* phenomenon is such because these books offer
exactly what we unthinkingly desire *within* our world and *because* of the
current condition of our world and *despite* the constitution of our world.
These are desires born in our world; these are not created by the *Harry
Potter* books, merely realized in them in a certain (attractive, readable,
undemanding) form.

This seems to me to be a plausible explanation of the *Harry Potter*
phenomenon, but one that will have to be left as a speculative matter
here. Books that engender phenomena such as the *Harry Potter*
phenomenon, no doubt do so (and I have argued this in Part I) both
because of their intrinsic qualities and content *and* because of the
contexts in which they are received and, in many ways, constructed. But
to examine this matter further would need a clearer understanding of
the social and political concerns of our world; would need, in other
words, a world-to-text approach to them. For this essay I have decided
to confine myself to a text-to-world analysis, and that, I feel, is done to
a sufficient extent. But as a matter of speculation it is worth indicating
that there has been a prodigious amount of sociological and political-
scientific scholarship on the characteristic features of our world that
may have a bearing on why we may desire the unthinkingly magical
within our world and *because* of the current condition of our world and
despite the constitution of our world. There is, for instance, evidence
that while our world grows increasingly dependent on science-technology
there is also a growing distrust of science-technology. This is, no doubt,
to a large measure because of the misuse of technology, but also because
of the intense specialization that different areas of science-technology
demand – often such that even scientists and technologists can have

only a limited apprehension of the field, and intelligent readers who are not scientists and technologists can hope for little more than a hazy understanding of these developments. But nevertheless science-technology in different ways is constantly and unthinkingly used in our world by almost all, and is certainly manifest almost everywhere: unthinkingly or necessarily ignorantly there is something magical about its ubiquity. Linked to this is also the growing sense of risks being multiplied in our world (environmental risks, health risks), of risks being factored into markets themselves (in terms of insurance assessments and policies, in terms of technologies designed to reduce risk as well as produce new risks, etc.). There is growing evidence of inequality across the world, and a steady increase in internecine and international conflict between all sorts of social categories – social classes, ideological alignments, ethnic groups, religious formations, etc. It is quite possible that these conflicts indicate a renewed and irrational conviction in innate qualities and chosen-ness. The manner in which national economies have gradually converged on international capitalism has something to do with all these factors: technological development, distrust of scientific rationality, increasing inequalities and conflicts. To a great degree these devolve from the power mechanisms that world economic organization entail, and the role of multinational corporations and state organizations therein. With this emerging world order there has also evolved concentrations of power which seem to be unfair and irrational to many, and which yet have to be accepted and reconciled. An interesting element within that is the growing preponderance of corporate managerialism in all sorts of sectors that affect social and political spheres, which is wilfully and determinedly anti-rational and ritualistic, and often promotes conviction in chosen-ness and innate qualities. And linked to all the above is the ever-expanding role of the mass media in our world, affecting more people more closely than anything else. The mass media both connects people together, informs people about events around the globe in an unprecedentedly efficient fashion, exposes people to different social and political and cultural contexts; and at the same time the mass media also distance these contexts and events from the immediate reality, conflates them with magical or fantastic images, gives them a game-like aura. Advertisements are another aspect of the emerging world order, teeming within both the immediate reality and the mass media screens and voices – advertisements that play magically with, for our world, perfectly rational financial calculations.

Put all that together and we have a picture of our world that would be recognisable in a very wide range of contexts therein. I think if we dwell on that picture and what the above-analysis of the *Harry Potter* books have clarified there is a meeting between the text-to-world and the world-to-text approaches that are possible. It is quite possible that the *Harry Potter* phenomenon grows unthinkingly but surely out of that meeting. More and more people in more and more contexts unthinkingly read the *Harry Potter* books, absorb their film versions and the advertisement images and computer and video games and other consumer products that derive from them, because they are inclined by our world to do so. The question is: are the *Harry Potter* books really *read* in the sense that some people speak of 'reading a face' or 'reading a situation' – *read*, that is, as being thinkingly understood?

Part III
World-to-Text

21
Reading *Re-Reading Harry Potter*

Continuing with the text-to-world argument

Readers of the first edition of this book (written in 2002) complained that I had represented the *Harry Potter* books as entertaining too black-and-white a view. I was fortunate in having responsive readers: not just reviewers and researchers, colleagues, students and friends, but also persons I don't know felt compelled to write to me. Some of these respondents took issue with my allegedly paying insufficient attention to the ambiguities of the *Harry Potter* books, particularly apropos the representation of class, race, gender and sexuality, and the politics of values (fascist 'evil' and liberal 'good'). It was averred, for instance, that my argument about the transposition of race relations on the Muggle–Magic relationship and the signification of 'blood' failed to take note of the constant interjections of hybridity. In other words, I hadn't noted that Harry and Voldemort being of mixed Muggle/Magic heritage, and Hermione being purely Muggle-born, etc., constantly undermine any over-signification of 'blood' and counter the fascist politics of Voldemort. Similarly, it was pointed out that my argument about characterising a class of servants – the house-elves – as a biogenetically determined species didn't account for the manner in which power relations are ambiguously distributed between the house-elves and wizards. Even with the first appearance of Dobby in *Chamber of Secrets*, it was clear that house-elves have at times as, if not more, powerful magic at their disposal; and later, in *Deathly Hallows*, Dobby's power overcomes Voldemort and the Death Eaters. Moreover, the house-elves are shown as constantly undermining their masters, as much in Dobby's betrayal of the Malfoys as in Kreacher's betrayal of Sirius. At one point Dumbledore suggests that the house-elves are not born into servitude but are subjugated by the social order of wizards:

> 'Kreacher is what he has been made by wizards, Harry,' said Dumbledore. 'Yes, he is to be pitied. His existence has been as miserable as your friend Dobby's. He was forced to do Sirius's bidding, because Sirius was the last of the family to which he was enslaved, but he felt no true loyalty to him.'
>
> (*Order of the Phoenix*, pp. 733–4)

None of the respondents took issue with my observations on gender and sexuality, but in a general way most objected that I should have taken account of ambiguities in the representation of norms in the books (broadly, fascist 'evil' and liberal 'good'). Almost all the key characters in the series, I was told, constantly test the reader's assessments: Defence Against Dark Arts teachers often straddle normative boundaries; it is not clear till the end whether Snape is 'good' or 'bad'; at times it seems that even Harry's father, James, and Dumbledore have lapsed into normatively questionable positions; and it is clear that Harry and Voldemort do have something of each other in them.

These points are all, of course, well taken, but as far as I can see they do not contradict anything I wrote in 2002. I had clearly signalled that hybridity introduces complexity into the argument about race relations (see first edition, pp. 104–5 and 108–9). My argument was that *if* Muggle–Magic relations are mapped on to race relations in our world (as they are, because some of the recognisable markers of racial discourse in multicultural contexts are deliberately pinned on this relationship) something worrying happens. Muggle–Magic relations are relations of *innate* inequality (certainly innate, even though the transmission of magical powers by bloodlines is questionable) and therefore opposition to them is a matter of virtue on the part of liberal wizards. By contrast, in our world racial prejudice is opposed both on the clear understanding of the natural equality of all humans and by rejecting the social construction of race itself. In short, in our world this is not a matter of virtue, but of reason. Similarly, insofar as I had outlined the representation of a class as a species, I had also clearly marked out the subversive potentialities that Dobby's role at that stage obviously presented (see pp. 113–14). In fact, my argument *followed* from that: since Dobby (and later Kreacher) is inevitably aware of the injustice of his condition as a rational being, it seems strange that his condition should be presented as somehow innate rather than socially imposed. I had presented both these arguments – and similar arguments about gender and sexuality, and about normative distinctions generally in the books – as being conceptual contradictions in the way the *Harry Potter* world is constructed. I had also suggested that these contradictions mirror something of the contradictions that operate generally about these issues in our world, even among the well-meaning liberal constituency.

The respondents whose views are summarised above often drew on material from the last three books – *Order of the Phoenix* (2003), *Half-Blood Prince* (2005) and *Deathly Hallows* (2007)[1] – to take issue with me, even though these hadn't been available when I was writing in 2002. Some felt that my argument may well have applied to the first four books (though most were annoyed that they were made even with regard to these), but by the end of the series enough complexity has been introduced for me to reconsider them. It is interesting that almost all the respondents, whether irate or earnestly seeking my reconsideration, expressed an underlying desire to keep the *Harry Potter* books free from any taint. This desire is itself worth exploring, and I will do so intermittently in this and the coming chapters. But first, to keep the record clear: I don't think that the completed series – the full *Harry Potter* text, so to speak – has in any way necessitated a reconsideration of my original argument made in 2002. On the contrary, the final three books have not only complied with the thrust of that argument, but rendered it more relevant, in a deeper fashion.

I do not mean to extend the argument made in 2002 by dwelling again on the categories of class, race, gender and sexuality in relation to the final three books of the series. Those categories have been examined elsewhere with reference to the *Harry Potter* books, and will no doubt continue to be, and have often reached similar conclusions.[2] Instead, I shall focus on outlining how the general thrust of my earlier argument chimes in with key strategies of the later books – strategies, that is, which enable the resolution and closure of the *Harry Potter* text. The general argument I made in 2002 was that the *Harry Potter* books place a consistent premium on what can be thought of as 'innateness'. Innateness works at various levels in the *Harry Potter* text: magic powers are innate (people are either born with them or not); social attributes are turned into biogenetic characteristics (as for the house-elves); heterosexual desire and gendered identity are innate qualities (encapsulated in the Veela, for instance); Harry's strengths – his ability to fly, his courage, loyalty, etc. – are qualities he is born with rather than acquires. I had observed that this premium on innateness is complemented by a downplaying of rational ability and by Harry being given things without working for them. Thus Harry is protected by his mother's extraordinary love, he inherits wealth, he is famous before he knows why, he is simply given efficient broomsticks, the Invisibility Cloak and the Marauder's Map, he enjoys headmaster Dumbledore's favouritism and protection, he is marked out by an optimistic prophecy. Hermione's considerable intellectual abilities, which save Harry repeatedly from the first to the last books, are predetermined to play second fiddle to Harry's innate qualities and advantages. In the later part of the text, as Voldemort's past is unravelled in *Half-Blood Prince*, we find the pattern of innate proclivities being repeated but with reverse effect. Voldemort is innately evil from childhood. Even in their first encounter, Dumbledore had observed in him 'obvious *instincts* for cruelty, secrecy and domination' (*Half-Blood Prince*, p. 259; my emphasis). Harry's and Voldemort's instincts determine what they become – otherwise both were orphans brought up in a hostile environment and socialised through adversity before they arrived at Hogwarts. The premium on innateness is critiqued superficially through Voldemort, only to be perpetuated tacitly by the very structure and conception of the *Harry Potter* text. That was the thrust of my argument in 2002, and it continues to apply to the series as a whole. In fact, it applies more firmly because the final three books deepen further the reliance on innateness and give it a religious turn.

There are primarily two magical devices around which the resolution of the *Harry Potter* series is constructed: the dark magic of Horcruxes, and the power of love. Horcruxes are explained to Tom Riddle (the youthful Voldemort) by his teacher Slughorn as follows:

> '...A Horcrux is the word used for an object in which a person has concealed part of their soul.'...'Well, you split your soul, you see,' said Slughorn, 'and hide part of it in an object outside the body. Then, even if one's body is attacked and destroyed, one cannot die, for part of the soul remains earthbound and undamaged.'...'Well,' said Slughorn uncomfortably, 'you must understand that the soul is supposed to remain intact and whole. Splitting it is an act of violation, it is against nature.'...'[You do it] By an act of evil – the supreme act of evil. By committing murder. Killing rips the soul apart. The wizard intent on creating a Horcrux would use the damage to his advantage: he would encase the torn portion –'
>
> (*Half-Blood Prince*, pp. 464–5)

It appears thereafter that Voldemort has managed to make seven Horcruxes of his soul, so the business of killing him would involve first destroying these. Horcruxes are things, as well as an animal (Nagini), and even a person – Harry Potter himself, who dies and comes back to life purified to defeat Voldemort in the final book. Slughorn's explanation makes it clear that the creation of Horcruxes is, first, predicated on 'the supreme act of evil...murder', and, second, consists in the splitting of the soul, which is itself 'an act of violation...against nature'. In other words, the *process* of forming Horcruxes – of externalising and splitting the soul – is *innately* evil: the process itself is evil, irrespective of causes and results. The strongest normative disapproval is imbued in Slughorn's description.

As it happens, the idea of a process of externalising and splitting the soul has a considerable basis in folklore around the world. James Frazer's *The Golden Bough* (1922), for instance, outlines folktales and folk rituals and customs from widely dispersed contexts, touching every continent, which are about external souls being stored in things, plants and animals, and which often conceive of the soul as split and stored simultaneously in multiple receptacles.[3] These myths and rituals all have a functional air, with underlying notions of maintaining souls in safety or enhancing life and power, and in some cases maintaining the consonance of social and natural order. Normative notions of good and evil are not conceived as innate to externalising or splitting the soul in any of these folktales and ritual practices, except, as Frazer notes, under certain circumstances:

> If a man has more vital places than one in his body, why, the savage may think, should he not have more vital places than one outside it? Why, since he can put his life outside himself, should he not transfer one portion of it to one animal and another to another? The divisibility of life, or, to put it otherwise, the plurality of souls, is an idea suggested by many familiar facts, and has commended itself to philosophers like Plato, as well as to savages. It is only when the notion of a soul, from being a quasi-scientific hypothesis, becomes a theological dogma that its unity and indivisibility are insisted upon as essential. The savage, unshackled by dogma, is free to explain the facets of life by the assumption of as many souls as he thinks necessary.[4]

By characterising the process of forming Horcruxes – externalising and splitting the soul – itself as implicitly evil, the *Harry Potter* text makes its first, directly compromising gesture towards dogmatic Judeo-Christian religiosity. Those Christian dogmatists who had been campaigning to ban the *Harry Potter* books in the early 2000s must have been pleased.

Onwards: in the last book, *Deathly Hallows*, when Harry is temporarily killed by Voldemort and meets Dumbledore in a kind of afterlife King's Cross station, the latter gives Harry (and the reader) a final explanation for Voldemort's ongoing failures against Harry and imminent final defeat. The key reason, in Dumbledore's words, is this:

> 'That which Voldemort does not value, he takes no trouble to comprehend. Of house-elves and children's tales, of love, loyalty and innocence, Voldemort knows and understands nothing. *Nothing.* That they all have a power beyond his own, a power beyond the reach of any magic, is a truth he has never grasped.' ... 'A part of his soul was still attached to yours, and, thinking to strengthen himself, he took a part of your mother's sacrifice into himself. If he could only have understood the precise and terrible power of that sacrifice, he would not, perhaps, have dared to touch your blood ... but then, if he had been able to understand, he could not be Lord Voldemort, and might never have murdered at all.' ... 'My dear boy, its [Harry's wand's] remarkable effects were directed only at Voldemort, who had tampered so ill-advisedly with the deepest laws of magic. Only toward him was the wand abnormally powerful.'
>
> (*Deathly Hallows*, pp. 568–70)

One may quibble with the details of this explanation, by asking: why is Harry's mother's love more powerful than that of Voldemort's other victims, who also presumably have those who love them? Is every kind of love equally powerful – Bellatrix Lestrange's love for and loyalty to Voldemort, for instance? Of more interest here, however, is the characterisation of the 'deep' structures of magic. It appears that just as the making of Horcruxes is in itself evil, at the deepest level, magic itself ('the deepest laws of magic') is inclined towards good and is predicated on the power of 'love, loyalty, innocence' ('a power beyond the reach of any magic'; 'the terrible power of that sacrifice'), and controls its instruments (wands) to work against anyone who disturbs that basis in good. In other words, magic can be used superficially for good or evil, but it is ultimately good that *must* prevail through magic because that is the basis for magic itself. There is innate goodness at the bottom of magic itself, manifested through but beyond human agency, intentions and causes. This characterisation of magic as good in its 'deepest laws' also bears a strong resemblance to what Frazer might have called 'theological dogma', specifically, to Christian *agapē*. The concept of an abstract selfless and all-embracing Christian love (*agapē*) – which in a sense is beyond human capacity and is understood as God's love, which characterises God's creations and which humans can aspire to – as differentiated from selfish physical love *eros*, has been much discussed, particularly since Anders Nygren's *Agape and Eros* (1953).[5] It is that sort of abstract power that seems fundamental to magic. Harry, who has distinctly messianic qualities (including a penchant for resurrection and an ability to overcome evil), turns out to be the instrument of these deep good laws of magic. Christian dogmatists who wanted the books banned should be very pleased with the ending of the series.[6]

What I am leading up to is that the two key devices which bring about the resolution of the *Harry Potter* series in the final books – Horcruxes and the power of love – deepen the concept of innateness around which the earlier books had already been structured. Unlike the earlier books, however, these devices have a religious ring to them. In the last two books, magic is no longer a neutral fantasy technology which can be wielded for good or bad ends by persons with good or bad intentions. Some critics have mistakenly thought that *Harry Potter* magic is analogous to science or technology as we understand it.[7] Actually, magic seems to be a quality embedded in the fantasy world at large, the various processes of which have normative content (good or bad), and the very constitution of which has a deep normative content (ultimately good). This characterisation of magic also robs the protagonists of agency. Voldemort is not really self-determining: as Dumbledore observes, he is innately such that he cannot comprehend this truth about the magic world; if he could, he would be otherwise. Nor is Harry self-determining. Rather, he is innately in tune with the deep qualities of the magic world and cannot but succeed. In a way, both are unthinking manifestations of the innate qualities and normative content of magic itself rather than free agents who pit their wits against each other and aspire to mould the world. Unless the reader has a deep-seated religious conviction in the goodness of our world, few fantasies can appear to be more debilitatingly anti-human (not just anti-intellectual) than the fantasy world (Magic and Muggle in a mutually defined bind) of the *Harry Potter* series. The success of the first four *Harry Potter* books, which I had put down to a pervasive ethos that is receptive to unthinking notions of innateness, may well have been consolidated by the later two books because the current ethos is even more receptive to unthinking innateness in its dogmatically religious forms.

Switching to a world-to-text view

Thus far in the first edition chapters (written 2002) and so far in this chapter (written 2008), I have stayed with the *text-to-world* argument – that is, re-reading the *Harry Potter* text and working out what associations from our world are called on to make sense of it. The idea is that any reading of the text necessarily, whether thinkingly or unthinkingly, calls on such associations in our-world terms to be able to make sense of the text, and my re-reading is an attempt to make that explicit. In undertaking this re-reading, some of the structural and conceptual fissures within the text, and their ideological connotations, are noted. I have not attempted so far that other approach which I briefly mooted earlier, the *world-to-text* approach. I described this as a method for clarifying the social and political implications of the *Harry Potter* phenomenon by 'delineat[ing] them from the midst of an informed understanding of processes of globalization, financial and market discourses, religious and other ideologies, specific cultural formations and cross-cultural perspectives (with the underlying linguistic and political presumptions), and the linkages between these' (p. 21). To be honest, I did not attempt it because I felt not only ill equipped to engage the range of information needed, but also because the world-to-text methodology itself was not then as clear to me as the text-to-world one. Now, however, I think I have a better conceptual grasp of the world-to-text methodology, and, though still ill equipped in the vast range of relevant information, would like to conduct a limited engagement with it. The remainder of this and the following three chapters are an attempt at a world-to-text approach to the *Harry Potter* phenomenon.

Becoming clear about the world-to-text methodology involved disabusing myself of two tacit – unthinking really – assumptions in my own argument so far. First, it occurred to me that my earlier analysis was based on a rather loose characterisation of *our world*, the contexts of which are not sufficiently marked. Consequently, it has the appearance of addressing a universally recognisable understanding of our world. While there are features in that characterisation which are in fact widely dispersed and recognised (globalised corporate activity and exploitation of markets, for example), there are also mixed among them features which are context-specific and conditional to my own location (the assumption that class/race/gender would be perceived in a particular fashion or would be perceived at all as significant issues). A world-to-text approach would require a considerably more contextually nuanced understanding of the *Harry Potter* phenomenon, without losing sight of the common ground shared by different contexts in our time. Second, the text-to-world methodology naturally assumes the primacy of the *original Harry Potter* text – the series penned and signed by Rowling and published in English by Bloomsbury. The idea was to look at those definitive original editions closely as the source from which, in a more or less linear manner, the *Harry Potter* phenomenon was generated, and to explain the latter accordingly. For the world-to-text approach, however, a quite different sense of the *Harry Potter* text is needed: the 'text' in the *text*-to-world methodology is not the same as the 'text' in the world-to-*text* methodology; the definitive original English editions are not returned as primary foci in the latter. What is needed here is a far more complex understanding of the *Harry Potter* text that is joined to the *Harry Potter* phenomenon; for the world-to-text approach we need, in fact, a grasp of *Harry Potter* as a 'fluid text'.

In a world-to-text perspective, the more widely the *Harry Potter* phenomenon is received and accommodated the more fluid the *Harry Potter* text becomes. I have used the singular '*Harry Potter* text' so far because the seven English books in the series appear now as a single continuous text with a beginning and an end. From the world-to-text perspective there is a larger dimension to this singular designation: if one thinks of the global dispersal of the *Harry Potter* phenomenon as surrounding a sprawling, expanding '*fluid* text', in John Bryant's sense (I haven't forgotten to quote, just momentarily deferred quotation to let the suggestive phrase speak for itself), then the seven original books are but a small part of this text and not a particularly stable part at that. The enormous marketing success which is denoted by the '*Harry Potter* phenomenon', and which materialises in a constantly swelling fluidity of *Harry Potter* textualisation, has increasingly only a perfunctory relationship to the Rowling-authored text. The *Harry Potter* fluid text constantly diminishes and undermines the *original* English books, the authority of the singular *author* Rowling, the publishers' (Bloomsbury/Scholastic) hold on the original editions. The fluid *Harry Potter* text bubbles out and beyond them, surrounds them and engulfs them, and relocates them and modifies their reception, despite the shrillness with which intellectual property claims and controlling authority are asserted on behalf of the author and the originals. (Some details of this will crop up in later chapters.)

Bryant's formulation of the 'fluid text' actually attaches to all literary texts and is a condition of textuality itself:

> The textual condition – encompassing processes of creation, editing, printing, and adaptation – is fundamentally fluid not because specific

words lend themselves to different meanings or that different minds will interpret the words fixed on the page in different ways, but because writers, editors, publishers, translators, digesters, and adapters change those words materially. Moreover, these material revisions can attest not simply to localized fine tunings but to new conceptualizations of the entire work. Thus, a literary work invariably evolves, by the collaborative forces of individuals and the culture, from one version to another. If we want to know the textual condition, we must get to the versions of a text, and there we will also find an even deeper condition of creativity within a culture.[8]

Bryant's 'fluid text' stretches both before and after what is usually received as a definitive edition, and has as much to do with the processes through which texts are made as with the processes through which texts are received and receptively reconstructed. By emphasising the processive nature of both production and reception, Bryant dilutes the presumption of textual unity, of the stability of originals and definitive editions, which we usually take for granted. This has an immediate bearing on the work of textual editing. But that's not my thing here: Bryant's account of the fluid text also flows into receptive processes. When Rowling's seven books appeared in the market as definitive editions of the *Harry Potter* text they entered an extraordinarily widely dispersed receptive field. They were translated into more than 60 languages and sold worldwide; they were produced as audio-books; they were adapted into films for worldwide distribution; they generated an enormous number of fan-sites and fan fiction (stories authored by fans for fans, using the *Harry Potter* characters and fictional worlds as scaffolding); *Harry Potter* computer games were produced; a vast range of *Harry Potter*-branded merchandise (picture books, postcards, posters, playing cards, cups, t-shirts, etc.) was churned out; textbooks and curricula at various levels excavated the books; an immense amount of mass media and academic writing was devoted to them – all these are part of the *Harry Potter* fluid text. The seven English editions are but flickering points in the *Harry Potter* fluid text, constantly modified by its expanding fluidity and constantly relocated within the contours of fluidity, but also constantly there as points of return and reference within the fluidity. Reading this *Harry Potter* fluid text is at the self-same moment a process of accounting for how different contexts and ideologies and socio-economic agencies worldwide act upon and are acted upon by that fluid text. That, effectively, is the world-to-text approach that the remainder of this book moves towards.

Staying with the self-reflexive note that I have already struck, one of the obvious receptive areas where the fluid *Harry Potter* text finds itself flowing into and out of is the academy. This has to do with education at the school and university levels, and the manner in which *Harry Potter* has been instrumentalised in this has received considerable attention.[9] I won't pursue this here. This has also to do with research and scholarship, which usually appear from the university and research institute levels of the academy. But much more important than the academic spaces within which research and scholarship are produced is the academic discourse through which they are formed and in which they are made available. In a way, the academy appears in research and scholarship less explicitly as an institutional space of production and work, and more obviously as an institutional discourse. This discourse is usually instantly recognisable in academic texts: through a combination of carefully delineated methodologies and arguments, usually a depersonalised tone, using a specialist disciplinary register, following conventions of citations and references and allusions, registering awareness of a field of discussion within which an academic text should be placed, etc.[10] Underlying academic discourse are practices and agreements that gesture towards the institutional space of the academy – the manner in which economic and cultural capital are distributed there, the rituals that identify academic community, the relationship the academy has with states and corporations[11] – so that, arguably, academic discourse and the academy as institution can be seen as inextricable expressions of each other. Both the academy as institutional space and the nuances of academic discourse have been extensively studied, separately and in relation to each other, but it is worth putting it into perspective here. This is partly because, by doing so, I have marked one of the world-to-text grounds in terms of which the fluid *Harry Potter* text and phenomenon can be placed, but also because this book itself was first written in 2002, and expanded in 2008, as within that academic discourse. And academic discourse is particularly worth dwelling on here because it has an anxious relationship with the *Harry Potter* text and an anxiety-ridden place in the *Harry Potter* phenomenon.

This anxious relationship seems to me to be manifested at various levels. Many of those responses mentioned above to the argument I made in 2002 were actually expressions of disgruntlement about my bringing the *Harry Potter* text within this discourse. It was tacitly suggested that to do so was not only to take the *Harry Potter* text outside its 'natural' sphere of children and fans, but also to take academic attention outside its 'natural' sphere of 'serious' writing. Reviews approached it either to discern whether there wasn't a fan 'dream[ing] of the Hogwarts Express arriving to take [the author] to join Harry at school'[12] behind this effort, or to cast it as a work that is 'curiously pedantic' and directs a 'beady gaze' on the 'sinister side' of *Harry Potter*.[13] Various e-forums accused me of 'missing the point', being 'pointless', 'stupid', 'pompous', 'heavy', 'convoluted' or 'simply wrong', and advised me to 'get a life'. Since none of these remarks derived from an engagement with the arguments made, it seems likely that these were expressions of resistance to my addressing the *Harry Potter* text within an academic discourse at all. In a different tenor, the growth of scholarly writings around *Harry Potter* has itself been marked by a tacit anxiety. As scholarly efforts took off, those that did *not* immediately place the *Harry Potter* books as 'children's literature' or 'fantasy literature' often spent time justifying the need for academic attention (as if academic attention needs to be justified for anything) or carefully positioning its academic claim. The very title of Lana Whited's edited *The Ivory Tower and Harry Potter* (2002)[14] is a self-deprecating self-positioning statement; in the edited collection *Reading Harry Potter*, Giselle Anatol devotes a section ('Why Engage in This Project?') to explaining why *Harry Potter* is 'critically significant and should be taken seriously',[15] as I did in the first edition of this book (pp. 14–23); Cynthia Hallett's edited *Scholarly Studies in Harry Potter* (2005) – also a carefully self-conscious title – came with several papers which agonise over the problem of bringing *Harry Potter* within academia, notably Laura Shearer's[16] about teaching the text in higher education and Evelyn Perry's wondering why *Harry Potter* is suffering from 'scholarly neglect'.[17] Such self-consciousness in scholarly approaches to *Harry Potter* has much to do with the unthinking resistance to academic discourse, especially in relation to the sacred text of a large fan-base, which I mentioned above. Those who did perceive *Harry Potter* as worthy of academic attention *as* 'children's literature' (which obviously seems safer) had a somewhat different and larger-than-*Harry Potter* anxiety to deal with: the place of 'children's literature' itself within an elitist academic discipline of literary studies, coming as it does from practitioner roots, was still being consolidated (an issue I have examined elsewhere).[18] And, chiming in with all that, there is a representational gap between the kind of knowledge institution described in the original *Harry Potter* text and academia as we understand it, which scholarship can only engage with by taking a text-to-world approach or by understanding *Harry Potter* as a fluid text in a world-to-text approach.

What needs to be understood is that there is no university, no institutional space for higher education or research, in the magic world of

Harry Potter. All the teaching and learning, and, more importantly, thinking and conceptualising and understanding the universe that is necessary in the magic world is confined to the secondary school of Hogwarts – essentially a pedagogic institution catering to young persons between the ages of 11 and 17. The appellation for those who profess specialist knowledge in universities in our world – professors – is transposed to school teachers at Hogwarts. These are teachers who are not necessarily specialists in the sense we normally understand: the qualifications and evidence of specialism for being a Defence Against the Dark Arts professor, for instance, seem to be very loosely defined indeed. Research and scholarship are not institutional or disciplinary activities in the magic world. In *Philosopher's Stone* readers gather that Dumbledore had done something like research when working with the alchemist Nicholas Flamel and had discovered the twelve uses of dragon's blood (*Philosopher's Stone*, p. 77). But there is no indication that there was any institutional or professional setting for this. The sort of research and discovery that are possible in the magic world can be accomplished by students in Hogwarts, as the extracurricular notes and spells in Snape's old potions textbook in *Half-Blood Prince* demonstrate. Unsurprisingly, when a researcher from our world engages in scholarship of the *Harry Potter* text she discerns not just a recognisable practice of school-level education, but also a comprehensive absence of the institutional pursuit of scholarship. And, appropriately, the engagement with *Harry Potter* in research and scholarship needs to come to grips with this lacuna. From a text-to-world approach this presents another slippage within suggested equivalences between the world (Magic-Muggle) represented in the *Harry Potter* text and our world (like those I charted in 2002) – in this instance, the slippage between the knowledge system that applies to Hogwarts school and the knowledge system that we understand and institutionalise in academia (in and *beyond* school).

Academic curiosity about this slippage in *Harry Potter* is well evidenced, and reveals as much about the nature of scholarship in our world as about the *Harry Potter* text. Some researchers have taken the Muggle world and our own to be uncomplicatedly identical and assumed a catholic attitude towards the Hogwarts curriculum and the magic knowledge system. Torbjørn Knutsen's view – inspired by ethnographic work on magic by Hubert and Mauss[19] – is a reasonably representative one in this regard:

> wizard and muggle scholars rely on different ontological assumptions. Both of them agree that a Real World exists. However, muggle scientists define this Real World more narrowly than wizards. For whereas

wizards acknowledge the existence of beings and objects that exist in both the muggle world and the wizarding world, muggle scientists acknowledge the *noumena* in the muggle world alone.[20]

Unfortunately, this is misleading. First, it suggests that there is a Muggle science represented as a knowledge system in the *Harry Potter* text. There isn't – there are some wizards (Mr Weasley obviously) who may be interested in Muggle technological devices, but only in incomprehension, as a sort of magic itself. It therefore mixes up Muggle world and science in our world, and talks of the nonexistent science in Muggle world (a fictional construct to complement magic world) as if it is the same as science in our world. Second, it thereby suggests that wizards are aware of our world science as a knowledge system *as well as* a discrete magic knowledge system that we are unaware of. Acknowledging 'the existence of beings and objects' in Muggle world is not at all the same as understanding science in our world – or, for that matter in Muggle world, if indeed there is science there. The wizards' dependence on magic comprehensively excludes the possibility of understanding science in any meaningful sense. Third, by citing Hubert and Mauss, Knutsen seeks to garner some kind of authority for the view that magic is objectively there with regard to a Real World. Mauss was considerably more circumspect: his view of magic was as a social accrual, of 'the expectations of successive generations, their tenacious illusions, their hopes in the form of magical formulas. Basically it is nothing more than this...'.[21] Closer to the mark are two essays in Neil Mulholland's *The Psychology of Harry Potter* (2006). Robin Rosenberg's, entitled 'What Do Students Learn From Hogwarts Classes?'[22], answers that question by observing that magic world lacks curiosity and therefore understanding of scientific enquiry and methods; basically, the school teaches memorising and learning by rote and practice rather than by problem-solving and creativity. That explains, in Rosenberg's view, the kind of helplessness that prevails in magic world and makes it vulnerable to Voldemort's machinations. It is fortuitous that Muggle-educated kids like Hermione and Harry are around to save the world. Charles and Emma Kalish, in their essay 'Hogwarts Academy', reach substantially the same conclusions after a closer look at the *Harry Potter* text, and conclude that 'Hogwarts is a kind of trade school' in our world terms.[23] Within their text-to-world limitations there is nothing wrong with the latter arguments, as they represent clearly an academic penchant for homing in on the misrecognition of academic work and knowledge systems in the *Harry Potter* text.

Understandably, engagement with the world-to-text approach to *Harry Potter* has generated more interest in scholarly circles. This has included coming to grips with the manner in which the marketing and publicity of *Harry Potter* have developed, media attention and corporate activity were generated, pedagogic interest was cultivated, adaptations and rewritings in different media appeared, reception in different contexts and through translation was conducted, and so on. In such scholarship, the *Harry Potter* text in its English editions has gradually ceased to have a definitive role and has instead become a node in the fluid text of *Harry Potter* readings and re-readings, translations, adaptations, rewritings and allusive textualisations. In an essay indicatively entitled 'Is There a Text in This Advertising Campaign?' (2005), Philip Nel struggles with both the marketing success that is known as the *Harry Potter* phenomenon and the scholarly criticism that interprets that phenomenon as symptomatic of a corporate capitalist ethos, to complain that these divert attention away from the perception that 'The Harry Potter novels represent the creative synthesis of a lifetime of reading, and to evaluate their literary qualities, we might consider how Rowling uses all that she has read'.[24] Nel then tries to correct this disregard by seeking out the texts behind the text. But this was already a somewhat *passé* exercise in valorising authorial ownership (Rowling's) and reviving confidence in the definitive novels' 'literary quality', perhaps undertaken to remind us all that Nel had written *J. K. Rowling's Harry Potter Novels* (2001)[25] along those lines. Meanwhile the world-to-text approach has gathered a far more dynamic pace in relation to the *Harry Potter* fluid text and phenomenon.

There are two directions in this world-to-text approach, each already opened to some extent in existing scholarship, which are taken up in the following three chapters: these concern the fluid text of *Harry Potter* in different linguistic/cultural *contexts*, and that fluid text in other *forms*. The next two chapters are devoted to the first of these: examining how the *Harry Potter* fluid text has been negotiated and reproduced in two specific linguistic/cultural contexts – namely, in Bulgaria and China. The English *Harry Potter* text offers the most fleshed-out 'foreign' (that is, outside Britain) link with regard to Bulgaria and Bulgarians. How the fluid *Harry Potter* text has circulated in Bulgaria and among Bulgarians is addressed in the next chapter. Arguably the thinnest trace of 'foreign' allusions – allusions so remote and slight that they serve more to erase than establish a link – in the English *Harry Potter* text is with regard to China. What happens to the fluid *Harry Potter* text in China occupies the chapter after that. Something analogous to this kind of approach has been undertaken from a broadly sociological perspective. In Nexon and Neumann's edited *Harry Potter and International Relations* (2006) there are two papers relevant to this approach. Jackson and Mandaville's

'Glocal Hero' argues that rather than regarding the *Harry Potter* phenomenon as global, in the sense of presenting homogeneous features worldwide, it should be understood as 'glocalization': 'worldwide distribution is sustained and enhanced by a process of *localization* whereby a cult product from one context is translated into different local contexts'.[26] Having placed the phenomenon within a familiar sociological register of globalisation studies, the authors then anchor it to the levels of translation that operate in localisation. The latter is undertaken, however, with so wide, and therefore so bitty, a range of information that it is impossible to arrive at a coherent sense of the nuances of localisation. Somewhat more successfully, in 'Foreign Yet Familiar', Towns and Rumelili discuss the reception of *Harry Potter* in terms of an over-schematic international politics model, focusing on Sweden as a context where *Harry Potter* represents the British, and Turkey as one where it represents the West.[27] The dominance of the sociology/international relations register in both papers, however, means that the *Harry Potter* text is lost entirely – even as a fluid one. *Harry Potter* becomes a somewhat incidental grid in which observations about and categories relevant to contemporary global and national societies can be framed.

Interestingly, the notion of 'glocalisation' and in relation to *Harry Potter* too appears also in an empirical study of the impact of media in children's fantasies, *Media and the Make-Belief World of Children* (2005). This outlines the fascinating case of ten-year-old Israeli Udi, who has created a complex fantasy life which brings together his reading of the *Harry Potter* novels with other media influences and local circumstances.[28] The authors categorise this as an instance of 'glocalization' too.

The last chapter here turns to fan fiction, thus picking up an example of the fluid *Harry Potter* text's different forms. A substantial amount of scholarly attention has been devoted to the many media and forms to, through and out of which the fluid *Harry Potter* text extends from a world-to-text perspective, particularly with regard to the films and computer games,[29] which I don't address here. Fan fiction has inspired some of the most interesting interrogations of textualisation, reading and worldly negotiation with regard to *Harry Potter* specifically and literature and criticism generally. This has already attracted scholarly attention – something I examine in the last chapter.

22
The Bulgarian Connection in *Harry Potter*

by Milena Katsarska

The Bulgarian connection

The Bulgarian connection in the *Harry Potter* text and phenomenon can be positioned between a brief explanation of the phrase 'the Bulgarian connection' and a quotation from EU Commissioner Guenter Verheugen's comments in January 2002. He had reportedly observed that 'Bulgaria would need magical powers, "a Harry Potter approach", in order to finish the accession talks by the end of 2003'. Extending the reference a month later at the Barcelona summit, the then Prime Minister of Bulgaria, Simeon Saxe-Coburg, was told how to do his 'homework' in order to strengthen Bulgaria's chances for early accession.[1] This may strike us as one of the least likely contexts in which a reference to *Harry Potter* would appear, and could be read simply as a rhetorical way of saying that Bulgaria's chances of accession in the near future were regarded as very slim at the time. My subsequent discussion shows, however, how the Commissioner's remark frames the particularities of the *Harry Potter* phenomenon in relation to its Bulgarian 'reading' or, more appropriately, 'reimaging', 'remapping' and 'rebranding'.

The *Harry Potter* phenomenon 'happened' in Bulgaria on a significant scale between 2000 and 2007 with the appearance of the authorised Bulgarian translations of the *Harry Potter* books, published by Egmont[2] Bulgaria EAD. The film adaptations are a part of the phenomenon in Bulgaria: these started to appear in February 2002 after an initial delay, which was followed by intensive exposure as the phenomenon caught on worldwide and Bulgaria set about catching up. Both acceleration and 'catching up' have a bearing here (I return to this below). As in other contexts, the success of the *Harry Potter* series and films was phenomenal, and their popularity cut across generations. In the context of a book market where the standard print circulation is 1,000 copies and 'each product which sells more than 3,000 copies is considered a hit',[3] Egmont Bulgaria EAD Executive Director Georgi Alexandrov's announcement, after the seventh book came out, that the *Harry Potter* books had a total print circulation of 355,000 copies speaks for itself.[4]

The title phrase here, 'the Bulgarian connection', is inspired by Alek Popov's essay in the Bulgarian Telegraph Agency (BTA) edition *100% Harry Potter* in December 2003.[5] This short essay, by a noted Bulgarian author born in 1966,[6] presents a superlatively enthusiastic endorsement of J. K. Rowling's decision to include Bulgarians in *Goblet of Fire* as Quidditch World Cup finalists (Bulgarian translation published in 2002) because, 'like every great work of literature, *Harry Potter* creates a parallel reality'. For Popov, this reality was shared by 'hundreds of millions' across the globe and referred to the football World Cup Finals in 1994, when 'Bulgaria was triumphant in stadiums, buzzed incessantly in the global flow of information, and Bulgarian footballers became media stars led by the famous Stoichkov. In practice, this was the most successful and the largest in scope PR campaign in the country's history over the last few decades'.[7] For his audience of *Harry Potter* fans Popov unpacks the 'authenticity of this collective image' of the Bulgarian Quidditch team: comparing Viktor Krum to Stoichkov; noting that the players' bellicose assertiveness before the referee, Mostafa, was reminiscent of the 1994 football World Cup Final; drawing attention to those typical representatives of Bulgarian folklore, the Veela, 'the most beautiful women Harry had ever seen' (*Goblet of Fire*, p. 93); recognising the realistic depiction of the typical Bulgarian bureaucrat, though in magic world he speaks English (*Goblet of Fire*, p. 104). For Popov, the fantasy *Harry Potter* Quidditch World Cup Final shows, as the real 1994 football World Cup Final had shown, that 'our team is a worthy rival to be taken seriously', and he revels in his conviction that 'the virtual champion Viktor Krum has already been generating a sense of national identity together with the real idols of the nation, such as Stoichkov and other geniuses'.[8]

Popov's essay highlights the motifs which gained momentum in the relation between Bulgaria and the *Harry Potter* phenomenon. Bulgarians focused on the tangible presence of compatriots in the fictional *Harry Potter* world (Viktor Krum, the Quidditch team members and the minister), that is, on that which literally constitutes a 'Bulgarian trace' in *Harry Potter*. The primary concern was 'tracing' the fictional trace into the real world of Bulgaria.

The reasons underlying this strategy have something to do with the quotations at the beginning, and are suggested in the title of Popov's essay itself *'Bulgarskata sleda v Hari Potar'*. He employed the phrase *'bulgarskata sleda'*, which corresponds to and has currency as 'the Bulgarian connection' in the English-speaking world, and alludes to the Cold War era. More specifically, it recalls the attempted assassination of Pope John Paul II in 1981 when a Bulgarian, Sergei Antonov, was implicated but eventually found not guilty.[9] This was widely covered in the press in what was then 'Western Europe' on the other side of the Iron Curtain,[10] and has since been considered a major blot on 'the image of Bulgaria abroad' and a difficult episode to deal with in the process of positively reimagining Bulgaria after 1989. The need for such a positive reimagining of Bulgaria *within* Bulgaria was necessitated after 1989 by dramatic socio-political and economic changes, accompanied by financial, governmental and demographic crises, which led to significant cultural transformations and crises of values and identity in the transitional 1990s.[11] After 2001, in the second phase of transition[12] in a climate of relative stability and economic growth, this renegotiation of 'Bulgarianness' *within* continued. But now, additionally, engaging the process of EU accession negotiations meant that the terms in which 'Bulgarianness' is conceived *outside* had to be considered too. The *Harry Potter* text and phenomenon appeared in Bulgaria at precisely this crucial juncture, and naturally *Harry Potter* came to be positioned between a post-communist legacy (past) and a (present) transitional period and an aspiration (future) to become an EU member state. 'The Bulgarian connection' in *Harry Potter*, therefore, went outside and beyond the actual 'Bulgarian trace' in the *Harry Potter* books and films. It started flickering between the slipping and fluctuating boundaries of past, present and future, and between the 'real' and 'fantasy' worlds of *Harry Potter*, and beyond that into the complexities of the 'reality' and 'fantasy' of Bulgaria itself – 'what Bulgaria fantasises about', which might be provoked by trauma or shaped by aspiration. 'The Bulgarian connection' accordingly became a matter of national identity reconstruction and performance, which was dispersed across several discursive axes: the very conception of identity (from essentialist and fixed to constructed and fluid); the socio-political transformation within Bulgaria (from national communism to capitalist liberal democracy); Bulgaria's location in a transitioning region, the Balkans; Bulgaria's location within Europe and as aspiring to EU membership.

Thus the discussion of 'the Bulgarian connection' and *Harry Potter* in this chapter expands on the arguments outlined above by working on three interrelated and intersecting planes. First, the Bulgarian reception and framing of the *Harry Potter* phenomenon in popular discourse as it has taken shape up to 2007 in mass media (newspapers, magazines, television), electronic forums and publicity campaigns will be drawn on. Second, critical (academic) discourse which the phenomenon has generated in Bulgaria will be examined with reference to one published book, a number of scholarly papers and an unpublished PhD thesis. Third, the two aforementioned discourses will appear to varying degrees as related to and even part of the fluid text of the *Harry Potter* phenomenon (books, films and marketing). These three planes are entwined in the following detailing of 'the Bulgarian connection' which is outlined above.

Viktor Krum – Stanislav Yanevski – Boris Mitkov

Viktor Krum or the importance of publicity

The Bulgarian 'trace' in the *Harry Potter* series became available to English readers in 2000 with the appearance of *Goblet of Fire*, but without attracting significant interest at the time.[13] Two years on, it was mostly through Egmont Bulgaria's publicity campaign that interest in the fourth book to be published in Bulgarian was considerably heightened, and the publishers were able to announce an initial print-run of 35,000. The press release articulated the Bulgarian connection in a way that went beyond the character of Viktor Krum:

> The anticipation of this book is higher because of the presence of Bulgaria in the novel – the Bulgarian team plays at the Quidditch World Cup Finals and one of the *main* characters is Viktor Krum. The author herself shares, *'I find the folklore of South East Europe exceptionally unique and different* from the British-Irish traditions. *I chose Bulgaria* as a finalist in the Quidditch World Cup, *after I had been touched by its folklore and history.'*[14]

> (emphasis added)

It doesn't matter whether the phrasing or sentiments attributed to J. K. Rowling are accurate. This initial press release was a way of constructing the Bulgarian connection in *Harry Potter* within a publicity initiative, anticipating that this could be an effective trope in the reception of the text and using its resonance with the tried-and-tested terms for constructing Bulgarianness, through history and folklore, as 'exceptionally unique'. This first articulation of the Bulgarian connection also had the advantage of fitting a worldwide phenomenon into the ongoing process of the country's attempts to renegotiate national identity and rebrand Bulgaria for internal and external consumption. Unsurprisingly, between 2001 and 2003, a British Council-sponsored project, indicatively titled 'Branding Bulgaria',[15] was undertaken, which brought together leading Bulgarian academics, journalists and intellectuals to work out ways of representing Bulgaria in a positive light. One of its recommendations was to capitalise on the fourth *Harry Potter* book's representation of Bulgarians and, by implication, Bulgaria.[16]

Two years down the line, while the Bulgarian edition of *Goblet of Fire* was still being vociferously discussed by readers like Popov, it was the process of organising its film adaptation that led to the new wave of public attention:

> This is, without doubt, God's intervention on behalf of a small country, which has experienced hard times in being recognized by the world and which has been conducting occasionally agonised negotiations with Brussels with regard to its accession to the European Union (envisaged for 2007). One of the characters in *Harry Potter and the Goblet of Fire*, the fourth work in the world-famous saga about the young wizard, turned out to be of Bulgarian origin![17]

This is the emotive opening paragraph to a 2004 article, '*Harry Potter* Ignites Passions in Bulgaria', in the Bulgarian language edition of the France-based newspaper *Parizhki vesti* (*Paris News*), written by a Bulgarian émigré of Popov's generation. The article, among a number of others,[18] was in response to Director General, Bulgarian State Agency for Tourism, I. Gyurov's announcements of a strategy for boosting the country's tourist industry made several months earlier. Between March and May 2004, Gyurov had been quoted as having identified that 'somewhat moody young man of few words', Viktor Krum, as the 'symbol of New Bulgaria'.[19] He discerned 'a unique opportunity [to have] millions of children and their parents globally [become aware of] one of Bulgaria's greatest rulers, Khan Krum – who has given his name to the Quidditch team player Viktor Krum'.[20] Gyurov hoped that having read the book, and after seeing the film, 'millions of kids will ask their parents to visit the country of the fearless seeker imagined by J. K. Rowling'.[21] Since the casting negotiations for the film adaptation of *Goblet of Fire* were underway, Gyurov expressed the hope that a Bulgarian boy would play the part, as that would 'open doors to tell the world about Khan Krum's glorious times, when the political map knew only about two great states in Europe – Bulgaria and the Empire of [the] Franks'. Heated e-forum debates followed, featuring both sceptical voices ('Do we really need a fictional hero to represent our country? Is that our only national pride?') and more optimistic, 'realistic' ones ('Let's be realists – can our museums, our nature and our hotels really attract kids and parents from all over the world?'). The casting of Viktor Krum was set to become a complex negotiation of contending ideologies and national allegiances.

Stanislav Yanevski or the importance of embodying nationality

Already enjoying a considerable following of young and adult admirers, as fan e-forums[22] indicated, the character of Viktor Krum ignited a new wave of passions as the news that a 'real Bulgarian boy' would be sought for the film adaptation was revealed. E-forum discussions became more animated: younger users were excited by the prospect, shared their disappointment or 'anger at the little word space Viktor Krum has in the book', felt anxious that 'the film might cut this even shorter' or 'exclude the love scenes with Hermione', and resolved to 'look down upon Warner Bros., if they change their mind' and cast a 'non-Bulgarian'. 'If the producers do not choose a Bulgarian for the part of Viktor Krum but some Brit kid, we'll find him and shoot him', one forum participant stated.[23] The turnout for the casting event in Sofia on 4 and 5 February 2004 was consistent with the enthusiasm expressed in the forums. Depending on the media source, between 2000 and 4000 young persons, aged between 15 and 19, came for the auditions from all over the country, some by truanting, others arriving in organised buses from the Vidin English Language High School, for example. The two most assertive refrains were, first, a Bulgarian casting agency[24] should make the selection, and do it in Bulgaria; and second, the boy must be Bulgarian. Consequently, the announcement that Stanislav Yanevski had been cast in London was met with some disgruntlement. Responses to it were contradictory and heated too, as the greater number of forums' participants wondered, 'Is Stanislav Yanevski Bulgarian enough?' given that he was not a resident of Bulgaria. Most of these entries resonated with the nationalistic discourse of the 1990s, the so-called 'brain drain period' which witnessed the two largest emigration waves from Bulgaria and was constructed as a national disaster and tragedy. Ten years later, while initial forum responses still expressed an ingrained isomorphism between nationality and territory, the actor was gradually recognised as a Bulgarian. In fact, he came to be seen as 'embodying nationality' by virtue of being born in Bulgaria, and was described thereafter as a 'typical' Bulgarian: 'swarthy, with thick eyebrows, and aquiline nose; tall, round shouldered; strong and sturdy'; 'our boy' and a 'true Balkan type'.

Get ready because...looking at the movie screen, your face will inter-
changeably express fear, hope, laughter, anxiety and...(not) a little
pride, when you hear how a multitude of thousands of wizards chants
the name of Viktor Krum.[25]

This is what the publicity discourse emphasised, while different voices
in the forums chimed in. 'Our Stan is number one. He is Bulgarian all
right....Stan is the most handsome Viktor Krum. He is the most handsome of all in *Harry Potter*', observed 'Mimi' and 'Dani', while a 'Fan'
opined:

> I am very glad that finally the image of Bulgarians will be connected
> with such a handsome and intelligent boy. It is really an honour to
> us to have such young, promising people, whose roots will never be
> severed. They will remain forever closely linked with what consti-
> tutes Bulgarianness, with our rich history and widely recognised
> intelligence. Way to go to Stanislav![26]

Since November 2005, when Mike Newell and Stanislav Yanevski
appeared in all Bulgarian media for the Sofia premiere, Krum, Yanevski
and 'Bulgarian' have blended seamlessly.

Boris Mitkov or the importance of lineage and kinship

At this point one might justifiably ask: 'What if the textual "trace" of
Bulgaria did not exist in *Harry Potter* – would there still be a Bulgarian
connection in the text?' The answer is yes. In 2002, prior to the translation of *Goblet of Fire* into Bulgarian and the unravelling of the Bulgarian
'trace' in Bulgaria, a Bulgarian 'blood-relation' has already been mapped
on the 'family tree' of the *Harry Potter* phenomenon – in the film adaptation of the first book. This was when the publisher Egmont offered as
the chronologically first entry of the 'Most Curious Facts about *Harry
Potter*' thread[27] the following, under the heading 'Boris Mitkov – the
Bulgarian kid who takes part in the Warner Bros. production *Harry Potter
and the Philosopher's Stone*':

> Bobby is 11 years old – exactly the age of the little wizard in *Harry
> Potter and the Philosopher's Stone*. Bobby's birthday, just like Harry's, is
> in July. The Bulgarian boy has been growing up in London too, even
> though he was born elsewhere – in Sofia in 1990. Just like Harry, the
> charming Bobby is also an offspring of a notable family tree – his

great-great-grand father is the famous Bulgarian writer Geo Milev,[28] whose daughter, Leda Mileva,[29] is Boris's great grandmother.[30]

Two immediate inferences can be made from this succinct account, one of a number about Boris published at the time.[31] First, by virtue of generation, sign, place of residence and a 'significant' lineage, Boris Mitkov is so much like Harry Potter that he could be regarded as Harry himself. Second, by virtue of origin, family and birthplace, he is Bulgarian. Hence, syllogistically, Harry Potter is Bulgarian – a claim which was very nearly, if not quite, made. It was certainly implied.

A complex series of negotiations can be discerned here. On the one hand, the construction of Boris's Bulgarianness as related to birthplace, origin, genealogy and history traces a line through his ancestors: a great-great-grandfather who is ensconced in the Bulgarian literary canon and a grandmother who represents the contemporary cultural elite in the country, both associated with the political left and a recent communist past. This emphasis on heritage suggests an understanding of national identity in ethnic historical terms. On the other hand, in order to construct Bobby's 'Potterness', the significance attached to such arbitrary facts as his generation, zodiac sign and place of domicile and development is emphasised. The latter are not seen as diluting his 'Bulgarianness' but accentuating it, since all these can be recruited to the idea of the 'new Bulgarian' – born and growing up in the post-1989 period and geographically mobile. The underlying rhetoric here is that of setting a claim for legitimate acceptance and inclusion on equal terms in which *Harry Potter* is signified as the world, or at the very least Europe. The passage quoted above goes on to report that Bobby was thrilled at being chosen to be one of the kids in Gryffindor House in the film, it was his 'greatest wish', which resonated with Bulgaria's aspiration to become a member of the 'EU club' at the time.

Viktor Krum – Dracula – the Other

Alongside popular enthusiasm, the *Harry Potter* phenomenon did not fail to attract significant academic and critical attention in Bulgaria, but without addressing explicitly the Bulgarian reception of *Harry Potter*. The academic discourse mostly revolved around textual analysis of the books and the role of film adaptations,[32] especially in relation to children's literature, teenage creativity and educational issues,[33] and some of the global responses which it generated, such as censorship.[34] Even though, as befits academic discourse, these critical writings are far less emotionally charged and more analytical, they often address issues similar to those outlined above, issues of identity and representation and their underlying ideologies and power relations,[35] and the relationship between real and fantasy worlds.[36] Here I present a survey of some of these discussions with a view to showing how 'the Bulgarian connection' has figured in critical terms, and how therein a sense of researchers' identities is conveyed.

Names and naming patterns in the *Harry Potter* series generated a number of popular accounts and academic publications. It is hard to say what impression the Bulgarian names made on English readers. Judging from two sample website entries in the 'glossary' of *Harry Potter* names, we can assume that 'Viktor' evoked the obvious association and 'Krum' was a grey area:

> **Krum, Viktor** Bulgarian seeker and Durmstrang triwizard champion. Close ::cough:: friend to Hermy-own-ninny . . .
> 'Viktor' is phonetically the same as 'victor', and he defeated Lynch in terms of catching the snitch. According to *A Harry Potter Fansite*, 'Krumm' is a German adjective used in phrases such as 'dont slouch' and 'sit up straight', and literally means 'crooked' or 'bent'.[37]

And:

> **Viktor Krum:** His first name means the 'victorious one,' appropriate for a forceful Quidditch player.[38]

Every Bulgarian aged seven (when school education begins in Bulgaria) and above, however, unmistakably identifies the surname with the historical Khan Krum (r. 803–14). During his reign the Bulgarian territory expanded twice, law and order were installed (the first known Bulgarian legal code was introduced) and enemies of long-standing were defeated (the Byzantines under Nikephoros I). In Bulgaria the name is immediately and universally recognised as indelibly associated with heroic national history – hence the 'added value' to the image of Viktor Krum, which would revive national pride, realise aspirations for new law and order, both recall past glory and quell 'enemies' (sceptics), and symbolise the elevation of the new Bulgaria in the world.

Scholars who recognised the importance of Viktor Krum as 'the primary symbol of Bulgaria'[39] and analysed the character[40] in terms of literary (and cultural) representation naturally made the connection to the historical Khan Krum. The scholarly account of this connection, however, was framed quite differently within the discourse of postcolonial criticism:

> Khan Krum was one of the most famous Bulgarian rulers who reigned during the IX c. and who defeated the army of the Emperor Niquephor and made a goblet out of his head with which he proposed a toast for the Bulgarian warriors. He was victorious and thus the association with the origin of the Bulgarian Quidditch player's first name Viktor. The name he has been given implies also the possibility of a noble origin. It also presupposes what Viktor will be competing for – he will be trying to win the goblet – a symbol of his victory. The historical fact is considered rather repelling and savage-like by westerners and to those familiar with this possible connection of the name of the Bulgarian star it would bring the association of the savage capable of cruelties and inflicting death.[41]

Thus in 2003 Cheshmedzhieva addressed the issue of how the name of Harry Potter's opponent in the TriWizard Competition can also be interpreted as the implied 'wickedness and difference of the Other'.[42] And, further on:

> The name of the Quidditch star adds to the perception of the Bulgarian player as an outsider who has taken the quest to compete with the British centre. However, he is not one of the centre, and this bodes the end of his quest for the goblet. The implication of victory that his name brings serves only the purpose to strengthen the contrast between him and the hero of the centre and makes the victory of the centre ever so important.[43]

In the same vein, the textual appearance of the character as well as the appearance of the actor Stanislav Yanevski who embodies him – 'thin, dark and sallow-skinned, with a large curved nose and thick black eyebrows...like an overgrown bird of prey' (*Goblet of Fire*, p. 95) – immediately seemed to suggest demonic, Dracula-like features. This perception is, it was argued, exacerbated by the almost 'inhuman' Veela,[44] who moreover gender the peripheral image of Bulgaria within the Balkans[45] and represent a threat to the stable English centre through, for example, their power over men. This argument then extended to the entire repertoire of Bulgarians in *Goblet of Fire*:

> The names of the Bulgarian team and the other characters in the book, invented or picked up from books and directories, definitely

sound difficult and weird to the British centre. They also give us a feel for the territories that Bulgaria covers in Rowling's understanding. Following the etymology of the names used, Bulgaria in its imagined form could be defined as covering the territories from Hungary to Russia.[46]

This critical account of the Bulgarian connection in *Harry Potter* used examples of names, descriptions of characters' appearances and personalities, plot developments, etc. and made numerous evocative associations, which mapped along the axes of periphery and centre, marginality and dominance.

One more illustration will serve to clarify this further. Viktor Krum's school, Durmstrang, is identified as 'mobile' and Bulgarian scholars have noted an association with Russia in it: by virtue of its northern location and landscape; the apparel of its members (fur capes and uniforms); and the Ivan Grozni or Koschei Bessmertnyi[47] look-alike headmaster, Igor Karkaroff, who sees double-dealing everywhere. As Cheshmedzhieva points out, 'these interchanging associations with Russians and Bulgarians are suggestive of the understanding and presentation of Bulgaria as a satellite of the ex-Soviet Union'.[48] Concurrently, there is a parallel association with the Balkans (e.g. Krum looks like Dracula), and the name of the school is easily linked with the German movement *Sturm und Drang* ('Storm and Stress'), which in turn 'perfectly matches...the image of the Balkans as a site of chaos and political turbulence'.[49] Consequently, the presentation of the school revives, as Bulgarian scholars pointed out, western stereotypical constructions of both the East during the Cold War, and of a racial Balkan 'other' in a nineteenth-century mould. Thus, it was maintained, *Goblet of Fire* can be placed within a strand of English literature from Bram Stoker's *Dracula* and G. B. Shaw's *Arms and the Man*[50] to Malcolm Bradbury's *Doctor Criminale*[51] and Julian Barnes's *The Porcupine*.[52]

The scholarly mapping of this fuzzy 'imaginative geography' (Said),[53] as it applies to Bulgaria, interestingly also turned in on itself to implicate the location from which the critical gaze was extended. Within the above arguments an assertive stance can be discerned, deriving from and embracing a real geopolitical location and sense of identity on behalf of the researchers making those arguments. The manner in which geopolitical location and cultural identity was *exercised* by the critical voice enunciating these arguments played in complicated ways with the manner in which these critical voices *incorporated* at the selfsame moment their academic status and authority (for instance, with reference to postcolonial theory).

The discernment of the researcher's identity being tacitly exercised through a critical text is not a straightforward matter, and has to do with recognising the critical choices that are made. Some Bulgarian *Harry Potter* critics have, for instance, been particularly interested in the connotations of colours:

> The colours of the two teams are of no less significance and carry *obvious* associations: the Irish are in green, while the Bulgarians [are] in red. Here there is the *inevitable* connection between the colour red and communism, and this contributes to the *marginalisation of the state*.[54]
>
> (Bulgaria in reference; emphasis mine)

An emphatic choice is made here in reading the colour symbolism. It was equally possible for the red strip of the Bulgarian Quidditch team here to recall the red worn by the Bulgarian football team when it beat Germany in the 1994 World Cup Finals (as Popov observes in the essay cited above). In this attempt to pass the choice made as *obvious* and *inevitable*, so as to support an argument about *marginalisation of the state*, a located ideological investment is revealed in the critical voice itself.

In Bulgaria between 2000 and 2007, the employment of the above postcolonial critical lens to deconstruct stereotypes and 'othering' strategies resonated with the social, political and cultural concerns of the country at the time. These contextual nuances were less explicit but also available in the first full-length book on *Harry Potter* in Bulgaria: Lidiya Denkova's *The Philosopher's Secrets of Harry Potter* in 2001.[55] This publication unpacked the philosophical dimensions of the series for the benefit of teachers and students. Addressed to adolescents and adults alike, Denkova touched on topics such as 'two worlds', 'the mixing of the two worlds' and 'freedom of choice' – all useful for drawing attention to philosophical principles and paradigms. These topics were, however, also increasingly central in socio-political developments in Bulgaria at the time, especially in the context of aspiring to accession within the EU. Similarly, essays by Bulgarian scholars related to *Harry Potter* and censorship in various contexts[56] outside Bulgaria in that period had a bearing naturally on the Bulgarian context itself. Bulgaria had just emerged from a period of official censorship and curbing of freedom of speech, and was facing a resurgence of moves towards censorship as sporadic representatives of Orthodoxy joined the 'crusade' against *Harry Potter*.[57]

A salutary example of academic work which has negotiated the researcher's identity and location in a more nuanced way while addressing similar issues is available in Ludmilla Miteva's essays and unpublished

PhD thesis 'Humour in late 20th-century British Children's Literature: Roald Dahl, Terry Pratchett, J. K. Rowling' (2008).[58] The third chapter of the work, 'Establishing and Crossing the Boundaries of Ethnic "Otherness"', deals with *Goblet of Fire*. The focus on humour allows the researcher not only to identify and deconstruct stereotypes, but to do so and distance the researcher's voice from those being unjustly stereotyped. This becomes effectively an exercise in looking for and finding stereotypical constructions both ways.

> The readers could laugh at the Bulgarian 'blighters', who want to trick 'us' and get hold of more seats...at the Bulgarian minister, who, it seems, hasn't heard of Harry Potter, at the grotesque figure of Krum and his absurd linguistic incompetence, at the Veela.... Laughter can be due to accepting that this is just a joke and 'we really do not think like that'. And yet, through humour we have seen through the contrasts and have come to realize that 'they', 'the blighters', could not have possibly been asking for tweezers, that Fudge is very stupid since he assumes that the Bulgarian minister does not speak English only because he comes from Bulgaria.[59]

Alongside such passages, where the critical perspective is carefully depersonalised, there are moments when it is explicitly personalised. When this occurs, however, the location and identity of the researcher is openly acknowledged. The following analysis of the Durmstrang headmaster's tantrum (*Goblet of Fire*, p. 487) is a case in point:

> I cannot deny the funny side of the scene, but to me it is funny in a different way. Unlike the younger audience for which it is intended, my mind is burdened (I cannot disregard my memories). I am laughing at the inadequacies of Karkaroff...with a degree of relief because even if the fictional depiction is exaggerated, things used to be more or less like that and now I can afford to laugh at the absurdity of the system, in which we used to live and at the preposterous leaders we used to have.[60]

Further on, by considering interchangeable views of an adult or a younger reader, and a reader coming from an English-speaking or a Bulgarian-speaking audience, Miteva manages to relativise her own position. In the process, the stereotypical representations of non-Bulgarian fictional characters are noted too (Dumbledore's, for instance), which allows her to observe that 'the stereotypical image of the West, the Centre, is just as implausible as the image of the Periphery or the former "enemy"',[61] and to conclude that 'the fixed imaginary boundary between "us" and "them" and especially its crossing are related to the interpretations and relativising of [dichotomies] such as West-East and Self and Other'.[62] Perhaps the balance that Miteva achieves has something to do with the fact that by the time she completed her work in 2008, the key source of tension in the Bulgarian connection of the *Harry Potter* phenomenon had been resolved – Bulgaria became an EU member state on 1 January 2007.

A very brief note on translation

In a generally 'faithful to the original' Bulgarian translation from the English text[63] it is worth noting a couple of tiny details which slightly modify the Bulgarian rendering of the text in terms of its Bulgarian 'trace'. Translating back from the Bulgarian these are:

- In relation to the portrayal of Viktor Krum: '*sallow-skinned*' (*Goblet of Fire*, p. 95) becomes '*pale*'; '*very surly* face' becomes simply '*surly* face'.[64]
- In relation to the Bulgarian minister: 'My *Bulgarian opposite number's making difficulties* and I can't understand a word he's saying' (*Goblet of Fire*, p. 82) becomes 'My *colleague on the Bulgarian side causes problems* and I can't understand a word he's saying' (Bulgarian edition, p. 76); 'The Bulgarian wizard suddenly spotted Harry's scar and started *gabbling* loudly and excitedly, pointing at it' (*Goblet of Fire*, p. 91) becomes 'The Bulgarian wizard suddenly spotted Harry's scar and *spoke* loudly and excitedly, pointing at it' (Bulgarian edition, p. 86); 'Good job too, *these Bulgarian blighters* have been trying to *cadge* all the best places...' (*Goblet of Fire*, p. 91) becomes 'Good job too, *these Bulgarians* have been trying *to get hold of* all the best places...' (Bulgarian edition, p. 86).
- In relation to the issue of accents, the English text renders the Bulgarian minister's English as follows:

> '*Vell, ve* fought bravely,' said a gloomy voice behind Harry. He looked around; *it was* the Bulgarian Minister of Magic.
> 'You can speak English!' said Fudge, sounding outraged. 'And you've been letting me *mime* everything all day!'
> '*Vell*, it *vos* very funny,' said the Bulgarian minister, shrugging.
> (*Goblet of Fire*, p. 104)

In the Bulgarian edition the foreign enunciation is not reproduced, and the difference in accent is transferred into descriptive/explanatory narration:

'Well, we fought bravely,' said gloomily in *correct English with a strong hard accent* somebody behind Harry. He looked around *and saw* the Bulgarian Minister of Magic.

'You can speak English!' said Fudge angrily. 'And you let me *wave hands and twitch [make faces]* all day!'

'Well, it was very funny,' said the Bulgarian minister, shrugging.

(Bulgarian edition, p. 98)

These small omissions and alterations for the most part and self-evidently neutralise expressions which cast Bulgarians in a negative light or which Bulgarians may find offensive. Instead of the hint of sickliness in 'sallow-skinned', the more neutral word 'pale' is used, which in Bulgarian can be associated with 'resolve and determination'. The Bulgarian minister is recognised as a 'colleague' by Fudge, and by a change of register as well since he is 'speaking' (Bulgarian to a Bulgarian audience) rather than 'gabbling' (an unfamiliar language to English-speaking audiences). Bulgarians are just 'these Bulgarians' and not 'blighters' ('*dosadnitsi*' is the Bulgarian equivalent), and they certainly do not 'beg' as the use of 'cadge' implies. Finally, in the scene depicting the exchange between Fudge and the Bulgarian minister, the slight changes transfer the comic culpability from the Bulgarian minister to Fudge, and that involves a slight shift in power relations too. The removal of the accent (actually more Russian-like than Bulgarian-like in the English text), is effectively the removal of something that English-speaking audiences are apt to regard with amused condescension. A 'strong, hard accent' it may continue to be in the Bulgarian text, but there's nothing wrong in attributing 'strong' and 'hard' to Bulgarian (whether in relation to the sound of the language or as a quality of the people). Moreover, emphasising the 'correctness' of the English spoken by the minister, while not contradicting the English source (the minister's English is indeed grammatically correct; it's the accent that is a problem), is to the credit of the Bulgarian minister's linguistic abilities.

At the moment when real Bulgarian politicians, government officials and diplomats were concerned with 'rebranding' and 're-imaging' Bulgarianness for internal and external consumption and were busy with negotiations for EU accession, the Bulgarian translator of the *Harry Potter* books was evidently doing something more or less similar – adopting the role of diplomat and politician.

23
Harry Potter in China

With assistance from Cheng Xiao

Beyond the pale

To come to grips to any extent with the *Harry Potter* phenomenon in China it is necessary to have the *Harry Potter* fluid text as a conceptual horizon rather than foreground the original text and try to establish a set of linear relations from it to the Chinese context. This is the case, as observed earlier, for any text-to-world approach, but this is especially pertinent when we focus on *Harry Potter* in China.

Insofar as a geopolitical location can be discerned *within* the original English *Harry Potter* text, China is placed beyond the pale. There is obviously a much discussed sense of location that readers of the English text are likely to be aware of. The Muggle–Magic world described marks its British locations and plays out its Britishness clearly: in the naming of places and persons, in the use of idioms and colloquialisms, in the rituals of social exchanges (in news, shops, schools, offices, etc.), in the manifestations of tacit class-consciousness. Working alongside these is a limited sense of an extrinsic world: the Quidditch World Cup has Bulgarian and Irish teams; there are magic schools abroad – the Beauxbatons in France and Durmstrang in an unnamed northern European location; there are stereotyped foreign characters; Charlie Weasley is a Dragonkeeper in Romania. In particular, as discussed in chapter 22, there is a clear 'Bulgarian connection'. Further, there is also a careful accounting of the multicultural world *contained* in Britain in the original text, especially in terms of names and ethnicities. At both the axes of alluding to a world outside Britain and taking into account the heterogeneous world inside Britain, the original text presents the merest trace of gestures towards the existence of China. This trace is so uncertain and self-effacing that it serves more effectively to put China beyond the pale than to bring it to the fore. Very incidental and low-key gestures efface a Chinese association by making it. So, at the axis of manifestations from the world outside, a Chinese Fireball dragon in the *Goblet of Fire* appears briefly. The origin of different families of dragons is one of the ways in which the extrinsic world is gestured towards:

> 'This is a Hungarian Horntail,' said Charlie. 'There's a Common Welsh Green over there, the smaller one – a Swedish Short-Snout, that blue grey – and a Chinese Fireball, that's the red.'
>
> (*Goblet of Fire*, p. 287)

Now the dragon (and also the phoenix) is more central to Chinese mythology and ubiquitous in Chinese iconography than anywhere else in the world – so much so that numerous texts in the West metaphorically refer to China itself as the 'dragon' (the 'sleeping dragon', the 'rising dragon', etc.). And those who are aware of Chinese iconography know that the Chinese dragon is not red (not unless political hues are being metaphorically united with the metaphor of the Chinese nation as dragon), and is associated with water and not fire (and is in fact quite different in all its associations from the western dragon). The red Chinese Fireball dragon therefore makes concrete in the *Harry Potter* magic world a western misreading and misrepresentation of Chinese mythology and iconography. While doing so, it diminishes the centrality of the Chinese dragon, which appears here in an incidental comment and is barely glanced at amidst other, more vividly visualised, more active dragons. It turns out in *Goblet of Fire* that the Chinese Fireball is faced by Krum, representing Durmstrang, in the first round of the Triwizard Tournament, and (by Ron's account) is dealt with by a blinding spell which leaves the floundering dragon destroying some of her own eggs. To try to make much of that would be to over-endow the slightness of the Chinese allusion, the near-absence of China. At the other axis of registering the world *within* multicultural Britain also there's the merest gesture towards a possibly Chinese association. Amidst the names indicative of different ethnic origins is that of Cho Chang's (Harry's first love interest), which sounds East Asian, and possibly Chinese. There is nothing in the original text to give that association substance – no information about Cho Chang's background – but in the films she is embodied as distinctly racially East Asian, Chinese. So there's only the name to go by. But even here things are murkier than the English reader might think. The other ethnically defined names or ethnically 'other' characters are unambiguously identified or identifiable: Angelina Johnson is described as black; it is a good bet that Anthony Goldstein is of German origin and probably an Ashkenazi Jew; Padma and Parvati Patil are very plausible Indian names, with probably Marathi Hindu origins (both first names redolent of Hindu religious significance). To the Chinese reader 'Cho Chang' poses a problem: it doesn't recall clearly any common Chinese name. The nearest sound equivalents to Cho have disagreeable meanings, unsuitable for names. In the Chinese translations of the *Harry Potter* books, the nearest sound equivalent which makes sense is chosen, 秋张 or Qiu Zhang (meaning Autumn), which sounds rather different. It might occur to the English reader that while Chang sounds like a generic Chinese name, Cho vaguely recalls that quintessential Oriental woman, the Japanese Cho-Cho-San in *Madam Butterfly*. Both Cho and Chang could be Korean family names rendered in English, but are unlikely first names. At any rate, the name presents a vague East Asian connection but a very tenuous Chinese one.[1]

The original *Harry Potter* text itself therefore promises little by way of an entry point towards its travels to China, but the fluid text of *Harry Potter* has made a remarkable inroad into China. And it is as a fluid text that *Harry Potter* in China needs to be engaged. This is not so much a matter of charting how the original text makes a passage to China, but of discerning how flows of discourse and translation operate in China to render the *Harry Potter* text malleable and fluid. The issue of translation is central to this, and that is the first to be addressed below. I examine translation here as an interlingual transfer – from the English to the Chinese – and also discuss the complicities and dissonances that arise at cultural interfaces and due to market forces. The final section is devoted to the reception of the *Harry Potter* text and phenomenon in China, which is framed by constructions of contemporary Chinese childhood.

Translations

Harry Potter came to wider attention in China with the simultaneous publication of Chinese translations from the first three books in the series by the People's Literature Publishing House in October 2000. Even then it was a remarkably confident entry: where children's literature books in China usually have a print-run of 10,000, the first three *Harry Potter* translations had initial print-runs of 200,000 each. The enormous success of the *Harry Potter* books in China is marked by the rising figures of first-print runs for subsequent translations: the fourth (*Goblet of Fire*) had a first print-run of 400,000, the fifth and sixth (*Order of the Phoenix* and *Half-Blood Prince*) of 800,000,[2] and the final book of one million.[3] The *Harry Potter* fluid text in China is concerned pre-eminently with the translated versions. Despite a strong drive to make English the second language in China,[4] consumption of the English editions there has been relatively negligible. However, there is a similar kind of quantitative increase to be noted there too: about 200 English editions of the first in the series were taken for sales in China, by the sixth (*Half-Blood Prince*) the figure was above 10,000.[5]

Translating the *Harry Potter* English text into any language presents a number of problems which need to be carefully negotiated. Reporting on translations of the *Harry Potter* books into different languages, Gillian Lathey points particularly to the following: markers of what is perceived as Britishness, such as tone and humour; proper names (these often work by aural assonance and verbal association rather than being straightforwardly meaningful or conventional); and the use of dialect and register, especially to indicate social status (for Hagrid and the house-elves, and in a different way for Fleur Delacouer, for instance, to mark foreignness).[6] Translating from English to Chinese puts particular pressure on some of these. This is principally because the written English alphabet consists of letters which roughly represent a phoneme or sound, while written Chinese characters (in practice, words usually have two or more characters) are each a word, morpheme or semantic unit and represents a meaning as well as a speech syllable. This means that in written Chinese phonetic variations in speech are less easy to convey – written Chinese is simply less malleable to represent non-standard speech. It can easily be comprehended that insofar as, say, social status or foreignness is suggested in English writing by the sounds of words enunciated (as is the case for Hagrid or Fleur) this is impossible to represent in written Chinese translation. Moreover, as I have noted, every Chinese character represents a sound and concurrently has a meaning embedded in it. Translating western proper nouns into Chinese, therefore, usually involves finding characters that convey the nearest sound equivalent, and either the meanings embedded in those characters are disregarded or, sometimes, characters are carefully selected to convey both something of the sound and some quality of the thing/person/place in question (even if that Chinese meaning is not contained in the western proper noun). Thus translating personal names into Chinese involves a complex level of cultural negotiation. The translation of *Harry Potter* names into Chinese is a good index of one of the levels of textual fluidity involved here.

I have already mentioned the cultural slippages that attach to translating the name of the possibly Chinese Cho Chang. Perhaps these slippages account to some extent for the remarkably scant interest that Chinese readers evince in Cho Chang in *Harry Potter* fan websites. The naming of this character is so full with ambiguity and ignorance from a Chinese point of view that it is difficult to accept the appellation without some misgiving. Other fascinating cultural negotiations in translating names can be discerned in the differences between the two available Chinese translations of the *Harry Potter* books – the Taiwanese ones and the ones produced in the People's Republic of China mentioned above.[7] The first name of Harry Potter itself is a case in point. In early Chinese media reports on the *Harry Potter* phenomenon 'Harry' was translated naturally and conventionally with the characters 哈里 (ha lǐ) where the character 'ha' is a pure sound character (as in the laughing 'ha ha') and 'lǐ' is the closer and smoother sound equivalent, but, incongruously, means something like 'inside' (that meaning could be disregarded). However, in the Taiwanese edition 'Harry' had already been translated with the characters 哈利 (ha lì), where the character 'lì', though less smoothly enunciated, carries the more suggestive meaning 'victory'. It was therefore decided that the Chinese edition would do the same. Incidentally, 'halì' and 'halǐ' are not exactly homophones, and are distinguished by different tones in Chinese (it is often difficult for westerners to distinguish between the four tones used in Chinese). The implications of 'Harry' immediately suggesting 'victory' in terms of understanding the character and his role are themselves not insignificant. However that may work for Chinese readers of either version, it would have no direct relationship to the English name 'Harry'. Further, a more telling example here appears with regard to the translation of the name 'Voldemort'. In the Taiwanese edition this was represented by the characters 佛地魔 (fo di mo) and in the Chinese by the characters 伏地魔 (fu di mo). The character 'di' means 'earth' and 'mo' means 'devil', the character 'fo' means 'buddha' and 'fu' means 'crouching'. To read 'Voldemort' as 'devil crouching on the ground' makes good sense; but any association of 'buddha' with Voldemort is desperately misplaced. None of this has any bearing on the name 'Voldemort', which to European ears may suggest something like 'stealing from death' or 'causing death'. Understandably, the English trick of having 'I am Lord Voldemort' as an anagram of 'Tom Marvolo Riddle' is impossible to convey in the Chinese.

The business of translating names is but a small thing, but it spins out into a mass of cross-cultural negotiations in translating from the

English to the Chinese. We must bear in mind that *Harry Potter* in China comes overwhelmingly in the Chinese. The Chinese translations *are* the *Harry Potter* text of China, and are parcel with the fluid text we are concerned with here. And the question of translating *Harry Potter*, for those who pay attention to these things in China, has been a matter of anxieties and uncertainties. One Mihepu (a pseudonym), for instance, has written many articles on different websites identifying mistakes made in the Chinese translations, and at one point called for the correction of 1,132 errors in the first eleven chapters of the Chinese edition of *Half-Blood Prince*.[8] Even the editor Ye Xianlian of the People's Literature Publishing House, which published the Chinese translations, observed that they are probably imperfect: 'there must have been some mistakes based on misunderstanding the original'.[9] I note this more to mark the anxiety of translation in evidence here than to dwell on troubled questions of authenticity and faithfulness to the originals. Insofar as I am dealing with the fluid text of *Harry Potter*, I may as well accept that it is in the nature of fluid texts that mistakes made in translations may nevertheless become a legitimately received aspect of that fluid text and let the matter rest there. But the scope of translational fluidity in question here needs a little more demonstration than those observations on names allow. Without presuming knowledge of Chinese, this can be conveyed to some degree by conducting exercises in back-translating.[10] This involves having someone who is fluent in both languages translate back into English from the Chinese translations without reference to the English originals, and then to compare the result with the originals. This can be a particularly revealing exercise when the passages in question are those that presented unusual linguistic features in the original text. By back-translating such passages it becomes possible to see whether the unusual linguistic features of the original had been conveyed in the translation.

To that end I have chosen two passages here from the first and last books of the *Harry Potter* series where arguably something unusual happens in the use of language in the original text. These passages stand out as unusual because the English of the original is generally idiomatic but uncomplicated, relatively free of linguistic opacity and experimentation. Back-translations of these are presented with comments below. In such exercises there are always intractable factors like a degree of bilingual competence, memory and contextual knowledge of the back-translator, prior familiarity with the texts, etc., which may somehow skew the results. Nevertheless the results are interesting.

The passage from *Philosopher's Stone* which I selected describes the moment when Harry steps into magic world for the first time, into Diagon Alley. Some of the passages which decided my choice are:

> The sun shone brightly on a stack of cauldrons outside the nearest shop. *Cauldrons – All Sizes – Copper, Brass, Pewter, Silver – Self-Stirring – Collapsible* said a sign hanging over them. . . .
>
> A plump woman outside an apothecary's was shaking her head as they passed, saying, 'Dragon liver, seventeen Sickles an ounce, they're mad . . . '
>
> A low, soft hooting came from a dark shop with a sign saying *Eeylops Owl Emporium – Tawny, Screech, Barn, Brown and Snowy*. Several boys of about Harry's age had their noses pressed against a window with broomsticks in it. 'Look,' Harry heard one of them say, 'the new Nimbus Two Thousand – fastest ever –'
>
> (Philosopher's Stone, p. 36)

The back-translation from the Chinese reads:

> Bright sunlight flashed on a pile of pots outside the door of the nearest shop. Above the pots hung a board with the words: 'big pots made of brass, tin, silver – all types – automatic-stirring, collapsible'.
>
> A fat woman stood outside a medicine shop. As they passed her, she shook her head and said, 'Dragon liver, seventeen sickles per ounce, they are mad.'
>
> From a dark shop came a low and soft woo-oo sound, the shop sign on the door said, 'Yila Owl Shop – grey forest owls, horn-sounding [like the French horn] owls, brown owls, snow owls'.
>
> Several boys of Harry's age had their noses pressed on the glass of a shop window. Inside the window there were flying brooms. 'Look,' Harry heard a boy say, 'that's the newest type of Halo 2000 – highest speed –'.

My reason for choosing this passage is that it performs, by the use of language, something that is seminal not just for Harry's but also the reader's entry into and continuing engagement with the magic world. It mixes two registers: first, a set of words that are immediately associated for English readers with something old-fashioned (often archaic words) and sometimes specifically with witchcraft (through fairy tale and folklore, through popular culture forms), such as 'cauldron', 'apothecary', 'broom', 'sickle' (associated with harvests and druidic rituals), 'pewter';

and second, the linguistic strategies of modern advertising, snappily referring to innovations for convenience ('self-stirring – collapsible'), listing types of products ('copper, brass, pewter...', 'Tawny, Screech, Barn...'), giving the catchy brand-name ('Nimbus 2000'). The manner in which the two registers are seamlessly mixed both brings alive in a contemporary sense, and updates the associations of, magic world. In the back-translation the second register (of advertising) is conveyed clearly enough, but the first is conveyed only to a limited extent – 'pot' doesn't have the specific witchcraft associations of 'cauldron', the 'brooms' have to be made to fly to bring out that nuance, 'medicine shop' doesn't have the air of quaintness of 'apothecary', the 'sickle' in Chinese is a pure sound translation and meaningless in itself. And yet the limited sense of old-fashioned fantasy of the first register is given a particular turn in the Chinese version, in that the whole passage comes with a stronger sense of the exotic – strange happenings and things made stranger by the unmistakable foreignness (from the Chinese point of view) of this environment. This sense of foreignness can be discerned in the slightly more laboured manner in which the back-translation reads compared to the original: it is more carefully precise, a bit more particular about positioning and explaining the relation of people and things in Diagon Alley. The negotiation with proper nouns also has a role to play here, but I won't go into this again.

The other passage I had chosen for back-translation, from *Deathly Hallows*, is of a completely different sort and describes the long-awaited final duel between Harry and Voldemort:

> A red-glow burst suddenly across the enchanted sky above them, as an edge of dazzling sun appeared over the sill of the nearest window. The light hit both of their faces at the same time, so that Voldemort's was suddenly a flaming blur. Harry heard the high voice shriek as he, too, yelled his best hope to the heavens, pointing Draco's wand:
> '*Avada Kedavra!*'
> '*Expelliarmus!*'
> The bang was like a cannon-blast and the golden flames that erupted between them, at the dead centre of the circle they had been treading, marked the point where the spells collided.
> (*Deathly Hallows*, p. 595)

There is an attempt here to perform through language the extra, almost excessive, significance of this climactic moment, appearing as it does after six earlier climaxes. The language itself is excessive: it comes with a close collection of words connoting an explosion (performing an explosive climax) – 'sudden', 'burst', 'hit', 'bang', 'blast', 'erupt', 'collide'; and a high density of words suggestive of burning (setting the stage alight, so to say) – 'red-glow', 'dazzling', 'flaming blur', 'golden flames'. And in thus stretching the language to perform the climax, the *sequence* of events described in this passage is overtaken by the enormity of this *moment*. Instead of appearing as a series of moves, the duel seems to become compressed into a speeded up, somewhat overwritten, blur. The back-translation of this passage comes up with the following:

> A flash of red light suddenly exploded from the end of the wand, burst out to the sky, flying over their heads, becoming brilliant like the halo around the sun. After that this beam of light crossed over the nearest window sill and shone on Harry's and Voldemort's faces, and Voldemort seemed like a fireball. Harry heard a sharp scream, so he collected all his concentration and, holding Draco's wand, shouted.
>   *Avada shoumingzhou!* [sound character for 'avada', the rest literally 'life-taking spell']
>   *Chouniwuqi!* ['expel-weapons' command]
>   A great sound like a canon came. Golden sparks spread between them. The circle they had been turning around became a circle of death at this moment. At the centre of the circle two spells clashed.

Though some of the blur of overwriting, linguistically performing the significance of the climactic moment, is preserved, it is interrupted by a need to clarify the sequence of events here. The slippage in identifying the first source of the red-glow is an understandable mistake which derives from the need to clarify causes and consequences. So is the qualification of the circle they were treading as a 'circle of death', as is the breaking down of one sentence into four after the spells are cast. Whether this is rooted in some way in the Chinese language or derives from this translator's inclinations is a moot point; it is part of the *Harry Potter* fluid text in China.

The kind of close, text-based approach to the negotiations that occur within the fluid text of *Harry Potter* as it disperses in China – the focus on interlingual translation – that I have dwelt on so far is only one aspect of the levels of translation involved here. The most important point to grasp here is that the interlingual translation of the English editions into the Chinese is a planned and relatively small part of a larger process of translation. What actually happens here is that the entire Harry Potter phenomenon, at all levels – as an advertising and marketing phenomenon, as a reading phenomenon, as a media phenomenon, as a phenomenon registered as such by academics and educationists, as a socio-cultural phenomenon – was systematically translated into China on an industrial scale. This is hinted at even if we take note of the manner in which the interlingual translation of the texts themselves was conducted. The Chinese translations of the first three books in the series were completed within three months: translators were commissioned in June 2000 and the translated books were available by October 2000. All the subsequent translations were produced within three months of the appearance of the English editions too (translators were only given the English versions once they had been officially released). The translation process was itself overseen by the publishers in a functional and efficient fashion for quick turnovers and consistency and with little opportunity for mulling over ambiguities and translators' equivocations. The most revealing overview of this grand translation project, and the place of interlingual translation within it, has been given by the Head of the People's Literature Publishing House, Ye Zhenning. In a 2002 speech on 'The Development and Marketing of Harry Potter in China'[11] he laid out the overall structure of the project to translate the *Harry Potter* phenomenon into China. It was based on the perception that despite their success in the West, the series might not do well in China. The expectations of children's literature in China seemed to be different, the record of foreign bestsellers wasn't encouraging and the *Harry Potter* books seemed at that stage not to have done well in the nearest comparable Eastern market, Japan. The project of bringing *Harry Potter* to China therefore became a considerably larger one than simply translating the books and making them available. The format of the book itself, as a physical object, was designed carefully to stand out in the Chinese context. The size of the books, the page layout, the colour of the paper (chosen to discourage piracy) and print quality were all carefully thought through. Chinese illustrators were invited to work on illustrations and covers, but were finally rejected in favour of the American design (with the covers embossed). Beyond the physical shape and appearance of the books, distribution and retailing were carefully organised. An extensive media campaign was orchestrated in advance of publication – through websites, and broadcast and print media. Posters were printed informing readers of the international acclaim of the series. The first three books were released simultaneously nationwide on 6 October 2000 at 10 a.m., with performances by Chinese actors in bookstores. Media awareness was maintained thereafter in a programmatic fashion. Harry Potter branded gifts and postcards were produced. Favourable scholarly articles and statements from intellectual authorities were engineered. Within a short period the entire apparatus of fandom and externally established frames for structuring individual and institutional reception was translated and transplanted into China in 2000, adjusted and modified for the Chinese social context, and maintained thereafter. In some sense, it thereby transformed literary production and reception in China. The interlingual translation of texts was a crucial but small part of the overall project.

The self-reflexive critical reception of *Harry Potter* that resulted in China was determined by this vast translation project. But critical reception and reflection also necessarily and almost always manage to escape any planning and engineering, and are uncontainable. How this has unfolded in China occupies the final section of this chapter.

Constructing childhood

In April 2008 I was fortunate in being given the opportunity to initiate and participate in a workshop on 'Harry Potter in China' at the Institute of World Literature, Peking University.[12] This consisted of two brief presentations and discussions between students ('post-1980s' and 'post-1990s' generations, i.e. those who were born in those decades and had grown up with the *Harry Potter* phenomenon in China) and academics. The issues covered seem to represent most of the strands of discussion of the *Harry Potter* phenomenon in China insofar as I have been able to gauge these from news features and scholarly publications. This section is in two parts: the first gives a summary of the deliberations in this workshop; and the second is a commentary on that summary, offering context-specific clarifications and linkages.

The workshop

Presentation 1

Wang Xiaoya, representing the People's Literature Publishing House, observed that, up to April 2008, ten million copies of the seven Chinese *Harry Potter* books had sold, and the last in the series alone had already sold one million copies. These were records for Chinese reading materials for children. Before publishing the *Harry Potter* books, the People's Literature Publishing House had focused primarily on classics of European literature. The *Harry Potter* books were also the first for which a Chinese publisher had bought rights, since prior to that such permissions were controlled by the state. The *Harry Potter* series was therefore the first to break into the Chinese market in an independent fashion, and has started a trend which has subsequently grown. Consequently, the number of books available in China has multiplied, and closer links have developed between China and the outside world.

Presentation 2

This was by Zhuang Zi, an editor of China Youth Publishing House, who has been responsible for publishing a series of *Harry Potter* fan fiction by Chinese authors. He took a more analytical approach to the *Harry Potter* phenomenon. By way of presenting a 'reading of the readers', he observed that the series has nourished two Chinese generations since 2000. In his view the texts are about a boy who is always 'running toward the future, and running to take up responsibility and assume a leadership role'. The boy grows as the series progresses and readers grow with him. In China these readers are primarily of the so-called 'I-generation' of the 'post-1980s' and 'post-1990s', and the success of these books shows that they have satisfied a desire to discover through reading what these generations are looking for.

According to Zhuang, since the 1990s Chinese society has entered a period of transition, and current social values are no longer the same as previous ones. However, the education system and attitudes to bringing up children that prevail in China have remained unchanged and are now anachronistic. Chinese books for children tend to be didactic and old-fashioned and construct children as passive instruments for social progress. Education and upbringing seem based on notions of devotion and dedication to social causes, which the 'I-generation' often regard as inauthentic. This generation is itself more focused on the individual self or 'I' (expecting social good to be achieved through individual fulfilment) and is not accustomed to thinking in terms of a collective 'we' – Zhuang cited some surveys to support these points. There is, therefore, a widening gap between the generations, and a vacuum in provision for the 'post-1980s' generations of China through education and intellectually stimulating reading. At the generational level, Zhuang understands this as a growing deficit of 'love', with parents functionally focusing on achieving success through their children, and children cultivating a more self-centred worldview. This deficit of 'love' is also ingrained in the education system, which is unable to bridge the generation gap and nurture the new generation's worldview. The latter is more global than before, in tune with a globalised and networked world. Zhuang discerns a broader political crisis behind this, since China is now opening up to and becoming an agent of globalisation itself (in contrast to the main agent of globalisation so far, the United States, which, particularly since

September 2001, has been retreating into protectionism), and it is incumbent on the Chinese to prepare future generations to embrace the opportunities available to them.

The *Harry Potter* books, with their unstinting ability to face up to human nature in a realistic rather than idealistic fashion (including depictions of cruelty, cowardice, betrayal, loneliness, death), while presenting both a strong concept of love and a powerful sense of individual ability as collective good, have served to stem the sense of alienation that the new generation in China feels. In this, they also mediate this generation's growing global consciousness. But the crisis is far from over, and China needs to respond to current educational needs and development more actively.

Discussion 1 – about generation gaps

Objections were voiced by some, who identified themselves as of the 'post-1980s' generations, to their being characterised as suffering from a deficit of 'love'. Perhaps these objections arose from misunderstanding Zhuang's observation as a criticism of that generation in itself rather than as characterising a prevailing socio-cultural formation. It was averred that the construction of the 'post-1980s' generations as lacking 'love' was a mistake commonly made by earlier generations. Such a construction has to do with the 'post-1980s' being the first generation in China to be almost entirely composed of single children, who are seen as spoiled and selfish. But such sweeping statements are no more than generalised nonsense. The generation gap in China has widened because of the cultural insularity of earlier generations compared to the greater openness and sense of being connected to others (through new media, for instance) in the 'post-1980s' generations.

Discussion 2 – about modes of communication

One of the respondents observed that she was first introduced to the *Harry Potter* books through a reading on the Central Broadcasting Radio Station, in the long-running radio programme 'Novel Reading' [xiaoshuo lianxu guangbo]. She felt that more than as texts which satisfy some abstract reading desire among children, the success of *Harry Potter* in China is due to their being available in media that children engage constantly – the internet, films, audio media. Another respondent argued that Chinese kung fu fantasy novels have been successfully transferred to different media, but that doesn't mean that they have become globally successful. The crucial factor is language: the *Harry Potter* books have reached a global readership because they were written in English, the world's dominant language. In some sense, it was felt, Chinese readers were responding both to the *Harry Potter* text's affinity with fantasy fiction in Chinese forms and to its strangeness in deriving from an exotic, western tradition and location.

Discussion 3 – about postmodern childhood

This strand drew largely on Buckingham's *After the Death of Childhood* (2000)[13] to argue that in the postmodern, globalised environment earlier constructions of childhood and adulthood as separate had been ruptured. The exposure to adult realities that electronic media have brought to children is part of this process, and in this Chinese children are partakers of a large global change in sensibilities. The *Harry Potter* books, with their unabashed representation of the darker side of life, chime in with this change. That also explains, as one respondent pointed out, why the phenomenon is not confined to children but extends to adults too – in China as much as elsewhere.

The prodigious quantity of Chinese *Harry Potter* fan fiction available on the internet was not discussed in the workshop despite Zhuang's presence and role in making such fan fiction available in print form. This is, however, a significant element of the fluid *Harry Potter* text in China, with context-specific nuances which cannot be disregarded. It also has a bearing on the discussion about generational divides above. I present some observations on Chinese *Harry Potter* fan fiction, along with fan fiction elsewhere, in the next chapter.

Commentary

The workshop arguments summarised above are pre-eminently addressed to the Chinese context that surrounds and receives the *Harry Potter* text, and do not really engage the text itself. This is consistent with pretty much all Chinese media coverage of and scholarly work on the *Harry Potter* text and phenomenon thus far. Just by being a success, by selling well, by being popular, by sustaining a phenomenon, the *Harry Potter* text is taken as *a priori* 'good' or 'worthy' (moral connotations intact). So Chinese critical reception of the *Harry Potter* text very rarely expresses the kind of scepticism about the text itself available in, for instance, Jack Zipes's or Andrew Blake's books[14] or in the 2002 chapters of this one. The congratulatory view of the *Harry Potter* text in China does, however, involve a constant restatement of the textual content in ways that resonate particularly there. Thus, at different times, it is the exotic, western roots of the text, the plotting, style and character development of the text, the representation of some value (love, heroism, individual achievement, realistic portrayal of human nature, etc.) in the text, that is highlighted as that which makes it 'worthy' or 'good'. But in every instance the 'goodness' or 'worthiness' of the text is taken as a foregone conclusion. Thus, an academic paper by Li Nishan maintains that the *Harry Potter* books arouse feelings of happiness and freedom full of 'western magic-colour' [xifang mohuan secai], encourage role-playing and childhood development, and 'moistens and lifts the soul';[15] one by Huang and Liang examining the double-world narrative argues that the books stimulate the 'creative force, and helps the spirit fly';[16] and another by Zhang and Kong on *Harry Potter* in the context of contemporary children's literature is largely a eulogy.[17] The argument typically goes as follows: the *Harry Potter* text is 'good' and 'worthy' – its success in China has done 'good' there – and the reason it has done 'good' in China is because there are such-and-such lacks, such-and-such unfulfilled desires and aspirations, in the social and cultural and political formation of China. The 'good' and 'worthy' impact of the *Harry Potter* text provides an opportunity to put those deficiencies into perspective and to correct them. There is an unmistakable and pervasive prescriptive strain of self-criticism, self-improvement, self-development in the Chinese reception of the *Harry Potter* text and phenomenon.

Along with that, the workshop discussions (also in keeping with published criticism) assume that the *Harry Potter* text and phenomenon are pretty much exclusively about and for children (in the broad sense of including early teenagers). This is actually not in keeping with indications of consumption in China: according to a survey reported in 2007, the majority of *Harry Potter* readers in China are aged between 14 and 24.[18] But it is generally taken for granted that if readers need to be considered, they are undoubtedly children and the books are clearly addressed to children. With these preconceptions in view, the Chinese critical response to *Harry Potter* typically makes two linked moves: first, use *Harry Potter* to characterise – and thus effectively construct – childhood in contemporary (2000 onwards) China; and second, discern how *Harry Potter* departs from, and may be used to modify, the provision of reading material and education for Chinese children.

The characterisation of childhood in the workshop deliberations interestingly revolve around decadal generational divides: 'post-1960s', 'post-1980s', 'post-1990s'. This terminology is prevalent in mass media and academic discourse in China at present. It is worth pausing briefly here because it demonstrates the precise manner in which characterising and constructing childhood are coeval. On the one hand, the artificiality and neatness of decadal generational distinctions seems to be at odds with what is obviously a flowing and continuous social process and experience. It is evidently used as a way to impose structure on an amorphous area, with arbitrary chronological markers to pin down a slippery process (much as historiography generally does sometimes in terms of decades or centuries). The decadal terminology also suggests that such a structure is not ideologically-led and has at least the appearance of neutrality. As Shao Yanjun observes in a paper on the Chinese phenomenon of 'pretty women writers':

> The so-called 'pretty women writers' derived from a young and gifted group of serious litterateurs who were called the 'post-seventies writers'. The latter term was consequent upon the earlier phrase 'post-sixties writers'. These purely chronological terms are different from earlier characterizations of literary groups in China, such as 'rightist writers', 'educated youth writers', 'root-finding writers', 'avant-garde writers', etc. Since the 1990s the tendency in China has been to demarcate writer groups not according to their experience and stylistic or ideological tendencies, but only according to the period they were born in. Through 'post-sixties', 'post-seventies', 'post-eighties', to the nascent 'post-nineties' writers, this method of chronological division has continued, demonstrating that Chinese literature has entered a phase in which there is no dominant theme and no mainstream.[19]

On the other hand, the device of decadal generational divides has caught on because it seems to make sense in China. This has something to do with the pace of social change in China, which is seen as being so rapid that each decadal generation could be meaningfully *assumed* to have significantly different formative experiences – especially in the first decade of childhood – in relation to each other. Thus, the 'post-1950s' generation would be the first to be entirely formed under the Chinese socialist system (after 1949); the 'post-1960s' generation would have their formative years marked by the Cultural Revolution; the 'post-1970s' generation would be the first to have grown in the post-Cultural Revolution and post-Mao (d. 1976) period; the 'post-1980s' and 'post-1990s' generations would be the first to consciously assimilate to a 1990 onwards market-socialist transformation, and also the first to be composed almost entirely of single children (following the one-child policy from 1979). Not uninterestingly, the *Harry Potter* phenomenon also appears in China at the significant decadal (indeed millennial) moment of 2000.

So, unsurprisingly, a structuring device that is assumed as a convenience (like a grid) for locating social processes begins to gather a life of its own. The characterisation of the 'post-1980s' and 'post-1990s' generations – the *Harry Potter* generations – as such seems to immediately construct them in analytically preconceived ways. Children become personified, as a whole, as individualistic or materialistic or media savvy in a market-socialist environment, which in China is corporate capitalism with centralised planning. And contemporary childhood generally comes to be assessed in terms of children being single progeny and therefore spoilt, self-centred and more dependent on friendships and extrinsic relationships. With such a construction of childhood in place, understanding the *Harry Potter* text and phenomenon in China involves fitting the phenomenon to the construction. This is clear in the workshop deliberations, and can also be evidenced in a range of mass media features and scholarly publications in China. The argument in the latter is also that the *Harry Potter* books and phenomenon *fit* this decadal characterisation of contemporary Chinese childhood in a way that children's literature and educational provision available in China does not. This has been a constant refrain: for instance, Zhang and Kong castigate Chinese children's writing for lacking originality, being 'adultised', having a lecturing tone, being too didactic in contrast to *Harry Potter*;[20] Ni Lishan argues that the Chinese educational system curtails thinking and enjoins responsibility in a soul-destroying fashion, from which *Harry Potter* has provided welcome relief;[21] using *Harry Potter* as an example, Xu Yurong wonders why Chinese children's literature deters children from reading while British children's literature give children pleasure;[22] and so on.

The *Harry Potter* text and phenomenon have been placed amidst that perceived slippage between the construction of contemporary childhood in China and the children's literature or educational system of China. *Harry Potter* is seen as repairing that slippage, constructing a bridge. Equally, *Harry Potter* is seen as highlighting the slippage. And, in doing so, another turn of the screw, so to speak, is revealed within the construction of contemporary Chinese childhood. *The perception of the slippage and consequent reception of* Harry Potter *are symptoms of a deep-seated anxiety about constructing childhood itself in China.* The idea is that Chinese educational systems and children's literature have in the past constructed, and still continue to construct, childhood in a way that has rendered children unhealthily passive. Children were constructed in terms of the 'greater good', some idea of a rigid, top-down social and moral order along socialist or, for that matter, Confucian lines. Children were constructed to absorb this order passively through education and books. The anxiety now is that for children of the 'post-1980s' generations this placing them in passivity is no longer desirable or possible. Children from the 'post-1980s' generation onwards have become active agents who are, at least tendentiously, outside the control of such determination and socialisation. They are spilling outside the confines of whatever is perceived as Chinese (very materially through new media), refusing to subscribe to formerly entrenched notions of social and moral order, and are interrogating the prerogatives of adults (parents). The extrinsic inflow of *Harry Potter* into China, and the embracing thereof by children, is therefore signified in the workshop, in mass media reports, in scholarly writing as symbolic of a coming to life of the child's agency in China.

It is difficult to say whether, and to what extent, this mode of thinking about *Harry Potter* in China stands up to historical experience and evidence. As in the workshop discussions, so in all the published sources cited above, the argument is made impressionistically. Little empirical and analytical research seems to inform their asseverations.[23] Their arguments involve a series of equally loosely founded constructions, based on few facts and few observations, as much of contemporary and past childhood, as of China's present and past educational systems, and as of Chinese children's literature now or earlier. In terms of the last, it is debatable whether such Chinese texts as were available to children during, say, the Cultural Revolution[24] – that most extreme pole of 'other' times – would have given them a social or political worldview that is radically different from the *Harry Potter* text. The children of the Cultural Revolution, for instance, had access to 'revolutionary martyr stories' in textbooks (such as stories about Liu Wenxue, Dong Cunrui, Huang JiGuang, Qin Shao Yun) which were redolent with violence and death and heroism. These would have conveyed to them a clearly morally divided universe of good and evil, dark and light. As in *Harry Potter*, the moral division could have been accounted as an external one: the 'good' or 'just' revolutionary social order in China as opposed to the imperialist capitalist reactionary western powers. And also as in *Harry Potter*, the moral schism could have been placed within the everyday psyche of Chinese people themselves: in terms of the 'reactionary' or 'bourgeois' tendency that may be discerned in anyone, even within the Party itself. Perhaps the difference is primarily that the *Harry Potter* books are unambiguously categorised in the genre of fantasy, and can therefore be taken light-heartedly, while those 'revolutionary martyr stories' were reality in their time, and therefore grimly serious; or perhaps the fantastic nature of the latter were not wholly unperceived even at the time, though it was expedient not to acknowledge it. And further back, the rich tradition of Chinese fantasy writing with Confucian overtones, and their contemporary renovation in the form of historical romances and martial arts fantasies, also calls for a complex accounting in this context. There are many inconclusively engaged questions and uncertainties here, and the prevailing reception of *Harry Potter* in China outlined above is, ultimately, far too schematic and impressionistic. Ironically, this overly schematic reception arguably reiterates, through its uncritical acceptance of the *Harry Potter* text and phenomenon as 'good' and 'worthy', through its unanalytical approach, something of the penchant for rigid ordering that such reception ostensibly seeks to counter.

But these uncertainties and ambiguities are part of something larger within China, something that exceeds the singularity of the *Harry Potter* text and phenomenon. The latter are a minuscule bubble in a much larger effervescence in the social and cultural and political formation of contemporary China. This is the effervescence of a prevailing sense of being in transition, of a ubiquitous sense of 'opening up' and 'catching up with the West', of a vaunted sense of assuming a significant place in globalisation processes – all clearly expressed in the workshop deliberations outlined above, and in numerous mass media and scholarly works. This sense causes a particular sort of anxiety in the China where *Harry Potter* appears. Equally, the recognition of 'China's rise' causes another sort of anxiety – a sort of fear – in the Anglophone West, where *Harry Potter* comes from. Numerous recent popular accounts of the rise of China written in the UK and USA are symptomatic of this.[25]

24
The *Harry Potter* Fan Fiction Text

Fan fiction text

The *Harry Potter* fan fiction text – a phenomenon in itself – has assumed its current, extraordinary, sprawling and expanding proportions almost entirely in the environment of the Internet, by exploiting the possibilities of global social networking. According to Tara Collins, by January 2006, popular fantasy fiction texts had attracted fan fiction writers in the largest quantities, especially the *Lord of the Rings* trilogy and the *Harry Potter* series; but whereas fan stories posted online for the former were estimated at 36,000, for the latter they exceeded 180,000.[1] The technology of the Internet is intricately enmeshed with the development of the phenomenon. Between the possibilities offered by the technology and the ability to exploit (and sometimes serendipity in working with) those possibilities the cultural form of fan fiction has dispersed and linked up, visibly and traceably, in ways that were impossible in the fanzine era. The entire *Harry Potter* phenomenon has unravelled as the electronic environment for social networking has been consolidated: within the frame of the development of blogging and web chatrooms from the mid-1990s, and the increasing popularity of social networking websites like MySpace and Facebook post-2000s. If the success of *Harry Potter* fandom demonstrates the success of niche media rather than large, centralised media corporations, then it also points to the facility with which niche media can now link up and generate new niches through networking, as Henry Jenkins observed in 2007.[2] Jenkins had by then theorised this process as one of 'convergence' in his book *Convergence Culture* (2006), where he reminds readers that such convergence is ultimately not simply through media appliances but in the 'brains of individual consumers and . . . their social interactions with others'.[3] The dynamic *Harry Potter* fan fiction text emerges from the *Harry Potter* fans and materialises through technologically facilitated convergence, wherein the textual creativity of *Harry Potter* fans is woven with the process of the *Harry Potter* series (which unfolded over ten years) and phenomenon. It is this interwoven quality that actuates the *Harry Potter* fluid text, of which the *Harry Potter* fan fiction text is as much an integral part (really a very large part) as the original *Harry Potter* text itself, and as indeed the various other textualisations of the *Harry Potter* phenomenon are. So integral is the fan fiction text to the *Harry Potter* fluid text that from a world-to-text perspective it can hardly be overlooked: it has become an auto-perpetuating area of textual production (with a guidebook for writing specifically *Harry Potter* fan fiction in the market)[4] and academic attention (the first book-length study was announced as this was being written).[5]

The *Harry Potter* fan fiction text, therefore, exemplifies much current thinking about fan fiction and textuality generally, often in ways that rebound into literary critical theory and practice at the broadest levels. To begin with, such fan fiction is predominantly in electronic text and hypertext form and is therefore available to writers and readers who can *interact* with the text. Electronic texts and hypertexts have been widely understood as involving various kinds of departure from conventional notions of print text because of the possibility of interactiveness. Thus, for Jay David Bolter, electronic texts opened up the possibility of 'interactive fiction': 'a nonlinear fiction, which invites the reader to construct a dialogue with the text'.[6] In this, writers would be called upon to think of their work not as 'a closed and unitary structure', but 'as a structure of possible structures', and readers would cultivate the ability to become a 'second author, who can then hand the same text to other readers for the same treatment'.[7] Similarly, Silvio Gaggi observed that hypertext entails an empowerment of the reader in that he or she can construct his or her own paths of reading and even interfere in the text by creating new links and inserting comments; that hypertext thereby challenges the concept of the author as a unitary presence and leads to 'encouragement of collaboration in the creation of knowledge and their capacity for a free, rapid, and unimpeded dissemination of knowledge';[8] and that, consequently, hypertexts lead to the development of an 'interactive literature', untrammelled by mediating authorities and industries.[9] Within the interactive electronic text/ hypertext, the contemporary fan fiction text is defined as being anchored to an original text (in this case Rowling's *Harry Potter* text), using characters and settings provided by it, and is typically circulated within a fan community, often while being available to a wider circle of fans outside the immediate community. Since the intertextual horizon and interactiveness of fan fiction is thus circumscribed, there is a *participative* aspect to it: fan fiction writers and readers are largely identified as such by participating in a fan community. Insofar as the fan fiction text is conceived at that nexus of participation, it is generally approached less as a stable and analysable entity in itself and more as expressing the interactive and participatory nature of fandom itself. Thus, Lanier and Schau's examination of three *Harry Potter* fan fictions demonstrates that the departures from the original text in these serve 'the creation of the symbolic structures and meanings of a particular form of pop culture', that is, they 'contribute to the "meta-text" that binds the Harry Potter community together'.[10] The fan fiction text, and fan communal participation in it, thus apprehended can be read and framed with distinct normative thrusts. So, on the one hand, Henry Jenkins's celebratory approach finds in and around the *Harry Potter* fan fiction text (he focuses on fan communities of children) evidence that children are:

> active participants in these new media landscapes, finding their own voice through their participation in fan communities, asserting their rights even in the face of powerful entities.... At the same time, through their participation, these kids are mapping out new strategies for negotiating around and through globalization, intellectual property struggles, and media conglomeration.[11]

In Jenkins's view, the fan fiction text gestures ultimately towards a new democratic global politics of participation through consumption communities.[12] On the other hand, in a less than celebratory vein, Cornel Sandross understands the fan text (in general, not specifically *Harry Potter* fan fiction) as possessing a superlative fluidity of textual boundaries at the level of both production and consumption, which makes it impossible to outline an aesthetic for such a text. To Sandross this is not so much indicative of emancipative possibilities, as indicative of entrapment in banality and Marcusean one-dimensionality – 'one-dimensionality arising out of a lack of alternative resources or "enabling devices" of the self'.[13]

On a related but different note, the constitutional fluidity and communal negotiability of the fan fiction text necessitate a less conventionally text-centred approach on the part of scholars who reckon with fan fiction – and, therefore, introduce a level of fluidity in critical practice itself, and call for reconsideration of critical conventions and academic categories. This is expressed succinctly by Busse and Hellekson:

> As fan academics, we inhabit a fluid space that needs to be continuously revised and reconsidered, where new influences, both internal and external, change not only the object of study, but our theoretical and methodological frameworks. Like the fantext, with its complementary and contradictory readings of the source text, the academic text seeking to describe and understand fandom also creates a work in progress as it attempts a larger understanding of fan culture.[14]

So from a literary studies point of view, the fan fiction text presents an *object* for literary analysis which doesn't subscribe to the conventional form of objects within the purview of that academic discipline, and by doing so puts pressure on the existing presumptions of the discipline of literary studies itself. It seems to call for what are at present marginal strategies (indeed, barely conceptualised as *strategies*) within the disciplinary practice of literary criticism: something like 'distant reading' (being able to assimilate the characteristics of a superlative textual field by not undertaking close reading),[15] or 'autoethnography' (fan fiction writers becoming critics/critics becoming fan fiction community participants), seem more to the purpose here.[16]

Given the plethora and complexities of the *Harry Potter* fan fiction text, one way in which it may be engaged here is in a symptomatic manner: i.e. it can be engaged insofar as it is symptomatic of something pertinent to this study. The world-to-text thrust itself recommends a foothold: the *Harry Potter* fan fiction text can be accounted insofar as it presents strands which exemplify *interventions* in worldly concerns, and interventions which disrupt the original *Harry Potter* text to spread the flow of the *Harry Potter* fluid text. In picking up such strands, this chapter continues the argument that has unfolded over the last three and yet in a different direction, and at the same time brings this study to an admittedly open-ended conclusion. The three strands that I pick up briefly below have to do with *Harry Potter* fan fiction, first, in relation to children's literacy, second, insofar as they play on homosexual desire, and third, in relation to its crossing-over into published book form in China. A few concluding remarks on the bearing that this discussion of *Harry Potter* fan fiction has on the understanding of fandom in general brings this study to a close.

Literacy – slash – China

Harry Potter fan fiction and literacy

That computer-mediated communication among fans evidences considerable creativity was observed even in the earliest fan communities: Nancy Baym, for instance, examined this with reference to exchanges on the USENET rec.arts.tv.soaps site for television soap fans, established in 1984.[17] The notion that fan fiction internet sites are a positive pedagogic environment for learning basic literacy for children was asserted influentially by Henry Jenkins in 2004 in his *Technology Review* blog entitled 'Why Heather Can Write: Not everything kids learn from popular culture is bad for them, some of the best writing culture takes place outside the classroom in online communities'.[18] Jenkins later expanded on this in *Convergence Culture*.[19] This argument was principally woven around the development from 1999 of the *Harry Potter* Daily Prophet fan website by Heather Lawver (then 14 years old). Like the fantasy magic world newspaper *Daily Prophet*, this site takes the form of an online newspaper, with children around the world assuming magic personalities and contributing reports about magic issues in the *Harry Potter*-related magic worlds that they have imagined in their – and in terms of their – specific locations and lives. Though anchored to the original *Harry Potter* text, the *Daily Prophet* website works by exploiting a lack or gap in it which has been noted in the previous two chapters: the predominantly British confines of the Muggle–Magic world in the original text leaves the magic world beyond open to speculation. The *Daily Prophet* website is effectively a participatory communication environment in which children as *Harry Potter* fans worldwide feel encouraged to read and write, to be communally creative fan fiction writers and readers. Its success was evidenced when Warner Brothers sought to control the use of the Harry Potter brand in fan websites by issuing notices ordering the closure of such websites in 2000–1. The *Daily Prophet* network initiated the Defense against the Dark Arts organisation, which called for a boycott of all Warner Brother products, and Warner Brothers capitulated by largely withdrawing the notices – the so-called 'Potter wars'. In *Convergence Culture* Jenkins extended his 2004 argument about the *Daily Prophet* website (it also picked up on other *Harry Potter* fan fiction sites, such as FictionAlley and Sugar Quill) by linking it squarely with its role in the 'Potter wars'. The latter seemed to confirm Jenkins's sense that children were taking possession of their creativity against establishment disapprobation. He regarded this as a positive step, and consistent with children taking possession of their education, by developing literacy – reading and writing skills – through participation and interaction in online fan fiction communities (affinity spaces). Jenkins regarded the latter as providing an alternative pedagogic space, possibly a more effective one, than the establishment pedagogic space of the classroom:

> Educators like to talk about 'scaffolding,' the ways that a good pedagogical process works in a step-by-step fashion, encouraging kids to try out new skills that build on those they have already mastered, providing support for these new steps until the learner feels sufficient confidence to take them on their own. In the classroom, scaffolding is provided by the teacher. In a participatory culture, the entire community takes on some responsibility for helping newbies find their way.[20]

And further:

> It is not clear that the successes of affinity spaces can be duplicated by simply incorporating similar activities into the classroom. Schools impose a fixed leadership hierarchy (including very different roles for adults and teens).... Schools have less flexibility to support writers at very different stages of their development. Even the most progressive schools set limits on what students can write compared to the freedom they enjoy on their own.[21]

Jenkins's point was that though fan fiction writers and readers may not necessarily be looking to learn, this is nevertheless a good medium for learning to *happen* because participants feel more in control, and fan fiction should therefore be encouraged. Soon after, Jenkins and his assistants published the McArthur Foundation report *Confronting the Challenges of Participatory Culture* (2006),[22] which argued that such technological resources as fan fiction sites, blogging, etc. should be garnered for new literacy purposes, which includes both basic literacy and media literacy in a cohesive fashion. The report also gave a defence of fan fiction writing against accusations of being derivative and unoriginal, by drawing attention to analogues with the respectable art form of the collage.[23] Meanwhile, since 2004, considerable academic research appeared, supporting the notion that such participative learning through online communities is an effective way of developing literacy skills, and especially through online fan fiction communities, in the work of Rebecca Black and others.[24] In the interim, the possibility of developing literacy through online fan fiction communities has been embraced by some of these communities, markedly the one that Jenkins had used as a case study to set out the argument in 2004. By 2008 the *Daily Prophet* website carried a paper entitled 'Making Progress toward Revolution' addressed to fellow *Harry Potter* fans:

> Let's make this the biggest grassroots campaign in the history of *Harry Potter* fandom! In 2001, The Daily Prophet and its fellow Potter fans were responsible for making huge waves on the international stage and setting legal precedents that protect all fans to this day through the infamous Potter War campaign. We can do this again, but for an even greater cause – literacy.[25]

On the website a letter from Heather Lawver also appeared, addressed to adults, explaining what the *Daily Prophet* is trying to accomplish in the following words:

> J. K. Rowling's Harry Potter series, I believe, merely opens the door to diving into a good book. By creating an online 'newspaper' with articles that lead the readers to believe this fanciful world of Harry Potter to be real, this opens the mind to explaining books, diving into the characters, and analyzing great lit. By developing the mental ability to analyze the written word at a young age, children will find a love for reading unlike any other. By creating this faux world we are learning, creating, and enjoying ourselves in a friendly utopian society.[26]

What Jenkins had observed as possibly happening in fan fiction online communities is here sought to be achieved actively by fans – or at least their spokesperson – in such communities.

A few pertinent observations about this argument for the possible literacy-enhancing function of fan fiction communities are worth making here. First, the argument is articulated through rhetorical tactics which are suggestive of normatively-loaded progressiveness. It is more these rhetorical strategies than evidence and analysis that push the argument forward. So, the neat oppositions that Jenkins sets up work more by the over-determination of oppositional placement than by meaningfully referring to anything: the hierarchical 'classroom' versus the communal sharing of online fan communities, the teacher/parent-controlled environment versus the alternative anti-establishment fan community, learners taking possession of their learning versus the imposition of learning from above. It is not clear where this 'classroom' is; it seems to be a

synecdoche for all institutional pedagogy. It is not clear whether allowances can be made for formal and informal modes of learning and
development which occur *within* all pedagogic institutions, inside and
outside classrooms. No one participating in a classroom – students or
teachers – seems to be consulted about what happens in a classroom and
why he or she is there; it is characterised by a series of assertions. While
the structure of online communities is outlined briefly, the everyday
life of such communities is not touched. The possibility and reality of
fractiousness, misunderstanding, misinformation, hierarchies, authori-
tarianism in online communities are not examined. Both the classroom
and the fan fiction community seem to exist in a political and economic
vacuum. It is the rhetoric of opposition, the discourse of alternative
spaces, the radical touch of self-possession and self-determination which
push the argument. By the time Lawver (as fan leader and as exemplary
child speaking to adults) sets about disseminating the argument within
her fan fiction forum, the rhetorical associations are crystallised and
foregrounded in an inflated verbiage which is reminiscent of and yet
detached from political application: 'progress . . . revolution', 'grassroots
campaign', 'greater cause', 'friendly utopian society'. The whole thing
sweeps along by an uncomplicated equation of fan fiction reading and
writing being equated with developing literacy skills (without pausing
on the conditions in which these may be equated) and by an uncomplicated equation of *Harry Potter* fans with children (as uncomplicated as
assuming that the original *Harry Potter* text is children's literature) – both
unexamined equations enabling a pat insertion of worldly concerns
about children's education and basic literacy into the *Harry Potter* fan
fiction text and phenomenon, with the effect of garnering normative
approval for fan fiction online communities *in general*. Second, in an
interesting way the polyvocal expansion of the *Harry Potter* Magic–Muggle
world by exploiting a gap of the original text which is *practised* on the
Daily Prophet website (and arguably many fan fiction websites) – and
the implicit subversions and interrogations of the originals that therefore
occur there – are constantly countered by harnessing them to an *enunciated assertion* of the normative position of the *Harry Potter* original text.
The latter serves as a frame for containing the former, and imposing
communal order in the online community – if the normative assertion
is accepted as an article of faith, any amount of critical and creative
practice and subversion can be accepted. This is apparent in the contradictions of Lawver's rousing calls for literacy: here the contradictions
of using fantasy as reality to a 'good' end struggle with the notion of
developing *analytical* skills. More importantly, these calls are predicated

on the understanding that any *Harry Potter* book is *a priori* a 'good book' or 'great lit' (a sort of Arnoldian touchstone) which will lead to a taste for and discernment of the good and the great. There are various ways in which this underlying article of faith may work in *Harry Potter* fan fiction communities which are not considered in the celebratory discourse of the above argument. It is possible that, despite allowances for the variety of readings and rewritings implicit in fan fiction stories, at the level of literacy the aspiration is to write as well as or in the style of the original *Harry* Potter text, thus setting an unquestionable standard for literacy. It is also possible that since the very structures of interactiveness in fan fiction communities (the 'scaffolding' of affective learning) that Jenkins lauds are premised on and made possible by the given, unquestioningly accepted, normative place of the original *Harry Potter* text, the use of those structures by specific fan writers and readers actually serve to constantly confirm that normativeness and to homogenise views of that original text as a rigid, unnegotiable entity. That this is likely to occur in fan communities was observed in another context (science fiction fandom) by Andrea MacDonald: 'Through computer networks, fans easily share their conceptualization of fictional universes, encouraging a more uniform understanding of the fictive universe.'[27] Third, the development of the above argument could be thought of as occurring amidst a renegotiation of fan identities: essentially, Jenkins takes certain examples of fan fiction writers, such as Lawver, and constructs them in a particular way, and then the fan fiction writer (Lawver again) strives to subscribe to that construction. It is worth asking to what extent something implicit in online fan fiction communities has been discerned in the above and to what extent the nature of such fan fiction communities has been altered through the above. And it is also worth pondering whether Jenkins's position and authority as expert have been devoted to describing an existing state of affairs or instrumentalised to moulding a new one.

The second of these observations is relevant also to the other two areas of the *Harry Potter* fan fiction phenomenon that I go into briefly below.

Harry Potter slash fan fiction

Much of the *Harry Potter* fan fiction that has appeared online explores sexual relations by imagining (often improbable) pairings of *Harry Potter* characters.[28] This is generally true of the fictional productions of different fandoms, but it probably has a particular resonance in the *Harry Potter* fandom. Since gender and sexuality are depicted along conservative lines in the original *Harry Potter* text (as I argued in 2002), the potentialities of magic in this regard are kept very low key (almost nothing apart from a few love potions are mooted) in that original text. But the concept of magic inevitably lends itself to exploitation along the lines of sexual drives and fantasies, and it is hardly surprising that the gaps in the original here have been rich resources for fan fiction. In keeping with fan fiction generally, almost as many works of *Harry Potter* fan fiction have been of the so-called 'slash' (describing same-sex pairings and sexual relations) as of the 'het' (describing heterosexual pairings and relations) variety. In a survey of *Harry Potter* slash fan fiction in 2006, Marianne MacDonald noted that: 'Although the "het" stories may still outnumber the slash stories, this would be a close call. Indeed the volume of Harry Potter slash fiction is rather staggering. A conservative estimate would peg the number at over 25,000 stories posted on the Internet, but the real total could be closer to 100,000.'[29] As with slash fan fiction generally, a majority of *Harry Potter* slash focuses on male-male pairings, and – as confirmed by a survey conducted by MacDonald – are written by women in their twenties. Exploration of the phenomenon of male-male slash fan fiction being produced by women pre-dates the case of *Harry Potter*,[30] and is an issue I don't go into here.

The impetus for slash *Harry Potter* fan fiction can be conceptualised along the lines of 'queering' the 'heteronomrativeness heroism' of the original *Harry Potter* text, as Hugh and Wallace have put it.[31] In an autoethnographic vein, this sort of impetus is described succinctly by the academic and *Harry Potter* slash fiction writer Ika Willis:

> It is through writing fan fiction that a fan can, firstly, make space for her own desires in a text which may not at first sight provide the resources to sustain them; and, secondly, recirculate the reoriented text among other fans without attempting to close the text on the 'truth' of her reading: but these desires and these demands circulate unpredictably, in ways conditioned by the discontinuities between the author's world and the fictional world, or by (for example) cross-gendered or multiply gendered identification.[32]

Willis demonstrates the workings of this impetus both by reading the ostensible absence and possibility of discerning implicit queerness in the original *Harry Potter* text and by reading two of her own slash *Harry Potter* stories as efforts at inserting or opening a queer space in Hogwarts. But this account is not of the slash fan fiction writer *as* fan, but of the queer theorist/activist who follows up a critique of the popular cultural original text by capitalising on its fandom and fan fiction communities – to bring to awareness and act on a queer political agenda. This is not discernibly the writer who is a fan writing fan fiction; this is a writer who writes fan fiction to be able to exploit the fan fiction online space for a specific political purpose.

While the insertion of the absent or silenced or coded (depending how one reads) queer desire in the original *Harry Potter* text with a view to assuming a political position might motivate some slash fiction writers, the relation to the original is arguably more complicated. MacDonald has suggested that the popularity of the Draco–Harry and Snape–Harry pairings in fan fiction shows 'an underlying humanism on the part of the slash writers in their desire to reconcile two enemies'.[33] If that is so, it also shows an underlying desire for reconciliation rather than confrontation as the mode for resolving the conflicts of the original text. In other ways too, slash fan fiction writers and readers seem to express as much a desire for reconciliation with the original text as sensitivity to its contradictions – in fact, paradoxically, the tendency is to *confirm* the normativeness of the original by digging into it, inserting into it, against its grain. In fact, often the apparently oppositional movement of slash fan fiction is actually expressive of a desire for containment within and recognition by the original text, the canon-holders, the authoritative author, the establishment underlying the *Harry Potter* phenomenon. The joy with which slash fans receive almost slightingly insignificant signs and gestures from that canonical proprietorship-exercising heart of the phenomenon attests to this. Along these lines a 2004 paper by Green and Guinery thus observed:

> Latterly, there is evidence that custodians of canon may be making subtle overtures to creators of fanon.... This sense within the fan community – that the holders of the canon have complimented them through an intertextual reference – is much prized and builds the momentum of the fan engagement.... Specifically, Harry/Draco slash fans have delighted in the hint of a blown kiss from Draco Malfoy to Harry (as Draco sends Harry an origami bird/graffiti message in a Defence Against the Dark Arts class in *Harry Potter and the Prisoner of Azkaban* [film]) as an acknowledgement of their cultural contribution to the Harry Potter phenomenon.[34]

In a similar vein, Rowling's 'revelation' in October 2007 that Dumbledore was gay and was in love with Gindelwald was generally received uncritically by fans and academic fan-watchers such as Tossenberger.[35] The *Observer* report on this concluded on an interesting note: 'Amazed by the warm reaction of the audience, Rowling, on her first US tour in seven years, joked: "Just imagine the fan fiction now".[36]

Chinese *Harry Potter* fan fiction in print

A certain amount of media interest in the US and UK has been devoted to *Harry Potter* 'counterfeits' or 'fakes' in China. These texts are derivative of the original *Harry Potter* text in the same way as fan fiction, but have appeared in print rather than simply online and may therefore be understood as produced to make profits, whereas online fan fiction in itself often explicitly eschews any such motive. Consequently, the media discussion has been characteristically dismissive. A couple of *New York Times* write-ups in August 2007, for instance, dealt with these as symptomatic of Chinese disregard for copyright regulation, and briefly outlined the plots of some 'fakes' by showing them up as evidence of bizarre Chinese tastes (the brief outlines were deliberately designed to make them appear completely nonsensical).[37] It is difficult to distinguish whether these were simply expressing moral outrage about copyright infringement in China or scoffing at Chinese fan fiction writers and readers in an implicitly racist fashion. Howard W. French observed: 'Here, the global *Harry Potter* publishing phenomenon has mutated into something altogether Chinese: a combination of remarkable imagination and startling industriousness, all placed in the service of counterfeiting, literary fraud and copyright violation.'[38] Perhaps French wasn't aware that such derivative *Harry Potter* fiction is legion in the US and elsewhere in online forums, that the Chinese are therefore not unique in writing and reading these (it is not 'altogether Chinese'), and that the imagination and industriousness in these are not '*all* placed in the service' of those dire, antisocial ends. All the Chinese 'fakes' named in the *New York Times* articles are fan fiction which appeared in print form after initially appearing online, and are distinguished from fan fiction elsewhere simply by virtue of appearing in print. Whether they appeared as such with the fan authors' consent, or whether the authors have profited from them, is not clear. It is, however, worth noting that the texts thus identified did not appear in print *as* fan fiction – the printed versions did not declare them as such. A 2006 paper by Lena Henningsen had already tried to engage with them 'not simply as an economic and legal dispute, but as a cross-cultural and multidimensional phenomenon',[39] which makes sense since they are as much within the *Harry Potter* fluid text as any fan fiction. With close attention to two such Chinese 'counterfeits' – the notorious *Harry Potter and Leopard-Walk-up-to-Dragon* (Hali Bote yu buozoulong), largely plagiarised from Tolkien's *The Hobbit*, and *Harry Potter and the Porcelain Doll* (Hali Bote yu ciwawa), both published as books in 2002[40] – Henningsen traces the Chinese and western traits in each. She finds that in both books Chinese readers are likely to find associations with the form of traditional knight-errant fiction (wuxia xiaoshuo), as well as resonances with some Chinese ancient and modern classics. Both have, at different levels, comments pertinent to contemporary China: the former touches on official corruption in a way that would be particularly meaningful in China, and the latter reads like a tourist guide for China and expresses the kind of nationalist sentiments that are current. Henningsen concludes that:

> the debate on the *Harry Potter* fakes should not be conceived as a matter of copyright infringement only. Rather, the counterfeit texts offer a number of different readings... – and thus offer different interpretations of *Harry Potter* and different visions of the world: Western dominance versus Chinese moral and strategic superiority; and the West as the source of evil or as a location for imagination and as the Other. These readings offer a better understanding not only of the *Harry Potter* phenomenon but also of the Chinese reality and its perception by both Chinese readers and authors.[41]

Chinese *Harry Potter* online fan fiction could be regarded as peculiarly Chinese in much the way that Henningsen understands the printed 'fakes' to be. The 'fakes' are distinguished as 'fakes' only by the print form and by their lack of acknowledgement of being fan fiction. That the switch from electronic publication to print publication can drive such a powerful categorical imperative into the *Harry Potter* fluid text, and such a morally loaded one, is worth pausing on. It says a great deal more about the contemporary legal and political control of the material forms of textual production and consumption than about what is contained, so to say, *within* the fluid text. But there is more to the transfer from online to print than that, and here too developments in the *Harry Potter* fluid text in China are indicative. More recently, the prestigious China Youth Publishing House (Zhonguo qingnian chubanshe) has been publishing as printed books some of the most popular *Harry Potter* online fan fiction. These are explicitly presented as fan fiction, and are based on valid agreements with their fan authors (usually teenage women). The two I have examined – *As Fallen as an Angel* (Xiang tianshi yiyang duoluo), 2005, and *Introduction of Plum Blossoms* (Meihuayin), 2005[42] – are quality paperback productions, in a consistent format and design. These present interesting contrasts and similarities, and are representative of a range. Both revolve around the Draco–Hermione pairing. The former is set entirely within Britain and with the original text characters, and is written in a style that would immediately suggest a foreign context to the Chinese reader (free of set phrases and quotations from Chinese literature, using a somewhat 'pretentious' register). Debates current in the Chinese media, however, resonate with some of the extended conversations in it, especially with regard to Harry's moral responsibilities and Draco's freedom. The latter book inserts a key Chinese character in Hogwarts, which is also a means for inserting a Chinese concept of magic and even takes the action to China. It is written in an obviously Chinese style – idiomatic, smoothly expressed, with occasional quotations from Chinese poetry. Both are reminiscent of Taiwanese romances which are immensely popular in mainland China. What distinguishes these quite standard fan fiction works in print from their online versions is not the textual content, but the manner in which they are *framed* in print. In particular, both appear with a 'Publisher's Announcement' (the same in both). This gives a definition of fan fiction, explains in what sense these could be regarded as derivative of the original *Harry Potter* text and in what sense they are original, and encourages potential readers to go through Rowling's books first (thus, arguably, seeking to expand their market rather than interlope). More interestingly, this also gives a reason for taking these seriously – not in their own terms, but as data which reveal something about fandom and about the current (in China 'post-1980s') generation:

> Another reason for publishing Harry Potter fan novels is to sieve, study and ponder the enormous phenomenon of Harry Potter fans, their thoughts and minds, the tide of the popularity of Harry Potter, and to thus better understand the psyche of the generation that has grown up with Harry Potter.... By publishing these novels we provide research data for society to be able to check the pulse of the young generation, study the direction of their thinking, and thereby guide their development. As the publisher with responsibility for providing a service toward the development of youth, this is our responsibility and ultimate aim.
>
> (translated from the Chinese)[43]

In other words, just by becoming available in the print medium it is expected that fan fiction will expand outside fan communities and come under the purview of academics, policy-makers and others with a scholarly interest in Chinese youth culture. The resonances of this purpose with the workshop debates in Peking University reported in the previous chapter are unmistakable. The print form deliberately takes the fluid *Harry Potter* fan text into establishment and institutional enclaves where conventional books still reigns supreme.

Fans

Studies of fans and fandom have gone through an interesting set of moves over the last couple of decades,[44] in which the last decade has seen quite a bit of the developing argument woven around the *Harry Potter* phenomenon. One significant strand in this has been occupied by attempts to conceive and reconceive fans as politically active agents in a consumer capitalist environment – increasingly, the world. This strand can be traced from, for instance, Lawrence Grossberg's 1992 characterisation of the political agency of fans in the following words:

> because the fan speaks for and to the question of authority, or from within an ideology of excess (which constructs a certain critical distance), the politics of the fan never entails merely the celebration of every investment or every mattering map. The fan's relation to culture in fact opens up a range of political possibilities and it is often on the field of affective relations that political struggle relates with popular concerns. In fact, the affective is a crucial dimension of the organization of political struggle[45]

to the following 2007 observations by Henry Jenkins – undoubtedly the academic who has invested most in activating the political agency of fans within an emancipative register – in view of recent commercial and economic commentaries:

> None of these commentators on the new economy are using the terms 'fan', 'fandom', or 'fan culture', yet their modes rest on the same social behaviors and emotional commitments that fan scholars have been researching over the past several decades. The new multipliers are simply a less geeky version of the fan – fans who don't wear rubber Spock ears, fans who didn't live in their parents' basement, fans who have got a life. In other words, they are fans who don't fit the stereotypes. These writers are predicting, and documenting, a world where what we are calling 'fan culture' has a real economic and cultural impact . . . [46]

Despite Jenkins's upbeat, future-gazing tone, the direction is clear: from the idea of the fan as an eccentric entity which can be activated and attributed political agency with effect on the establishment (in a 'political struggle') to the idea of the fan as a normal presence that is so completely co-opted and embedded in the establishment that it becomes meaningless to even name it a 'fan'. It is likely that the critical discourse which has tried to make common cause with the fan by observing/constructing/ becoming/deconstructing the fan is itself complicit with this process.

The hopes and failures of the critical discourse that plays the idea of the fan with political effect does so by exploiting a paradox that has been most cogently articulated in Matt Hill's autoethnographic exploration of the interfaces of academic and fan discourse. The paradox rests on the perception that the fan is at the core of a series of binary opposites that structure much critical discourse. One of the most obvious of these is the positioning of the fan between consumerism and resistance:

> While simultaneously 'resisting' norms of capitalist society and its rapid turnover of novel commodities, fans are also implicated in these very economic and cultural processes. Fans are, in one sense, 'ideal consumers'...since their consumption habits can be very highly predicted by the culture industry, and are likely to remain stable. But fans also express anti-commercial beliefs (or 'ideologies', we might say, since these beliefs are not entirely in alignment with the cultural situation in which fans find themselves).[47]

Hill proceeds to place fandom between other such binaries: community/ hierarchy, fantasy/reality, cult/culture, etc. This attempt at allocating complexity and fluid boundaries to the idea, which has been so enthusiastically irrigated by critical cultural theory, is a valuable one, mainly because it presents an optimistically misconceived tactic. Hill consistently presumes the in-betweenness of the fan, the ideational or conceptual space of the fan is *between* those polarities. It is a great deal more likely that the fan is actually always *before the fact*, before any critical enterprise along the lines of either binary pole, already there, available, ready to be observed/constructed/emulated/deconstructed in whatever direction critical discourse turns, seeping through the structures of critical practice itself. The academic engagement with fandom tries to make something of fandom that suits it from something that is already there in an unwieldy fashion. Depending on the critical expectation, the fan therefore appears and disappears in the span of two decades, flickers with promise and dims into normality, through the structures of cultural critical practice itself.

The *a priori* quality of the fan could be thought of as reflexive of the *a priori* presumptions which actuate fans and fandom. Even the very cursory account of *Harry Potter* fan fiction above conveys a sense of some of these presumptions. The immense creativity evident in fan fiction that stretches the *Harry Potter* fluid text constantly and in unexpected ways is premised on the normativisation of the *Harry Potter* original text. Even where the fan text seems to undermine the core assumptions and interrogate the basis of that original text, it is still with its normativeness unquestioningly reiterated as an article of faith or as an act of homage. The normativised object is pushed so far posterior to the practice of fandom that it cannot be dismissed as a norm: all creativity and subcultural activity and communal identification take place on the condition of the original text's normativeness. I have touched on this in the context of the argument about literacy and fan fiction writing. The normativeness also expresses itself in an anterior direction: in a desire to enter the canon, in the associative logic which super-signifies the authority of the author, the authorised corporations, and predictably and constantly consume their production and reproduction of the original text. That slash fans are beguiled by the little hints of approbation they perceive from Rowling and Warner Brothers and confirm themselves through these, as noted above, is symptomatic of the anterior desire of the fan for incorporation within the norm. The authorities that perceivably speak for the norm and from within the establishment can therefore easily set up a constant self-moulding and self-production of fans. All it needs is a bit of encouragement. When the academic fan guru Jenkins says an encouraging word or two about fan communities by taking up the virtuous cause of literacy, *Daily Prophet* fans accept it wholesale and turn it into a drive, a cheering agenda for 'revolution'. In the course of engaging this they may well question Jenkins's argument and critically explore the notion of literacy, but only after first normativising the original *Harry Potter* text and author and associated producers; second, the guru status of Jenkins and his disciples; and third, the pursuit of literacy as a social good – as if these are a coherent whole on which all else can be constructed. Just as suavely, fans can be encouraged into self-production and self-moulding by mainstream corporations. Prestigious publishers, in China for instance, can do this by deliberately making fan fiction the subjects and objects of their production and marketing; all they have to do is acknowledge the normative position of *Harry Potter*. Other corporations do it more tacitly and perhaps more effectively. A small instance of this is provided in observations by Mitchell and Reid-Walsh on the Warner Brothers website for fans before the release of the *Philosopher's Stone* film. The latter offered fans an expensive interactive environment with facilities for mutual engagement, role-playing, games and structures for the exclusion of *Harry Potter* non-readers, which in effect manufactured an online fan community and 'created an audience for the film before the product yet existed'.[48] Fans are reactive in every conceivable direction and can stretch the *Harry Potter* fluid text in every conceivable direction, but only *after the fact* of normativising that original *Harry Potter* text and accordingly placing it on an unassailable pedestal. Critical engagement with fandom is *after the fact* of fans being such. Every kind of manipulation is possible of ideas and products and consumption practices and political aspirations with fans so long as fans are already given and available as fans.

The world-to-text inferences made above from *Harry Potter* fan fiction are about fandom in general, and reflect on the world in general. These are not specifically concerned with children as fans or worldly concerns to do primarily with children. Focusing on children particularly in this context – in the way Jenkins does apropos the *Daily Prophet* website – is still conditional to the world in general, pervasively an adult world. In fact, it must be clear from this and the preceding two chapters that the *Harry Potter* fluid text, and therefore the *Harry Potter* phenomenon, has mostly to do with adults, and children, if they appear at all, are constructed in keeping with adult concerns and prerogatives. That, for instance, the Chinese construction of childhood in the context of the *Harry Potter* fluid text there coheres with wide-ranging socio-cultural changes in China at large has already been noted. Noting the all-encompassing complicity of adult interests in the *Harry Potter* fluid text takes me back, in a way, to the point where this project began when I started in 2002. At that time, arguing that the *Harry Potter* text and phenomenon have more to do with adults than with children was a relatively laborious business. Several chapters had to be devoted to making the argument. Interestingly, now this is barely necessary: the adult occupation of the *Harry Potter* text and phenomenon is not particularly hidden. This is especially clear when the part of fan fiction in the *Harry Potter* fluid text is in focus. Judging from a cursory survey of *Harry Potter* fan fiction websites, at least half are by definition adult and deal with adult concerns and sexually-explicit material. But even for the *Harry Potter* original text in itself, the subterfuge of thinking of it as children's literature and of its adult readers as deviants is beginning to be abandoned. In the early 2000s, much discomfort was caused by critics such as A. S. Byatt, Jennie Bristow and Stephen Pollard[49] who suggested that the adult readership of the *Harry Potter* books was a symptom of the infantilisation of contemporary society. They took it for granted that the whole *Harry Potter* phenomenon is a children's affair, wherein the presence of adult interlopers is a noteworthy and rather disgraceful quirk. It is now clear that the adult presence is not so much a deviation as the norm of the *Harry Potter* fluid text and phenomenon and is, by most indications, taking explicit possession of the original text itself. As the final volume of the series appeared in 2007, most of the indicators picked up by observers pointed to *Harry Potter* becoming ever more overtly an area of adult consumption. A Pew Research Centre survey showed that: 'Those aged 65 and older are among the least likely to buy the book (11% say someone in the household will buy the book). Among those aged 50–64, however, 26% say they have plans to buy the new book.'[50] For that age group that is a remarkably large number. The UK retailing chain Waterstone's reportedly found that there was a steady increase in pre-orders of adult cover *Harry Potter* books as the series progressed: for the initial editions the figure stood at 15 per cent of pre-orders, by the sixth volume it had risen to 23 per cent, and by the last book it was well over 45 per cent.[51] Perhaps most indicatively, a Book Marketing Limited survey of 2004 (questioning 10,000 individuals aged 12–74) found that more than 60 per cent of the *Harry Potter* books in 2003 were bought by adults. Moreover, as a summary of the survey in the *Bookseller* put it: 'The figures also suggest that Harry Potter has not helped grow the children's books market. Instead, sales to children under 12 years old are reported to have fallen in each of the last three years.'[52] Evidently, *Harry Potter* in all its aspects – as original text, as fluid text, as phenomenon – is a predominantly adult area and intricately entwined with the adult world, or the world at large.

The conclusion that this chapter, and this study as a whole, reaches is not a particularly complicated one and can be summed up in a couple of sentences. From a world-to-text perspective the balance of the world as a globally networked negotiation between regulated production/consumption for the profit of the few and unregulated fluid textuality for the benefit of the many is perceivable in the celebratory creativity of fans. From a text-to-world perspective unthinkingness, in the sense I explored in 2002, continues to thrive and expand and become consolidated within that balance.

Notes

Chapter 1

1. The following editions of the *Harry Potter* series are used for this essay: J.K. Rowling, *Harry Potter and the Philosopher's Stone* (London: Bloomsbury, 1997); J.K. Rowling, *Harry Potter and the Chamber of Secrets* (London: Bloomsbury, 1998); J.K. Rowling, *Harry Potter and the Prisoner of Azkaban* (London: Bloomsbury, 1999); and J.K. Rowling, *Harry Potter and the Goblet of Fire* (London: Bloomsbury, 2000). Different publishers and countries have different images on the covers of the *Harry Potter* books. A country-by-country view of book covers is available at www.openflame.com/harrypotter/book_covers.shtml. Most of these images are similar to those on the original Bloomsbury editions.
2. See Wolfgang Iser on the 'dialectical structure of reading' in *The Implied Reader: Patterns of Communication in Prose Fiction from Bunyan to Beckett* (Baltimore: Johns Hopkins University Press, 1974), p. 294.
3. Wolfgang Iser, *The Act of Reading: A Theory of Aesthetic Response* (London: Routledge & Kegan Paul, 1978), p. 34.
4. Stanley Fish's notion of interpretive communities and interpretive strategies is best given in Chapter 1 ('Introduction, or How I Stopped Worrying and Learned to Love Interpretation') and Chapter 6 ('Interpreting the *Variorum*') of his *Is There a Text in this Class?: The Authority of Interpretive Communities* (Cambridge Mass.: Harvard University Press, 1980).
5. See, in this context, Stanley Fish, 'Why No One's Afraid of Wolfgang Iser', in *Doing What Comes Naturally: Change, Rhetoric, and the Practice of Theory in Literary and Legal Studies* (Oxford: Clarendon, 1989), pp. 68–86; and Wolfgang Iser, on Fish in 'Interview 42', *Prospecting: From Reader Response to Literary Anthropology* (Baltimore: Johns Hopkins University Press, 1989), pp. 66–9.
6. For attempts at coming to grips with the actual reader see Norman Holland's *Five Readers Reading* (New Haven: Yale University Press, 1975), and David Bleich's *Subjective Criticism* (Baltimore: Johns Hopkins University Press, 1978).
7. Terry Eagleton, *Against the Grain: Essays 1975–1985* (London: Verso, 1986).
8. Jack Zipes, *Sticks and Stones: The Troublesome Success of Children's Literature from Slovenly Peter to Harry Potter* (New York: Routledge, 2001), pp. 170–2, explains why and what Zipes calls the *Harry Potter* 'phenomenon'. What this essay considers this phenomenon as consisting in is elucidated in Chapter 3.

Chapter 2

1. Dick Lynch, 'The Magic of *Harry Potter*', *Advertising Age* 72:50, 12 October 2001, p. 26.
2. Quoted in Kera Bolonik, 'A List of Their Own', in *Salon Magazine*, 16 August 2001, at www.salon.com

3. Ibid.
4. The figures given here are mostly available on the NPD web-site at www.NPD.com
5. Amelia Hill, 'Harry Potter Magic Fails to Inspire Young to Read More', *Guardian Unlimited* (www.guardian.co.uk), 5 May 2002.
6. For example, Bill Adler ed., *Kid's Letters to Harry Potter from around the World: An Unauthorized Collection* (New York: Carroll & Graf, 2001); Sharon Moore ed., *We Love Harry Potter* (New York: St. Martin's Griffin, 1999); Sharon Moore ed., *Harry Potter, You're the Best* (New York: Griffin, 2001).
7. Philip Nel, *J.K. Rowling's Harry Potter Novels* (New York: Continuum, 2001), provides a useful introduction to the early spate of reviews of the *Harry Potter* novels in Ch. 3 ('Reviews of the Novels').
8. Andrew Blake, *The Irresistible Rise of Harry Potter* (London: Verso, 2002), pp. 80–1.
9. Most famously, Marshall McLuhan, in *Understanding Media: The Extensions of Man* (London: Routledge & Kegan Paul, 1964), had provided some early explorations on how 'a new electric technology...threatens this ancient technology of literacy built on the phonetic alphabet' (p. 82).

Chapter 3

1. Reportedly Harold Bloom (author of *The Western Canon* [Basingstoke: Macmillan, 1995] and a highly regarded literary critic) said on the PBS interview programme 'Charlie Rose' of the *Harry Potter* books that: 'I think that's not reading because there's nothing there to read. They're just an endless string of clichés. I cannot think that does anyone any good. ... That's not *Wind in the Willows*. That's not *Through the Looking Glass*. ... It's just really slop.' Quoted in Jamie Allen, '"Harry" and Hype', 13 July 2000, www.CNN.com Book News. Also see Harold Bloom, 'Can 35 Million Book Buyers Be Wrong? Yes', *Wall Street Journal* 11 July 2000, A26.
2. Christine Schoefer, in a critical essay on the depiction of women in the *Harry Potter* books, 'Harry Potter's Girl Trouble', 13 January 2000, *Salon Magazine*, www.salon.com, observes: 'I have learned that Harry Potter is a sacred cow. Bringing up my objections has earned me other parents' resentment – they regard me as a heavy-handed feminist with no sense of fun who is trying to spoil a bit of magic they have discovered.' Similarly, Jack Zipes was reportedly severely criticized by callers in a phone-in programme on Minnesota Public Radio's *Midmorning* for expressing scepticism about the quality of the *Harry Potter* books. See 'Not Everybody's Wild About Harry', 19 July 2000, www.citypages.com
3. See 'All Time Best-Selling Children's Book List', edited by Diane Roback, Jason Britton, and compiled by Debbie Hochman Turvey, of 17 December 2001 at www.PublishersWeekly.com, and 'International Best-Seller in 2001 List' of 25 March 2002 at www.PublishersWeekly.com
4. 'Property Boom Keeps Duke Top of Rich List', www.Reuters.co.uk of 7 April, 2002. On J.K. Rowling's earnings from the *Harry Potter* books see also Philip Nel, *Harry Potter Novels*, pp. 71–2.

5. 'Survey – UK Middle Market Companies: Harry Potter Wield His Magic Wand', *Financial Times*, 9 March 2001, at www.FT.com
6. Ibid.
7. Simon Bowers, 'Bloomsbury Predicts Another Magic Year With Harry', *Guardian Unlimited*, 21 March 2002, at www.guardian.co.uk
8. Jim Milliot, 'Profits Jump 27% in Scholastic's Children's Publishing Group', www.PublishersWeekly.com on 9 March 2001.
9. Reported on biz.yahoo.com on 18 February 2002.
10. Reported on *Guardian Unlimited* (www.guardian.co.uk) on 28 February 2002.
11. Reported on www.Reuters.co.uk on 2 April 2001.
12. Reported at investor.cnet.com/investor/news on 30 January 2002.
13. 'Mattel Reports 2002 First Quarter Results,' 18 April 2002 at www.shareholder.com/mattel/.
14. 'Small-Cap Round-Up: 'Harry Potter' Magic Boosts Argonaut Stock', 12 March 2002 at www.Reuters.co.uk
15. 'Potter Creator Supports Lone Parents', *BBC News*, 4 October 2000 at www.bbc.co.uk
16. Reported in the Books section of the *Sunday Times*, 7 January 2001, at www.timesonline.co.uk
17. The auction in Wiltshire story was reported, 'Potter First Edition Nets 6000 Pounds,' on *BBC News* (www.bbc.co.uk) on 15 November 2000; the other, 'Potters Go under the Hammer', on *BBC News* (www.bbc.co.uk) on 12 February 2002.
18. For example, Stephen Brown, 'Harry Potter and the Marketing Mystery', *Journal of Marketing* 66:1, January 2002, 126–30; Stephen Brown, 'Marketing for Muggles', *Business Horizons* 45:1, January/February 2002, 6–14; Geoff Williams, 'Harry Potter and . . . the Trials of Growing a Business . . . the Rewards of Independence and Ownership', *Entrepreneur* February 2001, 62–5. Also see Ch. 2 n. 1 above.
19. See n. 3 above.
20. 'World Wide Wizard', *The Guardian (G2)* 8 November 2001, pp. 14–15.
21. 'Harry Potter Series Tops List of Most Challenged Books for Third Year in a Row', January 2002 at www.ala.org/news; Emma Yates, 'Harry Potter Tops US "Complaint" Chart', *Guardian Unlimited*, 10 January 2002 at www.guardian.co.uk
22. 'Harry Potter Series again Tops List of Most Challenged Books', January 2001 at www.ala.org/news
23. Reported on www.Reuter.co.uk on 28 March 2001.
24. 'Satanic Harry Potter Books Burnt', *BBC News* (www.bbc.co.uk), 31 December 2001.
25. This was posted on www.usccb.org
26. About the banning in UK – 'School Bans Harry Potter', *BBC News* (www.bbc.co.uk), 29 March 2000; in Australia – 'Schools Ban Potter "Occult" Books,' *BBC News* (www.bbc.co.uk), 29 November 2001; in Canada, 'Harry Potter Wins Round Against Canadian Muggles,' www.CNN.com, 20 September 2000; Germany, reported on www.CNN.com on 28 November 2000; UAE – 'Emirates Ban Potter Books', *BBC News* (www.bbc.co.uk), 12 February 2002; Taiwan, 'Harry Potter "Evil," Says Taiwan Church', www.CNN.com, 15 November 2001.

27. For example, Richard Abanes, *Harry Potter and the Bible* (Camp Hill, Penn.: Horizon, 2001); Connie Neal, *What's a Christian to Do With Harry Potter?* (Colorado Springs, Col.: WaterBrook, 2001).
28. See n. 2.
29. 'Harry Potter "Hate-Line" Launched', www.CNN.com, 28 December 2000.

Chapter 4

1. My use of 'our world' here looks forward to the second part of this essay, where in Chapter 11 a fuller treatment of its connotations here is given. For the moment it could be taken to possess something of the resonance that G.W.F. Hegel gave 'our world, our own time' at the end of his lectures in *The Philosophy of History*, trans. J. Sibree (New York: Dover, 1965), p. 442, but in a less triumphant spirit.
2. The qualifications made here are a kind of synthesis of a range of sociological and political theoretical studies. I have given my view of these matters elsewhere: in Suman Gupta, *Corporate Capitalism and Political Philosophy* (London: Pluto, 2002), Ch. 1.
3. In fact, I have some qualifications to make about this, as is explained in Chapter 6.

Chapter 5

1. From Umberto Eco, *The Role of the Reader: Explorations in the Semiotics of Texts* (Bloomington: Indiana University Press, 1979).
2. The quotations here are respectively from ibid., pp. 8 and 9.

Chapter 6

1. There is a large number of short biographies directed toward 9–12 year olds. Relatively extended efforts that are targeted toward older readers include: Sean Smith, *J.K. Rowling: A Biography* (London: Michael O'Mara, 2001), and Marc Shapiro, *J.K. Rowling: The Wizard behind Harry Potter* (New York: Griffin, 2000). Philip Nel, *Harry Potter Novels*, also begins with a well-considered exploration of Rowling's life so far in Ch. 1 ('The Novelist').
2. There is, in fact, a search engine devoted to locating and listing J.K. Rowling interviews at www.geocities.com/aberforths_goat/. Some of these are also listed in Nel, *Harry Potter Novels*, pp. 87–8.
3. Apart from almost every prize for children's writing going, J.K. Rowling has also received honorary degrees from the University of St. Andrews, the University of Exeter, and Napier University in Edinburgh; been awarded an OBE in the Queen's Birthday Honours List in June 2000; and been elected an Honorary Fellow of the Royal Society of Scotland in March 2002.
4. See Ch. 3 n. 4.
5. Gustave Flaubert believed that '*a novelist does not have a right to express his opinion on anything whatever*,' as he wrote to George Sand on 5–6 December 1866. Quoted from his letters in George J. Becker ed., *Documents of Modern Literary Realism* (Princeton: Princeton University Press, 1963), p. 95. Becker's

book contains a range of other statements on the ideal of realism from a range of nineteenth- and early twentieth-century European writers.

6. In James Joyce, *A Portrait of the Artist as a Young Man* (St. Albans: Granada, 1964/1916), the main protagonist (the artist) says the following in expounding a theory of art to a friend: 'The artist, like the God of creation, remains within or behind or beyond or above his handiwork, invisible, refined out of existence, indifferent, paring his fingernails' (pp. 194–5). T.S. Eliot, in his influential essay 'Tradition and the Individual Talent', argued that: 'the poet has, not a 'personality' to express, but a particular medium, which is only a medium and not a personality...' *Selected Essays* (London: Faber, 1932), pp. 19–21. Pound asserted that: 'The arts, literature, poesy, are a science, just as chemistry is a science. Their subject is man, mankind and the individual.' In 'The Serious Artist', *Literary Essays of Ezra Pound*, ed. T.S. Eliot (London: Faber, 1954), p. 42. These (and other such) are often regarded as manifesto statements from these most self-conscious 'modernists' of the early twentieth century.

7. W.K. Wimsatt and M.C. Beardsley, 'The Intentional Fallacy', *Sewanee Review* 54, 1946, pp. 468–88.

8. Roland Barthes, 'The Death of the Author', *Image–Music–Text*, trans. Stephen Heath (London: Fontana, 1977).

9. Karl Miller, *Authors* (Oxford: Clarendon, 1989), p. 164.

10. Sean Burke, *The Death and Return of the Author: Criticism and Subjectivity in Barthes, Foucault and Derrida* (Edinburgh: Edinburgh University Press, 1992), p. 154.

11. The much admired critic Paul de Man's controversial *Le Soir* essays, some of which seemed to express sympathy with fascist views, were rediscovered in the mid-1980s and published in Paul de Man, *Wartime Journalism, 1939–1943* (Lincoln: University of Nebraska Press, 1988). The agonies that these essays caused de Man's friends and like-minded critics is best gauged from the companion collection of critical essays: Werner Hamacher, Neil Hertz, Thomas Keenan eds., *Responses to Paul de Man's Wartime Journalism* (Lincoln: University of Nebraska Press, 1989).

12. T.S. Eliot's alleged anti-Semitism has been periodically rediscovered since the late 1940s, and on each occasion has caused a stir among the many admirers of his poetry and criticism. Most recently this occurred again when Anthony Julius's book *T.S. Eliot, Anti-Semitism, and Literary Form* (Cambridge: Cambridge University Press, 1995) appeared, and was greeted with a storm of impassioned reviews.

13. Binjamin Wilkomirski's *Fragments* appeared in 1995 as the memories of a Holocaust survivor in the death-camps as a child. It later transpired that in fact the author was not who he claimed to be and *Fragments* was an elaborately researched fiction. An account of the whole affair, including the complete *Fragments*, is available in Stefan Maechler, *The Wilkomirski Affair: A Study in Biographical Truth*, trans. John E. Woods (London: Picador, 2001/2000).

14. The book in question was purportedly by Rahila Khan and entitled *Down the Road, Worlds Away* (London: Virago, 1987). Virago specializes in publishing writings by women. It later turned out that the writer was in fact an English man called Toby Forward.

15. Roland Barthes, 'Novels and Children', *Mythologies*, trans. Annette Lavers (London: Vintage, 1972/1957), p. 50.
16. The link between Rowling's position as a single mother and Tory doubts about single mothers and call for family values in Britain in the early 1990s is made in Nel, *Harry Potter Novels*, p. 20.

Chapter 7

1. Tzvetan Todorov, *Genres in Discourse*, trans. Catherine Porter (Cambridge: Cambridge University Press, 1990/1978), pp. 17–18.
2. Tzvetan Todorov, *The Fantastic: A Structural Approach to a Literary Genre*, trans. Richard Howard (Ithaca NY: Cornell University Press, 1973/1970), p. 23.
3. Peter Hunt, 'Defining Children's Literature', in Shiela Egoff, Gordon Stubbs, Ralph Ashley and Wendy Sutton eds., *Only Connect: Readings on Children's Literature*, 3rd edn. (Oxford: Oxford University Press, 1996), pp. 16–17.
4. See Ch. 1 n. 3.
5. George M. O'Har, 'Magic in the Machine Age', *Technology and Culture* 41:4, 2000, pp. 862–3.
6. Roni Natov, 'Harry Potter and the Extraordinariness of the Ordinary', *The Lion and the Unicorn* 25:2 (2001), pp. 312–13.
7. Ibid., p. 323.
8. Jack Zipes, *Sticks and Stones: The Troublesome Success of Children's Literature from Slovenly Peter to Harry Potter* (New York: Routledge, 2001), p. x.
9. Ibid., p. 34.
10. Herbert Marcuse, *One-Dimensional Man* (London: Sphere, 1964).
11. Zipes, *Sticks and Stones*, p. 48.
12. Ibid., pp. 36–7.
13. The paradox of seeing the inviolability of one-dimensional thinking on the one hand, and feeling called upon to find a method of overthrowing it (seeing 'a great refusal') on the other. See Herbert Marcuse, *One-Dimensional Man*, p. 13.
14. Zipes, *Sticks and Stones*, p. 40.
15. Ibid., p. 44.
16. Ibid., in pt. 3 of the manifesto, p. 37.
17. Ibid., p. 65.
18. Kárin Lesnik-Oberstein, 'Essentials: What is Children's Literature? What is Childhood?' in Peter Hunt ed., *Understanding Children's Literature* (London: Routledge, 1999), pp. 15–29.
19. Zipes, *Sticks and Stones*, p. 171.
20. Ibid., p. 172.
21. Ibid., p. 183.
22. Andrew Blake, *The Irresistible Rise of Harry Potter* (London: Verso, 2002), pp. 17–19.
23. Ibid., pp. 29–46.
24. Ibid., pp. 76–80.
25. Ibid., especially Ch. 8.
26. Ibid., Ch. 2 ('Harry Potter and the Reinvention of the Past') and Ch. 9 ('Harry Potter and the Rebranding of Britain').

27. Jacqueline Rose, *The Case of Peter Pan or The Impossibility of Children's Fiction* (Basingstoke: Macmillan, 1984), pp. 1–2.
28. Ibid., p. 2.

Chapter 8

1. Tzvetan Todorov, *The Fantastic*, p. 33 (see Ch. 7 n. 2).
2. Explicitly disallowed in Todorov's definition quoted above. In ibid., Ch. 4 ('Poetry and Allegory') deals with this at some length.
3. Ibid., p. 54.
4. W.R. Irwin, *The Game of the Impossible: A Rhetoric of Fantasy* (Urbana: University of Illinois Press, 1976), p. 9.
5. Rosemary Jackson, *Fantasy: The Literature of Subversion* (London: Routledge, 1981), pp. 3–4.
6. Ibid., p. 9.
7. For example., Stephen Prickett, *Victorian Fantasy* (Hassocks: Harvester, 1979); Nina Auerbach, *Women and the Demon* (Cambridge Mass.: Harvard University Press, 1982); Fred Botting, *Making Monstrous* (Manchester: Manchester University Press, 1991); Margaret L. Carter ed., *'Dracula'* (Ann Arbor: UMI, 1988); W.P. Day, *In the Circles of Fear and Desire* (Chicago: University of Chicago Press, 1985); Christopher Frayling, *Vampyres* (London: Faber, 1991); Ken Gelder, *Reading the Vampire* (London: Routledge, 1988); Robert Mighall, *A Geography of Victorian Gothic Fiction* (Oxford: Oxford University Press, 1999); Ruth Robbins ed., *Victorian Gothic* (Basingstoke: Macmillan, 2000); Julian Wolfreys, *Victorian Hauntings* (Basingstoke: Palgrave, 2002).
8. As in, for example, Jane Donawerth, *Frankenstein's Daughters* (New York: Syracuse University Press, 1997); Casey Fredricks ed., *The Future of Eternity* (Bloomington: Indiana University Press, 1982); Gwyneth Jones, *Deconstructing the Starships* (Liverpool: Liverpool University Press, 1999); Damien Broderick, *Reading by Starlight* (London: Routledge, 1995).
9. Even an indicative list of critical studies of the sub-categories of 'women as fantasy writers' and 'children's fantasies' would inevitably be so long that I won't even try something like notes 7 and 8 above again.
10. Lucie Armitt, *Theorising the Fantastic* (London: Arnold, 1996), p. 3. Having made this point with the help of Armitt here, I should also mention Neil Cornwell's *The Literary Fantastic* (Hemel Hempstead: Harvester Wheatsheaf, 1990), in which the genre distinctions of Todorov are approvingly re-aired; however, insofar as the fantasy form is assessed from the perspective of political effectiveness Cornwell too accepts the subversive qualities of the genre to be more significant than the conservative.
11. Jacqueline Rose, *States of Fantasy* (Oxford: Clarendon, 1996).
12. John Pennington, 'From Elfland to Hogwarts, or the Aesthetic Trouble with Harry Potter', *The Lion and the Unicorn* 26:1 (2002), p. 79.
13. The book in question is Kathryn Hume, *Fantasy and Mimesis: Responses to Reality in Western Literature* (London: Methuen, 1984).
14. Pennington, 'From Elfland to Hogwarts', p. 79.
15. Ibid.

Chapter 9

1. David Jasper, *The Study of Literature and Religion* (Basingstoke: Macmillan, 1989/1992), pp. 138–9.
2. Graham Ward, *Theology and Contemporary Critical Theory* (Basingstoke: Macmillan, 1996/2000), pp. x–xi.
3. See, for example, George H. Smith's *Atheism: The Case against God* (Amherst NY: Prometheus, 1980) and *Why Atheism?* (Amherst NY: Prometheus, 2000); Daniel Harbour's *An Intelligent Person's Guide to Atheism* (London: Duckworth, 2001); Michael Martin's *Atheism: A Philosophical Justification* (Philadelphia PA: Temple University Press, 1992); Jim Herrick, *Against the Faith* (Amherst NY: Prometheus, 1985).
4. The other one, which I read shortly after writing this, is Connie Neal, *What's a Christian to Do with Harry Potter?* (Colorado Springs, Col.: WaterBrook, 2001). Despite its more temperate tone than Abanes's book, in broad structure this fits the arguments made about Abanes's book in this chapter.
5. Richard Abanes, *Harry Potter and the Bible: The Menace Behind the Magick* (Camp Hill, Penn.: Horizon, 2001), pp. 153–4, 191–2, 195, 197–8.
6. Ibid., pp. 41–2, 137.
7. Ibid., pp. 151–2.
8. Elizabeth D. Schafer, *Exploring Harry Potter* (London: Ebury, 2000). For Abanes on Schafer, see ibid., pp. 263–70.

Chapter 10

1. For Iser and Fish see Ch. 1 notes 2, 3, 4 and 5 above. Model 3 comes from Dan Sperber and Deirdre Wilson, *Relevance: Communication and Cognition* (Oxford: Blackwell, 1986).

Chapter 11

1. Andrew Blake, *The Irresistible Rise of Harry Potter* (London: Verso, 2002).
2. Colin Lankshear and Michele Knobel, 'Harry Potter', *Journal of Adolescent and Adult Literacy* 44:7, April 2001, p. 665.

Chapter 12

1. Schafer, *Explaining Harry Potter*, p. 6.
2. Zipes, *Sticks and Stones*, p. 175.

Chapter 13

1. Anne Sexton's poetic rewritings of fairy tales appears in the collection *Transformations* (1971) in *The Complete Poems* (Boston: Houghton Mifflin, 1981). Angela Carter wrote several versions of 'Beauty and the Beast' in *The Bloody Chamber* (Harmondsworth: Penguin, 1981). Angela Carter also edited *The*

Virago Book of Fairy Tales (London: Virago, 1990), to which she contributed a characteristically provocative introduction.
2. David Colbert, *The Magical Worlds of Harry Potter* (New York: Weatherhill, 2001); Allan Zora Kronzik and Elizabeth Kronzik, *The Sorcerer's Companion* (New York: Broadway, 2001). Schafer, *Exploring Harry Potter*, does this too.
3. J.R.R. Tolkien, *Tree and Leaf* (London: Grafton, 1992), pp. 62–3.
4. Such as Marina Warner, *From the Beast to the Blonde* (London: Chatto & Windus, 1994); Marina Warner, *Managing Monsters* (London: Vintage, 1994); Steven Swann Jones, *The Fairy Tale* (New York: Twayne, 1995); Ruth B. Bottingheimer, *Fairy Tales and Society* (Philadelphia: University of Pennsylvania Press, 1986); Jack Zipes, *When Dreams Come True* (New York: Routledge, 1999); Jack Zipes, *Happily Ever After* (New York: Routledge, 1997).
5. Vladimir Propp, *Theory and History of Folklore*, trans. Ariadne Martin and Richard Martin (Manchester: Manchester University Press, 1984), p. 5.

Chapter 14

1. Nina Auerbach, *Woman and the Demon: The Life of a Victorian Myth* (Cambridge, Mass.: Harvard University Press, 1982), Ch. 1 and passim.
2. I have used the deliberately open-ended 'our unconscious' of Sigmund Freud's *The Interpretation of Dreams*, trans. James Strachey (Harmondsworth: Penguin, 1976/1953), p. 775, rather than the later clarified 'superego'.
3. After a cursory examination of the matter this is what Philip Nel concludes in *Harry Potter Novels*, pp. 42–6. Nel considers class and race together; in this essay these are considered separately (class and servitude are the subjects of the next chapter) because, it seems to me, their treatment in the *Harry Potter* books are different.
4. Zipes, *Sticks and Stones*, p. 183.
5. Blake, *The Irresistible Rise of Harry Potter*, pp. 104–6.
6. Ibid., p. 108.
7. Malcolm X's awakening to the satanic qualities of white people in *The Autobiography of Malcolm X*, with the assistance of Alex Haley (Harmondsworth: Penguin, 1964), Ch. 10 ('Satan') is an instance of this kind. Toni Morrison in *Song of Solomon* (London: Chatto & Windus, 1978), pp. 154–61, presents a character, Guitar, who espouses a reverse racist ideology with terrible consequences.
8. Suman Gupta, *Marxism, History and Intellectuals: Toward a Reconceptualized Transformative Socialism* (Madison NJ: Fairleigh Dickinson University Press, 2000), pp. 221–44.
9. British Prime Minister Tony Blair's adviser, Robert Cooper, published an article in a Foreign Policy Centre pamphlet entitled *Reordering the World* in March 2002, recommending 'a new imperialism' in the wake of the terrorist attacks in the US on 11 September 2001. On this see Hugo Young, 'A New Imperialism Cooked up over a Texan Barbecue', in *The Guardian*, 2 April 2002.

Chapter 15

1. Robert Young, *Colonial Desire: Hybridity in Theory, Culture and Race* (London: Routledge, 1995), in Ch. 4 ('Sex and Inequality') gives an interesting account

of nineteenth-century attempts to negotiate between the commonness of human desire (and possibility of procreation irrespective of racial background) and the disposition towards racial discrimination.

2. Aldous Huxley, *Brave New World* (Harmondsworth: Penguin, 1932), Ch. 15.

Chapter 16

1. Some relatively recent arguments for and against class analysis are to be found in such overviews of the matter as R. Breen and D. Rothman, *Class Stratification* (London: Harvester, 1995), and particularly against in J. Pakulski and M. Waters, *The Death of Class* (London: Sage, 1996). The latter could be read in conjunction with the report on the 'Symposium on Class' in the journal *Theory and Society* 25:5, 1996, which carries a statement by Pakulski and Waters and responses to them.

2. About gender and class, see A. Pollert, 'Gender and Class Revisited: The Poverty of Patriarchy', *Sociology* 30:4, 1996, pp. 639–59; Heidi Gottfried, 'Beyond Patriarchy? Theorising Gender and Class', pp. 451–68, and Wendy Bottero, 'Clinging to the Wreckage? Gender and the Legacy of Class' pp. 469–90, in *Sociology* 32:3, 1998; Diane Reay, 'Rethinking Social Class: Qualitative Perspectives on Class and Gender', *Sociology* 32:2, pp. 259–75; and B. Skeggs, *Formations of Class and Gender* (London: Sage, 1997). About class and individual location, see Sighard Neckel, 'Inferiority: From Collective States to Deficient Individuality', *The Sociological Review* 44:1, 1996, pp. 17–34; Bill Martin, 'Knowledge, Identity and the Middle Class: From Collective to Individualised Class Formation?', *The Sociological Review* 46:4, 1998, pp. 653–86; K.K. Cetina, 'Sociality with Objects: Social Relations in Postsocial Knowledge Societies', *Theory Culture and Society* 14:4, 1997, pp. 1–30. For class and social mobility, see Kenneth Prady, 'Class and Continuity in Social Reproduction', *The Sociological Review* 46:2, 1998, pp. 340–64; Mike Savage and Muriel Egerton, 'Social Mobility, Ability and the Importance of Class Inequality', *Sociology* 31:4, 1997, pp. 645–72; R.M. Blackburn and K. Prandy, 'The Reproduction of Social Inequality', *Sociology* 31:3, pp. 491–509.

3. Karl Miller, 'Harry and the Pot of Gold', *Raritan* 20:3, Winter 2001, p. 136.

4. Blake, *The Irresistible Rise of Harry Potter*, pp. 108–9.

5. Ibid., p. 15.

6. Zipes, *Sticks and Stones*.

Chapter 17

1. Christine Schoefer, 'Harry Potter's Girl Trouble' (see Ch. 3 n. 2).

2. See Ch. 14 n. 4.

3. See Chris Gregory, 'Hands Off Harry Potter!' in *Salon Magazine* (www.Salon.com), 1 March 2000. Also see letters about this in *Salon Magazine* of 18 January 2000.

4. Michel Foucault, *The History of Sexuality Vol. 1: An Introduction*, trans. Robert Hurley (London: Allen Lane, 1979). Explorations of Victorian sexuality include: Michael Mason, *The Making of Victorian Sexual Attitudes* (Oxford: Oxford University Press, 1994); Ronald Pearson, *The Worm in the Bud*

(Harmondsworth: Pelican, 1969); Fraser Harrison, *The Dark Angel* (Glasgow: Fontana, 1977); Eric Trudgill, *Madonnas and Magdalens* (London: Heinemann, 1976); Roy Porter and Lesley Hall, *The Facts of Life* (New Haven: Yale University Press, 1995); Lynda Nead, *Myths of Sexuality* (Oxford: Blackwell, 1988); Judith Walkowitz, *Prostitution and Victorian Society* (Cambridge: Cambridge University Press, 1982); Andrew Miller and James Eli Adams eds., *Sexualities in Victorian Britain* (Bloomington: Indiana University Press, 1996).

Chapter 18

1. Raymond Williams, 'Advertising: The Magic System', *Problems in Materialism and Culture* (London: Verso, 1980), p. 178.
2. See, for instance, Jamie Allen, '"Harry" and Hype', at www.CNN.com (Book News), 13 July 2000.
3. Stephen Brown, 'Harry Potter and the Marketing Mystery: A Review and Critical Assessment of the Harry Potter Books', *Journal of Marketing* 66:1, January 2002, p. 127.
4. The language of advertising is usefully discussed in Geoffrey N. Leach, *English in Advertising* (London: Longmans, Green & Co., 1966); Guy Cook, *The Discourse of Advertising* (London: Routledge, 1992); Angela Goddard, *The Language of Advertising* (London: Routledge, 1998); Keiko Tanaka, *Advertising Language* (London: Routledge, 1999).
5. These techniques are unravelled with reference to a range of specific advertisements by Judith Williamson, *Decoding Advertisements* (London: Marion Boyars, 1978); Anthony Pratkanis and Elliot Aronson, *Age of Propaganda* (New York: W.H. Freeman, 1998).
6. Pennington, (see Ch. 8 n. 12), 'From Elfland to Hogwarts', p. 80.
7. Brown, 'Harry Potter and the Marketing Mystery', p. 129. The reference there is to Jagdish N. Sheth, 'The Surpluses and Shortages in Consumer Behavior Theory and Research', *Journal of the Academy of Marketing Science* 7, Fall 1979, pp. 414–27.

Chapter 19

1. John Ellis, *Visible Fictions* (London: Routledge & Kegan Paul, 1982), p. 77.
2. Ibid., pp. 78–9.
3. Richard Allen, *Projecting Illusions: Film Spectatorship and the Illusion of Reality* (Cambridge: Cambridge University Press, 1995), p. 82.
4. Siegfried Kracauer, *Theory of Film: The Redemption of Physical Reality* (Princeton: Princeton University Press, 1960), pp. 84–92.

Chapter 20

1. Lankshear and Knobel, 'Harry Potter', p. 665 (see Ch. 11 n. 2). The reference is to Daniel Bell, *The Coming of Post-Industrial Society: A Venture in Social Forecasting* (New York: Basic, 1976).
2. Donald Cardwell, *The Fontana History of Technology* (London: Fontana, 1994), p. 4.

3. O'Har, 'Magic in the Machine Age', p. 864 (see Ch. 7 n. 5).
4. In this context also see 'What if Quidditch, the Enchanted Sport of Wizards and Witches Featured in the Harry Potter Books, Were Regulated by the NCAA?', *Sports Illustrated*, 21 August 2000, p. 33.

Chapter 21

1. All references to the *Harry Potter* books are given in these chapters in-text, with the differentiating phrase from the titles (as here) and page numbers. All references are to the Bloomsbury editions.
2. On race particularly, see Elaine Ostrey, 'Accepting Mudbloods: The Ambivalent Social Vision of J. K. Rowling's Fairy Tales', in Giselle Liza Anatole (ed.), *Reading Harry Potter* (Westport, CT: Praeger, 2003), pp. 89–102; Mikhail Lyubansky, 'Harry Potter and the Word that Shall not be Named', in Neil Mulholland (ed.), *The Psychology of Harry Potter* (Dallas, TX: Benbella, 2006), pp. 233–48. On gender and class, see Farah Mandelsohn, 'Crowning the King: Harry Potter and the Construction of Authority', and Elisa T. Dresang, 'Hermione Granger and the Heritage of Gender', both in Lana A. Whited (ed.), *The Ivory Tower and Harry Potter* (Columbia, MO: University of Missouri Press, 2002), pp. 159–81 and 211–42; Brycchan Carey, 'Hermione and the House-Elves: The Literary and Historical Contexts of J. K. Rowling's Anti-Slavery Campaign', in Anatole (ed.), *Reading Harry Potter*, pp. 103–16. On sexuality, see Tison Hugh and David L. Wallace, 'Heteronormative Heroism and Queering the School Story in J. K. Rowling's Harry Potter Series', *Children's Literature Association Quarterly* 31:3, Fall 2006, pp. 260–81; Ika Willis, 'Keeping Promises to Queer Children: Making Space (for Mary Sue) at Hogwarts', in Karen Helleksen and Kristina Busse (eds.), *Fan Fiction and Fan Communities in the Age of the Internet* (Jefferson, NC: McFarland, 2006), pp. 153–70.
3. J. G. Frazer, *The Golden Bough: A Study in Magic and Religion* (abridged edition) (London: Macmillan, 1922), chs. 66 and 67.
4. Ibid., p. 903. Frazer's (and other ethnographers') characterisation of 'savage' or 'primitive' cultures and minds as such has understandably been superseded, especially in connection with his interpretation of totemism – which is implicit in his explanation of externalised and split souls – and influentially in Claude Lévi-Strauss, *Totemism*, trans. Rodney Needham (Boston, MA: Beacon, 1963). The quoted observation here, however, does not denigrate the 'savage' mind but discerns an internal rationale for totemistic practices, and in those terms also discerns the arbitrariness of dogmatic theology. ('Dogma', it seems to me, clearly suggests disapproval.)
5. Anders Nygren, *Agape and Eros*, trans. Philip S. Watson (London: Westminster, 1953). For a recent account of the debate about Christian love, see Amy Laura Hall, 'Love: A Kinship of Affliction and Redemption', in Gilbert Meilaender and William Werpehowski (eds.), *The Oxford Handbook of Theological Ethics* (Oxford: Oxford University Press, 2005), pp. 307–21.
6. In fact, there is plenty of recent work on the Christian content of the *Harry Potter* books: see e.g. Russell W. Dalton, *Faith Journey Through Fantasy Land* (Minneapolis, MN: Augsberg Fortress, 2003); John Granger, *Looking for God in*

Harry Potter (Carol Stream, IL: Tyndale, 2004); John Killinger, *God, the Devil, and Harry Potter* (New York: St. Martin's Press, 2004); Nancy Carpentier, *The Mystery of Harry Potter* (Huntington, NC: Our Sunday Visitor, 2007).

7. Such as Roger Highfield's *The Science of Harry Potter: How Magic Really Works* (London: Headline, 2002), which both examines how far magic in the series can be approximated or approached through science and technology, and gives an outline of the magical antecedents of science and technology.

8. John Bryant, *The Fluid Text: A Theory of Revision and Editing for Book and Screen* (Ann Arbor, MI: The University of Michigan Press, 2002), p. 4.

9. For a critical discussion, see Robin Truth Goodman, *World, Class, Women: Global Literature, Education and Feminism* (New York: RoutledgeFalmer, 2004). For advice on using the *Harry Potter* books for children's education, see e.g. Stefan Neilson, Joe Hutton and Nora Huston, *Character Education: The Legacy of the Harry Potter Novels* (Mountlake Terrace, WA: Vintage First Edition, 2001); Mary L. McNabb, *Literacy Learning and Networked Classrooms* (Newark, NJ: International Reading Association, 2006). For use in higher education, see Laura Baker Shearer, 'High-Brow Harry Potter: J. K. Rowling's Series as College Level Literature', in Cynthia Whitney Hallett (ed.), *Scholarly Studies in Harry Potter: Applying Academic Methods to a Popular Text* (Lewiston, ME: Edwin Mellen, 2005), pp. 199–215.

10. The characteristics of academic discourse are charted usefully in terms of linguistic analysis of academic writing, as in books and papers by Ken Hyland, *Hedging in Scientific Research Articles* (Amsterdam: John Benjamins, 1998); *Disciplinary Discourses: Social Interactions in Academic Writing* (Harlow: Pearson, 2000); 'Self-citation and Self-reference: Credibility and Promotion in Academic Publication', *Journal of the American Society for Information Science and Technology* 54:3, 2003, pp. 251–91; 'What Do They Mean? Questions in Academic Writing', *Text* 22:4, 2002, pp. 529–58; 'Options of Identity in Academic Writing,' *ELT Journal* 56:4, October 2002, pp. 35–43; 'Bumping into the Reader: Addressee Features in Academic Articles', *Written Communication* 18:4, Ocober 2001, pp. 549–75. Also relevant here are analyses of student academic writing, including Roz Ivanič, *Writing and Identity: The Discoursal Construction of Identity in Academic Writing* (Amsterdam: John Benjamin, 1997), and in most of the essays in Mary R. Lea and Barry Stierer (eds.), *Student Writing in Higher Education* (Buckingham: Open University Press and The Society for Research in Higher Education, 2000).

11. The relationship between academic discourse and the characterising features of academic institutions is examined in Tony Becher and Paul R. Trowler, *Academic Tribes and Territories* (Buckingham; Open University Press and The Society for Research into Higher Education, 2001; first edition 1989); Pierre Bourdieu, Jean-Claude Passeron and Monique de Saint Martin, *Academic Discourse: Linguistic Misunderstanding and Professorial Power* (1965), trans. Richard Teese (Cambridge: Polity, 1994); Pierre Bourdieu, *Homo Academicus*, trans. Peter Collier (Cambridge: Polity, 1988; original French edition 1984); Marjorie Garber, *Academic Instincts* (Princeton, NJ: Princeton University Press, 2001).

12. Peter Taylor-Whiffen, 'Harry Potter and the Social Order', *The Independent* 3 June 2003, p. 12.

13. Anna Thompson, 'Harry Potters on, and We Muggle through', *Times Higher Education Supplement* 19 September 2003.
14. See note 2.
15. Giselle Liza Anatole, 'Introduction', in Anatole (ed.) *Reading Harry Potter*, p. xiv. The 'Why Engage in this Project' section is from pp. xiii–xvi.
16. Laura Shearer Baker, 'High-Brow Harry Potter'.
17. Evelyn M. Perry, 'Metaphor and MetaFantasy: Questing for Literary Inheritance in J. K. Rowling's *Harry Potter and the Sorcerer's Stone*', in Hallett (ed.), *Scholarly Studies in Harry Potter*.
18. Suman Gupta, 'Sociological Speculations on the Professions of Children's Literature', *The Lion and the Unicorn* 29: 3, September 2005, pp. 299–323.
19. Henri Hubert and Marcel Mauss, *Outline of a General Theory of Magic* (London: Routledge, 2001; original French edition 1904).
20. Torbjørn Knutsen, 'Dumbledore's Pedagogy: Knowledge and Virtue at Hogwarts', in Daniel H. Nexon and Iver B. Neumann (eds.), *Harry Potter and International Relations* (Lanham MD: Rowman & Littlefield, 2006), p. 200.
21. Marcel Mauss, *A General Theory of Magic*, trans Robert Brain (London: Routledge, 1972, original French publication 1904), p. 171.
22. Robin S. Rosenberg, 'What Do Students Learn from Hogwarts Classes?', in Mulholland (ed.), *The Psychology of Harry Potter*, pp. 5–17.
23. Charles W. Kalish and Emma C. Kalish, 'Hogwarts Academy: Common Sense and School Magic', in ibid., pp. 59–71.
24. Philip Nel, 'Is There a Text in This Advertising Campaign? Literature, Marketing, and Harry Potter', *The Lion and the Unicorn* 29:2, April 2005, p. 245.
25. Philip Nel, *J. K. Rowling's Harry Potter Novels: A Reader's Guide* (New York: Continuum, 2001).
26. Patrick Thaddeus Jackson and Peter Mandaville, 'Glocal Hero: Harry Potter Abroad', in Nexon and Neumann (eds.), *Harry Potter and International Relations*, p. 46.
27. Ann Towns and Bahar Rumelili, 'Foreign Yet Familiar: International Politics and the Reception of Potter in Turkey and Sweden', in ibid., pp. 61–77.
28. Maya Götz, Dafna Lemish, Amy Aidman and Heysung Moon, *Media and the Make-Belief Worlds of Children: Where Harry Potter Meets Pokémon in Disneyland* (Mahwah, NJ: Lawrence Erlbaum, 2005), pp. 185–94.
29. See e.g. Andrew Burn, 'Potterliteracy: Cross-Media Narratives, Cultures and Grammars', *Papers: Explorations into Children's Literature* 14:2, 2004, pp. 5–17; Andrew Burn, 'Multi-Text Magic: Harry Potter in Book, Film and Videogame', in Fiona M. Collins and Jeremy Ridgman (eds.), *Turning the Page: Children's Literature in Performance and the Media* (Bern: Peter Lang, 2006); Deborah Cartnell and Imelda Whelehan, 'Harry Potter and the Fidelity Debate', in Mireia Aragay (ed.), *Books in Motion: Adaptation, Intertextuality, Authorship* (Amsterdam: Rodopi, 2005), pp. 37–50; Jyotsna Kapur, *Coining the Capital: Movies, Marketing, and the Transformation of Childhood* (New Brunswick: Rutgers University Press, 2005); Anna Gunder, 'Harry Ludens: *Harry Potter and the Philosopher's Stone* as a Novel and Computer Game', *HUMAN IT* 7:2, 2004, pp. 1–137. Also available etjanst.hb.se/bhs/ith/2-7/ag.pdf, accessed 1 May 2008; Ted Baehr and Tom Snyder, *Frodo and Harry: Understanding Visual Media and Its Impact on Our Lives* (Wheaton, IL: Crossway, 2003).

Chapter 22

1. Ivan Vatahov, 'Harry Potter Needed for EU Bid', *Sofia Echo*, 21 February 2002 and 21 March 2002. www.sofiaecho.com/article/the-big-story/id_3986/catid_ 29/search_1. Accessed 30 May 2008.

2. Egmont, one of Scandinavia's leading media groups, has been operating in Bulgaria since 1991 as the local licensee for the publishing products of major companies such as Walt Disney, Warner Bros., Mattel, National Geographic, Scholastic UK. It is an established leader in children publishing in the country. www.egmontbulgaria.com/. Accessed 6 May 2008.

3. Teodora Vassileva 'Small Wonders in Bulgaria too' [Malki vulshebstva i v Bulgaria], *Kapital*, 30, 27 July 2007.

4. Since there is hardly any official data on print circulation in Bulgaria, for comparison Bard Publishing House representatives are quoted to have said that neither Dan Brown's books nor Tolkien's *Lord of the Rings* have reached almost 60,000 copies sold, 18 December 2007. curious.actualno.com/news_ 139628.html. Accessed 30 May 2008.

5. Alek Popov, 'The Bulgarian Trace in *Harry Potter*' [Bulgarskata sleda v Hari Potar], *BTA – 100% Harry Potter*, December 2003. www.bta.bg/site/100per/ 2004/harry_potter/html/inside.htm. Accessed 6 May 2008.

6. In view of the chosen focus for our discussion, age (generation) plays a role, since the negotiations between a communist legacy and a transitional present are explicit mostly in the articulations of cited authors who have first-hand experience of both, i.e. they have come of age or lived in the years prior to 1989.

7. Popov, 2003.

8. Ibid.

9. In 2002, during the visit of the Pope to Bulgaria, the media's major focus was on his official remark that he personally believed Sergei Antonov was not part of the coup.

10. For more on the 'Bulgarian connection' in Cold War terms, see Antonic Savasta, 'International Terrorism and the "Bulgarian Connection"', Report of 19 March 1982, *Open Society Archives*. files.osa.ceu.hu/holdings/300/8/3/ text/8-10-58.shtml. Accessed 28 May 2008.

11. For a comprehensive account of the period in question, see John D. Bell (ed.), *Bulgaria in Transition: Politics, Society and Culture after Communism* (Boulder CO: Westview Press, 1998).

12. Indicative debates on the 'phases' of transition in Bulgaria can be found, among other related critical essays, in the records from the discussion held on 18 March 2003 'Bulgaria or the End of the Transition Paradigm?' organised by the *Razum [Reason]: Journal for Politics and Culture Theories*, 1, 2003. www.razum.org. Accessed 2 June 2008.

13. In the archives (www.cesnur.org/recens/potter_00.htm, accessed 2 June 2008) for newspaper articles related to religion and culture for this period, there isn't a single reference to Viktor Krum. In the *Guardian* archives, Viktor Krum is a factual reference in outlining the plot of the book.

14. Egmont Bulgaria, 13 May 2002. www.egmontbulgaria.com. Accessed 5 May 2008.

15. The project was supported by the British Council between 2001 and 2003. The major publication from it is Mila Mineva (ed.), *Take it Easy: Towards a Strategy for Representing Bulgaria* (Sofia: The British Council, IPK Rodina, 2003). Some details on the project activities are available in *Sofia Echo*, 25 July 2002. www.sofiaecho.com/article/bulgaria-branded/id_4975/catid_5, and 3 April 2003, www.sofiaecho.com/article/rebranding-bulgaria/id_6999/catid_47. Accessed 30 May 2008.

16. In the section 'Highlights of the Brand', the final recommendation reads as follows: 'The final branding resource is existing Bulgarians outside Bulgaria.... In *Harry Potter and the Goblet of Fire*, the best "Quidditch" player is a Bulgarian. An image campaign could exploit this and other elements that coincide with an overall prospective vision of Bulgaria for both domestic and international consumption.' In Mineva, *Take It Easy*, p. 59.

17. Alexander Levy, 'Harry Potter Ignites Passions in Bulgaria', *Parizhki Vesti* [*Paris News*], 4 November 2004, Translated from French and reprinted with the permission of LEMONDE.FR. www.parisvesti.com/?u_s=3&u_a=101& sid= Accessed 2 May 2008.

18. Samples available in English are 'Destination Bulgaria Promoted by Mythical Harry Potter Team', 11 June 2004, www.novinite.com/view_news.php?id= 35708; and 'Viktor Krum Looming as Bulgaria's Tourism Face', 10 March 2004, www.novinite.com/view_news.php?id=32055. Accessed 2 May 2008.

19. Levy, 2004.

20. www.novinite.com/view_news.php?id=32055. Accessed 2 May 2008. For some details on Khan Krum see quotation on p. 192.

21. Levy, 2004.

22. Among others: www.potter-bg.com, and http://www.pottermania.hit.bg. Accessed 27 May 2008.

23. Reports on the casting and forum entries can be found at life.dir.bg/stars/ 2/star2831c.html, www.standartnews.com of 4 February 2004. Accessed 27 May 2008.

24. The firm conducting casting in Sofia is Talent Partners Casting. www. talent-partners.com/content.php?lan=EN&op=home. Accessed 4 May 2008.

25. Egmont Bulgaria. www.egmontbulgaria.com, 2 December 2005.

26. Postings between 26 November 2005 and 5 April 2006. life.dir.bg/stars/2/ star2831.html. Accessed 27 May 2008.

27. Also published in the *Mickey Mouse* magazine, 7, 11–17 February 2002. www.egmontbulgaria.com. Accessed 30 April 2008.

28. Geo Milev (1895–1925), Bulgarian poet, critic and intellectual, educated in Sofia and Leipzig, visited London after the outbreak of the First World War. He is a key representative of literary expressionism in Bulgaria and, among other poets and intellectuals of his time, an activist of the political left. He was arrested and disappeared after the ultra-left bombing of 'St Nedelya Church' in April 1925. Later found buried in a mass, unmarked grave.

29. Leda Mileva (1920–), Bulgarian poet and author of children's books. President of the Bulgarian Union of Translators (1979–89), translator of Russian, English and French fiction.

30. 'The Most Curious Facts about *Harry Potter*', 11 February 2002. www. egmontbulgaria.com. Accessed 2 May 2008.

31. Including a later interview with his great-grandmother, Leda Mileva. Internet edition of *Sega* newspaper, *Nablyudatel* rubric, 15 July 2006. www.segabg.com/online/article.asp?issueid=2347&sectionid=5&id=0001201. Accessed 27 May 2008.
32. Iliyana Benina, '"Not in Slytherin, not in Slytherin": Audio-Visual Translation of *Harry Potter and the Philosopher's Stone* by J. K. Rowling' [Ne v Sliderin, ne v Sliderin: audio-vizualen prevod na Hari Potar i filosofskiyat kamuk]; Katya Nikolova and Sofia Angelova-Damyanova, '*Harry Potter*: Censorship and Literature Education' [Hari Potar: tsenzurata i obuchenieto po literatura], both in Margarita Slavova (ed.), *Adaptation as a Strategy of Children's Literature* (Plovdiv: Paissiy Hilendarski University of Plovdiv Press, 2005), pp. 206–14.
33. Ludmilla Miteva, 'Harry Potter Goes to America: Having Fun with Fan Works', CD-ROM edition of *Conference Proceedings: The Bulgarian Association for American Studies*, (Sofia, November 2003); Ludmilla Miteva, 'Harry Potter and His Fans' [Hari Potar i negovite pochitateli] *Vox Literarum* 3, 2004, pp. 26–34; Ludmilla Miteva, 'School Space as a Product and Mediator of Culture in Children's Literature', in Madeleine Danova and Milena Katsarska (eds.), *(Inter)Cultural Communication*. Conference volume. November 2006, Plovdiv (Sofia: Polis Publishing, forthcoming).
34. Galina Avramova, 'Is Harry Potter Dangerous?' [Opasen li e Hari Potar?], *Vox Literarum* 2, 2004, pp. 31–42; Ludmilla Miteva, 'Difficult Decisions: Huck Finn and Harry Potter', in Madeleine Danova (ed.), *The Transatlantic and the Transnational in a Changing Cultural Context* (Sofia: Polis Publishing, 2005), pp. 300–13.
35. Dessislava Cheshmedzhieva, 'The Same but Other: Igor Karkaroff – a Key Bulgarian Figure in J. K. Rowling's *Harry Potter and The Goblet of Fire*', *New Prospects Conference Proceedings*, Plovdiv, 1–3 November 2003 (forthcoming); Dessislava Cheshmedzhieva, 'Some Representations of Bulgarians in J. K. Rowling's *Harry Potter and the Goblet of Fire*. Viktor Krum: a Bulgarian Coming from an Imaginary Geography', in Svetlin Stratiev and Vessela Katsarova (eds.), *Spaces, Gaps, Borders* (Sofia: St Kliment Ohridski University Press, 2006), pp. 208–16; Ludmilla Miteva, *Humour in late 20th-Century British Children's Literature: Roald Dahl, Terry Pratchet, J. K. Rowling*. Extended précis of the PhD dissertation text defended at the Specialised Academic Board in Literature, at the Higher Attestation Committee (Sofia, 2008), 86 pp.
36. Lidiya Denkova, *The Philosopher's Secrets of Harry Potter (An Attempt on the Philosophy of 'Fairy-tales')*, [*Filosofskite taini na Hari Potar*] (Sofia, LIK, 2001); Gergana Apostolova, 'Are Dementors the New Guardians of the Golden Apple' [Dementorite li sa novite pazachi na zlatnata yabulka?], in *Jubilee Slavic Compendium* [*Yubileen Slavistichen Sbornik*] (Blagoevgrad, 2005); Gergana Apostolova, 'Bad Realism and Good Fantasy in Futile Attempt at Literary Representation in Julian Barnes' *The Porcupine* and J. K. Rowling's *Harry Potter*', presented at ESSE 8 Conference in London, 29 August–2 September 2006.
37. www.theninemuses.net/hp/4.html. Accessed 1 June 2008.
38. www.angelfire.com/mi3/cookarama/namemean.html. Accessed 1 June 2008.
39. Cheshmedzhieva, 2006, p. 210.
40. See Cheshmedzhieva, 2006; Miteva, 2008.
41. Cheshmedzhieva 2003.
42. Cheshmedzhieva 2006, p. 210.
43. Ibid., p. 211.

44. Ludmilla Kostova, *Tales of the Periphery: The Balkans in Nineteenth-century British Writing* (Veliko Turnovo: University Publishing House of St Cyril and Methodius, 1997).
45. Ibid., and Maria Todorova, *Imagining the Balkans* (Oxford: Oxford University Press, 1997).
46. Cheshmedzhieva 2006, p. 210.
47. The allusion to the Russian Tsar Ivan Grozni and the Russian fairy-tale villain Koschei the Immortal has been made by Ludmilla Miteva in her PhD précis, 2008, p. 46.
48. Cheshmedzhieva, 2006, p. 213.
49. Kostova, 1997, p. 10, referred in Cheshmedzhieva, 2006, p. 213.
50. By implication, through references to Kostova's argument in *Tales of the Periphery*, 1997, and also by direct allusions to these texts.
51. Again by implication through Miteva's 2008 reference to Ludmilla Kostova, 'Representing "Darkest Eastern Europe": Bulgaria in G. B. Shaw's *Arms and the Man* and Malcolm Bradbury's *Doctor Criminale*', in Martin Dengerfield, Glyn Hambrook and Ludmilla Kostova, *Europe: From East to West* (Varna: PIC Publishers, 1996).
52. Apostolova, 2006.
53. Along the lines 'imaginative geography', discussed in Edward Said, *Orientalism: Western Conceptions of the Orient* (Harmondsworth: Penguin, 1978), ch. 1, esp. pp. 54–5.
54. Miteva, 2008, p. 43.
55. Denkova, *The Philosopher's Secrets of Harry Potter*, 2001.
56. See notes 32 and 34.
57. By far less bellicose than their American counterparts, there were nonetheless church representatives who publicly opposed the *Harry Potter* books as the short publication in World Briefing 'Europe: Bulgaria: Church Warning on *Harry Potter*', as *The New York Times* 2 March 2002 indicates.
58. Miteva, 2008.
59. Ibid., p. 46.
60. Ibid, p. 47.
61. Ibid. p. 48.
62. Ibid. p. 49.
63. On scholarly attention regarding translation into Bulgarian, there is only one essay which comparatively analyses the proper names of the *Harry Potter* books in their English, Bulgarian and Hungarian versions: Ralitsa Stefanova 'A Glimpse at Harry Potter in Three Languages', *Literary Newspaper [Literaturen vestnik]*, 27, 10 September 2003.
64. Hereafter all page references in the translations from the Bulgarian edition are to *Goblet of Fire – Hari Potar i Ogneniyat bokal*, trans. Mariyana Melnishka (Sofia: Egmont Bulgaria, 2002).

Chapter 23

1. On this, see Richard Spencer, 'Harry Potter and the Cho Chang Mystery', 23 December 2005. blogs.telegraph.co.uk/foreign/richardspencer/dec2005/harrypotter.htm.

2. Jiang Wandi, 'Wild about Harry', *Beijing Review* 7 June 2007, p. 19.
3. Wang Shanshan, 'Latest Potter Book Now in Chinese, Officially', *China Daily*, 29 October 2007, p. 3. www.chinadaily.com.cn/cndy/2007-10/29/content_6212029.htm. Accessed 1 May 2008.
4. Described succinctly in Cheng Zhaoxiang, 'English Departments in Chinese Universities', *World Englishes* 21:2, 2002, pp. 257–67.
5. Ma Jianguo 'The Sixth Volume of Harry Potter is about to be Launched, the English Edition Has Arrived in Beijing', www.XINHUANET.com, 15 July 2005.
6. Gillian Lathey, 'The Travels of Harry: International Marketing and the Translation of J. K. Rowling's Harry Potter Books', *The Lion and the Unicorn* 29:2, 2005, pp. 141–51. Along similar lines, there is also Nancy K. Jentsch, 'Harry Potter and the Tower of Babel: Translating the Magic', in Gillian Lathey (ed.), *The Translation of Children's Literature: A Reader* (Clevedon: Multilingual Matters, 2006).
7. The Taiwanese and People's Republic of China editions were produced by different translators. Comparison of these could be a rich resource for translation studies, but I am not aware of much published academic research that uses this resource. There is an unpublished Auckland Technology University Master's dissertation which uses the Taiwanese and Chinese versions of a *Harry Potter* book: Yah-Ying Elaine Shiao, *Bewitched or Befogged in a Magical World? Chinese Translations of Culture-Specific Items in a Harry Potter Novel*, May 2006. The following have been consulted for this chapter. From the People's Republic of China: J. K. Rowling, *Hali Bote He Mofashi*, trans. Su Nong (Beijing: People's Literature Publishing House [renmin wenxue chubanshe], 2000); J. K. Rowling, *Hali Bote He Siwang Shengqi*, trans. Ma Ainong and Ma Aixin (Beijing: People's Literature Publishing House, 2007). From Taiwan: J. K. Rowling. *Hali Bote He Mofashi*, trans. Peng Qian-wen (Taipei: Crown Publishing, 2000).
8. Mihepu, 'My Reason for Writing "Preliminary Analysis of the Chinese Translation of Harry Potter 6 by the People's Literature Publishing House"', 2006. tieba.baidu.com/f?kz=66576189. Accessed 1 June 2008.
9. Jiang Wandi, 'Wild about Harry', p. 19.
10. Back-translation is usually used as a quality check in professional translating. However, its use to explicate the nuances of interlingual translation, as here, is also fairly common. It is used for this purpose, and with a similar awareness of its limitations, in Mona Baker, *In Other Words: A Coursebook in Translation* (London: Routledge, 1992), p. 8.
11. Ye Zhenning, 'The Development and Marketing of Harry Potter in China' [Hali Bote de zhengti kaifa he yingxiao], *China Bookmerchant's Newspaper* [*Zhongguo tushu shangbao*] August 2002. www.sinobook.com.cn/press/news-detail.cfm?iCntno=284. Accessed 1 June 2008.
12. I am very grateful indeed to Zhao Baisheng, Director of the Institute of World Literature, Peking University, for organising this. I am also grateful to students of the Institute who helped me follow the deliberations and followed up with explanations, particularly Wang Jiake and Wei Liping, and to Zhang Chunguang for making a full recording of the workshop for me.
13. David Buckingham, *After the Death of Childhood: Growing up in the Age of Electronic Media* (Cambridge: Polity, 2000).

14. Jack Zipes, *Sticks and Stones: The Troublesome Success of Children's Literature from Slovenly Peter to Harry Potter* (New York: Routledge, 2000); Andrew Blake, *The Irresistible Rise of Harry Potter: Kid-Lit in a Globalised World* (London: Verso, 2002).

15. Ni Lishan, 'Expedition of the Soul in the Game-Spirit of Harry Potter' [xinling de tanxian], *Journal of Fujian Educational College* [Fujian jiaoyu xueyuan xuebao], October 2005, pp. 79–83.

16. Huang Yunting and Liang Hongyan, 'On the Art of the Double-World Narrative in Fantasy Novels' [lu muohuan xiaoshuo zhongde shuangchong shijie], *Journal of the South China University of Technology* [huanan ligong duxue xuebao] 9:6, December 2007, pp. 63–7.

17. Zhang Ying and Kong Dan, 'Harry Potter and the Characteristics of Contemporary Children's Literature' [Hali Bote yu xinshiqi ertong wenxue de tedian], *Journal of the North East University: Philosophy and Social Science* [dongbei shida xuebao], 5, 2002, pp. 95–7.

18. Jing Xiaolei, 'Universal Potter', *Beijing Review* 7 June 2007, p. 23. The survey was conducted by Douban.com.

19. Shao Yanjun, 'A Study of the Phenomenon of Pretty Women's Writing: Weihui, Mianmian, Chunshu', *Wasafiri* (China Special Issue), 55, 2008, p. 14.

20. Zhang and Kong, 2002.

21. Li Nishan, 2005.

22. Xu Yurong, 'Children's Literature Should be Happy Literature: On the Revelations Available from Harry Potter' [ertong wenxue ying chengwei kuile wenxue], *Journal of Social Sciences* [chengdu daxue xuebao], 4, 2006, pp. 127–8.

23. In English the following are useful: Anne Behnke Kinney, *Chinese Views of Childhood* (Honolulu: University of Hawaii Press, 1995); Mary Ann Farquhar, *Children's Literature in China: From Lu Xun to Mao Zedong* (Armak, NY: M. E. Sharpe, 1999).

24. Productions of the Cultural Revolution could be expected to be, and generally are, about as ideologically black-and-white, reductive and propagandist as possible. The 'revolutionary martyr's stories' that I go on to mention are of that reductive mould. However, in children's writing of this period there are complexities that are worth keeping in mind. One of the best-known writers at the time was Hao Ran, of whose children's writings Farquhar (*Children's Literature in China*, p. 290) observes: 'despite all the rhetoric, the model writer of fictions for all audiences in China of this period ignored overt preaching, revolutionary propaganda, and model heroes in writing his children's stories. His works resurrected fifties' stories on children's work and play … but without the moral message that play was bad and work was good.'

25. Such as, recently, Michael Brown et al. (eds.), *The Rise of China* (Cambridge MA: MIT Press, 2000); Edward Timberlake and William Triplett II, *Red Dragon Rising* (Washington: Regnery, 2002); Ted Fishman, *China Inc.* (New York: Scribner, 2005); Jasper Becker, *Dragon Rising* (Westchester, OH: National Geographic Society, 2006); Peter Navarro, *The Coming China Wars* (New Jersey: FT Press, 2006); James Kynge, *China Shakes the World* (New York: Houghton Mifflin, 2007) – the titles speak for themselves.

Chapter 24

1. Tara Collins, 'Filling the Gaps: What's Happening in the World of Fan Fiction', *Library Media Connection* 24:4, January 2006, p. 36.
2. Henry Jenkins, 'Everybody Loves Harry', 21 May 2007, at *Confessions of an Aca-Fan: The Official Weblog of Henry Jenkins.* www.henryjenkins.org/2007/05/everybody-loves-harry.htm.
3. Henry Jenkins, *Convergence Culture: Where Old and New Media Collide* (New York: New York University Press, 2006), p. 3.
4. Linda Green, *Entering Potter's World: A Guide for Fanfiction Writers* (lulu.com, 2006).
5. Jane Glaubman (ed.), *Deconstructing Harry: Harry Potter Fan Fiction on the World Wide Web* (Durham, NC: Duke University Press, 2008).
6. Jay David Bolter, *Writing Space: The Computer, Hypertext, and the History of Writing* (Hillsdale, NJ: Lawrence Erlbaum, 1991), p. 121.
7. Ibid., p. 144.
8. Silvio Gaggi, *From Text to Hypertext: Decentring the Subject in Fiction, Film, the Visual Arts* (Philadelphia: University of Pennsylvania Press, 1997), p. 106.
9. Ibid., p. 122.
10. Clinton D. Lanier Jr and Hope Jensen Schau, 'Culture and Co-Creation: Exploring Consumers' Inspirations and Aspirations for Writing and Posting On-Line Fan Fiction', in Russell W. Belk and John F. Sherry (eds.), *Consumer Culture Theory* (Amsterdam: Elsevier, 2007), p. 324.
11. Jenkins, *Convergence Culture*, p. 205.
12. Ibid., pp. 240–60.
13. Cornel Sandross, 'One-Dimensional Fan: Toward an Aesthetic of Fan Texts', *American Behavioral Scientist* 48:7, March 2005, p. 835. 'One-dimensionality' here refers to Herbert Marcuse's phrase, which captures the notion that in advanced capitalist society all oppositional positions and agents tend to get co-opted within capitalism, in *One Dimensional Man* (Boston, MA: Beacon, 1964).
14. Kristina Busse and Karen Hellekson, 'Introduction: Work in Progress', in Hellekson and Busse (eds.), *Fan Fiction and Fan Communities in the Age of the Internet* (Jefferson, NC: McFarland, 2006), p. 7.
15. In the context of recent reconceptualisations of 'world literature', the notion of 'distanced reading' was controversially mooted in Franco Moretti, 'Conjectures on World Literature', *New Left Review* 1, January–February 2000, pp. 54–68.
16. For a useful recent discussion of the conceptual nuances of 'autoethnography' in various disciplines, see James Buzard, 'On Auto-Ethnographic Authority', *Yale Journal of Criticism* 16:1, 2003, pp. 61–91. In academic studies on the culture of fandom 'autoethnography' as a mode of both putting academic discourse into perspective and coming to grips with fan discourse is a much discussed area – in a sustained fashion in Matt Hill, *Fan Cultures* (London: Routledge, 2002), especially pp. 71–89.
17. Nancy K. Baym, 'Talking about Soaps: Communicative Practices in a Computer-Mediated Fan Culture', in Cheryl Harris and Alison Alexander (eds.), *Theorizing Fandom: Fans, Subculture and Identity* (Cresskill, NJ: Hampton, 1998), pp. 111–29; Nancy K. Baym, *Tune in, Log on: Soaps, Fandom, and Online Community* (Thousand Oaks, CA: Sage, 2000).

18. Henry Jenkins, 'Why Heather Can Write: Not everything kids learn for popular culture is bad for them, some of the best writing culture takes place outside the classroom in online communities', *Technology Review*, February 2004. http://www.technologyreview.com/Biztech/13473.

19. Jenkins, *Convergence Culture*, ch. 5.

20. Ibid., p. 178.

21. Ibid., pp. 184–5.

22. Henry Jenkins with assistants, *Confronting the Challenges of Participatory Culture: Media Education for the 21st Century* (Chicago: McArthur Foundation, 2006).

23. Ibid., pp. 32–3.

24. Rebecca W. Black, 'Access and Affiliation: The Literacy and Composition Practices of English-Language Learners in an Online Fanfiction Community', *Journal of Adolescent and Adult Literacy* 48:2, October 2005, pp. 118–28; Rebecca W. Black, *Adolescents and Online Fan Fiction* (Bern: Peter Lang, 2008); Len Unsworth, *E-Literature for Children: Enhancing Digital Literacy Learning* (London: Routledge, 2006), ch. 3; Dana J. Wilber, 'iLife: Understanding and Connecting to the Digital Literacy of Adolescents', in Kathleen A. Hinchman and Heather K. Sheridan-Thomas (eds.), *Best Practices in Adolescent Literacy Instruction* (New York: Guildford, 2008), pp. 57–77.

25. Heather Lawver, 'Making Progress toward Revolution'. http://www.dprophet.com/index2.html.

26. Heather Lawver, 'Open Letter to Parents, Teachers and Concerned Adults'. http://www.dprophet.com/hq/openletter.html.

27. Andrea MacDonald, 'Uncertain Utopia: Science Fiction Media Fandom and Computer Mediated Communication', in Harris and Alexander (eds.), *Theorizing Fandom*, p. 149.

28. Green, *Entering Potter's World*, gives a list of pairings on offer and on which websites which occupies 19 pages (pp. 25–44).

29. Marianne MacDonald, 'Harry Potter and the Fan Fiction Phenomenon', *Gay and Lesbian Review Worldwide* 13:1, January–February 2006, p. 28.

30. For example, Mirna Ciciani, 'Male Pair: Bonds and Female Desire in Fan Slash Writing', pp. 153–77; Shashanna Green, Cynthia Jenkins and Henry Jenkins, 'Normal Female Interest in Men Bonking', pp. 9–38, in Harris and Alexander (eds.), *Theorizing Fandom*.

31. Tison Hugh and David L. Wallace, 'Heteronormative Heroism and Queering the School Story in J. K. Rowling's *Harry Potter* Series', *Children's Literature Association Quarterly* 31:3, Fall 2006, pp. 260–81.

32. Ika Willis, 'Keeping Promises to Queer Children: Making Space (for Mary Sue) at Hogwarts', in Helleson and Busse (eds.), *Fan Fiction and Fan Communities*, p. 155.

33. MacDonald, 'Harry Potter and the Fan Fiction Phenomenon', p. 30.

34. Lelia Green and Carmen Guinery, 'Harry Potter and the Fan Fiction Phenomenon', *Media/Culture* 7:5, November 2004, at journal.media-culture.org.au/0411/14.green.php.

35. Catherine Tossenberger, '"Oh my God, the Fanfiction!" Dumbledore's Outing and the Online Harry Potter Fandom', *Children's Literature Association Quarterly* 33:2, Summer 2008, pp. 200–6.

36. David Smith, 'Dumbledore was Gay, JK Tells Amazed Fans', *Observer*, 21 October 2007. www.guardian.co.uk/uk/2007/oct/21/film.books.

37. Howard W. French, 'Chinese Market Awash in Fake Potter Books', *New York Times*, 1 August 2007. www.nytimes.com/2007/08/01/world/asia/01china.html?pagewanted=1&_r=1&ref=books, and Op-Ed Contributors, 'Memo to the Dept. of Magical Copyright Enforcement', *New York Times* 10 August 2007. http://www.nytimes.com/2007/08/10/opinion/10potter.html. The latter carries summaries of and translated passages from eight such 'fakes'.
38. French, ibid.
39. Lena Henningsen, 'Harry Potter with Chinese Characteristics: Plagiarism between Orientalism and Occidentalism', *China Information* 20:2, 2006, p. 277.
40. J. K. Luolin, *Hali Bote yu baozhoulon* [erroneously translated as *Harry Potter and the Leopard-Walk-Up-To-Dragon*] (Hohot: Neimenggu chubanshe, 2002); Zhang Bin, *Hali Bote yu ciwawa* [*Harry Potter and the Porcelain Doll*] (Beijing: Zhongguo mangwen chubanshe, 2002). The former was the subject of much discussion in the western media, and there's even a Wikipedia entry devoted to it: en.wikipedia.org/wiki/Harry_Potter_and_Leopard-Walk-Up-to-Dragon.
41. Henningsen, 'Harry Potter with Chinese Characteristics', p. 299.
42. Wadong Cangshu, *Xiang tianshi yiyang duoluo* [*As Fallen as an Angel*] (Beijing: Zhonguo qingnian chubanshe, 2005); Wushan, *Meihuayin* [*Introduction of Plum Blossoms*] (Beijing: Zhonguo qingnian chubanshe, 2005). I am grateful to Cheng Xiao for helping me with these.
43. The 'Publisher's Announcement' appears in both editions, ibid., p. 3.
44. This is traced usefully in terms of phases in Jonathan Gray, Cornel Sandvoss and C. Lee Harrington, 'Introduction: Why Study Fans?' in Gray, Sandvoss and Harrington (eds.), *Fandom: Identities and Communities in a Mediated World* (New York: New York University Press, 2007), pp. 1–16.
45. Lawrence Grossberg, 'Is There a Fan in the House? The Affective Sensibility of Fandom', in Lisa A. Lewis (ed.), *The Adoring Audience: Fan Culture and Popular Media* (London: Routledge, 1992), p. 64.
46. Henry Jenkins, 'Afterword: The Future of Fandom' in Gray, Sandvoss and Harrington (eds.), *Fandom*, p. 359.
47. Matt Hill, *Fan Cultures* (London: Routledge, 2002), p. 29.
48. Claudia Mitchell and Jacqueline Reid-Walsh, *Researching Children's Popular Culture: The Cultural Spaces of Childhood* (London: Routledge, 2002), p. 145.
49. A. S. Byatt, 'Harry Potter and the Childish Adult', *New York Times* 7, July 2003. http://query.nytimes.com/gst/fullpage.html?res=9A02E4D8113AF934A3575 4C0A9659C8B63, Jennie Bristow, 'Harry Potter and the Meaning of Life', *Spiked*, 19 June 2003. can www.spiked-online.com/Articles/00000006DE0C. htm, Stephen Pollard, 'I Worry for Harry's Adult Readers', *Sunday Telegraph*, 22 June 2003. http://www.telegraph.co.uk/opinion/main.jhtml?xml=/opinion/2003/06/22/do2209.xml&sSheet=/opinion/2003/06/22/ixop.html.
50. Pew Research Centre for the People and the Press, 'News of the Week Doesn't Grab Public's Attention: Harry Potter Books Widely Anticipated', 19 July 2007. people-press.org/report/343/news-of-the-week-doesn't-grab-public-attention.
51. See Nigel Reynolds, 'Adult Fans Taking Over Harry Potter', *Daily Telegraph*, 22 June 2007. www.telegraph.co.uk/arts/main.jhtml?xml=/arts/2007/06/22/nosplit/booldharry12.xml.
52. 'Adult Readers Grow Children's Market', *Bookseller*, 16 April 2004. http://www.allbusiness.com/retail-trade/miscellaneous-retail-miscellaneous/4668 034-1.html.

Bibliography

Harry Potter editions and translations

Rowling, J. K. *Harry Potter and the Philosopher's Stone*. London: Bloomsbury, 1997.
Rowling, J. K. *Harry Potter and the Chamber of Secrets*. London: Bloomsbury, 1998.
Rowling, J. K. *Harry Potter and the Prisoner of Azkaban*. London: Bloomsbury, 1999.
Rowling, J. K. *Harry Potter and the Goblet of Fire*. London: Bloomsbury, 2000.
Rowling, J. K. *Harry Potter and the Order of the Phoenix*. London: Bloomsbury, 2003.
Rowling, J. K. *Harry Potter and the Half-Blood Prince*. London: Bloomsbury, 2005.
Rowling, J. K. *Harry Potter and the Deathly Hallows*. London: Bloomsbury, 2007.
[In Bulgarian] Rowling, J. K. *Hari Potar i Ogneniyat bokal*. Trans. Mariyana Melnishka. Sofia: Egmont Bulgaria, 2002.
[In Chinese, PRC] Rowling, J. K. *Hali Bote He Mofashi*. Trans. Su Nong (actually two trans.: Cao Suling and Ma Ainong). Beijing: People's Literature Publishing House [renmin wenxue chubanshe], 2000.
[In Chinese, PRC] Rowling, J. K. *Hali Bote He Siwang Shengqi*. Trans. Ma Ainong and Ma Aixin. Beijing: People's Literature Publishing House [renmin wenxue chubanshe], 2007.
[In Chinese, Taiwan] Rowling, J. K. *Hali Bote He Mofashi*. Trans. Peng Qian-wen. Taipei: Crown Publishing, 2000.

Secondary reading

Abanes, Richard. *Harry Potter and the Bible: The Menace behind the Magick*. Camp Hill, PN: Horizon, 2001.
Adler, Bill (ed.), *Kids' Letters to Harry Potter from Around the World: An Unauthorized Collection*. New York: Carroll & Graf, 2001.
'Adult Readers Grow Children's Market.' *Bookseller*, 16 April 2004. www.allbusiness.com.
Allen, Jamie. '"Harry" and Hype.' *CNN*, 13 July 2000. www.CNN.com (Book News).
Allen, Richard. *Projecting Illusions: Film Spectatorship and the Illusion of Reality*. Cambridge: Cambridge University Press, 1995.
Anatole, Giselle Liza (ed.). *Reading Harry Potter*. Westport, CT.: Praeger, 2003.
Apostolova, Gergana. 'Are Dementors the New Guardians of the Golden Apple?' [Dementorite li sa novite pazachi na zlatnata yabulka?] *Jubilee Slavic Compendium [Yubileen Slavistichen Sbornik]*. Blagoevgrad, 2005. 606–18.
Apostolova, Gergana. 'Bad Realism and Good Fantasy in Futile Attempt at Literary Representation in Julian Barnes's *The Porcupine* and J. K. Rowling's *Harry Potter*.' Presentation at ESSE 8 Conference in London, 29 August–2 September 2006.
Aragay, Mireia (ed.). *Books in Motion: Adaptation, Intertextuality, Authorship*. Amsterdam: Rodopi, 2005.

Armitt, Lucie. *Theorising the Fantastic*. London: Arnold, 1996.

Auerbach, Nina. *Woman and the Demon: The Life of a Victorian Myth*. Cambridge MA: Harvard University Press, 1982.

Avramova, Galina. 'Is Harry Potter Dangerous?' [Opasen li e Hari Potar?]. *Vox Literarum* 2, 2004. 31–42.

Baehr, Ted and Tom Snyder. *Frodo and Harry: Understanding Visual Media and its Impact on Our Lives*. Wheaton, IL: Crossway, 2003.

Baker, Mona. *In Other Words: A Coursebook in Translation*. London: Routledge, 1992.

Barthes, Roland. *Image–Music–Text*. Trans. Stephen Heath. London: Fontana, 1977.

Barthes, Roland. *Mythologies*. Trans. Annette Lavers. London: Vintage, 1972/1957.

Baym, Nancy K. 'Talking about Soaps: Communicative Practices in a Computer-mediated Fan Culture.' In Harris and Alexander (eds.), 1998. 111–29.

Baym, Nancy K. *Tune in, Log on: Soaps, Fandom, and Online Community*. Thousand Oaks, CA: Sage, 2000.

Becher, Tony and Paul R. Trowler. *Academic Tribes and Territories*. Buckingham; Open University Press and the Society for Research into Higher Education, 2001. First edition 1989.

Becker, George J. (ed.). *Documents of Modern Literary Realism*. Princeton, NJ: Princeton University Press, 1963.

Becker, Jasper. *Dragon Rising*. Westchester, OH: National Geographic Society, 2006.

Belk, Russell W. and John F. Sherry (eds.). *Consumer Culture Theory*. Amsterdam: Elsevier, 2007.

Bell, John D. (ed.). *Bulgaria in Transition: Politics, Society and Culture after Communism*. Boulder, CO: Westview Press, 1998.

Benina, Iliyana. 'Not in Slytherin, not in Slytherin: Audio-Visual Translation of *Harry Potter and the Philosopher's Stone* by J. K. Rowling' [Ne v Sliderin, ne v Sliderin: audio-vizualen prevod na 'Hari Potar i filosofskiyat kamuk']. In Slavova, (ed.), 2005. 148–57.

Black, Rebecca W. 'Access and Affiliation: The Literacy and Composition Practices of English-Language Learners in an Online Fanfiction Community.' *Journal of Adolescent and Adult Literacy* 48:2, October 2005. 118–28.

Black, Rebecca W. *Adolescents and Online Fan Fiction*. Bern: Peter Lang, 2008.

Blackburn, R. M. and K. Prandy. 'The Reproduction of Social Inequality.' *Sociology* 31:3, 1997. 491–509.

Blake, Andrew. *The Irresistible Rise of Harry Potter*. London: Verso, 2002.

Bleich, David. *Subjective Criticism*. Baltimore, MD: Johns Hopkins University Press, 1978.

Bloom, Harold. 'Can 35 Million Book Buyers Be Wrong? Yes.' *Wall Street Journal*, 11 July 2000. A26.

Bloom, Harold. *The Western Canon*. Basingstoke: Macmillan, 1995.

Bolonik, Kera. 'A List of Their Own.' *Salon Magazine*, 16 August 2001. www.salon.com.

Bolter, Jay David. *Writing Space: The Computer, Hypertext, and the History of Writing*. Hillsdale, NJ: Lawrence Erlbaum, 1991.

Bourdieu, Pierre, Jean-Claude Passeron and Monique de Saint Martin. *Academic Discourse: Linguistic Misunderstanding and Professorial Power*. Trans. Richard Teese. Cambridge: Polity, 1994/1965.

Bourdieu, Pierre. *Homo Academicus*. Trans. Peter Collier. Cambridge: Polity, 1988/1984.

Bottero, Wendy. 'Clinging to the Wreckage? Gender and the Legacy of Class.' *Sociology* 32:3, 1998. 469–90.

Botting, Fred. *Making Monstrous.* Manchester: Manchester University Press, 1991.

Bottingheimer, Ruth B. *Fairy Tales and Society.* Philadelphia, PN: University of Pennsylvania Press, 1986.

Bowers, Simon. 'Bloomsbury Predicts Another Magic Year with Harry.' *Guardian Unlimited*, 21 March 2002. www.guardian.co.uk.

Breen, R. and D. Rothman. *Class Stratification.* London: Harvester, 1995.

Bristow, Jennie. 'Harry Potter and the Meaning of Life.' *Spiked*, 19 June 2003. www.spiked-online.com.

Broderick, Damien. *Reading by Starlight.* London: Routledge, 1995.

Brown, Michael et al. (eds.). *The Rise of China.* Cambridge MA: MIT Press, 2000.

Brown, Stephen. 'Harry Potter and the Marketing Mystery.' *Journal of Marketing* 66:1, January 2002. 126–30.

Brown, Stephen. 'Marketing for Muggles.' *Business Horizons* 45:1, January/February 2002. 6–14.

Bryant, John. *The Fluid Text: A Theory of Revision and Editing for Book and Screen.* Ann Arbor, MI: The University of Michigan Press, 2002.

Buckingham, David. *After the Death of Childhood: Growing up in the Age of Electronic Media.* Cambridge: Polity, 2000.

'Bulgaria or the End of the Transition Paradigm?' [Discussion]. *Razum [Reason]: Journal for Politics and Culture Theories.* 1, 2003. www.razum.org.

Burke, Sean. *The Death and Return of the Author: Criticism and Subjectivity in Barthes, Foucault and Derrida.* Edinburgh: Edinburgh University Press, 1992.

Burn, Andrew. 'Multi-Text Magic: Harry Potter in Book, Film and Videogame.' In Collins and Ridgman (eds.), 2006. 227–50.

Burn, Andrew. 'Potterliteracy: Cross-Media Narratives, Cultures and Grammars.' *Papers: Explorations into Children's Literature* 14:2, 2004. 5–17.

Busse, Kristina and Karen Hellekson (eds.). *Fan Fiction and Fan Communities in the Age of the Internet.* Jefferson, NC: McFarland, 2006.

Buzard, James. 'On Auto-Ethnographic Authority.' *Yale Journal of Criticism* 16:1, 2003. 61–91.

Byatt, A. S. 'Harry Potter and the Childish Adult.' *New York Times*, 7 July 2003.

Cardwell, Donald. *The Fontana History of Technology.* London: Fontana, 1994.

Carey, Brycchan. 'Hermione and the House-Elves: The Literary and Historical Contexts of J. K. Rowling's Anti-Slavery Campaign.' In Anatole (ed.), 2003. 103–16.

Carpentier, Nancy. *The Mystery of Harry Potter.* Huntington, NC: Our Sunday Visitor, 2007.

Carter, Angela. *The Bloody Chamber.* Harmondsworth: Penguin, 1981.

Carter, Angela (ed.). *The Virago Book of Fairy Tales.* London: Virago, 1990.

Carter, Margaret L. (ed.). *'Dracula'.* Ann Arbor, MI: University of Michigan, 1988.

Cartnell, Deborah and Imelda Whelehan. 'Harry Potter and the Fidelity Debate.' In Aragay (ed.), 2005. 37–50.

Cetina, K. K. 'Sociality with Objects: Social Relations in Postsocial Knowledge Societies.' *Theory, Culture and Society* 14:4, 1997. 1–30.

Cheng Zhaoxiang. 'English Departments in Chinese Universities.' *World Englishes* 21:2, 2002. 257–67.

Cheshmedzhieva, Dessislava. 'The Same but Other: Igor Karkaroff – a Key Bulgarian Figure in J. K. Rowling's *Harry Potter and the Goblet of Fire*'. *New Prospects* [Conference Proceedings, Plovdiv, 1–3 November 2003]. Forthcoming.

Cheshmedzhieva, Dessislava. 'Some Representations of Bulgarians in J. K. Rowling's *Harry Potter and the Goblet of Fire*. Viktor Krum: A Bulgarian Coming from an Imaginary Geography.' In Stratiev and Katsarova (eds.). 2006. 208–16.

Ciciani, Mirna. 'Male Pair: Bonds and Female Desire in Fan Slash Writing.' In Harris and Alexander (eds.), 1998. 153–77.

Colbert, David. *The Magical Worlds of Harry Potter*. New York: Weatherhill, 2001.

Collins, Fiona M. and Jeremy Ridgman (eds.). *Turning the Page: Children's Literature in Performance and the Media*. Bern: Peter Lang, 2006.

Collins, Tara. 'Filling the Gaps: What's Happening in the World of Fan Fiction'. *Library Media Connection* 24:4, January 2006. 36–8.

Cook, Guy. *The Discourse of Advertising*. London: Routledge, 1992.

Cornwell, Neil. *The Literary Fantastic*. Hemel Hempstead: Harvester Wheatsheaf, 1990.

Dalton, Russell W. *Faith Journey through Fantasy Land*. Minneapolis, MN: Augsberg Fortress, 2003.

Dangerfield, Martin, Glyn Hambrook and Ludmilla Kostova (eds.). *Europe: From East to West*. Varna: PIC Publishers, 1996.

Danova, Madeleine ed. *The Transatlantic and the Transnational in a Changing Cultural Context*. Sofia: Polis Publishing, 2005.

Danova, Madeleine and Milena Katsarska (eds.). *(Inter)Cultural Communication* [Conference volume, November 2006, Plovdiv]. Sofia: Polis Publishing, forthcoming.

Day, W. P. *In the Circles of Fear and Desire*. Chicago: University of Chicago Press, 1985.

Denkova, Lidiya. *The Philosopher's Secrets of Harry Potter* [*Filosofskite taini na Hari Potar*]. Sofia, LIK, 2001.

'Destination Bulgaria Promoted by Mythical Harry Potter Team.' *Novinite*, 11 June 2004. www.novinite.com/

Donawerth, Jane. *Frankenstein's Daughters*. New York: Syracuse University Press, 1997.

Dresang, Elisa T. 'Hermione Granger and the Heritage of Gender.' In Whited (ed.), 2002. 211–42.

Eagleton, Terry. *Against the Grain: Essays 1975–1985*. London: Verso, 1986.

Eco, Umberto. *The Role of the Reader: Explorations in the Semiotics of Texts*. Bloomington, IN: Indiana University Press, 1979.

Egoff, Shiela, Gordon Stubbs, Ralph Ashley and Wendy Sutton (eds.). *Only Connect: Readings on Children's Literature*, third edition. Oxford: Oxford University Press, 1996.

Eliot, T. S. *Selected Essays*. London: Faber, 1932.

Ellis, John. *Visible Fictions*. London: Routledge & Kegan Paul, 1982.

'Emirates Ban Potter Books' *BBC News*, 12 February 2002. www.bbc.co.uk.

Farquhar, Mary Ann. *Children's Literature in China: From Lu Xun to Mao Zedong*. Armak NY: M. E. Sharpe, 1999.

Fish, Stanley. *Doing What Comes Naturally: Change, Rhetoric, and the Practice of Theory in Literary and Legal Studies*. Oxford: Clarendon, 1989.

Fish, Stanley. *Is There A Text In This Class? The Authority of Interpretive Communities*. Cambridge, MA: Harvard University Press, 1980.

Foucault, Michel. *The History of Sexuality Vol. 1: An Introduction*. Trans. Robert Hurley. London: Allen Lane, 1979.

Frayling, Christopher. *Vampyres*. London: Faber, 1991.

Frazer, J. G. *The Golden Bough: A Study in Magic and Religion*. Abridged edition. London: Macmillan, 1922.

Fredricks, Casey (ed.). *The Future of Eternity*. Bloomington, IN: Indiana University Press, 1982.

French, Howard W. 'Chinese Market Awash in Fake Potter Books.' *New York Times*, 1 August 2007. www.nytimes.com.

Freud, Sigmund. *The Interpretation of Dreams*. Trans. James Strachey. Harmondsworth: Penguin, 1976/1953.

Gaggi, Silvio. *From Text to Hypertext: Decentring the Subject in Fiction, Film, the Visual Arts*. Philadelphia, PN: University of Pennsylvania Press, 1997.

Garber, Marjorie. *Academic Instincts*. Princeton, NJ: Princeton University Press, 2001.

Gelder, Ken. *Reading the Vampire*. London: Routledge, 1988.

Glaubman, Jame ed. *Deconstructing Harry: Harry Potter Fan Fiction on the World Wide Web*. Durham, NC: Duke University Press, 2008.

Goddard, Angela. *The Language of Advertising*. London: Routledge, 1998.

Götz, Maya, Dafna Lemish, Amy Aidman and Heysung Moon. *Media and the Make-Belief Worlds of Children: Where Harry Potter Meets Pokémon in Disneyland*. Mahwah, NJ: Lawrence Erlbaum, 2005.

Goodman, Robin Truth. *World, Class, Women: Global Literature, Education and Feminism*. New York: RoutledgeFalmer, 2004.

Gottfried, Heidi. 'Beyond Patriarchy? Theorizing Gender and Class.' *Sociology* 32:3, 1998. 451–68.

Granger, John. *Looking for God in Harry Potter*. Carol Stream, IL: Tyndale, 2004.

Green, Lelia and Carmen Guinery. 'Harry Potter and the Fan Fiction Phenomenon.' *Media/Culture* 7:5, November 2004. http://journal.media-culture.org.au/0411/14.green.php.

Green, Linda. *Entering Potter's Wold: A Guide for Fanfiction Writers*. lulu.com, 2006.

Green, Shashanna, Cynthia Jenkins and Henry Jenkins. 'Normal Female Interest in Men Bonking.' In Harris and Alexander (eds.), 1998. 9–38.

Gunder, Anna. 'Harry Ludens: *Harry Potter and the Philosopher's Stone* as a Novel and Computer Game.' *HUMAN IT* 7:2, 2004. 1–137. etjanst.hb.se/bhs/ith/2-7/ag.pdf.

Gupta, Suman. *Corporate Capitalism and Political Philosophy*. London: Pluto, 2002.

Gupta, Suman. *Marxism, History and Intellectuals: Toward A Reconceptualized Transformative Socialism*. Madison, NJ: Fairleigh Dickinson University Press, 2000.

Gupta, Suman. 'Sociological Speculations on the Professions of Children's Literature.' *The Lion and the Unicorn* 29: 3, September 2005. 299–323.

Gray, Jonathan, Cornel Sandvoss and C. Lee (eds.). *Fandom: Identities and Communities in a Mediated World*. New York: New York University Press, 2007.

Gregory, Chris. 'Hands off Harry Potter!' *Salon Magazine*, 1 March 2000. www.Salon.com.

Grossberg, Lawrence. 'Is There a Fan in the House? The Affective Sensibility of Fandom.' In Lewis (ed.), 1992. 50–65.

Hall. Amy Laura. 'Love: a Kinship of Affliction and Redemption.' In Meilaender and Werpehowski (eds.), 2005. 307–21.

Hallett, Cynthia Whitney (ed.). *Scholarly Studies in Harry Potter: Applying Academic Methods to a Popular Text*. Lewiston, ME: Edwin Mellen, 2005.

Hamacher, Werner, Neil Hertz and Thomas Keenan (eds.). *Responses to Paul de Man's Wartime Journalism*. Lincoln, NB: University of Nebraska Press, 1989.

Harbour, Daniel. *An Intelligent Person's Guide to Atheism*. London: Duckworth, 2001.

Harris, Cheryl and Alison Alexander (eds.). *Theorizing Fandom: Fans, Subculture and Identity*. Cresskill, NJ: Hampton, 1998.

Harrison, Fraser. *The Dark Angel*. Glasgow: Fontana, 1977.

'Harry Potter "Evil," Says Taiwan Church.' *CNN*, 15 November 2001. www.CNN.com.

'Harry Potter "Hate-Line" Launched.' *CNN*, 28 December 2000. www.CNN.com.

'Harry Potter Series Again Tops List of Most Challenged Books.' *ALA*, January 2001. www.ala.org/news.

'Harry Potter Series Tops List of Most Challenged Books for Third Year in a Row.' *ALA*, January 2002. www.ala.org/news.

'Harry Potter Wins Round Against Canadian Muggles.' *CNN*, 20 September 2000. www.CNN.com.

Hegel, G. W. F. *The Philosophy of History*. Trans. J. Sibree. New York: Dover, 1965.

Helleksen, Karen and Kristina Busse (eds.). *Fan Fiction and Fan Communities in the Age of the Internet*. Jefferson, NC: McFarland, 2006.

Henningsen, Lena. 'Harry Potter with Chinese Characteristics: Plagiarism between Orientalism and Occidentalism.' *China Information* 20:2, 2006. 275–311.

Herrick, Jim. *Against the Faith*. Amherst, NY: Prometheus, 1985.

Highfield, Roger. *The Science of Harry Potter: How Magic Really Works*. London: Headline, 2002.

Hill, Amelia. 'Harry Potter Magic Fails to Inspire Young to Read More.' *Guardian Unlimited*, 5 May 2002. www.guardian.co.uk.

Hill, Matt. *Fan Cultures*. London: Routledge, 2002.

Hinchman, Kathleen A. and Heather K. Sheridan-Thomas (eds.). *Best Practices in Adolescent Literacy Instruction*. New York: Guildford, 2008.

Holland, Norman. *Five Readers Reading*. New Haven, CT: Yale University Press, 1975.

Huang Yunting and Liang Hongyan. 'On the Art of the Double-World Narrative in Fantasy Novels' [lu muohuan xiaoshuo zhongde shuangchong shijie]. *Journal of the South China University of Technology* [huanan ligong duxue xuebao] 9:6, December 2007. 63–7.

Hubert, Henri, and Marcel Mauss. *Outline of a General Theory of Magic*. London: Routledge, 2001/1904.

Hugh, Tison and David L. Wallace, 'Heteronormative Heroism and Queering the School Story in J. K. Rowling's *Harry Potter* Series', *Children's Literature Association Quarterly* 31:3, Fall 2006. 260–81.

Hume, Kathryn. *Fantasy and Mimesis: Responses to Reality in Western Literature*. London: Methuen, 1984.

Hunt, Peter. 'Defining Children's Literature.' In Egoff et al., 1996. 2–17.

Hunt, Peter (ed.). *Understanding Children's Literature*. London: Routledge, 1999.

Huxley, Aldous. *Brave New World*. Harmondsworth: Penguin, 1932.

Hyland, Ken. 'Bumping into the Reader: Addressee Features in Academic Articles.' *Written Communication* 18:4, October 2001. 549–75.

Hyland, Ken. *Disciplinary Discourses: Social Interactions in Academic Writing.* Harlow: Pearson, 2000.

Hyland, Ken. *Hedging in Scientific Research Articles.* Amsterdam: John Benjamins, 1998.

Hyland, Ken. 'Options of Identity in Academic Writing.' *ELT Journal* 56:4, October 2002. 35–43.

Hyland, Ken. 'Self-Citation and Self-Reference: Credibility and Promotion in Academic Publication.' *Journal of the American Society for Information Science and Technology* 54:3, 2003. 251–91.

Hyland, Ken. 'What do they Mean? Questions in Academic Writing.' *Text* 22:4, 2002. 529–58.

Irwin, W. R. *The Game of the Impossible: A Rhetoric of Fantasy.* Urbana, IL: University of Illinois Press, 1976.

Iser, Wolfgang. *The Act of Reading: A Theory of Aesthetic Response.* London: Routledge & Kegan Paul, 1978.

Iser, Wolfgang. *The Implied Reader: Patterns of Communication in Prose Fiction from Bunyan to Beckett.* Baltimore, MD: Johns Hopkins University Press, 1974.

Iser, Wolfgang. *Prospecting: From Reader Response to Literary Anthropology.* Baltimore, MD: Johns Hopkins University Press, 1989.

Ivanič, Roz. *Writing and Identity: The Discoursal Construction of Identity in Academic Writing.* Amsterdam: John Benjamin, 1997.

Jackson, Patrick Thaddeus and Peter Mandaville, 'Glocal Hero: Harry Potter Abroad.' In Nexon and Neumann (eds.), 2006. 45–59.

Jackson, Rosemary. *Fantasy: The Literature of Subversion.* London: Routledge, 1981.

Jasper, David. *The Study of Literature and Religion.* Basingstoke: Macmillan, 1989/ 1992.

Jenkins, Henry, with assistants. *Confronting the Challenges of Participatory Culture: Media Education for the 21ˢᵗ Century.* Chicago: McArthur Foundation, 2006.

Jenkins, Henry. *Convergence Culture: Where Old and New Media Collide.* New York: New York University Press, 2006.

Jenkins, Henry. 'Everybody Loves Harry.' *Confessions of an Aca-Fan: The Official Weblog of Henry Jenkins,* 21 May 2007. www.henryjenkins.org.

Jenkins, Henry. 'Why Heather Can Write: Not everything kids learn for popular culture is bad for them, some of the best writing culture takes place outside the classroom in online communities.' *Technology Review,* February 2004. www.technologyreview.com.

Jentsch, Nancy K. 'Harry Potter and the Tower of Babel: Translating the Magic.' In Lathey (ed.), 2006. 190–207.

Jiang Wandi. 'Wild about Harry.' *Beijing Review,* 7 June 2007. 19.

Jing Xiaolei. 'Universal Potter.' *Beijing Review,* 7 June 2007. 23.

Jones, Gwyneth. *Deconstructing the Starships.* Liverpool: Liverpool University Press, 1999.

Jones, Steven Swann. *The Fairy Tale.* New York: Twayne, 1995.

Joyce, James. *A Portrait of the Artist as a Young Man.* St. Albans: Granada, 1964/1916.

Julius, Anthony. *T. S. Eliot, Anti-Semitism, and Literary Form.* Cambridge: Cambridge University Press, 1995.

Kalish, Charles W. and Emma C. Kalish. 'Hogwarts Academy: Common Sense and School Magic.' In Mulholland (ed.), 2006. 59–71.

Kapur, Jyotsna. *Coining the Capital: Movies, Marketing, and the Transformation of Childhood*. New Brunswick: Rutgers University Press, 2005.

Khan, Rahila. *Down the Road, Worlds Away*. London: Virago, 1987.

Killinger, John. *God, the Devil, and Harry Potter*. New York: St. Martin's Press, 2004.

Kinney, Anne Behnke. *Chinese Views of Childhood*. Honolulu: University of Hawaii Press, 1995.

Knutsen, Torbjørn. 'Dumbledore's Pedagogy: Knowledge and Virtue at Hogwarts.' In Nexon and Neumann (eds.), 2006. 197–212.

Kostova, Ludmilla. 'Representing "Darkest Eastern Europe": Bulgaria in G. B. Shaw's *Arms and the Man* and Malcolm Bradbury's *Doctor Criminale*.' In Dangerfield et al. (eds.), 1996. 33–48.

Kostova, Ludmilla. *Tales of the Periphery: The Balkans in Nineteenth-Century British Writing*. Veliko Turnovo: University Publishing House of St Cyril and Methodius, 1997.

Kracauer, Siegfried. *Theory of Film: The Redemption of the Physical Reality*. Princeton, NJ: Princeton University Press, 1960.

Kronzik, Allan Zora and Elizabeth Kronzik. *The Sorcerer's Companion*. New York: Broadway, 2001.

Kynge, James. *China Shakes the World*. New York: Houghton Mifflin, 2007.

Lanier Jr., Clinton D. and Hope Jensen Schau. 'Culture and Co-Creation: Exploring Consumers' Inspirations and Aspirations for Writing and Posting On-Line Fan Fiction.' In Belk and Sherry (eds.), 2007. 321–42.

Lankshear, Colin and Michele Knobel. 'Harry Potter.' *Journal of Adolescent and Adult Literacy* 44:7, April 2001. 664–7.

Lathey, Gillian. 'The Travels of Harry: International Marketing and the Translation of J. K. Rowling's Harry Potter Books.' *The Lion and the Unicorn* 29: 2, 2005. 141–51.

Lathey, Gillian (ed.). *The Translation of Children's Literature: A Reader*. Clevedon, OH: Multilingual Matters, 2006.

Lawver, Heather. 'Making Progress toward Revolution.' *Daily Prophet*, 2008. www.dprophet.com.

Lea, Mary R. and Barry Stierer (eds.). *Student Writing in Higher Education*. Buckingham: Open University Press and The Society for Research in Higher Education, 2000.

Leach, Geoffrey N. *English in Advertising*. London: Longmans, Green & Co., 1966.

Lesnik-Oberstein, Kárin. 'Essentials: What is Children's Literature? What is Childhood?' In Hunt (ed.), 1999. 15–29.

Lévi-Strauss, Claude. *Totemism*. Trans. Rodney Needham. Boston, MA: Beacon, 1963.

Levy, Alexander. 'Harry Potter Ignites Passions in Bulgaria.' *Parizhki Vesti [Paris News]*, 4 November 2004. www.parisvesti.com/.

Lewis, Lisa A. (ed.). *The Adoring Audience: Fan Culture and Popular Media*. London: Routledge, 1992.

Lilova, Dessislava. 'The Story of Viktor Krum: National Identity on the Internet' [Istoriyata na Viktor Krum: natsionalnata identichnost v internet]. *Kritika i Humanizum* [Critique and Humanism], 'Cultures in Movement' thematic issue. 25:1, 2008. 115–38.

Luolin, J. K. *Hali Bote yu baozhoulon* [erroneously translated as *Harry Potter and the Leopard-Walk-Up-To-Dragon*]. Hohot: Neimenggu chubanshe, 2002.

Lyubansky, Mikhail. 'Harry Potter and the Word that Shall Not Be Named.' In Mulholland (ed.), 2006. 233–48.

Lynch, Dick. 'The Magic of *Harry Potter.' Advertising Age* 72:50, 12 October 2001. 26.

Ma Jianguo. 'The Sixth Volume of Harry Potter is about to be launched, the English Edition has Arrived in Beijing.' *Xinhuanet*, 15 July 2005. www.XIN-HUANET.com.

MacDonald, Andrea. 'Uncertain Utopia: Science Fiction Media Fandom and Computer Mediated Communication.' In Harris and Alexander (eds.), 1998. 131–52.

MacDonald, Marianne. 'Harry Potter and the Fan Fiction Phenomenon.' *Gay and Lesbian Review Worldwide* 13:1, January–February 2006. 28–30.

McLuhan, Marshall. *Understanding Media: The Extensions of Man.* London: Routledge & Kegan Paul, 1964.

McNabb, Mary L. *Literacy Learning and Networked Classrooms.* Newark, NJ: International Reading Association, 2006.

Maechler, Stefan. *The Wilkomirski Affair: A Study in Biographical Truth.* Trans. John E. Woods. London: Picador, 2001/2000.

Man, Paul de. *Wartime Journalism, 1939–1943.* Lincoln, NB: University of Nebraska Press, 1988.

Mandelsohn, Farah. 'Crowning the King: Harry Potter and the Construction of Authority.' In Whited (ed.), 2002. 159–81.

Marcuse, Herbert. *One-Dimensional Man.* London: Sphere, 1964.

Martin, Bill. 'Knowledge, Identity and the Middle Class: From Collective to Individualised Class Formation?' *The Sociological Review* 46:4, 1998. 653–86.

Martin, Michael. *Atheism: A Philosophical Justification.* Philadelphia, PA: Temple University Press, 1992.

Mason, Michael. *The Making of Victorian Sexual Attitudes.* Oxford: Oxford University Press, 1994.

'Mattel Reports 2002 First Quarter Results.' *Mattel Shareholder News*, 18 April 2002. www.shareholder.com/mattel/.

Mauss, Marcel. *A General Theory of Magic.* Trans Robert Brain. London: Routledge, 1972/1904.

Meilaender, Gilbert and William Werpehowski (eds.). *The Oxford Handbook of Theological Ethics.* Oxford: Oxford University Press, 2005.

'Memo to the Dept. of Magical Copyright Enforcement.' *New York Times*, 10 August 2007. www.nytimes.com.

Mighall, Robert. *A Geography of Victorian Gothic Fiction.* Oxford: Oxford University Press, 1999.

Mihepu. 'My Reason for Writing "Preliminary Analysis of the Chinese Translation of Harry Potter 6 by the People's Literature Publishing House"'. 2006. tieba.baidu.com/f?kz=66576189.

Miller, Andrew and James Eli Adams (eds.). *Sexualities in Victorian Britain.* Bloomington, IN: Indiana University Press, 1996.

Miller, Karl. *Authors.* Oxford: Clarendon, 1989.

Miller, Karl. 'Harry and the Pot of Gold.' *Raritan* 20:3, Winter 2001. 132–40.

Milliot, Jim. 'Profits Jump 27% in Scholastic's Children's Publishing Group.' *Publisher's Weekly*, 9 March 2001. www.PublishersWeekly.com.

Mineva, Mila (ed.). *Take it Easy: Towards a Strategy for Representing Bulgaria.* Sofia: The British Council, IPK Rodina, 2003.

Mitchell, Claudia and Jacqueline Reid-Walsh. *Researching Children's Popular Culture: The Cultural Spaces of Childhood.* London: Routledge, 2002.

Miteva, Ludmilla. 'Difficult Decisions: Huck Finn and Harry Potter.' In Danova (ed.), 2005. 300–13.

Miteva, Ludmilla. 'Harry Potter and His Fans' [Hari Potar i negovite pochitateli]. *Vox Literarum* 3, 2004. 26–34.

Miteva, Ludmilla. 'Harry Potter Goes to America: Having Fun with Fan Works.' CD-ROM edition of *Conference Proceedings: The Bulgarian Association for American Studies*. Sofia, November 2003.

Miteva, Ludmilla. *Humour in Late 20ᵗʰ-Century British Children's Literature: Roald Dahl, Terry Pratchett, J. K. Rowling.* Extended précis of an unpublished PhD dissertation defended at the Specialized Academic Board in Literature, at the Higher Attestation Committee (Sofia, 2008). 86pp.

Miteva, Ludmilla. 'School Space as a Product and Mediator of Culture in Children's Literature.' In Danova and Katsarska (eds.), forthcoming.

Moore, Sharon (ed.). *Harry Potter, You're the Best.* New York: Griffin, 2001.

Moore, Sharon (ed.). *We Love Harry Potter.* New York: St. Martin's Griffin, 1999.

Moretti, Franco. 'Conjectures on World Literature.' *New Left Review* 1, January–Febuary 2000. 54–68.

Morrison, Toni. *Song of Solomon.* London: Chatto & Windus, 1978.

'The Most Curious Facts about *Harry Potter.*' *Egmont Bulgaria*, 11 February 2002. www.egmontbulgaria.com.

Mulholland, Neil ed. *The Psychology of Harry Potter.* Dallas, TX: Benbella, 2006.

Natov, Roni. 'Harry Potter and the Extraordinariness of the Ordinary.' *The Lion and the Unicorn* 25:2, 2001. 310–27.

Navarro, Peter. *The Coming China Wars.* New Jersey: FT Press, 2006.

Nead, Lynda. *Myths of Sexuality.* Oxford: Blackwell, 1988.

Neal, Connie. *What's A Christian to Do With Harry Potter?* Colorado Springs, CO: WaterBrook, 2001.

Neckel, Sighard. 'Inferiority: From Collective States to Deficient Individuality.' *The Sociological Review* 44:1, 1996. 17–34.

Nel, Philip. 'Is There a Text in This Advertising Campaign? Literature, Marketing, and Harry Potter.' *The Lion and the Unicorn* 29: 2, April 2005. 236–67.

Nel, Philip. *J. K. Rowling's Harry Potter Novels.* New York: Continuum, 2001.

Neilson, Stefan, Joe Hutton and Nora Huston. *Character Education: The Legacy of the Harry Potter Novels.* Mountlake Terrace, WA: Vintage First Edition, 2001.

Nexon, Daniel H. and Iver B. Neumann (eds.). *Harry Potter and International Relations.* Lanham Ma: Rowman & Littlefield, 2006.

Ni Lishan. 'Expedition of the Soul in the Game-Spirit of Harry Potter' [xinling de tanxian]. *Journal of Fujian Educational College* [Fujian jiaoyu xueyuan xuebao], October 2005. 79–83.

Nikolojeva, Maria. 'The Changing Aesthetics of Character in Children's Fiction.' *Style* 35:3, Fall 2001. 430–53.

Nikolova, Katya and Sofia Angelova-Damyanova. '*Harry Potter:* Censorship and Literature Education' [Hari Potar: tsenzurata i obuchenieto po literatura]. In Slavova, (ed.), 2005. 206–14.

'Not Everybody's Wild about Harry,' *Citypages*, 19 July 2000. www.citypages.com.

Nygren, Anders. *Agape and Eros.* Trans. Philip S. Watson. London: Westminster, 1953.

'Property Boom Keeps Duke Top of Rich List.' *Reuters*, 7 April 2002. www.reuters.co.uk.

O'Har, George M. 'Magic in the Machine Age.' *Technology and Culture* 41:4, 2000. 862–4.

Ostrey, Elaine. 'Accepting Mudbloods: The Ambivalent Social Vision of J. K. Rowling's Fairy Tales.' In Anatole (ed.), 2003. 89–102.

Pakulsi, Jan and Malcolm Waters, *The Death of Class*. London: Sage, 1995.

Pearson, Ronald. *The Worm in the Bud*. Harmondsworth: Pelican, 1969.

Pennington, John. 'From Elfland to Hogwarts, or the Aesthetic Trouble with Harry Potter.' *The Lion and the Unicorn* 26:1, 2002. 78–97.

Perry, Evelyn M. 'Metaphor and MetaFantasy: Questing for Literary Inheritance in J. K. Rowling's *Harry Potter and the Sorcerer's Stone*.' In Hallett (ed.), 2005. 241–75.

Pew Research Centre for the People and the Press. 'New of the Week Doesn't Grab Public's Attention: Harry Potter Books Books Widely Anticipated.' *People Press*, 19 July 2007. http://people-press.org/report/343/news-of-the-week-doesn't-grab-public-attention.

Pollard, Stephen. 'I Worry for Harry's Adult Readers.' *Sunday Telegraph*, 22 June 2003. www.telegraph.co.uk.

Pollert, A. 'Gender and Class Revisited: The Poverty of Patriarchy.' *Sociology* 30:4, 1996. 639–59.

Popov, Alek. 'The Bulgarian Trace in *Harry Potter*' [Bulgarskata sleda v Hari Potar]. *BTA – 100% Harry Potter*, December 2003. www.bta.bg.

Porter, Roy and Lesley Hall. *The Facts of Life*. New Haven, CT: Yale University Press, 1995.

'Potter Creator Supports Lone Parents.' *BBC News*, 4 October 2000. www.bbc.co.uk.

'Potter First Edition Nets 6000 Pounds.' *BBC News*, 15 November 2000. www.bbc.co.uk.

'Potters Go Under the Hammer.' *BBC News*, 12 February 2002. www.bbc.co.uk.

Pound, Ezra. *Literary Essays of Ezra Pound*. Ed. T. S. Eliot. London: Faber, 1954.

Prady, Kenneth. 'Class and Continuity in Social Reproduction.' *The Sociological Review* 46:2, 1998. 340–64.

Pratkanis, Anthony and Elliot Aronson. *Age of Propaganda*. New York: W. H. Freeman, 1998.

Prickett, Stephen. *Victorian Fantasy*. Hassocks: Harvester, 1979.

Propp, Vladimir. *Theory and History of Folklore*. Trans. Ariadne Martin and Richard Martin. Manchester: Manchester University Press, 1984.

Reay, Diane. 'Rethinking Social Class: Qualitative Perspectives on Class and Gender.' *Sociology* 32:2, 1998. 259–75.

Reynolds, Nigel. 'Adult Fans Taking Over Harry Potter.' *Daily Telegraph*, 22 June 2007. www.telegraph.co.uk.

Roback, Diane, Jason Britton, and compiled by Debbie Hochman Turvey. 'All Time Best-Selling Children's Book List.' *Publisher's Weekly*, 17 December 2001. www.PublishersWeekly.com.

Robbins, Ruth (ed.). *Victorian Gothic*. Basingstoke: Macmillan, 2000.

Rose, Jacqueline. *The Case of Peter Pan or The Impossibility of Children's Fiction*. Basingstoke: Macmillan, 1984.

Rose, Jacqueline. *States of Fantasy*. Oxford: Clarendon, 1996.

Rosenberg, Robin S. 'What Do Students Learn from Hogwarts Classes?' In Mulholland (ed.), 2006. 5–17.

Said, Edward. *Orientalism: Western Conceptions of the Orient.* Harmondsworth: Penguin, 1978.

Sandross, Cornel. 'One-Dimensional Fan: Toward an Aesthetic of Fan Texts.' *American Behavioral Scientist* 48:7, March 2005. 822–39.

'Satanic Harry Potter Books Burnt.' *BBC News*, 31 December 2001. www.bbc.co.uk.

Savage, Mike and Muriel Egerton. 'Social Mobility, Ability and the Importance of Class Inequality.' *Sociology* 31:4, 1997. 645–72.

Savasta, Antonic. 'International Terrorism and the "Bulgarian Connection"' Report of 19 March 1982. *Open Society Archives*, at http://files.osa.ceu.hu/holdings/300/8/3/text/8-10-58.shtml.

Schafer, Elizabeth D. *Exploring Harry Potter.* London: Ebury, 2000.

Schoefer, Christine. 'Harry Potter's Girl Trouble.' *Salon Magazine*, 13 January 2000. www.salon.com.

'School Bans Harry Potter,' *BBC News*, 29 March 2000. www.bbc.co.uk.

'Schools Ban Potter "Occult" Books.' *BBC News*, 29 November 2001. www.bbc.co.uk.

Sexton, Anne. *The Complete Poems.* Boston, MA: Houghton Mifflin, 1981.

Shao Yanjun. 'A Study of the Phenomenon of Pretty Women's Writing: Weihui, Mianmian, Chunshu.' *Wasafiri (China Special Issue)*, Issue 55, 2008. 13–18.

Shapiro, Marc. *J. K. Rowling: The Wizard Behind Harry Potter.* New York: Griffin, 2000.

Shearer, Laura Baker. 'High-Brow Harry Potter: J. K. Rowling's Series as College Level Literature.' In Hallett (ed.), 2005. 199–215.

Shiao, Yah-Ying Elaine. *Bewitched or Befogged in a Magical World? Chinese Translations of Culture-Specific Items in a Harry Potter Novel.* Unpublished Auckland Technology University MA dissertation, May 2006.

Skeggs, B. *Formations of Class and Gender.* London: Sage, 1997.

Slavova, Margarita (ed.). *Adaptation as a Strategy of Children's Literature* [Adaptatsiyata kato strategiya v detskata literatura]. Plovdiv: Paissiy Hilendarski University of Plovdiv Press, 2005.

'Small-Cap Round-up: "Harry Potter" Magic Boosts Argonaut Stock.' *Reuters*, 12 March 2002. www.Reuters.co.uk.

Smith, David. 'Dumbledore was Gay, JK Tells Amazed Fans.' *Observer* 21 October 2007. www.guardian.co.uk.

Smith, George H. *Atheism: The Case against God.* Amherst, NY: Prometheus, 1980.

Smith, George H. *Why Atheism?* Amherst, NY: Prometheus, 2000.

Smith, Sean. *J. K. Rowling: A Biography.* London: Michael O'Mara, 2001.

Spencer, Richard. 'Harry Potter and the Cho Chang Mystery.' *Telegraph Blogs*, 23 December 2005. http://blogs.telegraph.co.uk/foreign/richardspencer/dec2005/harrypotter.htm.

Sperber, Dan and Dierdre Wilson. *Relevance: Communication and Cognition.* Oxford: Blackwell, 1986.

Stefanova, Ralitsa. 'A Glimpse at *Harry Potter* in Three Different Languages' [Edin pogled kum Hari Potar na tri razlichni ezika]. *Literary Newspaper* [*Literaturen vestnik*], issue 27, 10 September 2003.

Stratiev, Svetlin and Vessela Katsarova (eds.). *Spaces, Gaps, Borders.* Sofia: St Kliment Ohridski University Press, 2006.

'Survey – UK Middle Market Companies: Harry Potter Wield His Magic Wand.' *Financial Times*, 9 March 2001. www.FT.com.

Tanaka, Keiko. *Advertising Language*. London: Routledge, 1999.

Taylor-Whiffen, Peter. 'Harry Potter and the Social Order.' *The Independent*, 3 June 2003. 12.

Theory and Society. 'Symposium on Class'. *Theory and Society* 25:5, 1996.

Thompson, Anna. 'Harry Potters On, and We Muggle through.' *Times Higher Education Supplement*, 19 September 2003.

Timberlake, Edward and William Triplett II. *Red Dragon Rising*. Washington: Regnery, 2002.

Todorov, Tzvetan. *The Fantastic: A Structural Approach to a Literary Genre*. Trans. Richard Howard. Ithaca, NY: Cornell University Press, 1973/1970.

Todorov, Tzvetan. *Genres in Discourse*. Trans. Catherine Porter. Cambridge: Cambridge University Press, 1990/1978.

Todorova, Maria. *Imagining the Balkans*. Oxford: Oxford University Press, 1997.

Tolkein, J. R. R. *Tree and Leaf*. London: Grafton, 1992.

Tossenberger, Catherine. "Oh my God, the Fanfiction!' Dumbledore's Outing and the Online Harry Potter Fandom.' *Children's Literature Association Quarterly* 33:2, Summer 2008. 200–6.

Towns, Ann and Bahar Rumelili. 'Foreign yet Familiar: International Politics and the Reception of Potter in Turkey and Sweden.' In Nexon and Neumann (eds)., 2006. 61–77.

Trites, Roberta Seelinger. 'The Harry Potter Novels as a Test Case for Adolescent Literature.' *Style* 35:3, Fall 2001. 472–85.

Trudgill, Eric. *Madonnas and Magdalens*. London: Heinemann, 1976.

Unsworth, Len. *E-Literature for Children: Enhancing Digital Literacy Learning*. London: Routledge, 2006.

Vassileva, Teodora. 'Small Wonders in Bulgaria Too' [Malki vulshebstva i v Bulgaria]. *Kapital*, Issue 30, 27 July 2007.

Vatahov, Ivan. 'Harry Potter Needed for EU Bid.' *Sofia Echo*, 21 February 2002 and 21 March 2002. www.sofiaecho.com/.

'Viktor Krum Looming as Bulgaria's Tourism Face.' *Novinite*, 10 March 2004. www.novinite.com/

Wadong Cangshu. *Xiang tianshi yiyang duoluo [As Fallen as an Angel]*. Beijing: Zhonguo qingnian chubanshe, 2005.

Walkowitz, Judith. *Prostitution and Victorian Society*. Cambridge: Cambridge University Press, 1982.

Wang Shanshan. 'Latest Potter Book Now in Chinese, Officially.' *China Daily*, 29 October 2007. 3. www.chinadaily.com.cn.

Ward, Graham. *Theology and Contemporary Critical Theory*. Basingstoke: Macmillan, 1996/2000.

Warner, Marina. *From the Beast to the Blonde*. London: Chatto & Windus, 1994.

Warner, Marina. *Managing Monsters*. London: Vintage, 1994.

'What if Quidditch, the Enchanted Sport of Wizards and Witches Featured in the Harry Potter Books, Were Regulated by the NCAA?' *Sports Illustrated*, 21 August 2000. 33.

Whited, Lana A. (ed.). *The Ivory Tower and Harry Potter*. Columbia: University of Missouri Press, 2002.

Wilber, Dana J. 'iLife: Understanding and Connecting to the Digital Literacy of Adolescents.' In Hinchman and Sheridan-Thomas (eds.), 2008. 57–77.

Williams, Geoff. 'Harry Potter and... the Trials of Growing a Business... the Rewards of Independence and Ownership.' *Entrepreneur*, February 2001. 62–5.

Williams, Raymond Williams. *Problems in Materialism and Culture*. London: Verso, 1980.

Williamson, Judith. *Decoding Advertisements*. London: Marion Boyars, 1978.

Willis, Ika. 'Keeping Promises to Queer Children: Making Space (for Mary Sue) at Hogwarts.' In Helleksen and Busse (eds.), 2006. 153–70.

Wimsatt, W. K. and M. C. Beardsley. 'The Intentional Fallacy.' *Sewanee Review* 54, 1946. 468–88.

Wolfreys, Julian. *Victorian Hauntings*. Basingstoke: Palgrave, 2002.

'World Wide Wizard.' *The Guardian*, 8 November 2001. 14–15.

Wushan. *Meihuayin* [*Introduction of Plum Blossoms*]. Beijing: Zhonguo qingnian chubanshe, 2005.

X, Malcolm. *The Autobiography of Malcolm X*. With the assistance of Alex Haley. Harmondsworth: Penguin, 1964.

Xu Yurong. 'Children's Literature Should Be Happy Literature: On the Revelations Available from Harry Potter' [ertong wenxue ying chengwei kuile wenxue]. *Journal of Social Sciences* [chengdu daxue xuebao], 4, 2006. 127–8.

Yates, Emma. 'Harry Potter Tops US "Complaint" Chart.' *Guardian Unlimited*, 10 January 2002. www.guardian.co.uk.

Ye Zhenning. 'The Development and Marketing of Harry Potter in China' [hali bote de zhengti kaifa he yingxiao]. *China Bookmerchant's Newspaper* [*zhongguo tushu shangbao*] August 2002. www.sinobook.com.cn.

Young, Hugo. 'A New Imperialism Cooked up over a Texan Barbecue.' *The Guardian*, 2 April 2002. www.guardian.co.uk.

Young, Robert. *Colonial Desire: Hybridity in Theory, Culture and Race*. London: Routledge, 1995.

Zhang Bin. *Hali Bote yu ciwawa* [*Harry Potter and the Porcelain Doll*]. Beijing: Zhongguo mangwen chubanshe, 2002.

Zhang Ying and Kong Dan. 'Harry Potter and the Characteristics of Contemporary Children's Literature' [hali bote yu xinshiqi ertong wenxue de tedian]. *Journal of the North East University: Philosophy and Social Science* [dongbei shida xuebao], 5, 2002. 95–7.

Zipes, Jack. *Happily Ever After*. New York: Routledge, 1997.

Zipes, Jack. *Sticks and Stones: The Troublesome Success of Children's Literature from Slovenly Peter to Harry Potter*. New York: Routledge, 2001.

Zipes, Jack. *When Dreams Come True*. New York: Routledge, 1999.

Index